Terror Undone

By Jessi Gage

A Turn Back Time Novel

Also by Jessi Gage

Highland Wishes Series

Wishing for a Highlander
The Wolf and the Highlander
Choosing the Highlander
King's Highlander

Love Under Construction Series

Hurt You
Tempt You
Keep You
Arouse You

Acknowledgements

Thank you, Barbara Towle, Martha Day, and Christine Morgan. You three made sure my kids got the education they deserve and that I got the writing time I needed to complete this book. Without you, this story would still be a fantasy rattling around in my head. Thank you for all the organizing, teaching, e-mail reading, attendance taking, and Chromebook troubleshooting. I know it wasn't an easy school year. I truly appreciate the contributions each of you made while COVID-19 forced us all to rethink how we educate our kiddos. I was more than happy to "be the bus" while you three did the hard work.

For every woman who has never known the joy of waking on a Saturday morning to a husband emptying the dishwasher, I can assure you, it is fantastic. Without the support of my amazing partner in life, I wouldn't be able to do what I do. Thank you, Shane, for all you do around the house, for proofreading, and for being my biggest fan.

Mom (Barbara Towle), you get a second mention, because not only did you make sure my kids got an education this year, but you also helped me with household stuff. Thanks to your efforts, Mt. Laundry has become a thing of the past, and my kitchen has been an orderly haven for dinner prep. Thank you for all your help! You are truly appreciated and loved. Thank you, also, for proofreading this manuscript. You caught some doozies!

Amy Raby, you continue to be my writing rock. No matter what's going on in the world or in our lives, you're always there to critique my writing. Your insights were vital to the shaping of this story. I value your friendship so very much and can't wait to resume our Bellevue breakfasts.

Thank you, Teresa Conner for all you do as my virtual assistant. From proofreading to promo graphics to organizing my marketing activities, you take all the stress out of birthing a book into the world.

To my neighbors and friends, Deborah Mystakidis and Miss T, thank you for your support and for checking in with me to make sure I got my writing done when I was supposed to. I couldn't ask for more enthusiastic cheerleaders. Allison Robinson, thank you for your support, advice, and friendship, as well as for beta reading this manuscript. Without you, I would be far less confident about Ian's background and how it affects his outlook.

Much appreciation goes out to the Quote Investigator website for locating the original source of the famous Joseph Pulitzer quote used as a chapter heading. Thank you, QI Guy, for posting the results at https://quoteinvestigator. com/?s=pulitzer.

Thank you, Piper Denna, for editing this book. It's always a joy to work with and learn from you. Thank you, Robynne from Damonza, for the beautiful cover you created for this book.

To you, my reader. You know that philosophical question, "If a tree falls in the woods and no one is there to hear it, does it make a sound?" Sometimes, I wonder whether a collection of words is a story without someone to receive it. Thank you for receiving my words. I hope you find some entertainment here, and maybe even some small bit of healing, like my heroine, Lydia Clay did, and I like I did through the process of researching and writing this book.

Author's Note

Dear Reader,

What we lost on 9/11 cannot be put into words.

Despite the time that has passed, that dark day continues to hold our fascination. Twenty years later, we still struggle to process the magnitude of what terrible people did to us in the name of extremist ideology. We struggle to understand how the attacks were able to happen and how we were caught so off-guard on our own soil. We struggle to find meaning in that day and its aftermath.

It's natural and normal to still grieve, to still ponder, and, yes, to still wonder what if. What if the terrorists didn't get away with murder? What if good triumphed over evil? What might that scenario have looked like? This novel explores that very question.

Fictionalizing a traumatic event might upset some people. Please don't read this book if you find the idea of this novel offensive. If, however, you enjoy indulging the impossible, if you've wondered "what if" and would like to see what one author's "what if" looks like, then read on.

This book is a work of fiction. It is not meant to educate about 9/11 but to provide escape and entertainment for those who still think about that day and wish it had ended happily for our nation. For more information about this novel, including a list of references, notes from the protagonist, and to explore what's fact and what's fiction, go to www.jessigage.com or see the appendices at the back of this book.

Sincerely,

Jessi Gage

Jessi Gage

*What separates us from the animals, what
separates us from the chaos, is our ability to
mourn people we've never met.*

—David Levithan

PROLOGUE

MOM AND DAD SAY Great Grandpa is just tired. Grandma says there's nothing to worry about. Pawpaw is the only one who tells me the truth. Great Grandpa is sick.

"Bodies wear out, Bean," he tells me on a sigh. I'm Pawpaw's jellybean. When he uses my nickname, I know everything will be okay, even if we talk about something sad.

We're sitting on the back porch. He's in his favorite lawn chair. I'm on his lap. It's wmidsummer, and the corn is as tall as the men when they go out to pull weeds the old-fashioned way that Pawpaw likes best. I'm full from dinner, and Pawpaw is smoking a cigarette. Mom, Dad, and Grandma are inside.

We all visited Great Grandpa today. He's in the hospital, and he has tubes like spaghetti all over him.

"Great Grandpa's body has seen a lot of years," Pawpaw says. I like that he doesn't talk to me like a baby. Pawpaw is my favorite. He makes the tip of his cigarette glow, then blows smoke into the air. "He's like an old hot rod. He was fast once. Now he's an antique, and he can't go very fast at all. Pretty soon, his engine won't be able to run anymore. When that happens, his soul—the inside part of him that makes him *him*—will go to heaven."

I think of the old cars Dad and Pawpaw like to look at, the ones with the big hoods and fins like sharks and wheels with white on them.

"Will he be an angel, then?"

Pawpaw crushes his cigarette in the ashtray and tilts his head. "That's a good question, Bean." I feel proud that he liked my question. Pawpaw thinks I'm smart. "May be." He says it like two words. "That's part of the mystery, I suppose."

"What mystery?"

"Why, the mystery of life and death." He smiles at me, then stares out at the cornfield. He likes watching the corn. Before, he used to farm it himself. Now Dad does it with a crew of men. I think Pawpaw misses the farming. He still talks with Dad about the corn all the time.

He gasps, and I jump, afraid. When I look at him, his eyes are joyful. I follow his pointing arm and look at the corn. No, above the corn.

"See that, Bean? A shooting star!"

I see it! Way up in the black sky. Lots of stars up there make me think of my Lite-Brite toy, but there's this one that is moving. It's moving fast, like it's in a hurry to get somewhere.

"Wow!" I've never seen anything so pretty.

"Did you know," Pawpaw says, "that every shooting star is an angel coming to Earth? When you see one, you're supposed to make a wish. If the angel likes your wish, you might be the lucky one he chooses to answer."

Pawpaw knows the neatest things! I watch the bright light sink closer and closer to the ground, and I wonder what kind of wish an angel might like. The star-angel is way far away. I'll make my wish nice and loud.

I cup my hands like a bullhorn and shout, "I'm gonna wish that Great Grandpa—"

"Ah-ah-ah-ah-ah! *Shh*!" Pawpaw interrupts my shouting, waving his hand like he's trying to forget what he heard. "You must never tell anyone your wish. It's a secret between you and the angel." He bops my nose with his finger and winks at me. Then his face grows serious. "Sweet girl. Don't waste your wish on Great Grandpa. Bodies wearing out is one of those things we aren't meant to change. Death from old age is as much a part of life as a new baby being born. It's just how things are. I'll tell you what. Great Grandpa would want you to make a wish for yourself."

"But the star is gone now!" I cry. I'm distraught. I've missed my chance.

"The star might be gone," he says. "But the angel can still hear your heart."

He sits quietly then, gazing out at the corn. He's giving me time to come up with something good to wish for. And I do. But it's not for myself, like Pawpaw wanted.

I make my wish, and I don't tell a soul.

Everyone stops, points up and gasps 'Oh look at that!' Then—whoosh, and I'm gone... and they'll never see anything like it ever again....

—Jim Morrison

CHAPTER 1

Lydia

Books.

Printed in permanent marker, my handwriting labels the contents of the box in the simplest of terms. Too simple, actually, for what this box means to me. It's so much more than a collection of bound writings. To me, this box represents my strength, my failure, and my future.

Books. I see them when I slice open the tape and part the folds of cardboard. One after another, I lift them out and slide them into the place of honor they'll occupy here at my parents' farmhouse—my farmhouse now, since Mom followed Dad to heaven and left it to me.

The built-in bookcase frames the wood-burning fireplace in the living room. Mom used to keep trinkets and mementos here. My bronzed baby shoes. An antique die-cast tractor. Ornaments of the season. And photos. Lots of photos. Her and Dad on their wedding day. Me as a kid, me as a bride, me as a mom. The only book was the family Bible, the cover of which I dusted many more times than I ever opened.

I'll put a few of my own mementos here, carrying on Mom's tradition. I've already unpacked some pictures of my kids. They're near the top, beside the baby shoes, tractor, and Mom and Dad's wedding picture. But I plan to use these shelves for books, too. The books in this box, to be precise. Because they're special to me.

And because I'm not ashamed anymore.

That will be the tradition I begin here and now in hopes Holly and Christian will carry it on for me. I'll show them that they can be proud of their passions, displaying them for all to see. They don't have to hide their interests from the people they love, only pulling them out from under the bed when they are alone, when no one can judge them.

There should never be shame in remembering.

The floorboards upstairs are creaking. Holly is moving around the bedroom I had as a child, unpacking her boxes like I'm unpacking mine. At nineteen, Christian is a college freshman now—jeez, time flies. But Holly is still in high school and has chosen to move to Nebraska with me for her senior year.

I tried to dissuade her—she's been in the same New Jersey school district since kindergarten. But she wouldn't have it. "I'm not letting you go back there alone! Not when you're grieving. Plus, I love Grandma and Grandpa's house." I suspect she tacked on the last part so it didn't seem like she was doing this for me, as if I would relent if her intentions were the tiniest bit selfish.

The farmhouse tells the story of her movements, letting me know when she's coming down the stairs. As I'm pulling the last book out of the box, she finds me in the living room.

"It's quiet out here," she says. Beneath the hem of her cutoff jean shorts, her legs are tan from a summer in the New Jersey sun.

"Sorry, baby," I say, because it's become my habit to lead with a spirit of apology. "It's going to be a boring couple of weeks for you before school starts."

As much as I want to spend every moment of those two weeks with her, I have to start my new job. While the county hospital in Ord, Nebraska isn't overwhelmed with COVID-19 cases, like Kindred in New Jersey, it's still much busier than the norm. I'm needed there, and I've become good at sacrificing family time for patients in need.

"No, I like it." Holly cocks her hip and stares me down. "You know you don't have to apologize for things that aren't your fault, right? Having to work isn't your fault. Taylor being quiet isn't your fault. Remember, you don't live with Dad anymore."

My little therapist. Okay, she's not so little anymore. At an athletic five-foot-seven, she's three inches taller than me.

"Sorry," I say with a smirk.

She rolls her eyes, but she's smiling too. I'm proud of the way she and Christian handled the divorce. I'm proud of myself for finally taking that step.

"*The Looming Tower?* What's that about?" Holly tilts her head to read the spine of the book I'm holding.

She hasn't seen these books before. No one has. Well, Tristan saw some of them, and his reaction is why no one has seen them since.

"It's not healthy the way you're fixated on 9/11, Lyd. What is it with you and death? It's been ten years. We weren't even close with anyone who died that day. Maybe you should see a therapist."

Every generation has its *where-were-you-when* moment. For my great grandparents, it was Pearl Harbor. No matter how much time had passed, they were always able to say exactly where they were and what they were doing when they heard the news that thousands of Americans had perished beneath the bellies of Japanese bombers. For my Grandma and beloved Pawpaw, it was the day JFK was shot, closely followed by the moment Neil Armstrong planted the American flag on the moon. For Mom and Dad, it was the fall of the Berlin Wall.

For me, it's 9/11.

As a media-saturated culture, we experience tragedies of this caliber collectively, but our individual minds need to process such events in their own intimate ways. For some, that looks like volunteering. For others, it looks like social action and slogans. For others, it's getting back to normal as quickly as possible. For some, like me, processing happens by reading everything they can about the event. In that way, acute interest in a national tragedy is natural. Healthy.

But that acute interest has a shelf life, or so I have learned.

When the attacks happened, Tristan and I were still newlyweds. He worked in a law firm in Manhattan, and I was a college graduate about to start a nursing program in Brooklyn. For months afterward, the attacks were all we talked about. Me, Tristan, fellow nursing students, strangers on the subway, everyone. The attacks had left deep scars, not just on the landscape but on the city's psyche, as well. And the shelf life was long.

Nine months after the attacks I transitioned into the clinical portion of my program. Patients and other health professionals were still talking about their close and not-so-close brushes with the event that had reshaped our city and nation. I listened to wives whose husbands had been on the island or at Ground Zero, husbands whose wives had been stuck in gridlock and unable to return home until late that night, parents of first responders, and grandparents of children who were supposed to go to orientation that week but had to wait for the delayed school year to start. Everyone had a story about where they were and what they were doing when they heard the news or saw for themselves. With each telling, that day in history became more and more firmly ingrained as our *where-were-you-when* moment.

And not just for those of us in the city. The whole of the U.S. was shell-shocked. Each day, the news programs and papers examined a new aspect of the attacks. The shelf life was long here, too. Related news stories continued to dominate the airwaves long after the debris had been trucked away. Terrorism, national security, domestic policies, the lack of communication between government agencies, survivor stories, conspiracy theories, rebuilding efforts. The list went on and on.

Then one day, a newscast aired without a single story mentioning 9/11. Eventually a week passed without a related story. Then a month. After a while, people stopped talking about it, except in passing, to comment on the Freedom Tower's grand opening or to sum up a visit to the 9/11 Memorial or to mark the day's anniversary with a few somber words.

Never Forget, we were told, but once the expiration date had passed, keen interest in 9/11 became morbid. Unhealthy.

So, I learned to keep my thoughts to myself. I learned that the one person I had hoped to share all of myself with, my husband, did not like the parts I dared the most to share.

I continued to buy my books, but I read them in secret and hid them where no one would see. Until now.

Holly reaches for the thick paperback in my hands. My instinct is to clutch it to me and hide the cover. To be ashamed. But that instinct belongs to a woman who failed over and over again to stand up for herself, to *be* herself without apology.

I place the book in her hands. Watch her flip it over to read the back. I hold my breath.

"Cool," she says. My lungs relax. "Did you get this because of the anniversary? Twenty years in just a couple days." She's giving me an acceptable reason to be interested.

"I've actually had it a while. These too." I show her the shelf. I'm not ashamed that I still read these books. I'm ready to own my interest. I'm ready to stand up for it.

No more apologies. I want Holly to know that she's allowed to be herself, no matter what others think. She's allowed her own inspirations and fascinations. I will always give her space to process things in her own way.

She tips her head to read the spines lined up on the shelf. "These are all about 9/11?" She runs her fingers over them, exploring.

"Yeah."

"Why haven't I seen them before?" She's curious, but there's a hint of hurt in her voice. Her mom has kept a secret from her.

No more secrets. Honesty is the new me. "I was embarrassed," I say. "So, I hid them. Not everyone wanted to talk about 9/11. Or be reminded of it." I sigh. "I needed to know more, but not everyone shared my interest. It was easier to do my research in private."

Holly nods. "Dad," she says, and her flat tone tells me she gets it. "Not everyone" means Tristan. *Tristan* didn't like me reading books about 9/11, and Tristan can be very adamant about what he doesn't like. To the point where you just give in to stop the criticism. But for all his faults, he's a great father. He adores Holly and Christian, and the feeling is mutual. I promised myself I would never make my issues my kids' issues.

"I can't imagine what it was like to be there," Holly says. "I mean, you were actually there, in New York when it happened. No wonder you wanted to know more."

Holly's words are a balm to my spirit. But I sense a need to stand up for others like me. "Yes. I was close to the tragedy, physically speaking, but I'm not sure that's why that day captivates me like it does." I lift the last of the books from the box and slide it into place. Standing back, I admire my handiwork. The shelf looks nice. It *feels* nice to put this part of myself on display for all to see. "I suspect it has more to do with being an American than being a New Yorker. You know?"

Holly's giving me a goofy grin. "Atta-girl, Mom. Way to own it."

I ruffle her hair, reaching up to do so. We make nose-kiss faces at each other, though we stopped actually rubbing noses long ago.

"Well, my darling, I am beat. What do you say we have some lemonade and take a spin on the old porch swing?"

Holly's game. We chat about our plans for the house and the school year as we mix up some lemonade and pour it over ice.

"Hey, Jes!" When we go outside, I greet Mom and Dad's faithful, long-legged hound. Jester came to me with the house and the farm. The porch is his domain, at least when he's not doing his rounds, protecting the property.

He butts his head against my thigh as I scratch behind his silky ears the way he likes.

"You know you can come in the house, now, right? Mom's not here to chase you out with a broom, anymore." I smile at the memory of Mom's empty threats as Jes made muddy puppy-prints across the kitchen linoleum.

He gives no sign of understanding. When Holly and I set the swing into a slow, rocking motion, he turns in a circle, then settles onto his dog bed.

The chains of the swing groan quietly while Holly and I sip and chat. Slowly, the stars begin winking into the velvety sky.

I'm grateful my girl is here with me. She's really something. Compassionate all the way to her bones. I bet she'll end up in a career where she can care for others. Like me, she can't help herself.

With nothing but ice in them, our glasses rest on the porch rail. Holly leans her head on my shoulder. "It's really peaceful out here. So clean and natural, you know? So different from New Jersey."

We're looking out over the cornfield. The moon looks like a Christmas ornament hanging above the acres of harvest-ready stalks. It casts the field in hues of blue.

"Soon, it'll be loud and bustling." The harvest equipment is coming next week. I don't have anything to do with the farming anymore, other than accepting the profit after Mom and Dad's account manager processes the income and pays the renters who do all the work. "You'll miss all the action, though. It'll happen while you're at school." I stroke her long hair, a habit I'll never be able to quit.

"Maybe I'll play hooky one day to see how a harvest is done."

I start to say, no way, then consider. "That's not a bad idea." Farming is an interesting process, with all the hands and machines working in harmony. "It could be like an educational field trip, but at home. Maybe I'll make you write a report." I grin, and she snorts, calling my bluff.

We're quiet for long moments, lost in our own thoughts. She gives me a glimpse into hers when she says, "It must have been so scary, living through that. 9/11," she clarifies. "For me it's something that happened in the past, before I was born.

It's something I learned about in school. But you actually stopped your day to watch the news. You walked past Ground Zero. It was real-time for you."

"I was about to start nursing school." In my mind's eye, I see the downtown skyline from the doorstep of our Spinney Hill apartment. The tops of the buildings always reminded me of an EKG. That morning, the highest peak on the readout bled black smoke into an otherwise spotless sky.

Holly has heard the *Cliff Notes* version from me a dozen times, always out of Tristan's earshot. I relate it one more time. It feels good to share an edited version of my *where-were-you-when* event with her, especially without having to look over my shoulder. "I was at home," I tell her. "A few miles from Manhattan, but your dad was there. Just blocks from the World Trade Center. I was so worried when I couldn't reach him. The cell carriers were overwhelmed. Traffic was a mess. The news showed people walking across the bridges to get home. I kept my eyes glued to the TV, trying to make out his face, but everyone was covered with this fine white ash. You couldn't make out hair color or clothing. There was nothing to help identify your loved ones from all the other people."

I'd felt so helpless sitting there on my couch while horror unfolded across the East River. Tristan had come home late that afternoon. We tossed his suit in the dumpster rather than deal with the ash. It was finer than chalk dust. Neither of us ever said so, but I think we both knew that dust contained more than pulverized concrete.

My husband had been spared, but thousands of New Yorkers hadn't been so lucky. *Thousands*.

It still boggles the mind, all that loss. For nothing. For anti-American, fanatical ideology. For an extreme interpretation of holy writings, as offensive to Muslims as it is to those of us targeted by the extremists.

"It's time to get over it, Lyd. It happened, yes, but it's over. Time to move the hell on."

My throat feels thick, and my heart is heavy. Old instincts prod me to shove the feelings down. No one needs to see them. They're not important because I'm physically fine. I wasn't harmed that day, so I have no reason to continue in my grief.

I ignore those instincts, because I'm not fine. The effects of that day may not be physical in my case, but they're no less real. I am still grieving, and that *is* okay.

"It *was* scary," I say. "If I'm honest, I'm still processing it." Almost twenty years has passed, and still, that day feels so *wrong*. So unbelievable. We should have been able to stop it. We, as a world power, a nation with a huge intelligence community, a strong military, and law enforcement agencies devoted to our security.

I shake my head, disgusted, distraught. I'm going to bring one of my books up to bed with me tonight. And I'm not going to hide it. I'll read it with pride, and I'll remember the lives lost.

"If you could go back and do things different, would you?" Holly's question collides with my thoughts about 9/11, and I'm confused. Images of smoking towers fill my head. As nice as it would be to go back and change a day like that, no one person could have stopped what happened. There were so many failures of communication leading up to the attacks, so many little errors and coincidences that made it possible for evil to win. "With Dad, I mean," Holly adds, and her question makes more sense. She picks at a hangnail and shrugs. "I know you weren't happy for a long time."

"Oh, baby." I hate that she was aware of my discontent.

"No, I mean, don't feel bad!" She hurries to soothe me, ever my compassionate girl. "I just wonder if you would have separated sooner. You know. Like if you had a do-over."

I've asked myself the same thing a hundred times and never settled on an answer. Honesty is the new me, but there are boundaries a mom keeps in place with her kids. Even her almost grown kids.

"That's a complicated question," I say. Honest. Safe. I pat her knee. "I certainly wouldn't want to change anything that would affect having you and Christian."

Holly accepts my answer with a wan smile, and before long, she goes upstairs with her phone to take advantage of our newly-hooked-up wireless internet. When I pass through the living room to look for the box with wine glasses inside, I notice a hole in the lineup of spines on the bookshelf. One of my 9/11 books is missing. I smile.

Glass of wine in hand, I return to the swing with a quilt to wrap up in. Jes perks up, happy to have extended company on his porch. I make a pad for him out of half the quilt and pat the swing. "Come on, boy."

He accepts the invitation and jumps up to sit with me, like he used to with Dad.

"I miss him, Jes." I scrunch my fingers over his smooth head and stare unfocused at the corn and the night sky.

He acknowledges my grief by opening his eyes to sleepy slits. Then closing them again.

Rich Petite Sirah cools my upper lip. But my blood is warm from the quilt and the alcohol. Holly's question teases at me, and I give in to a fantasy where I have as many do-overs as I want.

If I could go back and change things, I wouldn't waste the magic on myself. I would get Mom to a doctor to have her heart disease diagnosed. If she'd only known, she could have made healthy changes, taken medication. She'd still be here with me.

I would be more outspoken about Dad's smoking. Maybe I could find the right words to get him to quit, and the cancer wouldn't have taken him five years ago.

I would hire someone to cut down the tree in our yard that Christian fell out of when he was nine, breaking his leg in two places.

I would stand up for myself with Tristan. Maybe if I'd done that years ago, our marriage could have been saved.

As I reach the bottom of my glass, my fantasies grow bolder. I dare to imagine a do-over of epic proportion.

If I could go back in time, I would find a way to stop 9/11.

I nod, resolute, as I form the thought. It's utterly ridiculous and completely impossible, but I like it. It pleases me to consider where I would start, who I would contact, how I would warn everyone about what was coming.

My glass is empty. I frown at it and push out my lower lip. "No fair."

I would go back in time and pour myself a bigger glass.

I snicker at myself and start to get up to go to bed, but movement in the sky stops me.

Far above the cornfield, a pinprick of light swells in size. It grows brighter like a car turning on high beams. Then turning them up to an even brighter setting. And another. The brilliance makes me lift my hand to protect my eyes.

It's a shooting star, but no ordinary shooting star.

Pawpaw has his arm around my shoulders as we rock back and forth, back and forth. Our lawn chairs have been replaced by a brand-new porch swing that Mom painted red. I'm telling him about winning third place in the eight-grade science fair when he interrupts me.

"Look at that, Bean!" He points to the sky, and his face is surprisingly bright.

I follow his finger and see why. The moon is falling! At least that's what it looks like. But it can't be the moon, because the crescent shape hangs firmly in place off to the right.

"Do you know what that is?" he asks.

"A meteor?" I make it a question, even though I know it can't be anything else.

Pawpaw's gaze is fixed on the spectacle. It might as well be noontime for how bright everything is.

"There was a time you called them shooting stars," he says with a grin, without looking away from the sky. "Yes, Bean. That right there is a meteor, but it's

a very special one. When they're that big and bright, they're called fireballs."

"Should I make a wish?" My tone is teasing, but I'm transfixed too. I've never seen anything so magnificent. It's like the sun is whizzing past the farm, lighting up everything in its path.

"Oh, not just any wish," Pawpaw says. "A very special shooting star deserves a very special wish, a once-in-a-lifetime wish."

I'm fourteen now, too old for silly wishes. Or so I think until the magic of the fireball coaxes a moment of belief out of me.

I watch the huge spotlight in the sky sink toward the horizon, taking its silvery light with it, and in my heart, I make the same wish I've been making since I was little.

Please save the ones who aren't supposed to die yet.

Pawpaw taught me that natural death is a part of life. I've always accepted that. But *un*-natural death bothers me so much that I've devoted my career to thwarting it. As a trauma nurse, I've shoehorned myself between my patients and unnatural death, a practical application of the longing I've had since my very first shooting star.

The fireball drifts like a computer cursor from one corner of the sky to the other, just like the one I saw with my grandfather, only far brighter than any cursor could ever be. It burns a trail into my retinas, and I remember smoke billowing into the sky from a pair of towers that died an unnatural death. They went too soon, and so did everyone trapped inside when they fell.

With wine on my lips and a hound under my hand, I make a very special wish for a very special shooting star. It's fanciful and impossible, and Tristan would never approve, but I make it anyway. It's a wish that would have made Pawpaw proud.

*I dreamed I was a butterfly, flitting around in
the sky; then I awoke. Now I wonder: Am I a
man who dreamt of being a butterfly, or am I
a butterfly dreaming that I am a man?*

—Zhuangzi

CHAPTER 2

Lydia

SOMETHING IS WRONG.

My bare legs, free of days-old stubble, glide over silk
sheets as I stretch awake. This is unexpected, since I made
Mom and Dad's bed with cotton sheets last night, fell into
bed still wearing my leggings and *T*-shirt. Not to mention,
I haven't shaved since the motel Holly and I stopped at in
Iowa City.

Through my closed eyelids, I detect daylight. Also
unexpected, since I distinctly remember shutting Mom's
homemade blackout curtains before climbing into bed.
The memory is so clear because those curtains were a love
note from Mom to Dad, made for him despite her dislike of
sewing to help him get the sleep he needed as a farmer who
often went to bed before the sun. Last night, I'd fingered

the heavy fabric and treasured the memory of Mom cursing over her ancient sewing machine while stitching them.

No matter the hour, I should be waking up in pitch black, swathed in warm comfort. Instead, morning sunlight brings me awake to an odd sensation of being chilled and exposed.

Slowly, like prying the lid off a suspicious can of nuts, I open my eyes. And find myself in the bed Tristan and I shared when we were first married.

I'm dreaming. I have to be, because I haven't woken up in this apartment in twenty years. We moved out shortly before I had Christian, needing more space for the baby. I'd been glad to leave the Brooklyn neighborhood with its view of Manhattan. After 9/11, the skyline was a constant reminder to me that evil had struck all too close to home.

Memories of that awful day fill my mind as I close my eyes to go back to sleep. Black smoke staining a blue sky. Breaking news footage of dust-covered nine-to-fivers hoofing it across the bridge. Putting my 9/11 books on the shelf last night must have primed my subconscious to make me dream about that time in my life. I have a lot to do today to get settled in my new life in Nebraska, but I'm in no hurry to leave the dream.

Unpleasant as the memories are, I recognize that it's healthy to have them. So, I let them swirl while I wait to drift off again. Except I don't drift off again. I'm not tired in the least.

With alert, well-rested eyes, I take in the too-close walls of my long-ago bedroom. They remind me how small the apartment was, though it had been a generous size for its location within the city limits. Streaks of golden light stab across the wall opposite the window, courtesy of east-facing blinds. Outside, birds are making a cheerful racket. Oh, how I learned to hate those birds when they would wake me before my alarm when I had to get up early for my internship!

Smiling with the memory, I push up onto my elbows. Despite the obvious fact I'm dreaming, I feel acutely awake.

"Weird."

As I sit up, the sheets slide down, and I understand why my skin is chilled. My *T*-shirt and leggings have been replaced with a lacy boy-short-and-camisole set, and *everything* is visible through the lace.

"Ugh, Lyd." I look down at myself and cringe. Not only because all my bits and pieces are on display but also because of the gold band and one-carat princess-cut solitaire on my finger.

I tug the rings off and set them by the clock. I don't care if this is a dream, it feels wrong to wear them. Tristan and I have been divorced for almost a year now.

Rubbing my arms against the cold, I get up and search for something to cover up with. I might be stuck in a dream, but that doesn't mean I have to freeze to death.

I find what I'm looking for on the inside of the bathroom door. A cashmere Williams Sonoma robe with *Mrs.* stitched on the breast in gold. Tristan's hangs beside it, a gold *Mr.* beside the lapel. The set was one of many wedding gifts from my in-laws.

I'm about to wrap myself in luxurious softness when I'm distracted by the toilet. It's right there, and it's not in a nightmarish state. Usually, when my dreams include a bathroom, the conditions are utterly disgusting or lacking in privacy. It's an effective subconscious signal to wake up and do my business.

Not so with this bathroom. It's pristinely clean and there's a full roll of paper ready for use. I can't resist the temptation to take advantage of my dreaming good luck.

"That was a first," I say as I press the handle to flush. A successful bathroom trip has *never* happened in one of my dreams. I hope I haven't just wet the bed in real life.

While washing my hands, I blink at my reflection in the mirror. My dark blond hair is long and artfully streaked with the platinum Tristan liked. My face is fresh and young and free of sleep-smeared mascara. The caramel color of my skin tells me exactly what point in time I'm dreaming about. I'm still tan from The Caymans. I'm dreaming about the period of time shortly after my honeymoon.

Newlywed bliss looks good on me. I back up and turn this way and that, appreciating the perky breasts and narrow waist belonging to my twenty-three-year-old body. Between the planes of my skimpy lingerie, I'm toned and tight everywhere. Not a stretch mark in sight!

"Sweet."

I forgot how kicking my body had been. Either that or my subconscious is embellishing. Except everything else is spot on. Right down to the smudges on the mirror where Tristan used a hand towel to wipe away the fog before shaving.

I frown at those smudges. Dreams aren't usually this detailed. Not for me, anyway.

Somewhere at the back of my mind, a sense of wrongness puts down roots.

I hug myself, feeling exposed. The robe isn't going to help. I doubt even a full-body ski suit would do the trick. This vulnerability is more than skin deep.

I feel marginally better once I'm sheathed in a *V*-neck tee and a pair of low-rise jeans I found in the bedroom closet. I should be thrilled that I just zipped myself into a size four with no muffin top, but that sense of wrongness won't let up. I can't shake the feeling that something needs my attention, that I have to *do* something here in this dream.

That's when a mother's dread hits me. A sharp longing to lay eyes on my children is a knife in my chest. If I'm twenty-three and fresh off my honeymoon, my kids don't yet exist in this dreamscape. The realization shouldn't upset me—none of this is real. But for some reason, it does upset me.

I want to wake up. I try to wake up. I do all the things. Pinch myself. Slap myself. I even splash water on my face in the bathroom. To no avail. I'm still here. And my children are not. The farmhouse in Nebraska is not. It's like the years of my life beyond this point never were.

My hands shake as I turn off the taps and venture into the living room. I no longer view the apartment as the mildly interesting trappings of a dream, I begin inspecting it in earnest. I touch and explore, determined to find inconsistencies that will prove this to be a figment of my imagination.

A-ha! The dining room table is the wrong color! It's supposed to be mahogany, but here it is orange with purple polka-dots. And what is this kangaroo doing beside the coffee maker?

But the opposite happens. Never in my wildest dreams would my memory have supplied the exact shade of burnt orange for the couch Tristan's brother handed down to us or the precise location of the faded patch resulting from the sun's daily journey across the window of its former home. Never could I have conjured the pattern of dents, scratches, and water marks on the footlocker we used as a coffee table during the first year of our marriage, let alone that we'd *ever* used a footlocker for a coffee table.

I begin to realize that the level of detail before me transcends my ability to catalogue every-day objects and their features. Even the technology seems accurately dated beyond the capabilities of my memory. Smartphones are so much a part of life now, if someone asked me when they came about, I might have guessed wildly wrong. There were smartphones when Tristan and I got married in the summer of 2001, weren't there? But no, there weren't. Not according to the navy-blue Nokia plugged in to charge on the TV stand.

Seeing the device in front of me, I remember it, but I wouldn't have been able to pull its blocky shape or the gray buttons of its keypad or the greenish, two-inch screen from the recesses of my mind. Same with the Panasonic flatscreen on top of the TV stand. It's at least six inches thick and has a gray screen. Details I would never have remembered, yet I'm sure they're correct.

I pick up the Nokia and unplug it. Its shape and texture feel foreign in my hand. I lean down to the footlocker and brush my fingers over the four remote controls on top. We had a different one for the TV, cable, DVD player, and five-disk CD changer. Phone in one hand, remote control in the other, I plop down on the couch where Tristan and I used to watch movies rented from Blockbuster and make love while dinner got cold. My fingers search out the velvety rasp of the synthetic upholstery.

This doesn't feel like a dream. It's way too convincing.

My surroundings have an indescribable weight to them. I feel grounded, almost as if *this* time and place is the reality and the moment with Holly and Jes on the porch and my entire adult life up to that point were the dream.

I stare helplessly at the living room where Tristan and I had our first major blow-out fight. *What am I doing here?*

An answer to the question hovers just within my reach, but a sharp knock on the door drives it away.

I jump up, heart pounding. I'm trespassing and I'm about to get caught.

The knock comes again. "You home, Lydia?" Though it's been many years since I've heard that upbeat, accented voice, I recognize it, easily.

"Saraka?" The name is a whisper on my lips as I approach the door. Saraka and her husband, Sumit, lived in the apartment next to mine and Tristan's. The four of us hit it off and took turns hosting game nights on the weekends.

"Saraka?" I call out. "Is that you?"

"No, it's the tooth fairy! I have your paper. The boy tossed in our bushes again. Shall I leave it, or are you going to open the door?"

I reach cautiously for the deadbolt, remembering Tristan's frustration that the paper never came in time for him to read it on the subway.

When I ease open the door, I'm hoping for a hellscape populated with goat-footed demons and Saraka riding a feral unicorn, but there is no hellscape and no foaming-at-the-mouth mythical beast. Only my former neighbor with her beautifully-made-up eyes and cropped, silky hair. Behind her is an overcast Spinney Hill morning with rooftops sloping to a hazy view of the Manhattan skyline.

"Here you are," Saraka chirps, holding out the elastic-bound paper. She's dressed for work in a blouse and pencil skirt. A light trench coat drapes one arm. She's ready to walk to the subway stop three blocks from our apartment complex. It's ridiculously good to see her after all these years.

"Hey, you!" I drag her in for a hug. "How have you been? How's Sumit?"

She pats my back awkwardly. When she extricates herself from my hold, her sculpted eyebrows have climbed her forehead. "Ah, just fine, thank you. And so is Sumit. Same as last night when we played *Settlers of Catan* together. Are you all right?"

She acts like it's only been a few hours since we last saw each other, not twenty years. Just like me, she looks in her early twenties.

"Are you? All right?" she repeats, concern making graceful wings of those midnight brows.

I realize I'm staring at her. I wave away her concern. "Good! I'm good. Just...weird dream, *er,* last night."

Her expressive eyes hold many questions, but she nods in the if-you-insist fashion of a New Yorker with somewhere to be and no time to go digging into someone else's business.

I take the paper and thank her. From the doorstep, I watch her walk down the sidewalk and across the *S*-shaped courtyard. I'm bombarded with more frustratingly specific details. Like sprays of tall grasses and curved rows of azaleas on either side of the grassy area and like how the morning sun makes knife-blades of the slanted rooftops recently redone in trendy corrugated metal.

I came to love this neighborhood, but I remember being annoyed with Tristan for insisting on this place instead of the aging tenement I'd found before our wedding. The single-room walk-up would have been friendlier to our checkbook, not to mention only two blocks from my nursing school.

"Nursing school's temporary, Lyd." I remember Tristan spreading the catalog for The Heights on his parents' dining table. "My job is permanent, and this place has a good commute to Manhattan. I don't want us to choose a place just because it's convenient in the short term. Besides, don't you want to live somewhere, you know, more refined? Less urban?"

I grit my teeth at the memory. We weren't even married yet when I started letting Tristan steamroll me with his strong opinions. Ever the people-pleaser, I'd bought peace in our marriage with my white flags. I'd had a whole collection of them. It took me twenty years to realize the price for that peace was my happiness. It took me twenty years to truly believe that my opinions held just as much value as Tristan's.

"Water under the bridge," I mutter as I go back inside.

Or is it?

Holly's question from last night comes back to me with such force my legs go weak. *"If you could go back and do things different, would you?"*

My heart pounds like I've run a mile. Is that what this is? This not-so-dreamlike-dream? Is this some kind of mental-breakdown-cum-do-over with Tristan?

I don't want a do-over with Tristan! We're divorced. I fell out of love with him. Am I stuck in this alternate reality until I stand up to him the way I should have from the start? Would that have rewritten the destination of our marriage from divorce-ville to happy-ever-after-land?

I'm finding my happy-ever-after in Nebraska, and it doesn't involve romance of any kind. I don't want to participate in this therapy exercise or whatever it is.

"I just want to unpack boxes!" I shout at the apartment.

At my wits' end, I slap the newspaper on the kitchen counter. The rubber band snaps, and the paper unfurls. I scan the front page, and my gaze drifts to the top. Suddenly, everything clicks into place.

Panic explodes in my chest and propels me out the door. Bare feet on concrete, I peer through the haze toward Manhattan. From this doorstep on a clear day, you can make out the very tippety-tops of the buildings downtown. Today is not very clear. I can't tell the buildings apart from one another. But I can make out the overall shape of the EKG skyline.

With the desperation of a castaway, I comb over the dips and valleys. And I see it. Something that doesn't belong.

A very tall peak.

Even on the clearest day, that singular peak would be an illusion. It's actually two buildings. The twin towers of the World Trade Center.

They're still standing.

I stare for a full minute before dropping my gaze to the newspaper clutched in my hand. I know why this is happening.

This isn't a do-over for my marriage. It's not a dream.

Time has been rewound.

The fireball heard my wish.

The date on the paper stares back at me in black and white, and I can't look away. *Monday, September 10, 2001.*

We are an impossibility in an impossible universe.

—Ray Bradbury

CHAPTER 3

Lydia

"Okay. Okay. Okay." I wear a hole in the floor, pacing between the kitchen and living room. "Okay." I pace some more. Say, "Okay," some more.

But nothing is okay.

I check the date on the paper again. It hasn't changed.

My heart is frantic against my ribs. "This is impossible." I don't know who I'm trying to convince, but flinging my arms at the ceiling, I try again. "Seriously! This can't be happening!"

The only response I get is the sound of the refrigerator kicking on and the heavy weight of reality pressing in on me.

I don't feel like I'm dreaming, but I can't just concede this is reality. I mean, how could it be? I barely believe in the idea of God. Things like time-travel and wish-granting stars belong in the science-fiction section of the bookstore. They don't happen to real people.

Real people don't simply go to bed one night and wake up the next morning twenty years in the past. To the day. After witnessing the biggest, brightest fireball in history and making an impossible wish from the heart.

I wish they could all be saved. I wish someone could have stopped 9/11.

Could my wish have been heard? If so, there has been a terrible mistake. I wished that *someone* could stop 9/11. As in someone *else*. Someone *not* me.

I meant someone who could actually *do* something, like an agent with some intelligence organization or a law enforcement official. Someone with a gun and a badge and a reason to know about what was—or is—going to happen.

"I didn't mean me!" I say, my voice perilously close to a whine.

The apartment is indifferent. The walls don't care that I'm actually considering believing this craziness. The floor holding me up is unconcerned that I'm most likely losing my marbles.

I pinch the bridge of my nose. I need to think, but my mind is a tangled mess. Do I believe what I'm seeing and experiencing, or do I trust the science-based skepticism that comes far more naturally to me?

If I'm really here in the past, does that mean I'll have to live the next twenty years over again? What about my children? If time-travel movies have taught me anything, it's that time is fragile. If this is all real, I could be jeopardizing their existence simply by being here, where I don't belong.

Except this me *does* belong here. At least the physical me does. It's the mental me that belongs twenty years in the future. I am fractured. I'm a bone that's been broken in two and needs setting. But the raw edges are twenty years apart.

As terrifying as that feels, there's even more at stake than my children and twenty years of my life. Tomorrow is going to be *9-freaking-11!* And, if this is legitimately happening, that means *I'm* supposed to try and stop it.

"No pressure, or anything." The words come out half-hysterical. My chest feels tight. My breaths are coming too fast, and the edges of my vision fade to black. Years of training kick in. Hands on knees, I force myself to concentrate on not passing out.

Breathe. Slow and shallow. Breathe. Take it easy.

When the threat of hyperventilation passes, I stand up with the aid of a chair tucked in at the dining table. My gaze jumps around the apartment. I'm desperate for answers, guidance, anything. But I'm alone. I'm a tourist stranded far from home with no luggage, no passport or ID, and no one to help me.

Today's paper draws my eye. I must have set it on the table without realizing it. It sits by the chair I'm gripping, pretending to be innocuous. But the way it resolutely declares the date makes it feel like a pill with a lengthy warning label.

Used for the prevention of unprecedented terror attack.

Take on an empty stomach with extreme caution.

May cause interruption of reality.

Risk of permanent alteration of the space-time continuum.

I take a long, deep cleansing breath. "Okay, Lyd. Do not panic. You can think through this. You're good at solving problems."

The chaos of my thoughts keeps bringing me back to one problem in particular: whether or not this is reality. It's a problem I have to solve before I can entertain the possibility that I might be here to stop 9/11. Because once I start interacting with the outside world of September 10th, 2001, there will be no going back. I will have to assume that I'm here to stay. I will have to pretend to love Tristan long enough for my children to be born. I will have to hope and pray that they will be the same Christian and Holly as the ones I've already raised. If they aren't—I can't imagine the pain I'll feel. I'm already aching deep in the tissues of my beating heart at the thought of being separated from them, of having to wait to meet them again.

So, I need to be one-hundred-percent sure. But how?

I've already tried the pinch test. I've interacted with my environment and with another person. I've nearly hyperventilated. None of those things resulted in my surroundings melting away to reveal a truer reality beneath. I rack my brain for other ways a person can figure out whether they're dreaming.

Many years ago, I had an elderly patient who was misdiagnosed with dementia because her symptoms so closely resembled the illness. What she actually suffered from was a devastating case of chronic insomnia. Due to living in a sleep-deprived state, she often had trouble separating dreams from reality.

"Lucid dreaming," Inez says in my memory. Her face is pale. Her eyes are filled with wisdom and weariness. "You can train yourself to take control of a dream. If you're ever unsure whether you're dreaming or not, do something unexpected. Try to fly. Try to make something materialize in your hand. Break something." She nods sagely. "Dreams don't behave rationally. If you throw a vase at a mirror, you'd expect the mirror to shatter." She lifts a frail arm and mimics throwing something. "But if you're dreaming, the mirror won't shatter, at least not in the normal way. It might catch the vase and throw it back. It might absorb the vase like a portal." She chuckles. "My poor husband. Once, I threw our toaster through the kitchen window. Let's just say, I was not dreaming that day."

With Inez's words echoing in my ear, I face the bookshelf. The me that belongs here has begun lining up nursing textbooks in preparation for the coming semester. Beside the textbooks and a few novels Tristan and I had been reading, there are some decorations on the shelf, including a green ceramic vase.

I grab it and go into the bathroom. The vase is large and heavy in my hands, like a carved-out bowling ball with a thin neck for flowers. I wind up and hurl it at the mirror as hard as I can.

The vase and the mirror shatter as one into a million pieces that rain down on the counter and fill the sink. Only a few pieces of glass remain glued to the wall. My ears thrum with the deafening crash.

I blink at my fractured reflection.

Whelp. That was a pretty normal shattering.

Close on the heels of that thought comes this beauty: *Oh, man. Tristan's going to be pissed when he gets home.*

I'm beginning to think of things like consequences. My mind is starting to accept that I am here and not *there,* in Nebraska with Holly and Jes, where I belong.

Oh, sweet Holly. Dear Christian. I'm really here, and that means I will have to wait *years* to meet my children.

On one hand, the thought of raising them from infancy again fills me with soft, downy love. On the other hand, the thought of remaining married to Tristan long enough to have them is like drinking sour milk. It was hard enough the first time. I don't want to do it again.

With shards of glass and pottery around my feet, I acknowledge the worst-case scenario, that I may not have my children at all. The odds of the exact same sperm making it to the exact same egg are so slim as to be practically nonexistent. I might have two children, but they might not be *my* Holly and Christian.

I can't imagine a world without my kids. Holly, my compassionate girl, and Christian, my powerhouse athlete. Panic rises in my chest.

I can't do this. I can't risk my children for this.

I stop. I breathe. And I remember what's at stake. I remember what 9/11 will mean to this world I've invaded, which has no idea what's about to hit it.

I *can* do this. I *must* do this.

I have put my own wellbeing on the line for my profession before. I have wrestled drunk men twice my size. I have thrown myself into the fray to restrain an out-of-control patient while a doctor administers a sedative. I have quarantined myself from my family to battle COVID. Thank the stars, there has never been a situation where my kids have been seriously endangered. Until now.

To save three thousand lives tomorrow and many thousands more from environmental effects in the years to come, I must risk the two most precious lives to me.

What else can I do? I am here. I'm not going anywhere.

This is my life now. I am in the year 2001.

This is my life now. I am in the year 2001.

I tell it to myself again. And again. And yet again. Because I need to accept it.

It sucks to lose the last twenty years of my life. But there's something about all this that doesn't suck: Having a chance to undo the greatest wrong of my generation.

Reality settles on me like a lead apron. The longer I'm here, the more that apron feels like it belongs. Like I can't take it off, even if I want to. Surprisingly, now that I'm certain what's going on here, I don't want to be relieved of this burden.

Whoever heard my wish, if you can hear me now, please, please let my children still be my children.

Filled with purpose, I leave the glass-covered bathroom and tie on some comfortable running shoes. The clock on the bedside table reads 8:12 a.m. I don't take the time to sweep up my mess. I can't waste a single minute. Not when I have less than twenty-four hours to stop 9/11.

*When facing a difficult task, act as though
it is impossible to fail. If you are going
after Moby Dick, take along the tartar
sauce.*

—H. Jackson Brown, Jr.

CHAPTER 4

Lydia

STANDING IN MY FORMER KITCHEN, I'm gloved up with a sense of determination. I've lowered my face shield, an unshakable sense of reality. This is no dream or hallucination. I am here, and I have a job to do. All I need now is the right equipment.

I can't clean a wound or get fluids into a patient with my bare hands. And I can't stop 9/11 without some basic necessities. I just have to figure out what's available for my use.

I dash to the couch, where I dropped the Nokia when Saraka knocked. There it is, on the floor by the footlocker. I pick it up and look it over. It takes a minute to remember how to turn it on. Pressing and holding the button, I watch it come to life. Each component appears on the screen in due time, as if the phone is in no rush to provide me with connectivity. The battery symbol is black against the yellowish-green screen. The bars for signal strength appear next. Then the time. All the icons are huge and pixelated with laughably low resolution. There is no Bluetooth symbol. It's hard to believe this was the height of consumer-grade technology twenty years ago.

The phone is basic, but it'll do. It's the first item in my toolkit.

I'll also need a laptop. Internet access will be essential. Fortunately, Tristan and I always kept one at home. In two weeks, when the semester starts at nursing school, Tristan will present me with a shiny, new Mac. But at this point in time, we would be making do with the chunky Gateway PC I used in college. Where would it be, though?

I check the bedroom. The desk Tristan will get me for nursing school is absent. It should be crammed into the corner beside the closet, but there is nothing there except a vacuum cleaner too large to store anywhere else.

Moving briskly, I turn my attention to the living room. The footlocker is bare on top except for the remotes. Inside, Tristan and I kept mementos from our individual lives up to this point. I wouldn't have stored my computer in there.

My gaze falls on the small dining table. One end is cleared so Tristan and I can eat at it. The other end is cluttered with several days' worth of newspapers and mail. I see the corner of something smooth and gray poking from underneath the pile. Bingo!

I toss the papers to the floor so I can reacquaint myself with the old laptop. The rubber feet fight me as I drag it to the edge of the table. It can only come so far, because a power cord and an ethernet cable tether it to the wall. No wireless internet at this time, not at the apartment of a pair of newlyweds, anyway. Still, it's another item in my toolkit. I pry open the lid and power it on.

Next, I find a legal pad and pen in a drawer in the kitchen. While there, I notice the espresso machine I bought Tristan as a wedding present. Coffee. Coffee is definitely a tool I need right now.

Unfortunately, I am confounded by all the bells and whistles of the complicated machine. I knew my way around this thing at one time, but at the moment, all I remember is that the clear chamber is for grinding beans and the metal rod is for foaming milk. I've been spoiled by my single-pod Keurig for far too long.

I'm beginning to accept I may have to go without coffee when I remember the drip coffee pot I used in college. Tristan hadn't wanted to keep it after we got married. *"It'll take up space we don't have, Lyd."* But I'd hidden it away because I thought one day, I might like a simple cup of coffee again.

Standing on a chair, I find it at the very back of the coat closet on the top shelf. It's tucked behind a stack of magazines from my knitting phase. In a few minutes' time, the glorious scent of freshly-ground French roast fills the apartment.

"See, Lyd? You can do this." I give myself a pep talk while I stir in the perfect amount of creamer. "Take each problem as it pops up. Just like at work."

Coffee in hand, I line up the laptop, Nokia, legal pad and pen. My workstation is complete. Everything I need is at my fingertips.

I'm ready to do this thing. But my old Gateway is not.

It's been at least ten minutes since I powered it on, but it's still going through its start-up routine. Icons are sleepily blinking into place on the screen, one by one.

"Come on." I drum my fingers on the laptop casing.

Tomorrow, the world will witness the deadliest foreign attack on U.S. soil in our history. The loss of life and property will be catastrophic. I am the only one who knows about it. I am the only one who can stop it. And I'm stymied by a slow PC.

I take a soothing sip of coffee. Then another.

I use the time to plan what I'm going to do. It's not easy to focus. The task before me is overwhelming. Images of sharply banking planes, flaming towers, and dust-covered people fill my head.

How does one person stop something like this?

You can do this, Lyd. Just think about what needs to be done. This is no different from a critical patient coming through the door.

In the ER I left to move to Mom and Dad's farm, there was this red phone on the wall of the nurse's station. An installation just a few years old, it was used by paramedics and 9-1-1 operators to alert our department to emergencies in progress. The phone would ring, and on the other end would be a warning. A head injury is coming in, estimated time of arrival, seven minutes. Or a severe laceration, ETA 15. Or a heart attack, ETA 3. Whatever the emergency, the staff would gather the tools appropriate for the job, glove up, and brace for incoming.

That phone shaved precious life-saving minutes off the ER response to major traumas. That phone saved lives.

Today, I am that phone.

The United States needs to brace for incoming, and I am the only warning the country will get.

My challenge is that no one is listening for a ringing phone. No one's expecting what's coming.

"I have to make them listen."

But first I need to figure out who *they* are and what I'm going to tell them.

"All right, Lyd. What information do you have?"

I put pen to paper and start writing. I start with flight numbers and what I can remember of tomorrow's timeline:

American Flt 11 – North tower 8:46 a.m.

United Flt 175 – South tower 9:02

American Flt 77 – Pentagon 9:30 - 9:40

United Flt 93 – Southern Pennsylvania, 10-ish

But the times the planes reached their terminal destinations are not the important ones for my purpose. It's the take-off times that matter. Stop the planes from getting airborne, or at least prevent the terrorists from boarding, and 9/11 won't happen. It's as simple as that.

Beside my list of the four flights, I write, *Look up flight times. Stop from taking off.*

I don't dare look up the flight times myself. If I try with my Gateway, it'll take all morning. What I do know is that they all took off before 9 am. I also know where they took off from. I add the origin airports to each of the four flights, Logan for American Flight 11 and United Flight 175, Newark for United 93, and Dulles for American Flight 77.

I turn my attention to the terrorists. In my reading, I memorized the full names of the pilots. I know the last names of several of the other hijackers as well, but not all. I'm also positive I could recognize some of their faces if shown pictures.

I organize my list of terrorists by airplane, starting with American Flight 11, which was the first to take off. I make a large circle to represent the plane. Inside the circle, I write *Mohammed Atta – Pilot.* Omari was also on that plane. He and Atta entered Logan airport by way of an early-morning flight from Portland, Maine. I put *(Portland, 6 a.m.)* beside their names. There were also two brothers on Flight 11. I think their name was Sherri. I write the surname twice, probably butchering the spelling, but oh the heck well. If you kill people in my country, I reserve the right to misspell your name. There was a fifth hijacker on the plane, but I don't remember his name. Beneath the other four names, I draw a line representing a blank to be filled in.

I move on to United Flight 175. I make my circle and start with the hijacker pilot, *Marwan al-Shehhi.* I add Ghamdi beneath Shehhi. I remember the name because it reminded me of Gandhi, not that the peaceful activist would have appreciated the association. There were two hijackers by that name. Beneath the two Ghamdis, I draw two blanks and move on to a third circle.

The hijacker pilot of American Flight 77 was Hani Hanjour. Beneath his name, I add *Hamzi, Hamzi, Midhair,* and a blank.

Inside the circle for United Flight 93, I write *Ziad Jarrah* and three blanks for a total of four hijackers. Flight 93 was the only one to have four instead of five terrorists on board. Still, I draw a blank to represent a possible fifth, and I fill in the name *al-Qahtani,* followed by a question mark. Some dubbed Qahtani "The 20th Hijacker," believing he intended on rounding out the group on Flight 93. However, he never made the flight. He was denied entrance to the U.S. the month before the attack by an immigration official.

I read several articles about the supposed 20th hijacker, and I always thought Qahtani was the most likely of the suspects. Unfortunately, he was never convicted for being part of the plot. His case was thrown out due to the torture he'd endured in the detention camp at Guantanamo Bay. At this point in time, that torture hasn't happened yet. As far as I know, after failing to gain entry to the U.S., Qahtani was sent back to Saudi Arabia. It wasn't until after the attacks that he was caught. I make several notes about Qahtani, including *DO NOT TORTURE,* and sit back to review my work.

I've accounted for each of the 19 hijackers either by name or as a blank space, and I've connected as many of them as possible to individual flights and originating airports. Today, these names fill four circles on a page of lined, yellow paper. Tomorrow, they will be responsible for nearly three thousand deaths.

What would happen if I called TSA and gave them this list of names? Wait. I can't do that because the Transportation Security Administration doesn't exist yet. It came into being because of 9/11. I would have to call the airports directly, and they may or may not pass along the names to the private security firms responsible for passenger safety.

The fact is I don't know enough about how airport security works to be sure these men will be stopped. What if the airports simply referred me to local police who would have no reason to take me seriously? What I do know is that one, these men can't be allowed to fly, and two, they need to be caught and prosecuted.

Stopping 9/11 is paramount, but making sure the nation understands the threat is also important. Otherwise, some future date might become synonymous with tragedy and disaster.

If I'm going to do this right, I need to go deeper than airport security or local law enforcement. I need to contact officials who know who Osama Bin Laden is, who understand the threat al-Qaeda poses, and who have the authority to make arrests.

The first possibility that comes to mind is the FBI. On TV, their agents are always stepping around crime scenes in their black jackets with yellow letters on the back, looking capable and intimidating. My research on 9/11, however, tells a different story. Like millions of Americans, I read the *Commission Report*. The FBI knew about Bin Laden, but they hadn't made him a big priority. They knew al-Qaeda wanted to strike at Americans, but they envisioned another foreign embassy attack, or another bombing of a sea vessel, like the USS Cole. When it came to acts of terrorism, their focus wasn't on the homeland.

I imagine how a phone call to them would go.

"FBI Tip Line, what's your tip?"

"Yeah, hi. I'm calling to report an impending terrorist attack. It's going to happen tomorrow. See, al-Qaeda's going to hijack four planes from U.S. airports, and—insert nervous chuckle—*you're not going to believe this, but they're going to actually take control of the planes and turn them into guided missiles aimed at the World Trade Center and The Pentagon."*

I can already hear the likely responses. "Yeah right, lady. Ever heard of airport security?" Or, "Hijackers don't fly planes, sweetheart." Or, "Ma'am, this line is for serious tips only." And, of course, "How did you come by this information?"

And I'd have to respond that I'm just a nursing student from New York with absolutely no reason to know anything about enemies of the state.

I flip to a new page on the legal pad, and I write, *FBI—able to help, won't believe.*

Below that, I write, *CIA.*

Once again, TV and film-watching informs my presuppositions. I think of a secretive organization packed with gleeful torturers and hard-faced agents stationed in dusty bases overseas. I imagine counterterrorism units who live, eat, and breathe all things terror related. But that was all after 9/11. And heavily fictionalized.

All I remember about the CIA before 9/11 is that they knew some of the names of the nineteen terrorists. They even knew some of them were in the country. But they didn't share that information with other agencies. None of the names were put on no-fly or watchlists. Still, the CIA might take me slightly more seriously than the FBI because I'll be armed with names that I shouldn't know, names of al-Qaeda operatives.

I sip my coffee and wonder if they knew about some of those operatives enrolling in U.S. flight schools. How closely are they tracking them? Would they know about recent ATM withdrawals? Recently-bought plane tickets and cross-country travel carried out to gain experience with airport procedures and security?

Beside *CIA,* I write, *able to help, may be more likely to believe than FBI.*

I write *FAA* next. They will be the first to know when the planes are hijacked, but would they listen to a warning about terrorists getting on planes? From someone with no good reason to have the information? Would they stop planes from taking off based on such a warning, with no back-up from a law-enforcement entity?

I simply don't know enough about the FAA to make an informed decision, so I put a question mark beside the acronym.

Below that, just to be thorough, I write, *Local Police,* but I suspect at the mention of terrorism, they'd bring in the FBI, that is, *if* they even took me seriously.

In every scenario I come up with, the biggest problem is the same: me.

I am nobody. I have no reason to know the things I know. If that doesn't make my job challenging enough, the events about to unfold are so outlandish and the outcome is so far beyond the comprehension of anyone who hasn't lived it, that even if I were the most compelling of tipsters, no one would take this particular tip seriously. I might as well be alerting the nation to the impending alien abduction of George W. Bush or the flattening of the Statue of Liberty by Godzilla.

I check the clock in the lower corner of my laptop screen. It reads 8:49 a.m. At this time tomorrow, American Flight 11 will have already hit the World Trade Center's north tower.

Looking at the time makes me feel sick, so I force my attention away from the digits and onto the problem at hand. Who do I call, and how do I make them listen?

A scene from the movie *National Treasure* pops into my head. Treasure hunter Benjamin Gates, played by Nicolas Cage, and his tech-savvy counterpart, Riley, have learned some bad men are about to steal the Declaration of Independence to gain access to an invisible map on the back. Outside the FBI office, where they've apparently been turned away, Riley says something like the following to Gates: "Anyone crazy enough to believe us won't be able to help, and anyone who can help won't believe us."

I remember the gist of what comes after that, but I want the exact wording. Since my laptop is finally done booting, I open Internet Explorer, ready to hunt down the quote. And am met with an hourglass icon that tells me the webpage is loading. And loading. And loading.

Oh, jeepers. Internet is slow in 2001.

Hitting pause on the idea, I pour myself a second cup of coffee and make a bowl of cereal. At one time, I was the lady of this manor. But at the moment, I feel like a guest in a bed-and-breakfast, out of place and in the way. I'm happy to ignore the feeling and go back to my workstation with my sustenance.

When I sit down, Google is waiting for me like an old friend. The home page has changed remarkably little in twenty years. Gone are the artistic images that change daily to spell G-O-O-G-L-E. In their place is a simple heading in primary colors. Other than that, the page looks almost exactly like it does when I open the browser on my tablet or one of the computers at work.

I eat some cereal, sip some coffee, and feel like I'm in my element as I type into the search bar. After a minute, the results come back, and I learn there is no such movie as *National Treasure*. That's right. It came out well after I was done with nursing school.

I am reminded that while Google might look familiar, I'm a visitor in a world where I don't belong. The seriousness of my purpose goes down hard with a lump of cereal.

Soberly, I let my mind fill in the quote I had hoped to find, the gist of it, anyway. Benjamin Gates, consoling Riley, says something like, "We don't need someone crazy, but one step short of crazy, and what do you get?"

Riley answers, "Obsessed," and the droll look he gives Gates implies Gates, himself, embodies that word.

Gates corrects him. "Passionate." And in the next frame, they're at the National Archives waiting to meet with Abigail Chase, curator in charge of the Declaration of Independence. Though Dr. Chase seems an unlikely choice for an ally, she turns out to be just what the pair needs.

I need an Abigail Chase. Someone who's passionate about...what? National security? Terrorism? Someone with connections and knowledge, for sure. Someone accessible. Someone who might not only listen to what I have to say but who also has the power to *do* something about it.

Elbows on the table, head in hands, I put my neurons to work on the problem.

"Think, Lyd."

Who out there might take the time to listen to me? What kind of person might be motivated to look into my claims? A private investigator? I write down, *PI – motivated by cash*. I don't have much cash. I could empty Tristan's and my bank account, but after our honeymoon, we're not exactly rolling in dough. Furthermore, I'm short on time. I imagine calling a private investigator and having them schedule me for an interview later in the week. I need someone who can jump on this right away. I cross through *PI* and think about who might be able to act fast.

"A cab driver," I say with a snort. They move fast. But I don't imagine they're particularly well-connected, unless they happen to drive a lot of government officials around. Since this is New York, and not Washington, D.C., I don't bother writing that one down.

While I finish my second cup of coffee, my gaze drifts to the screen in front of me. The Google results are still up. All along the left side are news headlines. I remember when the internet used to look like that. Lots of blue font and underlined links enticing you to click over and read the latest developments in world news.

I freeze with my finger on the touchpad.

The news!

News stories are written by journalists. Who interview people in the government and have lots of connections. Who work fast and are motivated by their own curiosity and the desire to inform the public.

My neurons start firing like the Fourth of July. I finally feel like I'm getting somewhere. A plan begins forming.

I crack my knuckles and position my hands over the keyboard.

"Okay, Google," I say, knowing full well this version won't activate its microphone at the command. With my cursor in the search bar, I perform my second search of the morning. My Gateway seems to have warmed up, because the results come up faster this time. I take notes and do another search. And another. One hour and a few phone calls later, I've packed my workstation into a shoulder bag and am out the door.

In sneakers, jeans, and a hoodie, I jog down the hill to the neighborhood's main thoroughfare. I've got my eye on the entrance to the subway tunnel, but a cab for hire happens to be driving by. My lucky day! I hail it and get in.

"Where to?" the driver asks in a thick Brooklyn accent.

I ask him to wait while I check my wallet. I grabbed the purse by the door in a hurry, only checking to see that my ID was inside. I have no idea what I have by way of money. The leather of my pink billfold creaks with newness as I flip through it. I'll use this thing until it's coming apart at the seams, but at the moment, it's brand new. I remember Tristan buying it for me in the Caymans, the novelty of marriage coloring his gaze with indulgence.

For once, my ex's blanket declarations work in my favor. He always insisted I have cash on hand in case of emergency. Of course, he never approved of me spending that cash on frivolities like coffee and cab fare, at least not while we were living on a single income, but that's beside the point. I find a couple of credit cards and $180 in cash, which should be enough for this fare and for what I plan to do today.

"The airport, please," I tell the driver. "LaGuardia."

I can't believe I'm about to fly when 9/11 is barreling down on the east coast. If there were a faster way to get to Washington, D.C., I'd take it.

Put it before them briefly so they will read it, clearly so they will appreciate it, picturesquely so they will remember it, and above all, accurately so they will be guided by its light.

—Joseph Pulitzer

CHAPTER 5

Ian

I'M FIVE STEPS from the door of the coffee shop when I get a page from my editor. *My office now,* it says in blocky letters. Mournfully, I turn my back on the circular sign with the lusty siren and trudge upstairs to the fifth-floor cube farm also known as the *Washington Post* newsroom.

The back stairs are faster than the elevator, so I go that way. With each step, I regret my pitstop in the International District more and more. Detouring to the Persian Café before work had been a gamble. The source I needed to check in with was usually fifty-fifty on whether he'd be at the restaurant this early. Today, I lost the gamble. Now, I have to face Carmen without my triple shot cappuccino, and I have no new leads to show for it.

"What is this?" My editor's greeting is punctuated by a manicured finger jabbing at a printout clutched in her other hand.

"It's this week's column," I say cheerfully, assuming it's the piece I sent her at 11:59 last night. "Right on time."

Her expression does not change. She might be five-foot three in four-inch heels, but she's deadly as a velociraptor in red lipstick. She shoves the printout under my nose. "Try again, Greenberg."

Mindful of her talons, I take the page from her and turn it so I can read it. Belatedly, I realize my glasses are still in my pocket from the light mist outside. I flip them open and shove them on, and now Carmen appears even deadlier. Her em-dash eyebrows demand answers.

This time, when I study the paper in my hand, the headline jumps out at me. *City Youth Center Opens beneath Extremist Mosque.*

I force a breezy tone. "Ah. Yes. It's the feature piece I've been working on in my spare time. Had no effect on my workload."

See, Carmen? No big deal. Just an in-depth look at twenty-first century terrorist recruiting tactics happening right here in D.C., which had absolutely nothing to do with my late column. See how relaxed I am about it? Like it won't rip my heart out if you send it to the WAPO slush pile like you did with the piece I wrote last month?

Carmen is silent, but her predator gaze speaks volumes. She's freaky when she goes still like this. A hurricane could blow through the office and still, the edges of her Chanel suit wouldn't so much as flutter.

Never let them see you sweat. "Just an extracurricular favor for Miller. Not even sure why it came across your desk." I fold the printout and slide it into my messenger bag. Miller's going to hear from me. He promised this piece wouldn't hit Carmen's radar. "Nothing you need to worry about."

"Why don't you let me decide what to worry about." Her voice is deceptively quiet. I brace myself. "Like how a reporter on my payroll needs constant reminding that 'end-of-day' means close of business, not the stroke before midnight."

"Yeah, about that—"

"Like why a column writer in *my* bullpen keeps attempting to be a feature writer for goddamned Miller." Her arm becomes a perfectly tailored arrow pointing toward Miller's department on the other side of the floor. I don't know what personal vendetta she has against the feature editor, but I've suspected for a while now she'd have a lot less to say about it if I moonlighted for someone else.

Unfortunately, feature writing is where I want to be. It's always where I wanted to be. Growing up with a Jewish father, a Muslim mother, and complicated extended family dynamics sparked an interest in Middle-Eastern politics that carried me through a double major in Journalism and Middle-Eastern studies at Yale. It's always been my goal to use current topics to inform and educate about the part of the world I'm descended from and how it mixes with western culture. Misunderstandings need dispelling. Hidden dangers need exposing. And no one else is even trying.

But apparently, five years of paying dues as a local-politics column reporter isn't long enough.

"*Attempting* is rather harsh, Carmen. All I'm trying to do is—"

One of Carmen's eyebrows punches upward while holding its shape. That single motion stops me midsentence. "This is the last time I'm going to tell you this, so listen carefully, Greenberg. Stick to local politics unless I say otherwise, or I'll have you back to junior reporter so fast your head will spin."

It's not an idle threat. It never is with Carmen.

I decide to appeal to her humanity, because I *know* I have what it takes to be a feature writer. Hell, I *am* a feature writer. I'm proud of the piece I did last month about Saudis on tourist visas going to flight schools here in the States. I'm proud of the contrast I made between legitimate international students who go on to have careers at airlines or in their armed forces and students that should raise red flags because of their association with known terror cells.

I sent the piece to Miller, and he couldn't say enough positive stuff about it. I seem to remember the words, *interesting, important,* and *well-researched,* not that I read his email enough times to have it memorized or anything. Miller scheduled the feature to run in a weekend issue. And Carmen promptly cancelled it for "not being newsworthy."

Now she's doing it again. Any time I get close to printing something worthwhile, Carmen sucks me back down into column-writing purgatory. I'll do anything to get out. Even beg.

I spread my hands. "I hear what you're saying, Carmen. I do. I'm just asking for one longer piece once in a while. On something that matters, something thought-provoking that most people don't take the time to notice." Like last month's piece. Like the piece in my bag right now. Like the five other pieces on my hard drive that need to see the light of day. I do a good job of keeping the bitterness out of my voice. "Is that really so much to ask?"

Carmen's lips purse. Weirdly, on her, it's a softening of her expression. The line of her shoulders settles a fraction. She appears almost human as she studies me.

"If you had something to contribute to Miller's pool, I'd consider it. I know you think this is about interdepartmental bullshit, but it's not. This is about news. No one cares about Middle Eastern immigrants going to mosque." She waves a hand vaguely, as if that's what my latest piece is about. "And you haven't been consistent enough in local politics coverage to earn a higher word-count." She stabs a finger at the blotting pad on her desk. "Make a habit of impressing me on my turf, and we'll talk." She dismisses me by tapping a stack of papers into conformity.

Carmen has just given me a pseudo-concession. She's promised to revisit my feature writing at some point in the future. I would be a fool to compromise that in any way. Or to ignore her dismissal.

On the other hand, she has completely missed the point of my writing.

"Middle Eastern immigrants? That's what you think this is about?" My fingers dive into my bag and close on the printout.

Carmen looks up sharply.

Before I know what I'm doing, I'm waving the paper like a red cape before a bull. "This isn't about an ingredient in the great American melting pot. This is about the extremist fringe of a group most Americans don't understand. It's about possible terrorism. It's about New York in '93 and the extremely likely chance it'll happen again. It's about recruitment going on in our own back yard. It's about the influx of young people from other nationalities joining that fringe movement. No one cares that these kids are being indoctrinated to hate us on our own soil? Do you really believe that?"

One corner of Carmen's mouth curls up. Here I am mad as a hornet, and she finds me amusing, like I'm a toddler in the grips of a tantrum. "That's exactly what I believe. *No one's* writing about terrorism right now. It's a non-topic. Next time there's a bombing, you can send a piece across my desk—*not* Miller's—*if* you show me you can be on time with your column."

My face is hot. If I stay, I'm going to say something I'll regret. I'm lucky Carmen hasn't demoted me on the spot.

"I get it." I shove the printout in my bag. "I'll stick to debate summaries and polls on how locals feel about traffic congestion."

I'm striding out her door when she gets the last word in. "That's all I ask."

I have a ton of notes to organize and writing to do, and I need to get started ASAP, but my hands are shaking with the effects of Carmen's reprimand. I need a few minutes to calm down, get my head right.

"Remember my friggin' place," I mutter as I trudge to the breakroom.

Vending machines, microwaves, and an out-of-date refrigerator turn the small room into an overheated cave smelling of burnt popcorn and leftover lasagna. The coffee pot is empty of all but syrupy sludge. Not that drip would have done the trick after the all-nighter I just pulled. Carmen's hair would fall out if she knew the truth of how far behind that feature put me.

No more of that if I'm ever going to make feature writer. I've got to *impress* Carmen on *her* turf. As if the years I've already put in count for nothing.

I shove my fingers through my hair. I need more than a trip to the breakroom to settle down. A glance at my Blackberry shows the morning is still young. As long as the line's not too long, I should be able to get to the café downstairs and back to my desk in a reasonable timeframe. Having long legs has its advantages.

I'm tearing past reception when Renee calls out my name. "Ian, are you here today?"

She means am I at the office or on assignment. "I'm here. Writing day."

Renee's voice follows me to the stairwell entry. "Some woman called with a lead for you. I gave her your mobile because she said it was urgent, and I didn't see you come in!" The last part is muffled as the fire door bangs shut.

Fabulous. The last thing I need right now is a lead bothering me on my mobile. I'm neck-deep in local election fodder, and my focus is shot.

My Doc Martens make an unholy racket in the echo chamber of concrete and steel. The sound is egging on the headache I've got brewing behind my eyes.

Coffee. Coffee will make everything more manageable. I'll get my hands on some. Then, soon as I get back, I'll give Renee an earful for handing out my mobile number. *I'm* the one that calls my leads when the time suits *me,* not the other way around.

When I get to the café, the line is epic. Pinching the bridge of my nose. I take my place at the end and pull out my Blackberry to call Miller. Before I can pull up his contact card, the phone rings with an unknown number, New York area code.

"Greenberg," I answer, keeping my voice down—I refuse to be one of those uncouth loud-talkers who shout into their phones in public places.

"*Ian* Greenberg? Hi. You don't know me, but I got your number from the front desk."

The woman sounds young but professional. Her accent shows no obvious regional preference. This must be my mystery-lead lady.

"Look, right now's not a good time. Leave a message with Renee, and I'll—"

"You're right, you know." She cuts me off. "About terrorists using planes. You're exactly right. It's going to happen, and I have the details. I'm on my way to D.C. right now to meet with you."

It takes me a moment to catch up to the moving line. Mystery Lead has stunned me into inaction. "What did you say?" I ask even though the connection is crystal clear.

"They're going to use planes, just like you suggest in your article, 'New Face of Terrorism in the Twenty-First Century.'"

Last month's piece. The one Miller approved and Carmen shut down. My free hand clutches at my bag, even though the printout inside is a different piece than the one Mystery Lead just mentioned.

"That article was never sent to print. Did you get it from Miller? Who are you?" Is this another reporter trying to steal my work? Or someone trying to discredit me?

"I don't know about print, but it's online," the woman says. "The article is dated—" She pauses, like she's referring to notes. "August 26th. My name is Lydia, by the way. Lydia Clay."

"August?" I parrot. *Slow on the uptake* does not usually describe me. I blame lack of sleep and coffee. And the fact this conversation is taking me completely off guard. Terrorists and planes are topics best discussed while caffeinated. My brain skips right over them and latches onto the more personally relevant point. "Really? The piece is online?"

If I wasn't so close to the front of the queue, I'd break away and check the WAPO website this very minute. Renewed energy shoots through me. I'm bouncing on the balls of my feet.

"Um. Yes?" She makes it a question. I can tell it's not the existence of the article she doubts but the fact I hadn't known it was published.

I don't blame her. I should have known, but I don't even care that no one told me. I'm too excited.

Hot damn! Miller gave me my first feature! And he did it in a way Carmen—a print purist—would be unlikely to notice. Hell, *I* didn't even notice. Income from online readership is like a bucket of water compared to the inground swimming pool of profit from print ads. Publishing my piece there would have been a genius way for Miller to thumb his nose at Carmen. I make a mental note to buy him a beer. I'll buy him a whole keg for giving me my first feature. Even if it only appeared online.

And someone actually read it! Wait. My brain catches up to everything Mystery Lead—Lydia—said. "What do you mean, 'They're going to use planes?'"

I'm just beginning to register traffic noise on her end. She's in a car. A male with a thick Brooklyn accent says he's going to cut through Queens to avoid the backup on the parkway.

"Fine," Lydia says to him. "Just get me there quick as you can." When she says, "I have inside information about an impending attack," it's directed at me. "Yes, planes. It's... going to be bad. But I can't go to the FBI or CIA. At least not alone. I need your help."

"*My* help?" I resolve to begin speaking intelligently any moment now. When I ask, "Why me?" I make it a demand. It's past time I take control of this conversation. Ian Greenberg does not let a lead walk all over him. I don't have time for this today, but I'll be damned if I don't get to the bottom of a story when "terrorism" and "impending attack" are mentioned in the same breath as my piece.

Miller published my feature!

"In the article, you theorize that terrorists could up the ante on hijackings by learning to fly passenger jets themselves." If there's anything I appreciate about this phone call, it's that Lydia's wasting no time. Her speech is rapid and succinct. "Traditional hijackings are about hostages and negotiations. Pilots and attendants are trained to follow orders and let authorities on the ground solve the problem. But what if the terrorists don't want money or anything else in exchange for lives?"

The woman two customers in front of me hands over some bills. I'll be up soon.

Lydia is summarizing my feature with a familiarity that strikes me as both flattering and odd. My feature is so obscure *I* didn't even know about its publication. Yet this woman appears extremely knowledgeable about it. Or perhaps she's fascinated with the topic of terrorism in general, as am I. Either way, the clock is ticking on my patience.

Though Lydia can't see it, I wind two fingers in a circular motion, willing her to get to the point.

"Their goal with the USS Cole," she goes on, "with the embassy bombings of '98, was loss of life and property, not negotiation. If all they want is to cause damage, and they're not afraid to die for their cause, and we apply that thinking to commuter aircraft..." She trails off, but I'm well acquainted with the line of logic she's suggesting. I wrote it, after all.

"Hijackers of the future," I finish for her, "could bring down planes purely for the shock value."

"Exactly," she says, meaningfully, as if it's case closed. Except, I'm not sure what case she thinks she's made.

I wait a beat, and when she adds nothing more, I say, "Look, I'd be happy to meet later in the week to discuss this further, but today is no good. You said you're on your way D.C.? How long will you be in town?" I pull out my pencil and stack my notebook atop my wallet while pinning the phone to my ear. I'm ready to plan a meeting time out of sheer curiosity.

"It has to be today," she says.

The customer in front of me moves on, and the green-aproned cashier cocks her head impatiently. I'm holding up her line.

"Not possible." I have a living to make, and Carmen's making sure I do it in the most boring way possible.

Lydia is talking, but I'm not hearing her. I'm reciting my order and handing over my five bucks.

"Did you hear me, Ian? This attack is impending." I must have missed something, because it sounds like she's talking about a specific threat. "This is extremely important."

So's my job. "I appreciate your interest in my piece, Ms. Clay, but I'm very busy at the moment."

The cashier thrusts a few coins at me.

I wave at the tip jar and move down the counter. "As I said, Renee will set you up with a meeting—"

"It's Osama Bin Laden doing it." Lydia interrupts my blow-off with the very last name I want to hear in a conversation about terrorists and airplanes.

"What did you say?"

My pulse kicks into another gear. Another caffeine-seeker shoulders past me. I realize I'm standing stock still instead of following the protocol. Obediently, I move to the back of the queue crowding the counter. The people up front are eyeing each other warily, memorizing the order of arrival to ensure no one behind them gets their drink first.

"Osama Bin Laden," Lydia says. "And his group, al-Qaeda. They were responsible for the Cole and the embassy bombings. And the World Trade Center in '93. I shouldn't know that name, should I, Ian?"

She's listing the events driving my passion, the very events I just tried to get Carmen to acknowledge as portends of future violence. And she's right. Most Americans aren't familiar with UBL, as he's known based on the alternate spelling of his name, though they may have heard of al-Qaeda and they would have heard mention of the Taliban on the evening news.

"You might know that name. If you were well-read in Middle-Eastern politics." Or if she held a certain kind of government job. The Saudi millionaire is well known in the intelligence community, though he and his network of followers tend to appear in the middle portion of bureau briefings—right in the area no one pays attention to when they skim for the higher-profile cases.

I pay attention. I think al-Qaeda poses a significant threat to us, and I'm hoping to bring more public awareness, and thus government resources, to that threat. Hence, my constant petitions to Carmen to add me to the feature pool.

"Who did you say you work for?" I ask. She comes off as a civilian, but she has to have some kind of ties to intelligence.

"I don't work for anybody. I'm just a nursing student, but that's beside the point. Look," Lydia says, "in 1998, Bin Laden issued a fatwa. It went largely ignored by U.S. policy makers, but it was a war cry for extremists who love to hate us. In it, he specifically tells his followers that when they make jihad against us, they should not distinguish between military and civilian targets. Is this ringing any bells, Ian?"

Bells aren't ringing. They're screaming.

Just a nursing student, my ass. This woman has to be in some kind of intelligence outfit. No one else would still be talking about that fatwa. John Miller mentioned it in his *Frontline* interview with Bin Laden a few years ago, but what should have raised a whole army of red flags only made a blip on the mainstream news radar. People like me who wanted—and still want—to learn more about UBL's mission and capabilities are repeatedly told terrorism is a "non-topic."

"Clearly, you're well connected to know what you know," I tell her. "I'm not sure what help you think I can be. I admit you've made me curious, but this is not a good time." I glance at my watch, the weight of my local politics column bending my back.

"Ian, Bin Laden is going to make good on that fatwa, and we're not prepared to stop it. Thousands of Americans are going to die unless you help me *today*."

"Extra hot triple cap for Ian!" A barista shouts my order.

My feet are bolted to the floor.

Thousands of Americans?

That number eclipses the couple hundred that died in East Africa in the '98 embassy bombings. By a lot.

"That's impossible," I inform her. "Bin Laden's a threat, but not of that magnitude." I modulate my volume, conscious of the people around me. None of them are paying any attention, but still. "Even if he pulled off a coordinated attack with passenger jets, the number of casualties would be limited to passengers and crew." To reach the number Lydia just tossed out would take a level of coordination I tremble to fathom. They would have to crash dozens of 747's packed to the gills.

I'm tempted to write her off as a nut job conspiracy theorist who spends too much time in right-wing chat rooms. But I give her a grain of credibility because she read my piece and agrees with me.

"I'll admit, you're right about the fatwa," I say. "And maybe we're both right about the use of planes. But that doesn't explain why you're calling me instead of the CIA. If you think there's a threat to Americans getting on flights overseas, a D.C. journalist isn't going to be much help."

"It's not going to happen overseas, Ian." She cuts me off. "It's going to happen here. On the eastern seaboard. It'll be domestic flights."

I try to imagine a group of terrorists being allowed to board U.S. flights and struggle to find the scenario credible. A woman in a trench coat reaches for my cup. I shoulder through the thirsty throng, but I'm not in time to keep her from turning my drink to read the name on the side. I look pointedly at her and pluck the cup from her hand.

"Did you hear me, Ian? Ian, this is important."

I hate how Lydia keeps using my name. I hate that she uses the same word Miller used to describe my piece. I know what it's like to have something *important* to say and to have no one listen.

"I heard you." I move to the kiosk, my fingertips already singed, to find a cardboard sleeve. "But I'm still not sure what you want from me. If you think a crime is about to happen—here or abroad—you need to contact the authorities."

She sighs, and it's a heavy sound. "Maybe that's the best course of action. I don't know." She sounds uncertain. A little afraid. "Shoot. I'm at the airport. Look. Just give me an hour of your time. In person. If I can't convince you to help me, you can drop me off at CIA headquarters, and I'll bumble my way through trying to stop a terrorist attack. What's your email? I'll send you my flight info."

"I'm not meeting you at the airport. I don't even have a car." My Vespa, technically, can hold two, but not if the second person has luggage. I'm certainly not interested in taking my moped to the airport on a drizzly day.

"Then take a cab," she says. "I'll pay for it."

Persistence is usually a quality I admire, but this woman's timing could not be worse. "I can't today, Ms.—Lydia." I'm firm as I take the stairs two at a time back to the newsroom. If I ever want my features to see the light of day, I've got to play Carmen's game. "Look, I have to go."

I'm breathing hard from the climb. Standing by the big number 5 in the stairwell, I hear Lydia talking. It takes me a second to realize she's not talking to me. "There you go," she says. "Listen. Steer clear of the World Trade Center tomorrow. In fact, stay away from lower Manhattan altogether."

"Get my best fares in lower Manhattan." Ah. She's talking to the cabbie.

"Just, please. Stay away from there tomorrow. Just in case."

"In case of what?" he asks like he's waiting for a punchline.

"In case I fail." Her dark warning is punctuated by the slamming of a car door. "Ian," she barks. "Your email address."

I give it to her, because she has me off balance. And curious. One moment, I'm confident I can safely dismiss her. The next, the information she has and the tone in which she relays it has the hairs on the back of my neck standing on end.

World Trade Center? In case I fail?

I've got a sense about people. When I talk with them, I have a knack for cutting through the bullshit. Subtle cues tip me off. Tone of voice, facial expression, unintended gestures. My father calls me a human lie detector, like his sister, my aunt, who served her country with her gift during the Cold War Era.

Right now, even though I don't have a visual on Lydia Clay, I am certain of two things. One: she believes what she's saying, and two: she's deadly serious.

CHAPTER 6

Lydia

THE CURVED MURAL and larger-than-life bust of Fiorello LaGuardia give me a surreal sense of déjà vu. Less than a monh ago, I flew out of this airport for Mom's funeral. However recent that flight seems, it actually tock place twenty years in the future—or will take place twenty years in the future.

Strangely, the Marine Air Terminal hasn't changed one bit—or rather, it won't change. 2021 or 2001, it doesn't matter. LaGuardia remains too small, too dark, and kind of depressing. The only difference between then and now is that not a single passenger or employee is wearing a mask, and the only hand sanitizer in sight sits on a shelf of travel-sized toiletries in Hudson News.

I'm trying to ignore the fact I've gone backward in time. If I think about it too hard, I'll probably panic. This is not science or medicine or anything I've ever read about in a textbook. If this is like anything I've experienced before, it comes closest to the miracles of healing I've witnessed from time to time.

A father with three broken cervical vertebrae is told he will never walk again, but six months later, he strolls into the hospital with a single crutch on his arm to make the doctors cheerfully eat their words.

A baby born at a scant twenty-six weeks' gestation thrives and becomes a spelling bee champion in her state.

A mother on her deathbed is prayed over by her rabbi and turns a corner no doctor had read on the map of her test results.

A woman sees a shooting star and is sent back in time to stop her *where-were-you-when* moment.

In my hand as I race toward the security checkpoint is a ticket for the next available flight to D.C. I'm thankful there are several runs between the cities every day. Also, that it's Monday, and the flight is only half full, according to the ticket agent. I would not have had the patience to wait for a later flight. Not today.

As I join the line of travelers on this side of the luggage scanners and metal detectors, my mind is on how I'm going to convince Ian to work with me. Once I reach the front of the line, however, it hits me just how different things are from what I'm used to.

No one's stooping to awkwardly remove shoes. One man carries a travel mug and is motioned through the upright detectors with it in his hand. Laptop bags and suitcases are carried on a belt through *X*-ray units at a steady pace. None are stopped for closer looks. A security agent gives a dismissive answer when a woman asks something. Another woman tries handing her baby to an agent, I guess so she can take off the diaper bag slung across her torso. The agent wards her off with raised palms and waves mother, infant, and diaper bag through the upright detectors. No alarms sound. I wonder if the machine is even on.

Passengers seem stressed, but not overly so. The frustrations of air travel are taking their toll, but no one appears worried for their safety.

I'm not so lucky.

I've lived through something these people haven't, and it has made me ultra-alert. Maybe even a little afraid because here in this place and time I am so close to what happened—what will happen.

I hate myself for it, but every man I see with a certain coloring makes me uncomfortable. I'm practicing racial profiling, and it's wrong, but I can't help it. Tomorrow, nineteen men of Middle-Eastern descent will waltz through airport security stations just like this one, only instead of a laptop and a pink wallet in their bags, they'll have knives, cans of pepper spray, and instructions for carrying out their plans. Some of them will be given perfunctory additional searches that they will pass, and, ultimately, they will all be motioned through like the passengers in front of me today.

If any of tomorrow's four planes were to leave from this airport, I would be tempted to issue some kind of warning to these agents. Would they take me seriously or wave me off, calling me crazy or paranoid? Would they ask for more information? If so, I'd probably be taken somewhere to be interviewed, and I would miss my chance to meet with Ian. I'm glad I don't have to face that dilemma.

By the time I arrive at the gate, the digital sign says boarding will begin in twenty minutes. An airline employee stands behind the counter, looking harried but helpful. Her hair is in a short, feathered style I haven't seen in years. When there's a break in her line, I ask her where I can connect to the internet, and she points down the hall to a "business bank."

"You have time," she says, as if sensing my dilemma. Her customer-service smile strikes me as so terribly naïve. She has no idea that tomorrow, by eleven a.m., all air traffic in the nation will be shut down. If I told her that Air Force One and fighter jets will be the only things in the American skies, she would say, "Hon, that's just not possible," with that smile still in place.

I thank her and take a seat at a desk with four stations divided by partitions. A man in a suit is hunched over a land-line phone to my right, and a preppy guy in a Crocodile polo types away on a laptop to my left.

My laptop is still on. Before leaving the apartment, I saved a handful of webpages, including Ian's article.

I first learned about Ian when the rest of the country did, in the weeks after the attacks, when he was touted as "the reporter who predicted 9/11." His feature piece on the New Face of Terrorism, previously buried on the *Washington Post* website, was republished in every paper in the nation. Terrorism became the topic du jour, and with his insights and his easy way with words, Ian rode the forefront of that wave all the way to a Pulitzer. He later went on to write four *New York Times* bestselling books on 9/11.

"I predicted nothing," I remember him saying to Oprah, one argyle-clad ankle resting on his knee. "I simply saw a danger that no one else was looking for. I saw the danger, and I shone a light on it. That's what journalists do. I did my job." He smiled his relaxed smile, green eyes overflowing with charm behind tortoiseshell glasses while Oprah praised him with soft-spoken words heard around the world.

What I hadn't realized was that the lanky reporter-celebrity with the stylishly-tousled black hair and the swooning female fanbase had written only a single article about terrorism before 9/11, at least as far as I could find with my hasty Google search. Because that article happens to be the one everyone remembers, I tended to think of him as this larger-than-life expert on Middle-Eastern politics. But at this moment in time—the moment I'm stuck in—he's a simple column reporter who hadn't even known his feature article was published.

As soon as I thought about contacting a journalist, his name popped into my head. Of all the pages of newsprint dedicated to the attacks after the fact, Ian's name was the only one I associated with terrorism reporting beforehand. In his post-9/11 books and news stories, he comes across as genuinely passionate about counterterrorism. I'd hoped—I continue to hope—that I've put my eggs in the right basket. I need Ian Greenberg to be my Abigail Chase.

My laptop battery is in desperate need of a charge, so I thread the power cord through the hole in the desk and crawl underneath to plug it in. The plastic tip of an ethernet cable peeks from the hole. I plug it into my Gateway and follow the posted instructions for getting online.

I don't have to wait for the start-up routine. Still, getting to my email program is not a speedy proposition. Every page loads with as much enthusiasm as an eight-year-old told to clean his room.

Christian at that age pops into my mind. "Do I *hafta*, Mom?" Arms dangling, head lolling, he would trudge up the stairs, moaning the whole way. How that kid hated cleaning his room!

My eyes well with tears I can't afford to shed. I'll think about my children—and how what I'm doing might affect them—later. For now, I tap out my email to Ian, periodically checking the gate over my shoulder. A slow but steady stream of passengers trickles into the waiting area, but no one is queueing up to board yet.

Ian still hasn't agreed to pick me up at Reagan, but I'm not giving up. Typing at the speed of light, I compose my message. I let him know when my plane should land, and I dole out a little more information about tomorrow.

I focus on facts he can verify. Even if he's not yet the famous globe-trotting journalist he's going to be, he's still a journalist. If he can verify something I tell him, he'll take me more seriously.

As I hit send on the email, my phone rings. In my rush to answer, I nearly fumble the compact, little thing onto the floor.

"Hello, Lydia Clay speaking." I'm gearing up to make another pitch to Ian, but it's not him.

"Lydia *Clay?*" Tristan's playful purr is the last thing I expected to hear. "That's interesting. I thought I made it *very* clear last night that you are a married woman."

Gah! It's Tristan! Calling from work, sounding confident and oversexed.

Half the time we were married, he was a crabby jerk. I let him get away with it because he could ignite my libido so easily with that silky voice. Even now, after everything, his words make my stomach clench with desire.

My mouth opens and closes. My old habit of avoiding conflict urges me to correct my name to Lydia Watercrest, even though that is no longer the case.

"Lyd? You there, pumpkin?"

Jeez. He's in a good mood this morning. With a wince, I remember what I'd been wearing when I woke up. And I press the button to end the call.

I can't speak with Tristan. Not today. I have no mental energy to spare to pretend I'm the Lydia that belongs in this place and time. I have much more important things to do. Like convincing Ian to work with me.

I press and hold the button to turn off my phone. I'll deal with Tristan when this is over. Right now, there's only one man on my mind.

I need to do whatever it takes to get Ian to take me seriously. After talking with him on the phone, I can tell I was right about his passion for counterterrorism. Even though he hasn't written any of his best sellers yet—and he may never write them thanks to what I'm doing here—knowledge and insight roll off him in waves.

He won't dismiss my warning without good cause. I hope. Which means it's up to me not to give him cause. When I track him down in D.C., I'm going to make sure Ian Greenberg cannot, in good conscience, ignore me.

All I have to do is figure out how.

Any man who looks back on his past and feels he has been of some use need have no regrets.

—Ahmad Shah Massoud, anti-terrorist militia leader

CHAPTER 7

Ian

IF I EVER WANT TO WRITE FEATURES with Carmen's blessing, I need to buckle down and churn out columns like a good little lap dog. When I flop into my desk chair and wake up my computer, I have every intention of doing just that. The problem is I can't get Lydia out of my head.

She's not a nutjob. Not a conspiracy theorist. The things she knows are too specific, and her demeanor is too earnest. There isn't the slightest whiff of "unhinged" coming off her. Which means I can't ignore her.

They're going to use planes.

Bigger and more well-coordinated than you suggest.

Thousands of Americans.

World Trade Center.

In case I fail.

My list of works in progress is right there on the screen, staring at me as I sip scalding coffee. Do I open the first folder? Of course not. That would be the smart thing to do.

No. Ian Greenberg, reporter on notice of demotion, pulls up his contacts and dials an old friend to investigate a story that has nothing to do with his column.

While I listen to the line ring, I scratch out on a notepad, *Cat + Curiosity = .*

"Jewel here." Morgan answers on the fourth ring. He's eating his usual morning donut. I can hear crumbs peppering the receiver.

"Hey, buddy. It's Ian."

"Cock sock!"

I jerk the phone from my ear and ignore the look Sally gives me over her monitor. One Red-Hot-Chili-Peppers-inspired wardrobe mishap, and a guy's stuck with a fraternity-nickname forever.

"What's shaking, man?" Morg says. "Haven't heard from you in a while."

"Yeah. I've been crazy busy. What's up at the Bureau?"

"Same old, same old." I hear him slurp coffee. "We need to get together for drinks sometime."

"Sure. No problem. If I can get caught up in the next decade or so, I should be able to squeeze you in sometime around twenty-ten, twenty-eleven." I swivel in my chair to glare in the direction of Carmen's closed door.

"I get it. I get it. Not a social call." I swear, Morg's the loudest chewer on the planet. It sounds like he's mixing cement right over the mouthpiece. "Need some new software? Coming to old Morg for some fresh dirt?"

Morg's no stranger to my requests for help, so I cut to the chase. "I need you to find out who's on al-Qaeda for me." I need to know if Lydia's warning matches up with anything on the FBI's radar. I also want to review the fatwa she mentioned.

I write *1998 fatwa* and underline it two times.

"Al-Qaeda? Why you interested in those guys? Some local politician trying to drum up interest in terrorism to distract from 'personal indiscretions'?" I don't need to see him to know he's waggling his brows.

"Just a lead I'm checking out. Nothing special." It's fine if Morg thinks this is for my local politics column. "Who's investigating the group right now? Can you get me a contact? I want to get my hands on that fatwa from '98, but I don't see it in the public files."

The truth is I haven't looked. I don't have time to navigate the sluggish labyrinth that passes for the government-run website for public documents. Morg can get me the info much faster. If he can put down the damned donut.

He makes a noncommittal sound. "Not sure, bud. I'll have to get back to you. I can tell you it's not high priority."

"Do you have anything you can send me, even if it seems unimportant? I want to read up on what you guys know about his group and maybe talk to whoever's running the intel on them."

"Dunno. I can find out who's on al-Qaeda and get back to you."

Not good enough. "I'll wait while you look it up."

He snorts. "Nothin' special, huh?" In the background, I hear him clacking away at a keyboard. Good old Morg. I can always count on my buddy in forensics to dig up information for me—pun definitely intended.

"Want me to hang on while you get another donut?" I tease.

"Har-bloody-har-har. I'll have you know it's a Danish pastry, asshole."

"Always with the sweet tooth."

"Yeah, well, your mamma didn't complain about my sweet tooth last night."

"*Faaahck* you. Got anything yet?"

He laughs. "Yeah. I'm looking at last week's summary report. UBL fits the search terms, so he'll be in there somewhere. There's no obvious contact info, though."

Damn. "I could really use a contact. Tell you what. You get me a name within the hour, and I'll buy you a pitcher at Bulldog's Friday night."

"Deal!"

After I sign off with Morg, I notice a new email in my Outlook. It's from Lydiac3po@aol.com.

"Star Wars fan," I say under my breath, wishing my mystery-lead lady was less likable.

I have every reason to ignore the email and get to work on my column. But I'm thoroughly hooked. I open it and lean over my keyboard as I read. The short couple of paragraphs are littered with misspellings, as if written in a hurry.

Ian,

Thanks for taking my call this morning. I know you must be very busy, but I promise you;ll be glad you took the time to help me today.

I must sound like a lunatic, but here's som e infor you can verify to know I;m legit:

1. An afghan military leader in the anti-Taliban guerilla movement was assassinated yesterday. Name: Massoud. It hasn't been reported yet, but it will come out that the suicide bombers were likely al-Qaeda. Ask yourself how I could know this without having any government credentials (I'm a soon-to-be nursing student living in Brooklyn & a NYU graduate—a nobody).

2. Find contact info for Huffman Aviation flight school in Florida. I think the city is Venice. Ask if they had students named Mohamed Atta and Marwan al-Shehhi.

3. There's a flight school in SandDiego—Montgomery Airfield. Ask why Kalhid Midhair and Salem Hamzi flunked out.

See you soon.

Lydia

At the end, she includes her flight number and arrival time, which is a scant fifty-five minutes away. I roll my eyes.

As if I'm going to drop everything to be your chauffer for the day. Please.

I absolutely do not have time to meet Lydia today, but I can't help taking the time to re-read her message over sips of cappuccino.

An assassination in Afghanistan. Flight students with Middle-Eastern names. Hooked, indeed. This woman has me practically wriggling on the line for more information.

Not to mention curious about how she knows what she claims to know. She's a simple nursing student with no ties to the government, she claims.

"All right, Lydia. I'll bite."

I jot down Massoud's name and do an internet search, the special kind I had to do some hacking to set up with a little password help from Morg. The kind Carmen would crap herself to know runs in the background on the WAPO mainframe.

With Massoud's name and a few keywords entered into the program, I let it run. Meanwhile, I scribble notes from Lydia's email, including the four Middle-Eastern names she mentioned in relation to U.S. flight schools: *Atta, Shehhi, Mihdhar, and Hazmi.*

It's automatic for me to correct the spelling of the last two, with which I'm familiar thanks to my research on my first piece for Miller.

"How on Earth do you know about Mihdhar and Hazmi, Ms. Clay?"

In the feature article we spoke about on the phone, I mentioned how easy it would be for international students with terror-cell affiliations to enroll in U.S. flight schools. I proposed the scenario as a possibility when, in fact, I knew of two such students, each revealed to me through different sources. Unfortunately, I wasn't satisfied with the level of verification I was able to obtain, not on the enrollment of the men in flight schools but in their affiliation with terror cells. Unwilling to risk false accusation, I refrained from printing the names.

But they existed in my notebook. And in my memory.

Somehow, Lydia managed to find them, and two more as well.

I think back to when I first heard of Hazmi. It was from my source at the Persian Café, the same one with which I'd failed to connect this morning. Several months ago, this source told me about an acquaintance of an acquaintance by the name of al-Hazmi who had described taking lessons at a flight school somewhere in California. The kid was on a tourist visa and had bragged that the money for his enrollment came from al-Qaeda. A brother or cousin of Hazmi's claimed the kid was lying, but later was heard scolding him for blabbing.

"What I heard was that the elder Hazmi put the younger in his place," my source relayed. "Reminding him that his flight instructor sent him home for not being bright enough to fly planes." The conversation outside the Persian Café is prominent in my memory because it piqued my interest in terrorists and airplanes. Without that tip, the article Lydia found online never would have existed.

Shortly after meeting my source, I hit the phones. Armed with a name and a state, I'd called flight schools in California until I found one that confirmed they'd had a student by the name Hazmi. The school was Flight Training International, or FTI, at Montgomery Field in San Diego—the same school mentioned in Lydia's email. Unfortunately, FTI wouldn't confirm whether Hazmi had been dismissed from the program or whether he was on a student visa. All I learned was that his lessons had been paid in full with cash and he was no longer enrolled.

Mihdhar's name came to me by an entirely different route. Sharon Hansen's desk phone was the highest I could get in the chain of command while researching terrorist activities on the CIA's radar. She worked as an aide for Bill Peterson, a foreign intelligence officer specializing in Middle-East relations, and agreed to meet at a pub to answer some questions, off the record, of course.

I finish my cappuccino and unlock my desk drawer. I still have my handwritten notes from the conversation with Sharon. Reviewing them brings me back to that June happy hour.

"So," I start out while Sharon peels off her rain-dappled trench coat. "Crazy busy at the office, huh?" They were the same words she used on the phone when we arranged this meeting.

"Oh, my God, yes." With a messy bun on top of her head and a fuzzy, pink, cashmere sweater, she brings to mind an Easter bunny perched on a barstool. "I've been working for Peterson for two years, and I've never seen him so stressed."

I order a white wine and a hefeweizen. "What's he stressed about?" While we wait for our drinks, I let my gaze lazily roam around the bar. My notebook remains tucked away in my pocket. Sharon is the kind of source that'll spook if I seem too eager for information.

She leans in, scandal shining in her eyes. "Since last week, the Agency has been on alert for something major. The pressure is on for Peterson to make sense of the scattered intel we're getting."

The arrival of our drinks makes it easy to hide the keen interest her confession inspires. "Stressful, indeed," I say and sip my beer. "I'm glad I don't have the kind of job where The White House *puts pressure on me." I lean back in my stool and grin at my own wit, like I imagine someone here for a casual get-together would do.*

"Totally." She huffs a petite chuckle and sips her chardonnay. She's pretty in a bookish way I might have found myself attracted to under other circumstances.

Some men make it a rule never to mix women with work, but since my life is all work, I don't need those kinds of rules. The sad truth is that I tend not to view women as potential romantic partners. That doesn't mean I'm above using flattery to acquire the information I need.

I use it now to help relax Sharon's tongue. "I bet Peterson relies pretty heavily on you to organize all that scattered intel. Cheers, by the way." I tilt my pint her way.

She clinks her glass with mine and sits up straighter, preening. "I mean, I guess he relies on me, a little." She shrugs. "But really, I'm just a glorified secretary." Her shoulders droop. "I don't get to see the most sensitive emails. What are you researching for the Post *again?"*

"I'm looking into how terrorist organizations are changing tactics for the twenty-first century." I swirl my pint glass with practiced nonchalance, like someone making idle conversation. "Like I said on the phone, I'm just starting my research. No one's in a better position than you to give me some direction."

I'm hoping that direction points to any existing hijacking threats and, ideally, leads to verification of Hazmi's name as a terror-cell associate.

"Okay," Sharon says, eyes wide with interest. "What do you want to know?"

"Well, you mentioned the Agency being on alert. That sounds intense. Is your boss anticipating some kind of attack? Something like another USS Cole?"

Sharon peers at me, as if debating how much she can safely divulge.

I try to look as cherubic as humanly possible while sipping beer. "Off the record, of course," I add. And I mean it. Sticking to my word means I can call Sharon again for future stories. Or better yet, get her to vouch for me with her boss so I can land a high-profile interview with a senior intelligence agent.

Sharon's face relaxes. She cocks a crooked smile, as if she has judged me a safe receptacle for a thimbleful of information. "That's exactly what we're worried about. Another Cole. Another bombing like at the embassies in Kenya and Tanzania. All the intel points to something big coming soon, but we don't know what." My skin erupts in goosebumps at that ominous prediction. Oblivious, Sharon goes on. "Security is ramping up at all our overseas interests. Bennet's even been pushing The White House for more resources—Peterson's always griping about how the director isn't doing enough. He expects miracles but wants us to pull them off with our hands tied behind our backs. Anyway, we know something's coming soon, but without specifics, it's hard to prepare, and Peterson's the one getting blamed. It's driving him crazy."

Everyone knows evil is out there, and that our people overseas can potentially be targeted. But hearing specifics like this makes it hard for me to continue my nonchalant act. "I'll bet," I say. "Out of curiosity, where is the threat coming from? It was al-Qaeda that did the USS Cole bombing, right?" I make it a question, even though I know it to be fact. "Are they the big concern, or is it another group?"

Sharon sips from her glass, then looks to the side to make sure no one's eavesdropping. "You didn't hear this from me, but there is an increase in chatter linked to al-Qaeda. There's a higher volume of communication within the group and a higher rate of transfer of funds."

I perk up at "transfer of funds," but Sharon shakes her head, telling me not to get excited.

"We're not talking large amounts," she says, disappointed. "If we were, the alert would go wide."

"Go wide?"

"To the other agencies. As far as I know, this chatter is only known to Peterson, the CTC, and MI6. Peterson and Peck—he's the director of the CTC—they met with MI6 in London last week to share intel and to decide if al-Qaeda warrants more attention. The meeting went really well. Peterson thinks he might be up for promotion to Deputy Director of the CTC."

I feel my eyebrows climb my forehead. She probably shouldn't be so open with a reporter about her boss's movements and aspirations. On the other...
"What was the verdict? Do they? Al-Qaeda, I mean. Do they warrant more attention?"

"Not sure. All I know is when Peterson got back, he put me to work tracing materials that could be used in car bombings. The focus was Saudi Arabia, but so far, nothing's come of it." She shrugs one shoulder. "Maybe MI6 stopped it."

This is all fascinating information, but it doesn't help me with the piece I'm working on for Miller.

I try being more direct. "Has anything about using explosives on aircraft come up in this chatter? Like, hijackings or anything like that?" I hold my breath, hoping to hear Hazmi's name.

She shakes her head, bun leaning to one side after bearing up under a full workday. "Not specifically, but Peterson is always on the lookout for any kind of lead where explosives are concerned. It's certainly possible that those materials could be used on planes, trains, vans parked in front of embassies, you name it." She finishes her wine and lifts her glass to get the bartender's attention.

I buy another round.

"You know," she says, while waiting for her second drink. "I actually do remember something weird about planes. I mean, it's probably not relevant to what your researching, like, at all, but there was this one name I remember Peterson mentioning when he was talking on the phone about foreign air travel."

I lean forward, practically falling off my barstool. "What was the name?" Hazmi. Say Hazmi.

"It was weird. I think it stuck in my head because, at first, I thought Peterson was saying something was going to happen 'mid-air.'" She makes air quotes with her fingers. "But the context was off. Then I realized 'mid-air' was a name, like, of someone he wanted intel on. After that call, he had me look up a phone number for a flight school in California. Later, the name Mihdhar—M-I-H-D-H-A-R—popped up in an email. Peterson was trying to find out if a Saudi national by that name was here on a tourist visa."

We talk through our second round, but Sharon makes no mention of Hazmi and knows nothing more about Mihdhar. After Sharon leaves the bar, I dial FTI to ask if Mihdhar had been a student along with Hazmi. I get a non-answer along the lines of, We don't give out information on former students, sir. *In other words, someone had gotten in trouble for talking to me last time I called, and the school tightened their security protocol. I content myself with the fact that I uncovered two Saudi names linked to California flight schools and leave it at that.*

Finished reliving my interview with Sharon, I crumple my coffee cup and toss it in the wastebasket at my feet. I'm puzzled at how Lydia came to know both of the names I uncovered in my research. The odds of her having spoken with Peterson's aide *and* my restaurant source are slim to none. Yet she knew not only about Hazmi and Mihdhar attending the same flight school, but her suggestion they flunked out is the closest thing I've gotten to verification of my source's statement that Hazmi got sent home for not being bright enough to fly planes.

And she brought two more names to my attention, names I haven't seen before.

Somehow, I doubt Lydia is a simple nursing student. Letting my fingers fly, I do some digging in the public records. I find three Lydia Clays living in the New York metro area, none of them young enough to be the woman I spoke with.

I could broaden my search. After all, I don't know where, exactly, Lydia lives, only that she called from a New York area code. Before expanding the search to outlying areas, I try court records.

"Let's see if you have any speeding tickets, Ms. Clay."

Within a few minutes I find a record that looks promising. There is a Lydia Clay, age 23, who recently filed for a marriage license in New Jersey. Now Lydia Watercrest, she has a Brooklyn address on file. Her husband's name is Tristan, and they've been married about a month. With zero citations and no other information available, it's difficult to ascertain anything about this Lydia, including whether she's my would-be source.

Dismissing the dead end, I move on to the other two names in her email.

The Florida White Pages provides a number, and a Google search sends me to a website touting the school's safety record and its many prestigious clients who have gone on to fly with NASA, the military, and U.S. and foreign airlines.

I dial the school, and a man with a friendly southern drawl asks how he can help me.

"Yeah, hi. This is Ian Greenberg from *The Washington Post*. Is there someone I can speak to about Huffman Aviation's excellent reputation attracting the best of the best international students?"

With a little coaxing and a lot of flattery, I'm able to confirm Atta's and Shehhi's enrollment. They attended at the same time and tended to keep to themselves. Mohamed Atta stood out to the man I spoke with, who also happened to be an instructor, for being a dedicated student with a serious demeanor who always paid his tuition on time. In cash.

I let the instructor go with profuse thanks.

The rhythmic *tap-tap-tap* of my pencil on my desk helps focus my thoughts. That's two more flight students with Middle-Eastern names, but how do Atta and Shehhi tie in to al-Qaeda?

My watch tells me I'm due to hear from Morg soon if he wants that pitcher at the pub. I'll ask him if the two men appear in any interdepartmental communications.

But not even Morg will be able to tell me how Lydia knew about Atta and Shehhi. Or Mihdhar and Hazmi. Again, I'm brought back to her reliability as a source. I have nothing concrete to suggest she's credible, and yet my gut tells me she's the real deal.

I'm tapping my No.2 on my notebook when I get an alert that my super-secret search on Massoud is finished. Morg's program has brought up four results. A table at the top of the page shows that none of the four originated with the AP, UPI, or any of the other standard international news agencies. That means my four "hits" are all from confidential information services that are typically only available to those in the intelligence community.

On this version of the software, I can't get into the reports themselves, but the data tags, which appear like news headlines, often reveal a wealth of information. I click on the first tag and read the couple of lines that come up.

Transcript 8404 10 September 2001, the headline reads. I blink. That's today's date. That means the data tag is fresh, like hours-old fresh. I keep reading.

Massoud Assassination: Guerilla commander Ahmad Shah Massoud of the Northern Alliance coalition confirmed dead at Khoje Bahauddin base in northern Afghanistan.

"Holy shit."

The Northern Alliance is an anti-Taliban movement that has U.S. support. If a Northern Alliance commander was assassinated at a base in northern Afghanistan, that means he was ambushed on his own turf.

My pulse quickens. I'm seeing something I'm not meant to see. This news hasn't hit the mainstream media yet. In other words, only a handful of people in the intelligence community know about it. Plus Lydia.

There is absolutely no way she could get this info without a high-level government ID. This is the kind of stuff a columnist like me only reports if he wants to end up on the wrong side of an interrogation table.

I don't take any notes before clicking on the next tag.

The second headline, dated in April this year, reads, *Massoud shares intel re: imminent large-scale terrorist attack by al-Qaeda, possibly on U.S. soil; Requests humanitarian aid for Afghanistan from European Parliament.*

The text does nothing to calm my racing heart. If anything, I'm even more on edge now. If he warned us about al-Qaeda, that might have been what led to his assassination just a few months later.

My eyes jump to the third headline, even though I'm still processing the first and second. It's dated in February this year and reads, *Massoud—U.S. agreement. Aid released to Afghan militia leader in exchange for intelligence on Taliban.*

The fourth headline is from 1998 and links to a report on Massoud's success driving Soviet troops out of the Panjshir Valley not just once, but multiple times.

I don't need access to the linked reports to understand the significance of these headlines. Massoud was a badass and a US ally against the Taliban. A few months ago, he warned of an "imminent large-scale" attack by al-Qaeda, and now he's dead, assassinated on a base that should have been a place of safety for him.

Holy Smokes. Could al-Qaeda be behind Massoud's assassination, like Lydia suggested? How imminent is imminent? How large scale is large-scale? If those questions don't make the hairs on my neck stand up, the phrase, "possibly on U.S. soil" certainly does.

I delete the search and cover my tracks with a few keystrokes. My heart won't stop pounding.

Where my notes read, *Cat + Curiosity = ,* I finish with a sketch of a skull and crossbones.

"Who are you, Lydia Clay?"

The nation was unprepared.

—9/11 Commission Report, Executive
Summary

CHAPTER 8

Lydia

As I board the plane, a Boeing 757 like two of the planes that will be hijacked tomorrow, my thoughts spin out in every direction like marbles dumped from a jar.

One marble. Getting on a plane today feels like playing Russian Roulette, even though logic reminds me nothing happened on September 10th.

Another marble. Which set of authorities do I turn to? Who is most likely to listen and act?

Another marble. How do I alert them to tomorrow's danger without making them dismiss me as paranoid or in need of psychiatric meds? I can't exactly say, "I know what's going to happen tomorrow because I lived through it twenty years ago."

I've never been in a situation before where I possess a truth no one else could reasonably believe. It makes me feel alone, adrift.

Another marble. Even if I can get the authorities to listen, how can I convince them that what's coming is going to be a hijacking unlike any we've seen in the past?

On today's date, there is no precedent for hijackers taking control of a cockpit and turning a passenger flight into a suicide bomb. There is no precedent for a passenger jet being used as a missile to strike an inhabited building on U.S. soil. If there's no precedent for such a thing happening to a single plane, there's certainly no precedent for it happening to multiple planes simultaneously.

How do I make the authorities understand that four jets and several huge buildings are in immediate peril? That if those jets get airborne with terrorists on board, people are going to die? That there will be no room for negotiation or counterstrike? That by the time they figure out what's happening, it will be too late.

Another marble. Even if I can get someone to listen to me, how much should I say? Should I mention the World Trade Center at all? The Pentagon? Will that distract from the goal of stopping the hijackers from getting airborne? Will talking about targets raise more questions than I have answers for, like how I know the specifics of an al-Qaeda plot when no one in intelligence has gotten a whiff of it?

Another marble, this one dark and large. How will I manage to live the next twenty years over again without losing my mind? What if my children are never born?

I allow myself the time it takes to buckle into the airline seat to feel overwhelmed. After that, I find my resolve.

You can do this. You will *do this.*

Why else would I be here, if not to succeed? I look out the plexiglass window and see baggage handlers loading the plane's belly from boxcar-like trailers. It's sunny out, the morning gloom is burning off as afternoon approaches. The luggage truck turns to drive away, and the windshield reflects the sun. I'm reminded of last night's fireball.

I chose to wish on a shooting star. What if the star also chose me? Maybe I'm the best person for this job. Maybe I have what it takes to stop what's coming.

I embrace the idea. It gives me strength.

I'm all the way at the back of the plane in a seat that can't recline because it abuts a partition. I don't mind. It's not like I'm going to be napping.

A flight attendant runs through the safety precautions midway up the fuselage. Instead of paying attention, I get out my legal pad. The flight from New York to D.C. is a short one, and I have a lot of marbles to organize.

Ian's skepticism when I spoke with him on the phone reinforces the need for verifiable facts. No matter who I end up talking to, I'll have zero credibility unless I present information that can be checked out. I start with writing down what I remembered in the cab and included in the email to Ian.

Massoud assassination in Afghanistan (probably al-Qaeda).

Midhair & Hamzi flunked out of flight school – instructors alarmed because only interested in controlling a plane mid-air, not in takeoffs or landings. Montgomery Field.

I search my mind for more about the terrorists' time in the U.S., and I remember several things that can, hopefully, be verified.

Some were in U.S. on tourist visas, reported lost passports, got replacements to remove record of suspicious travel.

They used their real names.

Abided by law, kept heads down, trained to fly or to be muscle, attended non-extremist mosques, had gym memberships.

Midhair & at least one other on watchlist for other countries for al-Qaeda association.

CIA knows some are in U.S. Did not share with FBI or place on watch lists or no-fly.

No-fly list useless, has only 16 names on it at this point in time, no one knows who maintains it or how it's used to screen passengers.

FBI knows Bin Laden was interested in planes as weapons as early as 1996.

U.S. had a terrorist in custody who confessed to plans of crashing a plane into the CIA building - Not sure if CIA, FBI or other govt org.

Facts about the hijackers' flight training becomes clearer in my mind the more I think about my reading on the topic. The same happens when I have a patient with a rare condition. Skimming a chapter in a textbook brings back more than just the contents of that one chapter. I remember clinical trials, studies, and bits of trivia that help me anticipate my patient's needs. It's like warming up my neurons helps them fire more rapidly.

They're firing like mad now, and I'm getting carpal tunnel trying to write as fast as I can.

> *Atta already had pilot's license (from Egypt, I think).*
>
> *Several hijackers spent time in Hamburg, Germany – Atta & Shehi met and came to U.S. from there.*
>
> *Dekker, Owner of flight school in Florida.*
>
> *Airman something or other, Flight school in Oklahoma.*
>
> *Several carried out cross-country travel, multiple trips to learn airport security & procedures.*

Once these facts are verified, there should be enough information to warrant the arrest of these guys. I focus on what I remember from the days and hours leading up to 9/11. What were the terrorists doing? Where did they go? How did they arrive at the airports?

I continue making notes.

> *ATMs used to get out cash, empty bank accounts.*

Letters or packages, cash sent to family, girlfriends in FL, Germany.

Blue Nissan Altima, Atta & Omari drive from Boston to Portland on evening of 9/10 for early morning flight.

Some stay at hotel in Newton, MA (I think) – hookers hired.

Preparations underway for end of life, religious martyrdom - prayer, reflection, shaved body hair.

Rolling luggage that looks like pilots' bags.

Atta's checked bag will get lost & never make the connecting flight from Portland. FBI will find it at Logan. Items inside will confirm suicide plan - Arabic instructions for carrying out attack, including night-before - how to prepare to die.

Items in carryon bags: folding knives under 4", mace, VHS for flying Boeing jets, flight computers, red bandanas, Koran.

By the time the drinks are done being served, I've added two full pages to my legal pad. My fingers are numb as I put down my pen, and I have to gently stretch my wrist.

I sip a small cup of water and roll my neck on my shoulders. I'm tense, and I feel the beginnings of a headache. My forehead finds the cool, hard surface of the window. I close my eyes and take a moment to breathe.

It's funny. I was always ashamed of the 9/11 books I bought. I kept them secret, afraid of ridicule. But if not for those books, the ones I carefully arranged on a shelf last night, I wouldn't be able to access so many of these details.

Some of the books described the events leading up to 9/11 in the context of the terrorists and their preparations. Some laid out how the law enforcement and intelligence communities failed to communicate with one another. Some highlighted flaws in existing airport security protocols. Some discussed how the common thinking on hijackings hindered our ability to imagine something grander and more sinister than what history taught us was possible.

Tristan called my fascination with these books macabre and unhealthy, and I felt ashamed. I'm not ashamed now. I'm glad I read them over and over. I just hope I've remembered enough to help.

My water cup rests empty on the fold-down table. I review what I've written, adding clarification or newly remembered information here and there.

My pages of notes take the facts from several different 9/11 accounts and tie them together. They reinforce the end result, that, whether knowingly or unwittingly, the terrorists managed to slip through the gaps in our systems of protection, intelligence, and travel. They took advantage of our failure to anticipate a large-scale suicide attack using planes. Men who hated Americans hid in plain sight while plotting to kill us.

The warning signs were there, but we didn't heed them. Like with speed limit signs on a road travelled every day, our eyes skipped right over them.

Hindsight has laid out the signs for the people of the post-9/11 world. Some of them seem so obvious now, but at this present time, no one's paying attention.

It's my job to make them pay attention.

It's up to me to point out the signs to the *pre*-9/11 world. No, to shove the signs in the faces of those who are supposed to protect us. I have to get them to connect the dots and understand the severity of what's coming, and I have to do it STAT.

Which brings my attention to the most problematic marble of all. Ian Greenberg.

All the information in the world will be no use to me if I can't get anyone to listen. And no one high enough in the food chain to *do* something with the information will listen without someone to vouch for me, someone with an iota of credibility who can verify certain facts. Someone with a Rolodex full of D.C. connections. That someone is Ian.

He is my basket, and I'm about to hand him all my eggs. Unfortunately, the plane will touch down in D.C. in twenty minutes, and I still don't know how I'm going to convince him to help me.

On the phone, I did what I could to make him curious. In my email from LaGuardia, I demonstrated that I know things I should have no way of knowing. But something tells me that's not enough. Without more, he'll find it all too easy to dismiss me. I just don't know what that *more* could be.

Think, Lydia. What do you know about Ian?

I know from his writing that he cares deeply about the truth. That's why I've decided not to lie to him. Lying will buy me a one-way ticket to losing Ian's trust. However, I can't tell him the whole truth, either.

So, yeah. I'm from twenty years in the future—well, not my body, only my consciousness, and I think I'm here because—get this, right?—I made a wish on a shooting star.

I barely believe the truth, and I'm living it.

Yet somehow, I have to impress upon him the fact that I know things that should be impossible for me to know. I need to convince him to trust in the information without focusing on where it's coming from. In short, I need him to believe in *me.*

The seatbelt light comes on, and the pilot announces the weather in D.C. My stomach leaps with jitters. I fold the rickety table and lock it into the seat in front of me. We're close enough to landing that I can make out individual plots of land below. Houses with yards, office buildings, freeways with cars like marching ants.

How does the landscape below look today compared to how it will look in twenty years? Probably not much different. But on the ground, things will be very different. 9/11 changed this city, maybe not as obviously as it changed Manhattan, but significantly, nonetheless.

The Department of Homeland Security will come into existence, employing more than a quarter of a million people from the neighborhoods below this plane. Airports will completely change how they handle passengers and screen luggage. Muslims will suffer an increase in hate crimes. News about 9/11 and terrorism will eclipse all other newsworthy events for weeks and months to come.

The heaviness of what I'm trying to do seeks to overwhelm me, but I won't let it. I shut my window shade and flip to a blank page in my legal pad. Writing on my lap, I create the heading, *Ian Greenberg*. Below that, I list the titles of his books. I take a moment to recognize that these few lines represent hundreds of thousands of words that, if I'm successful today, will never be written. I think about adding his articles too, but they are too many to number. What I do make note of is how Ian's writing changed our country for the better.

Somehow, Ian was able to take the complex political and cultural atmospheres that led to the attacks and make those concepts accessible to the layman. People who never paid attention to Middle-East relations before 9/11 could suddenly hold intelligent conversations about them on the subway and around the dinner table with their families.

Unfortunately, none of his future accomplishments will help me relate to Present-Day Ian, and that's exactly what I need to do.

Sitting back, I clip the pen to the pad and stretch my cramped fingers. The plane hums, and I feel a mild jolt as the landing gear is lowered.

My neurons fire like mad, racing against the sharply decreasing distance between the plane and the ground.

This morning, when I Googled Ian, I was expecting a long list of results befitting a prestigious and prolific journalist. But my expectations were based on a reality that exists twenty years in the future. What I actually got was a handful of relevant hits, including a six-year-old graduation announcement from Yale. At this point in time, Ian Greenberg is a young journalist.

He is not a household name. But by the end of the week, if the attacks happen, he will be. And that will be just the beginning for him.

In Oprah's voice, I hear the introduction. "You know him as 'the reporter who predicted 9/11.' Welcome *New York Times* Bestselling Author of *9/11, The Whys and Wherefores,* Pulitzer Prize winning journalist Ian Greenberg."

The audience cheers while a very tall man with artfully mussed hair strides onto the platform. After an affectionate, two-handed shake and a few cordial words murmured to his beaming host, he folds himself into an overstuffed white chair. He waves away the audience's clapping with an elegant, long-fingered hand, but the eyes behind his tortoiseshell frames shine with appreciation.

It's three short years after 9/11. Ian is on the show to promote his first book, but he has been in the public eye since shortly after the attacks. The article I had to scour the internet to find is every bit a part of the cultural consciousness by this time as the latest snarky episode of whatever show tops the TV charts and whoever Beyoncé is dating—was Jay-Z in the picture yet?

Oprah praises Ian for his book. I know it well, since it's among those I placed on a shelf in Nebraska yesterday, or twenty years in the future, if one wants to nitpick. One part of Oprah's interview pops into my head.

"In the introduction, you describe a childhood riddled with landmines of prejudice and racial tension. The son of a Jewish father and a mother from a Muslim family, you made it your mission to understand both sides of your family, even though your mother's side refused to acknowledge you. This passion led you to a double major in Middle Eastern studies and journalism at Yale, where you graduated top of your class. I'm dying to know, and I'm sure everyone watching is, too. Given your devout Jewish upbringing, do you, Ian Greenberg, believe in God?"

"I don't believe in God," Ian said. "But that puts me in the minority. Most people believe in some form of deity or deities. I simply haven't witnessed evidence in my own life to support such a belief."

"But you believe in miracles," Oprah said. "You cite several cases of them in your feature report 'The Miracles of 9/11,' calling them 'the documented unexplained.' If you don't believe in God, who or what is responsible for miracles?"

"An excellent question. I may not believe in God," Ian answered. "But I do believe in truth. I believe in what can be observed, documented, and verified." He held up a cautionary finger. "Notice, I don't say explained. The literal definition of *supernatural* is that which occurs by some force that *cannot* be explained by scientific understanding or the known laws of nature." He smiled his charming smile and spread his hands in an engaging manner. "Many people find it difficult to acknowledge what cannot be explained. I don't. Truth is truth, regardless of our ability to explain it or identify its impetus."

I remember being transfixed during that interview. He seemed so self-assured in his beliefs. He voiced his passion for truth and integrity in reporting, and I could tell his integrity went deeper than just the words he chose to share with the world. I saw in him inherent honor. It was during that interview that Ian became more than a household name to me. He became a hero of sorts. Of all the authors who wrote about 9/11, he was the one who helped me the most. He informed me, yes, but through his honesty, he also helped me process what I felt about the attack.

I turn the interview over in my mind, looking for tidbits that might help me today. I jot down, *OK if things can't be explained,* and below that, *No God, but miracles OK. Supernatural = unexplained. Truth is truth.*

The plane touches down, and my upper body is thrust forward as the brakes are applied.

I have a page filled with notes about Ian, but I still don't quite know how to mesh it all together into a strategy to secure his help. I had hoped he would meet me at the airport, but now, I'm kind of hoping he doesn't. I need more time.

When the passengers begin disembarking, my lungs relax. I hadn't realized it, but I've been in a state of tension since boarding back in New York. My leg muscles clench and unclench with the need to flee the plane, but I'm near the back and have to wait my turn. It's with no small relief that my feet join the pounding vibrations of the jetway.

I'm on the ground. No one took over my plane. Four groups of passengers won't be so lucky tomorrow if I fail.

I can't mess this up. I've got one shot to set things right. I'm not going to blow it.

By the time I enter the gate area, I'm in full-on charge-nurse mode. Passengers stream around me as I dig my phone out of my laptop bag and power it on. I plan to call Ian STAT and find out where he is so I can take a cab to meet him. If he won't tell me where he is, I'll camp out at the *Washington Post* office until he agrees to see me. Worst-case scenario, I won't be able to convince Ian to help, and I'll have to go to the CIA headquarters by myself and make them take me seriously.

While my phone powers up, I scan the ceiling for signs pointing toward ground transportation. But something else catches my eye first. *LYDIA CLAY* is scrawled in black marker across two pieces of paper joined with a perforated seam, the kind you would see being fed through a dot matrix printer. The makeshift banner is pulled taut between the hands of a lanky young man with a windswept tangle of black hair and a light-weight jacket. Tortoiseshell glasses frame alert, green eyes that fix on me when I stop dead in my tracks. He appears younger than I'm used to seeing him, but then, so do I.

Ian.

A flutter of excitement rises in me, birds of purpose taking flight. He came!

But panic quickly follows. I'm not ready!

I haven't figured out what to say, yet, but I better come up with something, because my feet are taking me toward him.

"I've never been met at the airport with a sign before," is what comes out of my mouth. "Did you bring a limo, too?" My attempt at humor lands like a soggy pancake on the tiles. "I'm Lydia Clay." I adjust my bag on my shoulder and reach to shake his hand.

Ian clasps my hand in his much larger one and pumps it professionally.

He towers over me, six-five if he's an inch. I have to look up to meet his eyes, which are a little too wide as he takes me in. I remember I'm in jeans and a hoodie.

If I wanted to convince government officials to take me seriously, I should have put on a suit. Unfortunately, as a twenty-three-year-old up to her ears in college loans, I owned exactly zero suits. The closest I could have come would have been either a button up blouse and pair of khakis or one of the cocktail dresses I kept for socializing with Tristan's family and friends. I'm kicking myself for not dressing up at least that much, but it's too late now.

"No limo, today," he says. "But I happen to know where all the best seats are on the Metro." In his there-and-gone grin, I glimpse the larval stage of the charm he'll use to woo his future public.

Ian's mixed heritage expresses itself in unapologetic brushstrokes. Thick, dark brows lend him an academic sternness while high cheekbones and an aquiline nose bring to mind an Ottoman emperor presiding over a bloody battlefield. A messenger bag slung across his body has dragged his loosely-knotted tie off-center and caused one side of his collar to wrinkle. Corduroy slacks show signs of wear at the knees and look a size too large, reinforcing how much styles of dress have changed in the last twenty years. His demeanor is that of a community college professor who's been cajoled into teaching summer term.

"I'm going to cut to the chase, Ms. Clay. Or should I say, Ms. Watercrest?" He wears a superior look as he folds the sign bearing my name and slides it into a trash receptacle.

Mentally, I slap my forehead. I should have given him my married name. It is, after all, my legal name at this point in time.

"I'm here because you've piqued my interest," he informs me. "But that interest is hanging by a thread. You asked for an hour of my time, but I can't afford that much. You have thirty minutes—over lunch—to convince me I haven't ruined my career by coming here."

He marches off, and I follow in his wake, feeling chastised.

"You're buying," he tosses over his shoulder.

I'm not on Ian's good side, and I've only got half an hour to fix that. This is going to take a miracle.

CHAPTER 9

Ian

"PUT THAT AWAY," I say when Lydia slaps a legal pad filled with handwritten notes on the table.

I've found us a booth in a quiet corner of the airport Chili's, where a server has promptly delivered two ice waters and taken our drink order. My would-be source sits across from me in an oversized hoodie, looking far less confident than she sounded when we spoke earlier. Though, now that I've barked an order at her, I'm catching a glimpse of the assertive caller who's managed to tie up my entire morning. Her blue eyes flash with affront, and she clutches at the legal pad.

I look pointedly at it while I pull out my own notebook.

"Now," I say, holding my pencil ready. "Tell me—"

"Why do you get to use a notebook?"

I look up sharply, annoyed at the interruption. I'm here at her behest, and she's interrupting me and questioning my methods?

"I get to use a notebook because I'm the reporter."

She sits up taller, drawing an aura of authority around her like a queen's mantle. Her fresh, make-up free face is that of a woman in her early twenties, but she's staring me down like someone with decades of experience in directing personnel. I'm reminded of being taken to task by Carmen this morning.

"I'm the one with the information," she says loftily. "This—" She jabs a finger at her legal pad. "Is the information. If you get to take notes, I should get to refer to mine."

After dragging my tired ass to the airport—and probably losing my job in the process—I'm in no mood to listen to a recitation of facts from a set of notes. If I'm going to spend a single second more with Lydia Clay, I need her to convince me I'm not making a huge mistake. That's not going to happen with her reading from a pad of paper.

Patience worn to a nub, I say, "You have twenty-eight minutes left."

She arches one eyebrow, and I brace myself for an argument, but it doesn't come. "Fine," she says. "We'll do this your way. But I may need to refer to these at some point." She flips the pad over, resting her joined hands on top. She's channeling a teacher who has temporarily assumed the role of pupil.

"As I was saying," I begin. "Let's start with your name. Your *real* name."

Her lips pinch like she's sucking a lemon. "My legal name, at the moment, is Lydia Ann Watercrest."

As I thought. She's the same Lydia Clay whose marriage license I found in the court records this morning. She's been married about a month, according to the license, time enough to become accustomed to a new name.

She lifts her waterglass with a left hand free of matrimonial jewelry and takes a bracing sip. "I'm—right now, I'm newly married." I've never heard a newlywed use that funeral-march tone when announcing their happy news. When she notices me looking at her fingers, she adds, "I took off my rings this morning." The tip-of-the-iceberg statement is delivered with an unspoken warning: Proceed at your own risk.

I heed the warning. Whatever drama surrounds her personal life is irrelevant to my purpose here. I withhold the customary congratulations at her newlywed status and simply record her full name.

Lydia's alert eyes follow the movements of my pencil.

"I prefer to go by my maiden name, Lydia Clay."

I make brief eye contact with her, but her face gives nothing away other than a strong desire not to be called by her married name.

When I underline *Clay* two times, she nods, appearing satisfied.

I position my pencil below her name. "What's your address?"

"My address?" she asks, as though she's unprepared to answer.

"It's a standard question I ask all my sources."

"It's—" Her eyes dart up and to the left. Combined with the consternation carving a pleat between her brows, her eye position indicates an honest attempt to access information. "Shoot. I don't remember." She sucks in a breath. "Wait!" She unzips her bag and rummages for a moment. "Ah-ha! Here is it." Reading from her drivers' license, she gives an address in New York. It's the same one I found in the court records.

"Why do you have to read your address off your driver's license?"

She crosses her arms in front of her chest and looks away, this time to the right. "I haven't lived there long."

She's lying. Not about residing in Brooklyn for only a short time. I believe that, seeing as she's newly married. What she's lying about is the *reason* she isn't able to rattle off her address automatically.

Perhaps there has been significant trouble in paradise and she's been living separately from her husband. That would fit, seeing as she isn't wearing her wedding ring, and she prefers to go by her maiden name. If she hasn't had to give her legal address in many instances, I suppose I could understand not having it memorized. But why dance around it? Troubled marriages are common enough.

Shrugging, I move on to the meat of this interview. For most sources, I would jump right into the Who, What, Where, and When of the story. But Lydia is not most sources. I set down my notebook and pencil.

"Why am I here, Ms. Clay?"

"Please, call me Lydia."

"All right. Lydia. You claim to know about an impending terror plot. You have names, and you know it will involve planes. But you say you can't go to the FBI or the intelligence community. Instead, you contact me."

I'm interrupted by the arrival of our iced colas. The server slides them onto the table between us and takes our orders. When we're alone again, I finish.

"Why a simple column reporter and not some network news anchor? Your story could get a lot more attention in broadcast news, and there are plenty of outlets where you live. Why fly to D.C.?"

Lydia draws a long breath. She grabs my gaze with hers. "You think you're here to write a story? Ian, no. That's not why I called you."

I blink. Anger rushes up and makes my face hot. I've given up my morning for her, and she doesn't even have a story for me? I don't get to report something big about terrorism that will prove Carmen wrong when she claims it's a "non-topic"?

"What am I doing here, then?" I force the words past gritted teeth. "Why did you fly here to talk with me?"

"You're not here to report a story," Lydia says, face solemn. "You're here to help me stop the story from happening."

Lydia

It was the wrong thing to say.

Behind his tortoiseshell frames, Ian's eyes are flames of green fury. He jams his notebook and pencil into an inner coat pocket so hard I'm worried the pointed lead will punch a hole in the fabric.

"I hope you like fajitas, Ms. Clay," he growls, and he slides out of the booth. "Because I've lost my appetite."

I jump up and grab his wrist. "No! You can't leave."

He shakes me free with a look of warning, and I hold up my hands to show I'm not a physical threat. I won't stop him from leaving, not with force. But I need to do *something*.

I can't do this without him. It has to be *him*. There's no one else I can think of who, on this day in history, understands the threat our nation is facing. There's no one else who will believe me that what's about to happen is even possible. If I can't convince someone who warned of a scenario like this in a recent news article, how will I convince the government intelligence machine whose blind spots will allow it to happen?

I have to think of something. Quick.

Ian jerks on the sleeve of his coat. His glare tells me I've unforgivably rumpled the material with my touch. I'm not put off by his ire. Instead, I'm struck by how young he seems compared to the Ian whose image I've seen countless times in various forms of media over the last twenty years.

He's going to age well. Distinguished lines around his eyes and salt and pepper at his temples will only deepen his natural attractiveness. His lanky body will fill out, making him a paragon of academic fitness. His fashion sense will set trends in business couture. The inquisitive light in his eyes will shine even brighter with inner confidence and experience, experience he'll gain turning his interest in terrorism into hundreds of thousands of words that will educate millions.

All that potential turns his back and walks away from me.

"You're going to win a Pulitzer," I blurt out.

He stops. I have his attention, even if he refuses to face me.

"Two of them, actually," I say. "One for feature writing in journalism, and another for a book you'll write about how what's going to happen tomorrow was able to happen."

He cocks his head as I come around to stand in his path. We're blocking the entrance to Chilis, but no one's trying to get around us at the moment.

It occurs to me none of what I'm saying will make sense to him, but he's listening, so I keep going.

"If you leave right now, you'll be forever known as the 'reporter who predicted 9/11.' You'll be a household name by the end of the week and a full-fledged celebrity by the end of the year. Your career will be made in the shade."

He frowns. "9/11? That's tomorrow's date."

"It is."

For the first time since meeting him, I see real concern pass across his face.

"Let me get this straight," he says. "You're predicting a major terrorist attack will happen tomorrow. And that if I leave right now, somehow, I'll become famous because of it?" He scowls. I can see he's offended at the thought of benefitting from a tragedy.

Elation makes me feel light on the balls of my feet. I was right about him. His reputation for altruism is no act.

I nod in answer to his question.

He scoffs, but the blow-off doesn't reach his eyes. "First of all, no one knows the future. Second, if you want me to stay and hear you out, you're not exactly selling it. Quite the opposite, actually. I'd really like a Pulitzer. That would get me out from under Carmen's thumb for sure." He says the last bit to himself and gets a distant look in his eye.

I have no idea who Carmen is, but judging from the grin on his face, getting out from under her thumb would be immensely satisfying. Perhaps not enough to overcome the moral affront at benefiting from tragedy, but satisfying, nonetheless.

"I don't want you to leave," I say. "I need you. America needs you. But by staying, you'll be giving up a lot. It's important to me that you know that."

"Why on Earth would I stay, then?" He turns so he's facing the booth again, and I breathe a sigh of relief. He's not walking out.

"Because it's the right thing to do." I motion to the booth. The server is coming with our plates. "And because it's dumb to turn down a free meal."

His anger melts away. He appears thoughtful for a moment, then shakes his head ruefully.

"I must be a glutton for punishment." He slides into his seat.

I gambled on his good nature, and I won. The mere suggestion of him giving up something valuable in order to do the right thing was enough to recapture his interest. Unfortunately, I doubt altruism will get him to stay if I tell him *how* I know what's going to happen tomorrow.

"No one knows the future."

He's right. And wrong. And that's going to be impossible to explain.

Good thing a plan is beginning to form in the back of my mind. If I can implement it just right, I have a shot at securing his belief in a way that might help him overlook the question of where I'm getting my information.

I thank him for sitting down again as the scents of sizzling meat and sauteed vegetables fill the space between us. Ian trades the implements of news reporting for those of dining. Fork in hand, he begins piling fixings onto a warm tortilla.

"You do realize that a journalist who stops the news is a journalist out of work." He rolls up the fruits of his labor and takes a massive bite.

"Not necessarily." I nibble at my chips and salsa, but I'm not that hungry. Instead, I focus on my diet cola. Icy cold and refreshing, it steels me for what I need to do, which is to appeal to an Ian who doesn't yet exist, but who will. "By stopping one story, you might find yourself in the best possible position for reporting a different story."

He chews, face thoughtful. "So, you're saying I might not have to give up everything if I listen to you, just the dazzling career I'm supposed to have if this attack you predict takes place."

"I don't think you can do anything *but* have a dazzling career," I say honestly. "As for the attack, the plot is underway. Whether it's carried out or stopped, al-Qaeda is still going to be big news tomorrow. You'll still be the only journalist who saw it coming." I smile brightly. "Maybe you'll still get a Pulitzer."

Ian barks out a laugh that makes nearby patrons stare. "Ah, well," he says when he recovers. "I'm good as fired, anyway. I might as well hear you out. What is it I'm supposed to have seen coming?"

"I'm sorry about your job, but I think you'll find it worthwhile to indulge me. I'll tell you everything I can," I promise. "And I'll be completely honest."

"More honest than you've been, already, I hope." I take offense at his raised eyebrow.

"I have been honest!"

"Sure. All honest people give out false names and don't know where they live." He's smirking, but the censure still stings.

"The situation is complicated."

"Uncomplicate it for me."

If only I could.

He finishes off his first fajita and begins making a second. "Start with how you know about Massoud. That's highly classified information at this point. I shouldn't even admit to you that I was able to verify it. And how did you know about those flight school students? You say you can't go to the CIA, but you have to be with some kind of intelligence outfit to know the things you know."

"I'm not. I'm just a civilian."

"A journalist?"

"No."

"Then you must work for one of the flight schools. Or manage some kind of government database. Come on. Out with it. How do you know what you know?" He flips open his notebook one-handed while using the other to make quick work of his second fajita.

I feel my half hour slipping away.

"How about instead of you asking me questions and writing down answers, you let me talk to you? Morally responsible person to morally responsible person?"

He blinks. He has long lashes for a guy, and mixed in with the green of his irises are specks of golden brown. His eyes are like a glass of Scotch sitting in a patch of sunshine on the lawn. "That's not how an interview works."

"But this isn't a story. Remember? This is two people trying to do the right thing."

He looks skeptical. I get the feeling his notebook and pencil are extensions of his person, like stethoscopes and blood pressure cuffs are for me.

"It's my half hour," I say. "And I choose to spend what's left of it just...talking."

I see the moment he relents. His shoulders lose their rigid line, and his mouth softens. For the first time, I realize how full his lips are. Which is, of course, completely irrelevant.

"All right," he says, tucking away the offending objects. "Talk."

To be Jedi is to face the truth, and choose.

—Yoda

CHAPTER 10

Ian

D ressed for comfort in the lecture hall, aversive bordering on combative about the state of her marriage, and clearly lying—or at least withholding information— about her ignorance of her own address, Lydia Clay has not exactly inspired confidence so far. But there's a flip side to the coin. Such as her knowledge about Massoud and those flight students. Her sincerity in reaching out to me for help. Her unfeigned concern that lives are at stake. It's that side of the coin that keeps me in this booth.

Okay, yes, and the free food.

And maybe, if I'm honest, a tiny wish that her warnings are legitimate, and I might have a hand in preventing this attack she's worried about. It's strange, to wish for something bad to almost happen. But such is my ego. The part of me that perked up when Lydia mentioned a Pulitzer wants to be known for doing good with his journalistic talents, and to do good, there must be evil afoot.

Rather than think too hard about that, I enjoy my meal and tune my ears to listen, not for the eventual composition of a story, but for the solving of the mystery that has taken over my morning. A mystery, apparently, about tomorrow.

With her vague warnings and dire projections, Lydia has set out a series of dots. As a journalist, I make my living connecting such dots. She's given me enough that I've formed a complete, if contradictory, story. But it's not a story I like. I'm hoping that by listening to her, I will find the contradictions explained and my fears allayed.

I know I've made you think something terrible is going to happen tomorrow, but it's really not as bad as all that, I wait for her to say. *I've led you to think that maybe, just maybe, a small group of terrorists will try to hijack some airplanes with the intention of crashing them. I've made you think thousands of Americans could be at risk. But I've grossly exaggerated. Besides, the authorities will have no trouble catching these guys before they can do harm.*

"Okay," Lydia says, bolstering herself. Her chips and salsa sit forgotten. "Okay. Ian." She makes my name a sentence all by itself. "I'll answer all your questions, and I'll be completely truthful. But first, I need you to put your faith in me. Because what I have to say will be hard to believe."

I snort. "I'm not big on faith."

"I know," she says, surprising me, because how could she possibly know such a thing about me?

"You were a devout Jew growing up," she says, leaning forward and talking with her hands. "You attended synagogue with your parents and had a bar mitzvah and did all the things you were supposed to as a young Jewish man. But when you graduated high school, you learned your mother's family disowned her for converting to Judaism. Your faith was shaken. As soon as you were able, you tracked down your extended family in Iran. When you travelled to meet them, your grandfather refused to acknowledge you. He wouldn't let you enter his home, and he forbade your aunts and uncles from taking your calls. He made it impossible for you to meet your cousins. You lost your faith on that trip."

I'm in danger of catching flies, as my paternal grandmother would have said. My jaw just about hit the table as Lydia described the family history I've always kept close to my vest.

"And the religious prejudice wasn't limited to the Muslim side of your family." She goes on, unperturbed by my reaction. "Your father's parents actually divorced over it. Your grandmother wanted to be part of your life, but your devout Jewish grandfather refused. Your grandmother came to live with you and your parents, but she never really got along with your mother.

"You witnessed so much hatred from people who were supposed to love you and love each other. All that hatred entered your life because of religion. You decided that religion was overrated, and you decided to put your faith not in God or spirituality, but in—"

"Truth," I finish for her.

She smiles sadly. "Truth," she echoes, as if she had been about to say the exact word that has become my life's purpose.

I stare at her, speechless. I'm racking my brain for any possible avenue for her to discover these intimate details about my life. Could she be someone who attended synagogue with me? No. I would recognize her. And my parents never discussed family issues outside their home. Nor did I.

The only possible explanation is that she's been a fly on the wall throughout my childhood, but not even that covers it all. I haven't discussed my faith or lack thereof with anyone, not my closest university friends, not even my parents. That little nugget lives in my heart and nowhere else. I've let my family believe I don't attend synagogue anymore simply because my work demands too much of my time. If they knew how I really felt, they would badger me endlessly.

The server picks that moment to deliver our check. Lydia drags it toward herself as the server leaves again.

When we're alone, I lean forward. "How do you know all that?"

"I shouldn't, should I?"

"No. You shouldn't." Not for the first time, I wonder if she has some kind of connection to U.S. intelligence. But that doesn't jive. No one in the government would have reason to spy on my family, well, with the exception of my ex-CIA aunt. I wouldn't be surprised if someone somewhere was keeping tabs on her. But my parents and I should be of no interest whatsoever.

"But I do know," she says. "I also know you don't believe in God. And after all you've been through with your family, I don't blame you. But I'm hoping you believe in miracles."

Unruffled doesn't begin to describe how Lydia has made me feel in the last five minutes. My only solace is that she seems to take no pleasure in these personal revelations. The slant of her brows, and the compassion in her gaze tell the story of a woman who desires not to best an adversary but to forge a connection.

I wish, not for the first time, I could walk away from Lydia Clay and her vague warnings of doom. But, as she has demonstrated once again, she knows too much. This time, the knowledge is not something she could have gleaned from a government database or a darknet chatroom. This time, she has shown me something I cannot ignore.

She has shown me myself.

"Miracles," I say. I reposition myself in the booth. My fingers cramp with the urge to hold my notebook and pencil. I want to go back to interviewing her. I want to wrest back control of this meeting. At the same time, I crave whatever understanding Lydia wishes to reveal to me.

"Do you believe in them?" Again with the compassion and sincerity. Her focus is so honed on me, I can practically feel her imploring me to engage with this line of reason, to really search myself and be honest to the point of vulnerability. I also sense that she will treat my vulnerability with care.

Like an experienced nurse. The thought manifests out of the ether, but somehow, it fits. Again, I'm assaulted with a discordant feeling that Lydia Clay is older than she appears.

I feel the moment I decide to give in. With a sigh, I begin piling meat and veggies on my last fajita and restate the question.

"Do I believe in miracles?"

My first inclination is to say no, but I can't deny there are things that go on in the world that science can't explain. Whether I believe in the supernatural or not, certain events are recorded in the fact-record of history. I chew slowly while my mind wanders back to Yale, to a course I took on journalistic objectivity.

"An adult voice calling for help guides Montana rescuers to a car," I say, thinking out loud. "An infant is found strapped in the car seat of an overturned sedan partially submerged in a river. The water is inches from the baby's head. The driver, the infant's mother, is found to have been dead for hours. No source of the voice is every found, and yet six rescuers all confirm hearing it."

Lydia gives me her rapt attention.

"A statue of the Virgin Mary weeps and is documented by hundreds of visitors over several generations. A scientific study of the statue reveals no explanation for the occasional appearance of the liquid, which contains human DNA."

Lydia's eyes widen. I see tentative hope in them.

"Numerous members of a Syrian army in the tenth century document a burning fireball that led them to a life-saving oasis after weeks lost in the dessert. Their drawings of the phenomenon on goatskin parchment are a perfect match to those carved into stone at a holy site miles away, down to the size of the orb, its height in the sky, and the width of its star-shaped, seven-pointed corona, proving there were multiple witnesses.

"An ancient Jewish teacher is tortured, crucified, definitively killed and wrapped in graveclothes. Numerous witnesses report seeing him alive three days later."

"The resurrection of Jesus Christ," Lydia says.

I nod. "I could go on. There are dozens of documented examples like these, where no one can explain the *how,* but witnesses confirm the *what.*" I sip my drink. "I may not understand how events like these were possible, but that doesn't mean I'll dismiss them out of hand. Some journalists will, mind you."

"But not you," she says with satisfaction.

"Not me."

She slouches back in the booth with a look of relief softening her face.

I hold up a finger. "Don't get excited. I don't dismiss stories like these, because the presence of witnesses is a strong indicator of truth. But I hesitate to call them miracles. The word implies some sort of benevolent engineer overseeing the event. It implies the existence of God. It takes the objective account of the event and adds an unwarranted layer of subjectivity."

Lydia munches on her triangular chips. She shakes her head in that way someone does when they joyfully make a connection in their own mind.

"So, you would report on an event you couldn't explain," she says. "But you wouldn't call it a miracle."

"If there were multiple credible witnesses. Yes."

She wipes sweat from her glass with her thumb. "So, it's the word you take umbrage with, not the concept?"

"You could say that. Why? Do you have a miracle for me, Lydia?"

Lydia

SITTING ACROSS A restaurant table from Ian is surreal. Yesterday, he was a celebrity with salt-and-pepper hair and a CV any journalist would covet. I viewed him as an untouchable icon several years my senior. Today, he's a young, idealistic man who hasn't quite realized yet how charming he is. Coming face to face with his youth is as startling as seeing myself in the mirror. Despite being rewound twenty years, he still has the same intellectual charm that will help make the man as popular as his writings. When he gestures with his long-fingered hands, he makes me want to debate world issues with him for hours on end.

Maybe when all this is over, we'll have that chance. I'll have twenty years to kill, after all. Of course, Tristan won't like me getting together with another man for any reason, even just to socialize, but this time around, I'm not going to let Tristan set the course for my life.

This time, I'll create healthy boundaries in my marriage and maintain them as long as needed to bring Christian and Holly into the world. I'll show Tristan that my opinions and desires count just as much as his, and I'll pray every day that the children I have in this second round of life are the same two wonderful creatures who stole my heart and had so much promise in the previous one. I refuse to dwell on the epic improbability of the same exact sperm and ova coming into contact a second time. I imagine the improbability matches that of wishing on a shooting star and being sent back in time.

But these considerations are for another time. Right now, I'm focused on Ian. He asked if I have a miracle for him. His tone was teasing, his eyes sparkling.

I prefer the laid-back charmer to the wigged-out Ian who froze with a fajita halfway to his mouth when I summarized his childhood for him. But neither of those Ians is the one I need right now. I need future Ian. I need the Ian who's seen terrible events unfold and has comforted the masses with his insights, the Ian whose writings rally government officials to an improbable cause.

How do I tell the Ian before me that I don't *have* a miracle for him, but that I *am* the miracle?

What I know is impossible to explain, but it's the God's honest truth, and much of it can be verified, like where the terrorists will be tomorrow morning and what they will have in their bags. I just need people in the right places to take a chance on me. Ian can help me get in touch with those people. But he needs to really believe in me in order to wield that power of conviction.

If I can't secure his unshakable belief, I will have blown my chance to stop 9/11. Because if Ian can't believe, no one else will be able to, either.

I slip my credit card in the folded holder and set it at the edge of the table. My half-hour is up. I've laid the groundwork as well as I can. All that's left is for me to spit it out and leave it up to Ian as to whether he believes me or not.

I start by answering Ian's question with a question of my own. "Would you say it's a miracle that I know so much about your background?"

He studies me. "If you are who you say you are, a nursing student with no government connections, then I suppose that word could apply, my preferences notwithstanding."

"Okay. Yes. Good. Let's not call it a miracle, then. Let's call it—" I remember the as-yet-nonexistent interview with Oprah. "The documented unexplained."

He ponders the phrase with unfocused green eyes. "I like that. Documented unexplained. *Documented,* because I can verify that what you've told me about my upbringing is accurate. *Unexplained,* because I can't come up with a reasonable explanation for how you know so much about me." His fingers fidget and tap on the table. "It helps me not to freak out if I think about it academically, so thanks for that."

"Any time."

He returns my smile.

"I shouldn't know anything about your background," I reiterate. "But I do. I know certain things about you, Ian, that have no rational reason to exist in my head. I know these things the same way I know about Massoud's assassination and about Hamzi and Mihdhar flunking out of flight school."

"Hazmi," he interjects.

I draw myself up. He's jolted my train of thought clear off the tracks. "What?"

"It's Hazmi, not Hamzi. You're putting the *z* in the wrong place. By the way, I didn't get in touch with FTI in San Diego. They weren't open yet when I called."

My momentum goes *poof* as Ian critiques my spelling. Then I realize what he's saying.

"You didn't verify the facts in my email?" If he hasn't checked the veracity of what I've presented him with so far, he's not going to believe anything else I have to say. Panic rises in my chest. I'm blowing this whole thing.

"Hey." Ian's voice makes me look up from my twisting hands. "Hey, it's okay. I believe you. I verified Atta's enrollment at Huffman. And I'm familiar with the names Hazmi and Mihdhar from other sources. I'm not doubting their legitimacy as persons of interest. I'm just pointing out the discrepancy. Out of curiosity. Why *did* they flunk out?"

I fall back against the booth. He has no idea what the words "I believe you," do for my confidence, even if their meaning is limited to what I've told him up to now.

"They flunked out because they told their instructor they wanted to learn how to fly big jets, but they didn't care about learning how to take off or land."

His eyebrows go up. "Bold move."

"More like stupid. The official reason for letting them go was lack of aptitude." I lower my voice because the server is coming our way. "You mentioned looking into Massoud's assassination. So, you were able to verify that?"

The server drops off the receipt that needs signing, and I push it aside. I can't focus on calculating a tip right now.

When we're alone again, Ian says, "I did. How did you know about that?"

Here we go. "That's the one question I can't answer. That's my whole point in prepping you for what I have to say. I have important information about tomorrow, but I can't tell you how I got that information." I spread my hands, imploring. "I know it's going to be really hard for you to move forward without knowing, but I *need* you to. I need you to trust in *what* I know and to be okay not knowing the how. Do you think you could, like, treat it like a case of documented unexplained?"

I hear myself, and I sound far from confident. I remind myself of the me that used to couch everything I asked of Tristan in promises and concessions. I don't want to be that way with Ian, but I'm not sure how else to be. I'm asking a lot, and I really need his cooperation.

To keep from making a desperate fool of myself, I grab up the pen and begin working out the tip. When I look up again, Ian's staring at me like he doesn't know what to make of me.

I fall back on my nursing experience, reminding myself that I am the expert in this scenario. I need Ian, yes, but he doesn't owe me his cooperation. If a patient refuses my care, I must respect that. I'll do the same with Ian. If he won't help me, I *will* find another way.

Self-assured but humble, I lift my chin, and I wait for his answer like the professional I am.

"You're asking for a blank check of trust," he says. "Obviously, I can't give you that."

My stomach drops.

"But," he says with a raised finger. "You've earned an extension." He's talking about my thirty minutes. "Consider me prepped. I'll forget the 'how,' for now. Go ahead. Lay it on me."

I suspect it's as good an offer as I'm likely to get.

It's time.

Stick to things that are possible to know, Lyd. Tell him what the hijackers are planning and leave it at that.

I meet his gaze head on. "Tomorrow, nineteen terrorists plan to hijack four passenger jets with the intent to crash them into populated areas on the East Coast. Their goal is to take as many lives as possible. One target is the World Trade Center. Bin Laden wants to take those towers down. He's determined to finish what was started in '93. Another target is The Pentagon. The White House may also be a target."

Ian stares at me. I think I've shocked him expressionless.

"You've given me thirty minutes of your time," I tell him. "Now, I'm giving you—" I do a quick calculation in my head. "Twenty hours to help me stop a major terror attack."

*Does al-Qaeda have to hit The Pentagon
to get your attention?*

—Michael Sheehan, State Department's
ambassador-at-large for counterterrorism
in 2001

CHAPTER 11

Ian

I PRIDE MYSELF on my poker face. Learning how to appear unflappable has served me well as a journalist. Lydia has managed to put every ounce of my training to the test.

I sip my water, letting the ice cubes cool my upper lip. I focus on the sensation instead of the wild improbability of her claims coming to fruition.

Across from me, she leans forward, hands on the table. Her blue eyes are intense on me. She awaits a response with no small amount of desperation, judging by the winged slant of her brows, but how can I give her one when my mind is going in a million directions?

What she suggests is impossible. Of course, it's impossible. I mean, sure, I suggested terrorism could move in this direction—involving planes with skilled pilots willing to die—but what Lydia's talking about is a large-scale operation the likes of which the intelligence community is always on alert for.

The odds of such a large group of al-Qaeda-affiliates being in the country and being able to purchase airline tickets is so unlikely it borders on absurdity. The movements of persons of interest like this would be rigorously monitored. Their finances would be observed. Their names would be on no-fly lists.

Setting aside intelligence considerations, for arguments' sake, and presuming nineteen terrorists *could* obtain tickets on passenger jets, they would never be allowed to board. They would need weapons to carry out a hijacking. Airport security would reveal those items, and the supposed plot would end there.

If, by some wicked miracle, these hijackers managed to breeze through airport security and board the planes, and *if* they could take control of the cockpits, like Lydia suggests, they would have to possess great skill at flying and navigating in order to strike specific targets.

Say all those obstacles could be surmounted and nineteen men willing to die took control of passenger jets and aimed them at major urban centers in Manhattan and D.C., military jets would be scrambled to intercept them before they could do harm, limiting the loss of life to those onboard—a tragedy, but not on the scale of the thousands she mentioned during our phone call this morning.

Even if all laws of probability failed, and the hijackers managed to crash into actual buildings, the casualties would still fall far short of the "thousands" she suggested. Evacuations would take place as soon as the threat was realized.

The improbabilities mount atop each other to the point where something like this simply could not happen. Perhaps—and that is a monumental *perhaps*—an attack like this could take place overseas, in, say, a country where airport security is not as stringent as here in the U.S. If the targets were located in Europe, national boundaries would create a communications nightmare. It would be difficult to coordinate a counterattack against four airplane-missiles flying toward several different countries. Still, I struggle to fathom an outcome anywhere near what Lydia seems to be worried about.

I study her as the ice water chills a line down my esophagus. The concern on her face is real. What has she seen or heard to make her fear something so beyond the scope of reason? I would ask if I thought she would tell me.

Instead, I say, "Nineteen? That's awfully specific. How did you arrive at that number?"

The hope in Lydia's expression is banked by some cooler emotion. Chin lifted, she says, "In the ER, I hear doctors use that word when they don't believe a single thing coming out of the patient's mouth. 'Those are *awfully* rhonchi lung sounds for someone who quit smoking years ago.' 'That's an *awfully* high blood sugar for someone who doesn't eat sweets.' 'That was an *awfully* big coincidence that upside-down stool happened to be right behind you when you fell.'"

My jaw falls open at her last example.

She plows ahead. "People only say 'awfully' when they're being condescending. Nineteen isn't an 'awfully' specific number. It's the exact number. The correct number. It's the number of hijackers who will change our country forever by this time tomorrow. Are you going to help me stop them or not? If not, I have to go. I have a lot of work to do."

"That's supposed to be my line," I say. "I'm the one who dropped everything at the whims of a stranger. Tell me, Ms. Clay. How long have you worked in an ER? I thought you were just a student."

Her eyes widen. I've caught her in a lie—or something like a lie. Lydia has my knack for sensing truth going haywire. But even without it, I can spot the discrepancy between her young façade and the years of experience she draws around herself like a cloak...or like nurse's scrubs.

She clamps her lips shut. For a brief moment, panic flashes across her face. There's no reason her panic should cause a flutter of discomfort in my stomach, but it does.

I decide not to press her for an answer. Something about her squared shoulders and the amount of white showing in her eyes suggests she might bolt. While the possibility would allow me to salvage part of my day and maybe hang onto my job by a thread, I find the thought of losing Lydia unpalatable. She is a mystery I must solve.

"Look, the good news," I say at last, hoping to allay some of her fear, "is that a plan like what you just described could never happen. There are multiple hurdles men like that would have to overcome. Intelligence, for one. Airport security. And as a last resort, the Air Force." I smile broadly. "So, it's okay. You don't have to worry. It can't happen." I wait for her to see the reason in what I'm saying. I'm also starting to wonder if

Lydia might be not quite right in the head, because the look on her face is not relief.

Lydia slowly sits back in the booth. Her jaw works like she's clenching her teeth. Her eyes flash.

"Gee, thanks for mansplaining and putting my worried little brain to rest. I can fly back to New York now that you've declared 9/11 is utterly impossible." She grabs up her legal pad and scoots out of the booth. "Enjoy being the reporter who predicted the impossible."

Bag on her shoulder, she stands and storms off.

I give chase, confused and, if I'm honest, a little hurt.

Mansplaining? What the hell is that supposed to mean? Does she think I'm being sexist?

She's speed-walking toward ground-transportation. Fortunately, my legs are longer than hers.

"Lydia," I say, striding directly behind her.

"Go back to work, Ian. You've got Pulitzers to win, and I've got to go to the CIA."

"Come on. Lydia. Stop." She's angry, and I'm at a complete loss as to why.

I'm starting to get angry, too. I didn't ask for any of this!

I'm as good as fired for letting this woman take over my writing day. Not to mention, I don't know where my bruised feelings are coming from. Lydia is nobody to me. Why should it matter if she rejects my attempt to soothe her fears?

She gets on a descending escalator, destination, baggage claim. I get on behind her.

"What will you do at the CIA?" I ask.

She sniffs. When I try to lean around to see her face, she turns away. "I don't know, but I won't make the same mistake I made with you."

Her tone is final, and it twists the blade on my hurt feelings.

Does she really think she can walk away when she's made me so curious? When I can tell she's holding back information? If I've learned anything as a reporter, it's to recognize when a story is incomplete.

I put a hand on her shoulder. "How can I help you if you hold back from me? Give me a real chance, Lydia. Tell me the whole story, not just bits and pieces."

She goes still, then chances a peek at me. Her red-rimmed eyes are conflicted.

At last, she says, "I can't," and she steps off the escalator. Passengers flow around her as she stops to take in the signage on the ceiling.

I hate the word *can't*. Most of the time when people say it, what they mean is they *won't*. They're afraid. Or stubborn. Or in the case of Lydia Clay, as I suspect, both.

"Yes, you can," I say, and I do something I'm not proud of. Before she can make a beeline for ground transportation, I swipe the legal pad out of her hand.

"Hey! Give that back!"

"No."

I don't know what's come over me. I've never asked a source for another chance before or taken liberties with their personal property, but Lydia's different. She has written me off as a lost cause when I'm not ready to be a lost cause.

She has asked me to believe in her, but she won't believe in me enough to give me the whole truth. If what she's trying to warn about has any merit and thousands of lives are truly at stake, then invading her privacy is warranted. Or so I tell myself.

She reaches for the legal pad, but I've reverted to seventh grade playground tactics. I hold it over my head, oddly satisfied, not at the power granted me by the mismatch in our statures, but at being the object of her laser-like attention.

"Give it back, Ian." She's mad as a hornet. She's also very afraid. I can tell from the hitch in her voice.

"You're a nursing student, but you talk like you've been working in an ER for years. You're a newlywed, but you hate the sound of your married name. You know things that are supposedly going to happen tomorrow, but you won't say how you know them. Call me curious, Ms. Clay. Call me rude, but I have to know what you're not telling me."

I have to know why I can't let her walk away.

"Very mature," she mutters, but I'm not looking at her.

I'm craning my neck to read her feminine, efficient handwriting.

"Ian, stop. Please."

The *please* tugs at my heart, but I don't stop. I *can't*. Because what I'm seeing has overruled my sense of journalistic integrity. It's overruled everything.

At the top of the page is tomorrow's date and a list of four flight numbers. Beside each flight is a landmark: North tower for American Flight 11, South tower for United Flight 175, The

Pentagon for American Flight 77, and Southern Pennsylvania for United Flight 93.

My stomach drops like a bowling ball as I remember.

"One target is the World Trade Center. Bin Laden wants to take those towers down. He's determined to finish what was started in '93. Another target is The Pentagon. The White House may also be a target."

The White House isn't listed here, but the other targets are. *North tower* and *South tower* clearly mean the World Trade Center, and there, in blue ink on yellow lined paper, is the chilling word, *Pentagon*.

Beside the landmarks are times. At first, I think they're departure times, but then I see a note to one side reminding the reader to *look up flight times* and *stop from taking off*. If the times listed here aren't take-off times, what are they? Could they be when the terrorists plan to storm the cockpits? Could they be projected times of impact?

A chill snakes down my spine.

Lower on the page are four circles, each representing one of the listed flights. Inside each circle are four or five Middle Eastern names or dashes to represent a missing name. Most of the names don't mean anything to me, but I recognize two of them. Her misspelling of Hazmi sits in the same list as a misspelled Mihdhar.

At the bottom margin of the page is a squished note about a Saudi denied entrance to the U.S. in August. My eyes linger on an all-caps warning: *DO NOT TORTURE!!!*

9/11/2001

American Flt 11 - North tower 8:46 a.m.
United Flt 175 - South tower 9:02
American Flt 77 - Pentagon 9:30 - 9:40
United Flt 93 - Southern Pennsylvania, 10-ish

Look up flight times.
Stop from taking off.

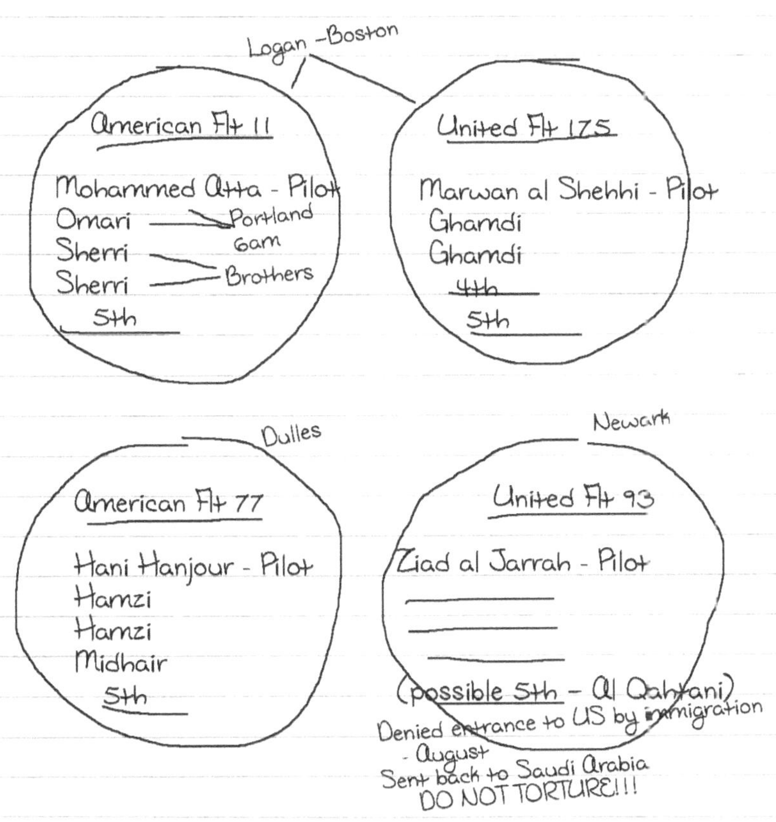

My mysterious friend has put in writing a terrible prophecy. Four planes, four crash sites, maybe even projected crash times. A few minutes ago, sitting in a restaurant booth, she told me of this plot, but seeing it in writing somehow gives the predictions more weight. Seeing it in writing makes me imagine it.

A Boeing jet banking sharply, then diving toward the five-sided bastion of military might, another jet picking up speed as it aims straight for one of the two towers that make up Manhattan's tallest building complex. The crashes would be heard for miles around. The fireballs would be massive, the jets carrying full tanks of fuel after east-coast departures. Boston, Dulles, Newark.

How long would it take the planes to reach their targets after take-off? Would there really be enough time for evacuations?

I seek comfort in the impossibility of the scenario. Intelligence, airport security, locked cockpits. Hijackers could never make it far enough to actually take control of passenger jets.

But swirling in my gut is a type of dread reserved for the possible.

The top page of Lydia's notes has a rounded fold in it, showing it's been flipped to the back of the pad for access to the pages underneath. A nudge of my finger swings the first sheet into its flipped position. I keep reading.

On the second page, Lydia seems to have considered places where she might go for help. She lists the FBI, CIA, FAA, and local police. Her conclusion is that *No one in right mind will listen to me. I am _nobody_.*

I bristle at the thought of such a determined, well-spoken woman thinking of herself as a nobody. I read on, skimming over a name I don't recognize, *Abigail Chase,* and I see that Lydia considered going to a private investigator. However, she crossed through that avenue for help in favor of one she underlined two times. *Reporter.*

There's something else underlined two times. My name.

I'm not surprised to see it, knowing she sought me out, but reading my name in her notes gives me a strange sense of something being off. The feeling grows when I read the sentence containing my name.

Where is Ian Greenberg in 2001?

Following is a grouping of notes that seem to have appeared through the course of some research: my place of employment, the title of my feature piece, and some highlights pulled from it. The highlights center on my warning about terrorists using planes as enormous suicide bombs. I wrote those words dreaming of Miller's feature department, taking pleasure in the imagined criticism I would be sure to garner once my piece made it to print. The reality was that my first feature got published quietly online without my knowledge and didn't generate a single phone message or email of complaint. Did anyone even read it? Other than my biggest fan, that is?

Thinking of Lydia brings back my presence of mind. For a moment, there, I became lost in the strangeness of her notes, in the writing out of the present year in the manner reserved for dates from the past, in the location of the *Washington Post* building written under the heading, *Old address,* in the times listed beside those flights, in the groupings of supposed

FBI - able to help, won't believe.
CIA - able to help, may be more likely to believe than FBI.
FAA - ?
Local Police -

Problem is ME - No one in right mind
will listen to me. I am <u>nobody</u>.

Need an Abigail Chase!

- ~~PI - motivated by cash~~

* <u>Reporter!</u>

Where is <u>Ian Greenberg</u> in 2001?
    - Washington Post
    - "New Face of Terrorism in the
       Twenty-First Century" - Aug 26, 2001
        - suggest planes as means
        - builds on Cole & embassy bombings. If we
         apply same motivations (to cause as much
         damage as possible) to planes scenario,
         "we could see major air-travel catastrophes
         the likes of which we've never before imagined."
         "It would be a mistake of deadly proportions
          not to consider the terrorist mind capable
          of evolutionary thinking."

Margin note (upper right): not yet located at One Franklin Sqaure Old address: 1150 15th Street NW

Margin note (left, diagonal): First person to suggest planes as terror implements. Still no idea planes can be used as missiles

Margin note (circled, lower left): Don't think he knew abt his article being online!!

hijackers, neatly assigned to individual jets, and, of course, that *DO NOT TORTURE!!!*

I come back to myself with her legal pad held at chest height. I'm no longer trying to keep it out of her reach, and she's no longer trying to snatch it back. In fact, she's nowhere to be seen.

My stomach lurches.

I've lost her!

No sooner does the thought petrify me than my gaze falls on her. She's sitting a few steps away at one end of a row of adjoined leather chairs, dark blond head in her hands.

I take the seat beside her feeling like a shit. "I'm sorry."

She looks up. I expect to see tears, but her face is calm, resigned. "Those notes are private," she says, but the reproach lacks heat.

There are more pages filled with her writing, at least three more, as evidenced by the paper's memory of being bent. They tempt me with glimpses of ink and evidence of more page bending. What other shocking, impossible details might those pages contain? I suppose I'll never know.

"I'm sorry," I say again, and I hold the legal pad out to her.

She doesn't take it. "I didn't mean for anyone else to see them." Her mouth forms a hard grimace of self-incrimination. She's certain she's blown her chance at getting me to help her.

"I don't know if you've noticed," I say. "But I'm still here."

She smiles. "Making sure I don't run while you call the guys with white coats, huh?"

I lean back in the chair and prop an ankle on my knee. "I'm playing it by ear. Look, I didn't mean to imply you hadn't thought through the hurdles to a plan like this." I wiggle the legal pad. "Clearly, you've given it a lot of thought."

"A lot of thought," she says with a huff. "Right."

Thought. Notes. Plans.

Something about her notes is off. Or maybe it's something about her reactions. I can't put my finger on the problem. All I know is I'm as desperate to get to the bottom of this plot as Lydia seems to secure my help.

I've come to a decision.

I'm in.

As far as Lydia wants to take me, I'm in. She says I'm not here to write a story, that I should go along with her plan today because it's the right thing to do. I'm not entirely convinced that hijackers are on the verge of a major terror attack, but I'm not entirely confident they're not, either.

If Lydia's wrong, I figure at the very least, I'll get a story out of this day. It won't be *WAPO* that publishes it. Carmen will see to that. But I'll carry on writing for someone somewhere, and I'll start with a story of an unbelievable warning by a civilian with inexplicable access to information. My day won't be wasted, and my curiosity will be satisfied.

If Lydia's right, on the other hand, that puts me in a position to save lives at best and be first reporter on the scene at worst. Lydia suggested as much in Chili's.

"Maybe you'll still get a Pulitzer."

That might be a stretch, but my gut tells me I'm onto something with Lydia, and my gut is rarely wrong.

"Who's Abigail Chase?" I ask.

Lydia gets that secret smile again, the one that says I wouldn't understand the answer. I expect her not to answer, but she surprises me.

"She's a fictional character in a film about a treasure hunter and his technologically-gifted sidekick who try to warn the FBI about a plot to steal the Declaration of Independence."

Seems easy enough to understand. Maybe I misread that secret smile. "Is she an FBI agent?"

"No. She's a curator or something at the National Archives, an expert on old documents. The treasure hunter guy, he's played by Nicolas Cage, his name is Ben. So, Ben and Riley go to the FBI, but they're laughed right out the door. 'It's impossible,' the FBI tells them. 'The Declaration of Independence can't possibly be stolen. It's too well protected.' But Ben and Riley know better. See, they have inside information." She taps the side of her nose. "They know the crooks who want the Declaration, and they know how well funded they are. If anyone's capable of stealing the Declaration, these guys are, which is unacceptable to history-loving Ben.

"So, after leaving the FBI, they go to the National Archives and meet Dr. Abigail Chase. Her reaction is the same as the FBI's. 'The Declaration can't be stolen.' With nowhere else to turn, Ben and Riley decide to steal the Declaration themselves, you know, to protect it from the bad guys. Plus, there's an invisible map on the back that could lead them to 'the treasure to beat all treasures.'" She makes air quotes with her fingers.

"Sounds like a good movie. It's got Nick Cage in it, huh? I'm surprised I haven't heard of it." A movie about the Declaration of Independence would find a lot of viewers in Washington,

D.C. I would have gone to see it or at least looked forward to it coming out on DVD. "How old is it?"

"It hasn't been made yet."

I feel my eyebrows climb my forehead. "First Massoud and Hazmi and Mihdhar. Now you've got access to screenplays for movies that haven't come out yet?" I shake my head. I've stopped trying to make sense of what she knows, and that's saying something. I'm kind of a stickler for verification. "So, this Abigail Chase. She doesn't end up helping them?" Why write her name down, then?

"She *does* end up helping them." Lydia stands and takes her notes back. "Because she realizes they were telling the truth when the impossible actually happens. The bad guys show up and try to steal the Declaration. At the same time, Ben and Riley are actively stealing it. It's supposed to be impossible. Security is supposed to be infallible. But on that day, it's not."

"It's not?"

She shakes her head. "The Declaration is out of its usual case for cleaning. There's a replica on display in the National Archives. Meanwhile, there's a gala going on in the building, distracting the security guards."

"I see where this is going," I say, "The circumstances are just right for the impossible to become possible."

She holds up her legal pad and taps it with two fingers. "Just like they will be tomorrow."

Her statement sucks the air out of my lungs. "What do you mean, 'like they will be tomorrow?'"

"Time's a'wasting," she says. "How about I fill you in on the way to the CIA?" She motors off to ground transportation.

I stand and follow. She's my Pied Piper, and that legal pad I'm itching to read the rest of is the music.

CHAPTER 12

Lydia

I'VE GOT HIM. I don't know exactly when it happened, but somewhere between Chili's and baggage claim, he went from skeptical and annoyed to skeptical but curious. Maybe it was my notes. Maybe instead of convincing him I'm crazy, they convinced him there's more to me than meets the eye. Or maybe it was my giving up and walking away. Maybe he saw that as a challenge. He was ready to walk away not long before, but when it was me ready to do the walking, he couldn't abide it.

Whatever the reason, relief floods through me as he climbs into the cab. He's all knees and elbows as he settles himself on the bench beside me in the Crown Vic. The car feels dated to me, but for all I know, it's a late model in the year 2001.

"Where to?" the driver asks.

"The CIA building," I say.

"What's the address?"

Why do cabbies always need an address? They should know where major places are. With a huff, I admit I don't know. The clock is ticking on tomorrow's attack, and here I am digging my Nokia out of my bag, and not even sure it'll help me. In a world without smartphones, I don't know how to look up an address on the go. Does 4-1-1 work for more than just phone numbers? I don't remember, since I haven't used the service in ages.

Before I can turn on my phone, Ian says, "1000 Colonial Farm Road, McLean, Virginia."

"McLean?" I whip my head around. Ian takes up entirely too much room in the cab. He's not even manspreading, but somehow, his long body invades my half of the backseat. A knee here, an elbow there, shoulders that seem to have doubled in width in the confined space. "I thought the CIA was in Langley."

"Langley is technically an unincorporated community in Fairfax county," Ian says while the cab takes us away from the airport. "The name has stuck since the eighteenth century, when the tract was bought by Thomas Lee. He named it after his family's estate in England." I get the impression he knows a lot about the history of this area. I expect him to keep talking about Langley, but instead, he says, "Why the CIA? Why not the FBI? They're closer."

He's finally asking the right questions. I turn in my seat, excited to dig into the bits and pieces of information that might actually help stop what's coming.

"Right, so the agencies know different things, and they're not talking to each other. They're not sharing information. That's one of the circumstances that makes tomorrow possible."

I flip to the page in my legal pad with the heading: *Verifiable Info*. Judging by the hungry look Ian gets as he fixates on the page, he hasn't read this one yet.

"See, here. I wrote it all down so I wouldn't forget." I point and angle my notes so Ian can follow along while I read from my bullet list. "The FBI knows Bin Laden was interested in planes as weapons as early as 1996. The U.S. had a terrorist in custody who confessed to plans of crashing a plane into some government building. It may have been the CIA building. I forget."

I move to another bullet point and keep my voice low as I talk, conscious of the cab driver just a couple feet away. "The CIA knows about some of the terrorists already. They know they're in the country and that they have ties to al-Qaeda."

I look up and find Ian devouring the page with his eyes. Snapping in front of his face, I get his attention. "That's why I think the CIA will take us more seriously. They have more specific information. If we go to them with these names—" I flip to the first page and point to my circles. "They'll have to listen, right? Because they already know some of these names. They know they're potentially dangerous dudes. Then we give them *this* information—" I'm back on the *verifiable info* page. "To prove we know things we shouldn't. Then—" I flip to another page. "We tell them where the terrorists will be and when, and they can stop them from boarding those planes."

I sit up tall and triumphant. With Ian by my side, helping me convince the CIA to listen, and with the information on our side, we should be golden.

Ian doesn't look convinced. He reaches for my notes but pauses. "May I?" he asks.

I don't see why not. He's already read some of it, and he hasn't run away screaming.

I hand him the legal pad and try not to pick at my cuticles while he turns to the *Verifiable Info* page. This is where I made notes about Massoud and the flight students who flunked out at Montgomery Field. I also wrote down everything I could remember about the terrorists that could possibly be verified to support my case.

"Some of the terrorists are on tourist visas," Ian says, eyes scanning. "That should be easy to check out. 'Reported lost passports,'" he reads. "'Got replacements to remove record of suspicious travel?'"

I should have written more next to that point. "Some of them flew cross-country multiple times. Probably to learn airport protocols. You know, like how tight security is, to study cockpit access, flight attendant behavior, etcetera."

Ian's eyebrows go up. He keeps reading. "They're using their real names?"

I nod. Out the windows, the Potomac streaks past like a gunmetal-gray silk ribbon winding between industrial brick buildings and sloping banks of soggy grass.

He reads aloud, "Abided by law, kept heads down, trained to fly or be muscle, attended non-extremist mosques, had gym memberships." He looks up. "Just a bunch of regular Joes."

Verifiable Info

- Massoud assassination in Afghanistan
  (probably al Qaeda)
- Midhair & Hamzi flunked out of flight school
  - instructors alarmed because only interested in
    controlling a plane mid-air, not in takeoffs or andings.
    - Montgomery Field.

- Some were in US on tourist visas
  - reported lost passports, got replacements tc remove
    record of suspicious travel
- Used their real names
- Abided by law, kept heads down, trained to fly or
  to be muscle, attended non-extremist mosques,
  had gym memberships
- Midhair & at least one other on watchlist for otner
  countries for al Qaeda association
- CIA knows some are in US
  - Did not share with FBI or place on watch lists or no-fly
    (No-fly list useless, has only 16 names on it
    at this point in time, no one knows who maintains it or
    how it's used to screen passengers)
- FBI knows Bin Laden was interested in planes as weapons
  as early as 1996. US had a terrorist in custody who
  confessed to plans of crashing a plane into the CIA building.
  Not sure if CIA, FBI or other govt org

"Exactly. Nothing to see here, right?"

Ian nods. "Mihdhar and at least one other on watchlist for other countries for al-Qaeda association." He looks to me for clarification.

I shake my head. "From what I remember, we never had any of the terrorists on our watch list. Other countries did, but not us. Again, lack of communication proves to be our downfall."

Ian gives me a skeptical look. "From what you remember?"

"Like I said, I just know these things." It's the truth, just not the whole truth. "They're memories for me, and my memory, while good, isn't perfect." A shame it is, too. If I had a perfect memory, this would be a lot easier.

Ian studies me a moment, then he keeps reading.

"Wait," he says suddenly. "Our no-fly list only has sixteen names on it?"

"Crazy, huh? And no one really knows how or if it works to actually stop those people from flying."

"None of these guys—" He flips to the first page and points at the circles filled with the names of the hijackers. "Are on that list?"

"Correct."

"Holy Smokes."

"Be careful, Ian. It almost sounds like you're starting to believe me."

His eyes are wild. He's taking in a lot of information. But he manages a small smile. "Almost."

He turns to the page with the heading, *More about Terrorists' time in U.S.* It's a hodgepodge of facts remembered from various books written about 9/11, a lot of which I hope can be verified.

He reads aloud. "Atta had a pilot's license already, from Egypt. Several hijackers spent time in Hamburg. Atta and Shehhi met there. Dekker, owner of flight school in Florida. Airman something or other, flight school in Oklahoma. Several carried out cross-country travel, multiple trips to learn airport security and procedures."

He looks up, acknowledging what I'd said a few minutes ago.

I remain silent.

"ATMs used to get out cash, empty bank accounts. Letters or packages, cash sent to family, girlfriends in Florida, Germany. Blue Nissan Altima?" He pauses and checks in with me.

"Keep reading."

"Atta and Omari drive from Boston to Portland on evening of 9/10 for early morning flight." He swallows hard before continuing. "Some stay at hotel in Newton, MA. Hookers hired. Preparations underway for end of life, religious martyrdom. Prayer, reflection, shaved body hair?" He makes the last bit a question, but he plows on, not waiting for an answer.

"Rolling luggage that looks like pilots' bags. Atta's checked bag will get lost and never make the connecting flight from Portland." I hear the question in his inflection. His curly head gives a shake before he continues.

"FBI will find the bag at Logan airport. Items inside will *confirm suicide plan*—that part is underlined," he says.

"Yes," I nod eagerly. "That's the evidence they'll need to bring these guys to trial, along with the other stuff in their bags. Keep going."

Behind the bristly shadow of unshaved black hair, Ian has lost some of his color, but head bent over my notes, he goes on.

"Arabic instructions for carrying out attack, including night-before—how to prepare to die. Items in carryon bags: folded knives under four inches, mace, VHS for flying Boeing jets, flight computers, red bandanas, Koran."

He flips to the next page, but I don't want him to read that one. It's about him.

I lift my legal pad out of his limp fingers. He offers no resistance.

"My God, Lydia. This reads like an itemized receipt for evil."

"Good. That was my intention." I tuck my notes into my messenger bag and pat the flap closed. "All that, plus the names and flight numbers—we have everything we need to stop this attack. We can totally do this, Ian."

An urge to grab up his hand and hold it in solidarity comes and goes. I let it slip away without acting on it.

Ian does not look as confident as I feel. His focus is on some point a foot in front of his face. His eyes dart back and forth.

At last, he says, "It's not enough."

"What's not enough?"

"Your information. Us. Two people with a list of facts that will take time to verify. It's not enough." He meets my eyes. "Whoever we go to, CIA, FBI, whoever—we need them to act fast, yeah? We're talking high-level, decision-maker, command-giver action. A low-level agent isn't going to be able to wipe his ass—pardon my French—without getting the go-ahead from his superior, and the mere act of getting approval takes time. If we get into Langley—and that's a big *if*—we'll be shuttled straight to the lowest man on the totem pole. More likely we'll be turned away like your Ben and Riley."

I start to argue, but Ian holds up a finger. He's looking out the window, but not at the trees and strip malls sliding past. It's more like he's looking into space, or into himself. I'm recognizing this as his thinking face.

A long minute goes by before he says to the cabbie, "Forget McLean." He gives an address in Maryland instead.

"We're not going to the CIA?" I hear the panic in my voice. From everything I know, that's the best place to take our information.

"You asked me to give you a blank check of trust," he says. "To treat what you know as a case of 'documented unexplained.'" His eyes bore through me with intellectual energy. "I'm the most likely person to believe you, and I'm barely there. I mean, the amount of detail alone is hard to argue with, but still, it's a stretch. And *I'm* trying. I *want* to believe. Add in the inconsistencies surrounding you—"

"Hey! What inconsistencies?"

He ticks off fingers. "Let's see. You're a newlywed, but you prefer using your maiden name. You don't know your own address. You talk like you've been working in a hospital for years, but you're just a nursing student. I'm a pretty big Nick

Cage fan, and you describe a movie he's in that I haven't heard of, then you tell me it hasn't been released yet. Shall I go on?"

I fold my arms.

"You think trained intelligence agents aren't going to recognize there's something off about you?"

"*Off* about me? You make it sound like I'm an escaped asylum patient."

"For all I know you could be," he states baldly. "I'm indulging you because you make me curious. And you said I'll win a Pulitzer. Of course, I'd like to believe you when you toss in that little gem." His rueful smile softens his critical words. "And I happen to find you irritatingly credible. But that's after, what, a couple hours? You think a CIA agent will give you that kind of time to convince him of something he considers impossible? You think they won't kick us out the second you refuse to say where you got your information? You think they won't interrogate you for possessing classified information? We walk into the CIA right now, we have no control. None."

I feel myself deflate as I consider what he's saying. I was hoping having him by my side would lend me credibility, but he's presenting a totally different picture, one that's bleak and hopeless. Worse, I fear he's right.

He gestures with a long-fingered hand and echoes my thoughts. "It's not enough."

"It's not enough," I agree.

He's not done. "My point is, what if we had some way to 'document and explain' the things you know *before* we go to the CIA?"

Well, yeah. That would be nice. But I don't see how that's possible. "Are we going to the *Post* so you can do some research?" I hear the skepticism in my voice. That will take time, and time is exactly what we don't have.

He must be able to tell what I'm thinking, because he grins. "It's your turn to trust me, Ms. Clay."

There is no good reason why we should fear the future, but there is every reason why we should face it seriously, neither hiding from ourselves the gravity of the problems before us nor fearing to approach these problems with the unbending, unflinching purpose to solve them aright.

—Theodore Roosevelt

CHAPTER 13

Ian

WE'RE ABOUT TO EXIT onto Route 123 when I give the cabbie a Bethesda address that's familiar to me, even if I haven't been there in a while. My change of direction is issued just in time. With a glare in the rearview, the driver swings out of the exit lane back into the flow of traffic on the G.W. Parkway.

Lydia's face is taut with nerves as we continue toward 425 instead of exiting for McLean. She's trying to trust me. From recent experience, I know just how hard that can be, especially when the person asking for your trust is a new acquaintance and insists on drastically changing your plans.

Perhaps I should find pleasure in the irony of the shoe being on the other foot, but I don't. The more I talk with Lydia, the more I'm beginning to believe what she's saying.

The scenario she describes is becoming real to me, and there's nothing pleasurable about it.

"The circumstances are just right for the impossible to become possible."

"Just like they will be tomorrow."

"Tell me about the circumstances," I say as the cab makes its way northwest.

Lydia has a question in her eyes when she meets my gaze.

"You said the FBI and CIA aren't talking to each other," I remind her. "That's one of the circumstances that will make tomorrow possible. What else?"

She nods with understanding and adopts an air of confidence she only gets when she's talking about tomorrow. "NORAD," she says like a professor introducing a new topic in the lecture hall. With a glance at the front seat, she leans closer and adjusts her volume downward. "The northeast offices of—" She says *"KNEE-ads,"* but I recognize the acronym for the Northeast Air Defense Sector, N-E-A-D-S, "are planning a military exercise for tomorrow. Normally, across the nation, there are fourteen fighter jets armed and ready to go at a moment's notice. But tomorrow, the jets in the northeast quadrant won't be armed. Do you know what that means?"

She doesn't wait for me to answer.

"If those four passenger jets get airborne tomorrow, and if they head for the World Trade Center and The Pentagon, which they will, there won't be any way to stop them from reaching their targets. Well—" She cocks her head. "Short of crashing our F-16s into them, which *will* be considered as a last resort."

Just when I think I've had enough shocks for one day, she keeps surprising me. "Hold on." I glance at the cabbie, who's singing along with a song on the radio and, thankfully, ignoring us. My voice just above a whisper, I say, "You're saying NORAD will scramble fighter jets tomorrow, but those jets won't be armed?"

Lydia nods solemnly as our cab joins the crawling traffic on the American Legion Bridge.

"But the point is practically moot," she says. "It'll take so long for us to figure out what's happening that three of the four planes will have already crashed before any kind of organized response can be mounted."

I blink at her, speechless. I should be used to this by now, her stating things that no civilian ought to know with the kind of certainty a reporter craves from witnesses to some major event.

Witnesses.

My mind stutters over the word and tries to link it with that odd sense I keep having that something is off about Lydia. There's more to her than she's telling me, but I don't have time to puzzle out the problem because she's still talking about tomorrow.

"Two fighter pilots will start tracking the fourth plane over Pennsylvania, United Flight 93. They'll have authorization to take it down before it reaches Washington, but the only way would be to literally fly into it. Fortunately, the pilots won't have to make that call. Ninety-three won't make it to D.C. The passengers will hear about the other three planes crashing into populated areas. They'll revolt, and the terrorists will ditch the plane into a field rather than risk having the passengers take back control of the cockpit."

She's done this before, spoken as if what tomorrow holds is written in stone. It's not right the way she applies future tense to her verbs.

"Thousands of Americans are going to die."

"You're going to win a Pulitzer."

"If you leave right now, you'll be forever known as the 'reporter who predicted 9/11.'"

"The plot is underway. Whether it's carried out or stopped, al-Qaeda is still going to be big news tomorrow."

I've learned not to ask how she knows these things or why she states them as though their occurrence is a foregone conclusion. That's not to say I'm no longer curious—I definitely am. I'm just waiting to ask again until I know I can trust her answer. Soon. I'll be asking her soon.

For now, I say, "Hard to believe we'd disarm a significant proportion of our defense system for the purpose of an exercise."

"Right? But necessary to keep skills fresh. Vigilant Guardian is far from the only exercise the military is taking on around this time. In fact, it's just one arm of a larger exercise. But it's the one that'll get the most attention."

"Vigilant Guardian?"

She shrugs. "The goal is to practice defense against Russian missiles or something like that. Everyone's getting ready for it as we speak. Tomorrow, when the flights are hijacked, it'll take precious minutes to communicate that what's happening isn't training. It's real world."

I'm gob smacked at how readily she communicates such terrifying images. My fingers drum on my knee with eagerness to get to the bottom of all this.

We can't reach our destination soon enough. Lydia has no idea what she's in store for, but if she agrees to the little test I plan to give her, and if she passes it, we'll gain an ally who could help us bypass a shit-ton of bureaucracy. If, on the other hand, every instinct in my body is wrong, and Lydia's full of crap, this test will reveal as much, hopefully, in time for me to salvage my career.

"The other circumstances," she says, "is that no one's considered a scenario remotely like this. For all our training exercises, not a single one has dealt with bad guys taking control of cockpits and using passenger planes as missiles. Pilots and flight crew are taught to cooperate with terrorists and let the authorities on the ground figure things out. They won't know that the hijackers don't care about negotiations. They won't know that the only way to survive is to fight.

"If those planes get airborne tomorrow, we're going to watch a terrible disaster unfold. The military will fail miserably. How can they possibly stop a scenario they've never even imagined?"

With every word she speaks, she convinces me more and more that tomorrow is absolutely possible. I want those flights grounded as badly as she does. I'm hoping being on her side will help her forgive me when we reach our destination.

"What's the 'DO NOT TORTURE!!!' about?" I ask to keep her talking. We're finally on the Maryland side of the Potomac and have about ten more minutes to drive. I don't want to tell her what I have planned until the last minute.

She blinks, then looks at her legal pad. I'm referring to the first page, the one with the circles representing tomorrow's flights and the lists of hijackers. She wrote that note at the bottom, next to a line that read, *Possible 5th*.

"Oh, Qahtani," she says. "Right. So, there are nineteen known hijackers, but some people think he would have been the twentieth. He never made it into the U.S., though. He was denied entrance at immigration and returned to Saudi Arabia. Eventually, we captured him, and he ended up at Guantanamo Bay, where he wasn't treated so well. Okay, that's putting it mildly. The guy was tortured. So, his evidence about the plot for 9/11 was dismissed. They don't admit testimony obtained under torture."

I frown at her use of past tense all of a sudden. "*Was* captured? Evidence *was* dismissed?"

Lydia looks startled for a moment, but she quickly recovers. "Like I said. These things are like memories for me."

The talent I have for sensing truth—my bullshit meter, as Morg calls it—prickles a warning. She's not being completely honest.

"When is this trial supposed to happen?" I ask. "The one where Qahtani's evidence is dismissed?"

She looks sideways at me. "Sometime in the future," is all she says.

"Before or after that Nick Cage movie comes out?"

She narrows her eyes. "After. I think." She crosses her arms tightly over her chest. "The point is, when we capture Qahtani, he should be treated well. His testimony will be critical to convicting the others." Defiance shows in her lifted chin.

I hold up my hands. "I'm not doubting," I say honestly. "Just asking." Just trying to tease apart the truth in what she knows from the evasiveness surrounding how she knows it. To lighten the mood, I say, "So, you know the future, huh? Who's going to be president after G.W.? Will he go two terms?"

"I'm not a crystal ball," she says in a voice that tells me I missed the mark with my attempt at humor. "But yes, he'll go two terms. Beyond that, I'm not talking about future stuff. Not if it doesn't help us stop this attack. Trust me. There's a lot you don't want to know, especially where The White House is concerned." She faces away from me, watching southern Maryland drift past in hues of pewter and concrete. "Besides," she says, voice melancholy, "After tomorrow, things might change."

"That's good, right? We want things to change. Stopping a major terrorist attack and saving thousands of lives will surely have an effect on the future."

"I'm sure it will," she says, and then she swallows hard.

I want to ask about a million questions. If her goal is to save lives, why does the prospect of succeeding upset her? How many more details about the future does she know? Do her predictions delve into the realm of winning lotto numbers and hot stocks in which to invest? How many years forward she can see? What is the level of her certainty? Her notes lead me to believe it's one hundred percent, but is there some chance, however small, the things she knows won't happen?

I refrain from asking. I'll have my chance soon enough. Instead, I leave her to her thoughts and focus on ordering my own.

The way I see it, I have a big decision ahead of me. Indulging Lydia one-on-one has likely cost me my position at the *Post*. But taking the next step—the step she demands—by facing the authorities with her information? That's another kettle of fish. I can get a job reporting anywhere. But if I lose my credibility by crying wolf, my work will never be taken seriously again.

I'm leaning toward helping Lydia no matter the consequences. My truth sense and my sense of integrity are conspiring to ruin me. The woman beside me needs a very specific sort of help, and I can't shake the gut feeling that I'm the only person who can deliver that help. But before I can commit, I need to know what she's holding back.

If I'm going risk everything, Lydia has to trust me with the absolute truth. She has to lay her soul bare for me. And for one other person.

At last, the cab turns up a hill into one of Bethesda's most exclusive neighborhoods. The private road is immaculately paved and wide enough for two panel trucks to pass without bumping mirrors. Lawns like dry-cleaned blankets on freshly-made beds stretch for acres on either side beyond tidy fences of varying heights and materials. Every so often a pair of iron gates punctuates a driveway. These are few and far between as the estates in this neighborhood are some of the oldest and largest in Maryland.

I'm familiar with the scenery, having viewed it dozens of times from the backseat of my parents' station wagon, usually with wrapped presents in a pile behind me.

"Where are we?" Lydia asks, no small amount of alarm in her tone.

I have the decency to feel slightly bad about what I'm about to do to her, but if she's telling the truth and thousands of lives are at stake, she'll forgive me.

I don't answer her question. Instead, I say, "I'm going to make you a deal."

She tears her gaze from our surroundings and gives me her attention. "Okay," she says cautiously.

"I'll help you today. However you need, whatever that looks like, I'm totally, one-hundred percent in."

Her eyes widen with hope that cannot possibly be faked.

"But—" I lift a cautionary finger. "You have to give me the full, unedited truth. That's my price, and I won't budge an inch. Do you accept?"

Her lips part. She holds my gaze for a beat before sighing and returning her gaze out her window. "I can't, Ian. There's no way you would believe the 'full, unedited truth.'" Her sad smile strikes me as utterly, painfully honest. "Seriously, where are we? This does not look like a place where government agents hang out."

"You'd be surprised," I say mildly. "If you must know, we're going to my Aunt Marge's house."

She looks at me like I've lost my mind. "Ian, we don't have time for a family visit. This is serious."

The pavement ends, but the road continues for another half-mile. Gravel crunches under the tires as the cab slows its speed.

"I know it's serious," I tell her. "So am I. If you promise to tell me the full, unedited truth, I promise to believe you. I'm already half-way there. If I weren't, we wouldn't be here."

"Here, at your aunt's house?" she says, her pitch rising. She's starting to panic.

"Hey." I take her hand and squeeze it. It's cool and pliant, and it squeezes back. "You're not in this alone, anymore," I tell her. "This stop we're making? It's not just for me. You need to bring your information to someone with government connections, yeah? Someone who can actually stop these guys?"

She nods. "Ideally, yes. Someone who can enter the airports tomorrow and detain the hijackers, search their bags and find the proof of what they're planning. Someone who can process evidence and prosecute these guys. Stopping the attack is just one part of what needs to happen." Her passion for her mission bleeds into the space between us. She grips my hand harder for emphasis. "We also have to make sure no one can do something like this again. The country needs to change how we handle air travel, how we think about terrorism. We need someone who can convey the scope of this threat to the powers that be so those changes can be mandated. This is a lot bigger than just stopping a terror plot, Ian. A *lot* bigger."

"If everything you're saying is the truth, my aunt's place will be the perfect launching pad for all that."

Lydia looks sideways at me.

"You've sought me out. You've asked for my faith. Now, I'm asking for yours." I crave her trust to an alarming degree. I want to stop a terror attack, if, indeed, there is a plot afoot. But, irrationally, I also want to be Lydia's hero.

"My help, my belief in exchange for the full, unedited truth." I slip my hand from hers and hold it out to shake on it.

She tosses her hands in exasperation. "You don't get it. I literally *can't* tell you the 'full, unedited truth.' There's no possible way you would believe it. I barely believe it." The last is muttered to herself while she glares out the window.

We're driving through gates that stand open during daylight hours. Aunt Marge's passion is her yard, and it shows as the cab drives us beneath a canopy of green. In springtime, it's pinkish-white, since cherry blossom trees line her curving drive.

"First of all, you're using the word *literally* wrong. Unless you have some sort of selective speech impediment, you *can* tell me the full, unedited truth. You're just choosing not to because you're afraid I won't believe it. Second, I'm not a fan of the word *can't. Can't* says, *I won't negotiate with you.* It says, *I give up and I want you to give up too.* But giving up is overrated. No one's ever learned something about themself after giving up. Third, what if I could promise my belief?"

She snorts. "If you could promise your belief, I could promise the full, united truth. But you *literally can't—*" She emphasizes the last two words.

"Oh, but I can," I say as the cab crunches to a stop.

Truth is what stands the test of experi-
ence.

—Albert Einstein

CHAPTER 14

Lydia

THE CAB CRAWLS COUNTER-CLOCKWISE around a circular drive and rolls to a stop next to a stone fountain before a two-story turn-of-the-century Colonial. White with forest green shutters, the house is modest in size, but its finishes give it a grandness impossible to replicate with newer architecture. Square columns support a covered porch with a peaked pediment, and marble lions flank the front steps.

The grounds are equally grand. Stone pavers create a path that disappears into artfully placed manicured shrubs. Leafy cherry blossom trees and purple maples spread their branches over a sitting area with a cast-iron bench and a flowerbed bursting with colorful chrysanthemums.

"Here we are," Ian announces, and he climbs out of the cab, leaving me to pay for the ride, as promised. The fee takes most of the cash I had on hand. Fortunately, I still have plastic I can use if I run into more expenses, like another cab trip or a plane ticket back to New York—and back to an apartment with too many memories and a husband I don't love.

When I slam the door of the cab, I leave all those worries inside. They'll find their way back to me, eventually, but I can't handle them right now. I'm too unsure, too curious, and far too frustrated with Ian.

We were on our way to the CIA when he changed the plan on me. Now, we're at his aunt's home, of all places, where he claims he can guarantee his belief and where he expects me to furnish him with the "full, unedited truth."

He has no idea what he's asking. Or how badly he's tempting me by promising his unwavering support in exchange. Because I know Ian from the many works he hasn't written yet, I know he's a man of his word. If I tell him the unflinching truth, he will try his very best to believe me. But how can he possibly succeed? The truth is impossible.

Worse, I fear he's right. If he can't believe when he's trying, no one in a position to stop this attack will believe, either. Where does that leave me? Where does that leave four planes of passengers scheduled to take to the skies tomorrow? Where does that leave Pentagon workers and Windows on the World patrons and the entire staff of Cantor Fitzgerald and hundreds of New York first responders?

Ian asked for my trust. It's only fair that I give it, since that's what I also happen to be asking of him. But it's difficult. This home doesn't exactly scream, "Let's stop some terrorists!"

The cab disappears down the drive, and I clench my fists against the urge to panic.

If Ian has reservations like I do, it doesn't show as he strides up the front steps.

Shaking out my hands, I join him as he lifts a lion's head knocker and raps three times on a door painted to match the shutters. There is no answer. The house emits no sounds indicating its dwellers are aware of our presence.

"Um, should we have let the cab go?" I'm back to clenching my fists. I have the feeling we just stranded ourselves here. We'll have to call another cab, and while we wait, we'll lose precious time.

"Must be out back," Ian says, ignoring me. He leaps down the steps, using the head of a lion for leverage as he rounds the porch. A pathway of stone pavers carries him past the hedges lining the front of the house.

I trot after him, grumbling about his long legs. When I catch up, he has come to a stop in the center of a wide gravel path terminating at a brilliant-white gazebo. Potted petunias overflow hanging baskets all around the structure, and painted benches provide respite beneath its shady beams. Beyond the gazebo is a view of rolling hills dotted with houses and patches of forest.

In the city, the skies were yellowish-gray, and the air was cool and damp. Here, spots of blue punch through the cloud cover, and a soft breeze carries a hint of late-summer warmth. The ground has been recently saturated by rain but is starting to dry. The air smells like freshly-cut grass.

A high-pitched droning sound fills my ears, growing louder, as if its source is coming closer. Suddenly, a gardener bearing a weed-whacker rounds the gazebo. Tall decorative grass obscures him from the waist down, but on top, he's wearing what looks like a fisherman's vest, a stars-and-stripes bandana over the lower half of his face, protective goggles, and a sombrero.

Ian waves his arms wildly as he nears the gazebo.

The gardener looks up. The weed whacker stops.

"Ian, is that you?" I'm surprised to hear a woman's voice come from behind the bandana. Gloved hands reach up to remove fluorescent orange ear plugs, which hang from a cord around her neck.

"Aunt Marge! You've been busy!" He makes a sweeping motion. "The yard looks amazing!"

The woman, Aunt Marge, apparently, tugs down the bandana and goggles and whips the sombrero off her head. Coming out from behind the tall grass, she strides to Ian and embraces him. She's shorter than him, but not by much, standing at six feet tall, if not an inch or two more. Below the waist, she's protected from the elements by denim culottes and a pair of rubber rainboots that look like they were purchased in the men's aisle of a bait and tackle shop. Strands of gray hair stick to her sweaty cheeks, having fallen loose from a ponytail cinched tightly at her nape.

"It's been too long," she says, leaning back while holding Ian's face between her gloves. "To what do I owe this surprise visit?" Smile lines frame her wide mouth as eyes a familiar green turn my way.

I give a finger wave while Ian says, "It's not a social call, unfortunately. Aunt Marge, we need your help."

Ian

I'VE HAD AN INSTINCT for spotting truth all my life, but I've never treated it as infallible. There is, however, one person I know who can infallibly parse out truth from lie. My Aunt Marge. It's a talent she was born with, like with me, but which she's devoted years of her life to developing and enhancing in order to use it for the service of her nation.

I see her, for a moment, as Lydia must see her, dressed in her garden gear, dirty from a hard morning's work, smelling of sweat and potting bark. For me, these scents herald memories of kneeling in the soft soil of the garden and picking fresh rhubarb for pies, collecting eggs from the henhouse, and playing Scrabble at the kitchen table with my cousins, the kinds of wholesome activities a lot of kids don't get to experience anymore. Lydia won't have the advantage of these happy memories.

To the casual observer, Marge might not seem it, but she is our very best bet to stop what Lydia insists is going to happen tomorrow. Not only will Marge be able to tell whether Lydia is, in fact, telling the truth, but if our next step is to visit the CIA with Lydia's information, Marge will open doors for us that wouldn't normally be available to private citizens.

I place a reassuring hand on Lydia's shoulder and address my aunt.

"Aunt Marge, this is Lydia Clay. We met when she called me this morning with what might just be the tip of the century. At first, I thought she wanted me to write a story, but it's much bigger than that. Lydia claims to have information about a terrorist attack that will happen tomorrow. I need to know if she's telling the truth. And if she is, well, I'm hoping you'll help us get the information to the right people so they can try and stop it."

Marge has never cared for certain social conventions, including eyebrow plucking. Like my father's—her brother's—her brows are Frida-esque in their fullness and as dark as her hair used to be before age and experience turned it gray. Those brows shoot up with surprise, putting horizontal creases in her forehead.

"My," she says as she extends a gloved hand to Lydia, who shakes it with a smile that fails to conceal her skepticism.

"Lydia, you need someone with government connections to share your information with, and you need someone to vouch for you when you get there. As much as I'd like that person to be me, it can't be."

Lydia's eyes go wide with panic.

"Because," I hurry to add, "there's someone better. Better at being able to tell when someone's lying, better at having connections. I'd like to introduce you to my aunt, retired CIA Agent Margaret Greenberg."

To my aunt I say, "What do you say? Are you up for an interrogation?"

"Interrogation?" Lydia says, voice sharp.

I grin in response.

Marge's eyes, so much like my father's, shine with excitement. "Always," she says, and she leads the way inside.

Lydia

LEMONADE IN HAND, Ian and I sit at a rough-hewn table in Mrs. Greenberg's kitchen, which is decorated in a farmhouse style more authentic than the trend popular in the time I'm from. The floors are wide plank, gently worn in high-traffic areas, and host a colorful collection of oval rag-rugs. The countertops are buttercream yellow tile, and the curtains are red-and-white checkerboard with little flower motifs inside each square. A basket of eggs in the center of the butcher-block island tells me there is a chicken coop on the premises.

The appliances are an eclectic blend of old and really-old. The icebox is an aqua Frigidaire with chrome accents. The cooktop is an electric model with labels etched in gilt cursive beside the dials. The eighties-brown wall-oven sits inside a brick alcove that looks like someone may have baked bread in it two hundred years ago. Either the appliances have been gently used and are remarkable for their longevity, or their owner has both the money and desire to refurbish antiques.

Mrs. Greenberg's boots, along with Ian's and my shoes, are lined up beneath a bench in the mud room we came through from the backyard. The floor is cool on my stocking feet as I sit at the kitchen table. I'm not sure what Ian means by "interrogation," but when his aunt sets out a plate of fork-pressed peanut butter cookies and takes a seat beside me, I suspect I'm about to find out.

"When I woke up this morning," Mrs. Greenberg says. "Terrorism was the last thing I imagined on my agenda." She crosses her legs and folds her hands primly on the table. Her manners are *Pride and Prejudice*. Her wardrobe is *Duck Dynasty*. "Well, then. What's all this about?" There's a bit of old New England in her accent, a slight softening of the vowels that brings to mind British nobility. "Give me the nutshell version, and I'll decide where to begin."

I don't know if she's addressing me or Ian, who sits across the table from us, but I'm happy to let Ian answer between bites of cookie.

"The nutshell version is that Lydia knows an impossible amount of information about a terrorist attack she claims will take place tomorrow morning. Against my better judgment, I looked into some of that information, and it checked out. Based on that and on the feature I wrote for the *Post*, she wants—"

"A *feature*," Mrs. Greenberg says, impressed.

Ian pats the air, telling her to lower her expectations. "It got published, but only online. The point is the piece was about how an attack like the one Lydia describes could be a possible next step for terrorists. That's why she called me. She thought I might listen because of what I wrote, and she was right. Between my research and her information, she thinks we have enough to go to the CIA. Unfortunately, I don't think it's enough. See—" he brushes crumbs from his hands and motions with them as he talks, "what Lydia knows is so specific, it'll raise questions. Like where she got her information—which, by the way, don't bother asking, because she won't tell you. In other words, we need more than unsourced information and a journalist's half-assed theory that something like this could be possible. We need documentation. We need clout. Basically, if what Lydia says is true, we need you."

I try to imagine what Ian's aunt must make of me based on Ian's introduction, and I cringe. My story sounds outlandish, and my plan sounds juvenile. Hearing him state the problem drives home just how far we are from being able to approach anyone in authority for help.

Ian said his aunt used to work for the CIA, but she strikes me as more the type to write for *Home and Garden* or *DIY Magazine* than to advise about issues of national security. If Ian's right, and somehow, this woman is a good launching pad for a makeshift anti-terror operation, then everything rides on her willingness to help. I try not to wring my hands as I wait for her response.

Finally, she looks from Ian to me, and says, "I don't think my nephew understands the term *nutshell.*"

A laugh bursts from my anxious lungs.

Ian chuckles, and so does he aunt. Despite my reservations about how helpful she'll prove to be, I find myself liking her.

She raises an eyebrow at Ian. "I surmise you've come to determine whether Lydia's warning is legitimate."

"It is," I say.

At the same time, Ian says, "That's the gist of it."

Mrs. Greenberg steeples her fingers. "If you're here at all, that means she's already passed the test for you."

Test? What test?

"She has," Ian says.

"Interesting," Mrs. Greenberg says. "Very interesting."

I'm about to ask what they're talking about when Mrs. Greenberg asks me, "What sort of attack are we talking about, dear?"

I meet her eyes, noticing they're green and highly intelligent, like Ian's. "Multiple, simultaneous passenger jet hijackings," I say baldly because nothing about Mrs. Greenberg suggests I should mince words. "We're talking about terrorists taking control of cockpits and turning planes into missiles aimed at populated areas in Manhattan and D.C. We're talking a coordinated attack by four teams of al-Qaeda operatives, and by ten o'clock tomorrow morning, almost three thousand Americans will be dead, unless we can stop it."

Ian and Mrs. Greenberg aren't the only ones who can administer tests. My words are a test. If this woman is really a retired agent, if she really does have the experience to help us, she won't flinch when I drop the scenario at her feet.

I study her for any sign that this kind of attack is too much for her delicate sensibilities—or for signs of disbelief. I wait for her to dismiss me as paranoid or ridiculous, but she does none of those things.

Mrs. Greenberg sits stock still as she absorbs my words. At last, she says, "Russians aren't our primary concern anymore, are they?" It's more a commiseration than a question, and it makes me wonder what, exactly she did for the CIA. Drawing herself up in her chair, she looks me dead in the eye, "But what I'm wondering is where a nice girl like you learned about a terror network The White House is only just beginning to take seriously? What is it you do for a living, dear?"

"I'm a nurse," I answer automatically before remembering that's not exactly true. "—Er, nursing student." I make the correction, but I'm more interested in what Mrs. Greenberg just said about The White House only recently beginning to take al-Qaeda seriously. "You're talking about the September fourth meeting, aren't you? You know about that?"

If she knows about last week's meeting between the CIA and CTC directors and the National Security Advisor, then she must keep in touch with someone high up in the CIA. I'm becoming more and more hopeful that Mrs. Greenberg can actually help.

She arches one eyebrow, the action dragging at the opposite one. "The question is, how do you know about it?"

"What meeting?" Ian says.

With a tilt of her head, Mrs. Greenberg indicates I should field the question.

For the first time since waking up this morning, I feel part of a team. I'm beginning to feel like my old self. If I can organize nursing staff in a busy ER, I can explain the current situation and communicate what needs to be done.

"I didn't write about it in my notes," I say to Ian, leaning forward in my chair. "But on September fourth, CIA Director Bennet and Colin Peck—he's the head of the Counterterrorism Center," I add in case Ian doesn't know—I certainly didn't before 9/11. "They met with some White House bigwigs, including the National Security Advisor. They asked for the meeting months ago, when UBL was becoming a bigger concern, but The White House kept putting them off. Finally, last week, they got to make their case to the powers that be that the al-Qaeda network needed more attention, like STAT.

"Based on their intel, Bennet and Peck predicted an attack could be 'imminent' and that it would be 'spectacular.'" I make quotes with my fingers. "Still, The White House remained unconvinced. All they did was authorize the arming of the Predator drone with missiles—that's the drone surveilling Bin Laden, and up to now it hasn't been armed. I don't even know if the authorization has been carried out yet. I haven't been able to find that information. Unfortunately, by tomorrow Bin Laden will disappear. We won't get him for another ten years. Basically, that meeting resulted in too little too late. In other words," I make eye contact with both members of my team, "stopping tomorrow is up to us. No one else has any clue what's happening—what's going to happen in—" I glance at the rooster-shaped clock over the oven. It's almost 2:00 pm. "Eighteen hours."

Ian looks shellshocked as he stares at me.

Mrs. Greenberg studies me. I feel penetrated by her gaze, realizing for the first time how hawklike her features are.

"Which is it?" she says.

I blink. I expected her next question to be about what, exactly, is going to happen in eighteen hours. "Which is what?"

"Nurse. Or nursing student. And do tell the truth. I'll know if you don't."

I swallow a lump in my throat. She'll know if I don't tell the truth? How? Is she trained in catching suspects in lies, like through pupil dilation and mannerisms? Is that why she's watching me so closely?

I look to Ian. His mouth tilts into a grin that says he's glad it's me under her scrutiny and not him.

I remember that he told me she was better at spotting lies than he was. By introducing me to his aunt, he's somehow putting me to the test. If I convince Mrs. Greenberg I'm telling the truth, he'll believe me.

I want him to believe me. I want him to believe *in* me. I want it so bad.

But it doesn't really matter what I want. The truth is utterly impossible. If I tell the truth, I risk alienating my only allies. I can't afford honesty.

Both sets of eyes are on me.

I turn to Mrs. Greenberg and say the most truthful thing I possibly can. "I'm not sure how to answer your question."

In 2021, I'm a senior nurse with two decades of experience. But in 2001, I've only just been accepted to nursing school. I haven't even attended my first class yet. I want to tell the truth, but which truth do I tell? The one that belongs twenty years in the future, or the one that belongs in the here and now?

"Be that as it may, I'd like it very much if you tried."

I shake my head, frustrated. I *am* trying. They have no idea how hard I'm trying.

"Tell her," Ian says. "This is your chance to say everything you think can't be believed."

I toss my arms in the air. "How? How is this my chance? I told you. The truth is unbelievable. And it's irrelevant. Wherever I came from, it doesn't change what those nineteen men are doing right now, what they're preparing to do tomorrow."

Ian starts to answer, but Mrs. Greenberg stops him with a look. Her hand lands gently on my shoulder. "If your claims about tomorrow are true," she says. "You'll be glad my nephew and I interrogated you here in my kitchen. That way you won't have to sit through one at Langley. However—" She holds up a cautionary finger. "If you aren't completely honest, and I can't vouch for you with confidence, all bets are off."

So, this "interrogation" is about her being able to vouch for me. Given her familiarity with last week's meeting and with al-Qaeda, I'm guessing her endorsement will be worth its weight in gold. But she and Ian don't know what they're asking for.

I squirm in my seat. "But I've given Ian verifiable information. Can't we put together some kind of operation to stop these terrorists based on the facts I know, like where the terrorists will be tomorrow? Why does my background matter?"

"It's not your background that matters," Mrs. Greenberg says. "It's the truth."

I plead with her with my eyes. "But the truth is impossible."

"It's still the truth," she says, and in her green gaze, I see a sincerity that tempts me to bare my soul. It would be freeing, telling the truth. Carrying it alone is a heavy burden. But no one, no matter how sincere, could ever believe it.

"You can trust her," Ian says. "And me."

I look at my hands, clasped on the table. Cookie crumbs make a constellation on the tabletop beside my napkin. I remember the catalyst for all this. The fireball.

"You've heard the saying, 'Truth is stranger than fiction,'" I say. "If there was ever a time that saying applies, it's now." I look at Mrs. Greenberg. "If I tell the truth, the whole, unedited truth—" I glance at Ian. "You will definitely *not* believe me, and tomorrow will happen." My eyes get hot with memories from two decades ago. "It will happen, and like Bennet and Peck told The White House, it will be spectacular."

I can't help grabbing Mrs. Greenberg's hand, which is larger than mine and toughened from a lifetime of hard work. "Ma'am, if we do nothing, almost three thousand people will die tomorrow. Please. Please, help me get this information to the right people. I have terrorist names. I know where they'll be tomorrow morning. I know what they're planning to do. Please. We can stop this, but we have to act quick.'

"Then you better answer the question, dear. Are you a nurse or a nursing student?"

I feel my lungs deflate. I won't secure Mrs. Greenberg's help on the merit of my information alone.

"Would it help if I reminded you that I believe in miracles?" Ian says. "We can document the unexplained. We can do it right here, right now. But you have to tell the truth. Show my aunt that you have something worth documenting, and you'll see you can trust us."

I stare at him. This is the second time he's asked for my trust. It's no more than I've asked of him.

I sigh, and as the breath leaves my lungs something shifts inside me. Chains fall from the secret I've been carrying since waking this morning. Suddenly, I want to tell the truth. I want allies in more than just stopping tomorrow's attack. I want these two people to join me inside this impossible situation.

I take a deep breath, and I say, "I'm both. I have memories of being a wife, a mother of two grown children, and a nurse for more than twenty years, but this body I'm in belongs to my twenty-three-year-old self. In the here and now, I'm newly married, have no kids, and haven't even started nursing school yet. Next week, I'm supposed to start classes at Helen Fuld, but the beginning of the semester will be delayed because of the attack. This present feels like my past. Only, in my past, there was no warning that 9/11 was about to happen. Somehow, I've been sent back here with the knowledge that can stop the worst terror attack on U.S. soil in our nation's history. I can't explain how, but I also can't deny the memories I have." I look down at my hands, clasped on the table. "That's the truth, crazy as it sounds."

When I look up, I expect Mrs. Greenberg to stare at me like I'm crazy, but that's not what she does. She beams at me like she did with Ian when he described his feature article.

"Thank you, dear. I know that cost you. Ian," she says, rising from her chair. "Fetch the old polygraph from the basement. Scrounge up a video camera, too, something modern enough to play back at Langley. Set everything up. We'll need more than my word for it if we're going to present a case to Bennet this afternoon." She strides from the kitchen, but reappears a moment later to add, "Don't start without me." I hear her pad up the stairs to the second floor.

Ian sits stock still until the sound of running water moving through old pipes jogs him into motion. "Yeah. Um—yeah, I'll go—get that." He's answering his aunt, even though she's no longer here.

He pushes away from the table and disappears down the hall.

I'm all alone in the kitchen. But less alone in my fight. Mrs. Greenberg seemed to accept my answer as honest. I think she believes me. She said we would present a case to the CIA Director this afternoon.

I sag back in my chair, beyond relieved. Ian told me to trust him, and I'm beginning to see why. His aunt might just be the best possible person to help stop this attack.

All I have to do now is pass a lie detector test.

I know
The past and thence I will essay to glean
A warning for the future, so that man
May profit by his errors, and derive
Experience from his folly

—Percy Bysshe Shelley

CHAPTER 15

Ian

I'M STANDING IN MY AUNT'S BASEMENT with no memory of how I got here. All I can think about are the words Lydia just spoke.

"I have memories of being a wife, a mother of two grown children, and a nurse for more than twenty years, but this body I'm in belongs to my twenty-three-year-old self."

I'm not sure what I expected, but it wasn't *that*.

All morning, I've been trying to figure her out. I've been collecting information, listening not only to her words but to her tone. I've been watching her, processing her mannerisms, looking for any reason to discount her warning about tomorrow. And I've come up short.

All morning, I've battled the suspicion that Lydia is telling the truth. My truth sense suggests she is, but logic says there's an impenetrable wall between her and the information she knows. There's no reasonable way she could have obtained that information.

Yet she has it.

She knows about Massoud's assassination. She knows about Hazmi and Mihdhar. She's right about me—about my family and my beliefs. She knows about a meeting at The White House last week where UBL was discussed.

The question is how?

Memories, she says. Marge seemed pleased with her answer, but I'm confused. Memories come from experience. Is Lydia saying she has experienced twenty years beyond this point in time, and that somehow, that experience included exposure to details about this attack? Or is she saying she had a dream or some kind of vision about points in her future, like, major life and career moments, oh, and a terror attack on our homeland?

Whether she likes it or not, the answer to the *how* is vital. It will be the first question asked by anyone at Langley, and without a good answer, all three of us, Lydia, me, *and* Marge, will be dismissed.

It's time to put my curiosity to rest, one question at a time.

The familiar aged-paper-and-laundry-detergent smell of my aunt's basement fills my lungs as I weave my way through stacks of storage bins and neatly labeled cardboard boxes. I know exactly where I'm going, having played with the old polygraph machine countless times. While other kids were riding bikes and playing basketball, I was giving my cousins "lie-detector" tests with questions like, "Have you been snooping for Christmas presents?" and "Did you have lasagna for dinner last night?"

I find the plastic suitcase housing the device and run my fingers over it. This machine, when used correctly, is capable of parsing truth from lie. Even better, it gives a readout that data-driven folks, like those in the CIA, can't easily dismiss. Machine in one hand, I heft a crate filled with audio-visual equipment under my other arm and make my way upstairs.

I'm about to get to the bottom of what Lydia knows and how she knows it, and I'll have more than just my truth sense to help me decipher the results. I'll have this device. And I'll have Marge.

As I make the turn into the kitchen, I find Lydia at the sink, drying our lemonade glasses with a dishtowel. Aunt Marge had the countertops designed for her six-foot-one frame. They're a few inches taller than what you'd find in a standard cabinet shop. Standing in Marge's kitchen, Lydia appears smaller than I know her to be.

She has removed her sweatshirt and stands with her back to me in *T*-shirt, jeans, and stocking feet on the rectangular rag rug that's cushioned unshod feet for all the years I've known this old house.

Uninvited, my gaze drops to the rhinestones dotting the pockets of her jeans. Those pockets hug a nicely shaped rear end, the sight of which warms my blood. But the heat is more than the spark of carnal possibility. Something in my chest tightens at the sight of this girl in my aunt's kitchen. My desire to help her runs deep. Maybe even deeper than the compulsion to solve the mystery she presents.

Leave it, Ian. She's married. Unhappily, perhaps, but still married.

I'm not meant to be Lydia's hero. But maybe Marge can be.

I set my load on the table, and Lydia faces me with concern etched on her features. Her slanted brows rouse protective instincts I work to quell.

"So," she says, hands clasped nervously in front of her. "Your aunt keeps a lie detector in the basement?"

"Technically, it's a polygraph. It doesn't detect lies, but with a skilled operator, it can help detect physiological changes that suggest untruthfulness."

She blinks.

I feel like a pedantic shit. "Yeah, she keeps a lie detector in her basement. She's ex-CIA. There's lots of weird stuff in her basement."

Lydia meets me at the table and passes a curious gaze over the equipment as I pull items from the A/V crate. "What did she do for the CIA?"

"She was a spy during the Cold War Era," I say while setting up a table-top tripod. "Speaks fluent Russian, Polish, and German. Not that she talks about those days, it's just things I've heard from my dad. As long as I've known her, she's just been Aunt Marge. But she would teach me things that she must have picked up in the Agency."

"Like how to give a lie detector test?"

I grin. "I've subjected all my cousins to my interrogations."

"Should I be worried?"

"Very." I lock the camcorder onto the tripod and start connecting cables.

"You said something about your aunt being able to tell if I'm lying. Is that because of this?" She flips the latches on the polygraph and swings the lid open, revealing the boxy device inside with its spool of paper and delicate needles. Pressed into holders in the lid are the attachments she'll soon be wearing.

I shift on my feet. I haven't told Lydia about my talent for sensing the truth. "I haven't been completely honest with you," I admit. To avoid her no-doubt accusing gaze, I keep mine on the equipment. I'm unwinding the cable for a lapel mic that will be clipped to her shirt in a moment. "Yes, in part, my aunt's ability is because of this, but there's an innate aspect to it as well."

Lydia cocks her head, confused.

I'm mucking this up. "Marge is amazing at using devices like this, but it's not just the device that tells her what she needs to know. It's something inside her that recognizes truth. It's a talent she was born with, and it's why she went into the CIA. She was never normal, my aunt. According to my father, she had trouble making friends. Growing up with her was a challenge." I smile ruefully, remembering stories. "He could never get away with anything when she was around. She always seemed to know when he was fibbing, and she was the tattle-type. Going into the spy game must have seemed like a no-brainer. Someone like her? With her passion for truth and justice. Dad says that when she entered the CIA, she found her calling." I look up from the camera and find Lydia's gaze on me. "What Marge has? I have it too."

"What she has?" Lydia frowns while her finger tests the smoothness of the polygraph paper.

"Whatever natural ability she has," I elaborate. "Whatever she was born with that earned her the nickname 'Human Lie Detector' at the Agency. Whatever you want to call it, I have it too, but not as strong." I tilt my head, considering. "At least, I haven't honed the skill like she did at the Agency."

Lydia keeps frowning. "Natural ability. For…recognizing truth."

I nod.

"You have it too." She makes it a dubious statement.

"Yep." I offer a smile. "Helps me as a journalist. Makes me miserable at relationships."

Lydia stares at me, then gives her head a shake. "I don't understand. You're telling me you—and your aunt—are, what? Good at knowing when people are lying? Like, you know on a supernatural level or something?"

I make a scoffing noise while digging through the A/V crate. I'm looking for a blank tape to no avail. "No. Like, on an instinctual level. Like, I see through what people say, and pay attention to the signs. You know? Eye movement, tone of voice, mannerisms. There's nothing special about it. It's just how I'm wired, how Marge is wired."

"Sounds pretty special to me."

I clear my throat. "Especially annoying, maybe." There are no tapes in the crate. "Can I trust you not to tamper with the device while I go get something?"

Her gaze sweeps the table. "I wouldn't even know how to tamper with it."

I enjoy a reprieve from her curiosity while I search the tech-corner of the basement for blank media. I don't tell people about my truth sense. It feels strange to talk about it. It makes me different. It makes me unpopular. Or uncomfortable. Or awkward. Usually, all of the above.

I always know when people don't mean the things they say. You'd think that would be helpful, but it's really not. Not in my personal life, anyway. It's one of the reasons I don't have many friends, and have had even fewer girlfriends.

When I return to the kitchen, tapes in hand, I'm ready to change the subject. I've prepared a speech about the technology in my hands. These tapes are a Digital Audio Tape-Digital Video hybrid developed by the U.S. government in the early nineties. They fit in your pocket, but they hold ten times what you can put on a VHS tape from the same period and can be played back from the camera onto any video monitor with the right attachment.

But I don't get to share any of that.

As soon as Lydia sees me, she says, "What does your wiring say about me?"

I glance at the tangle of cables on the table. "My wiring?"

"Your 'nothing special' wiring that makes you more sensitive to lies than the average homo sapiens." Ah. Guess we're still talking about my truth sense. Her grin tells me she suspects there is, in fact, something special about it despite my protest. It also makes me want to spill my guts to her. It makes me feel like I won't be judged. "What does it say about me?"

I punch the tape into the camera and switch it to record mode. "It says you believe what you're saying." I keep my eyes on the equipment, nervous about admitting I've been reading her all day. At her silence, I look up.

"That all it says?" She's not balking, not preparing to disbelieve me. She's being honestly curious.

I sigh. "It says you believe what you're saying, one-hundred percent."

She nods. "But I could be crazy, or delusional, or mistaken."

"You could be."

"Do you think I am?"

I take my time answering. "Mistaken, maybe. Delusional, nah. Crazy—" I smile at her. "Definitely."

Lydia

"A LARGE PART of detecting lies," Ian says, "is actually detecting what type of person you're dealing with. See, everyone lies, but some people lie for altruistic reasons, while others lie for selfish reasons. Some people tell lies as a last resort. Others make such a habit of it they struggle to remember what's true, themselves."

He's setting up the lie detector—sorry, the *polygraph*—and he's chatting as he does so. I'm learning that he changes the subject when he gets uncomfortable. Flirting by calling me crazy made him uncomfortable, judging by the red splotches that crept into his cheeks. Pontificating about lie detection is helping his color return to normal.

To be fair, my cheeks may have flushed a little, too.

"Have you ever taken a polygraph exam before?" he asks me.

I shake my head no.

"You'll be wearing a blood pressure cuff." He lifts said item from the plastic case. "An electrode on the forefinger of both hands, and a pneumatic chest tube."

"Chest tube? You don't have to put something down my throat, do you?" I'm imagining being intubated in Mrs. Greenberg's kitchen.

"Don't worry. Nothing involved in the polygraph procedure is invasive." He waggles his brows. "Unless you have something to hide."

"Ha-ha."

His grin is contagious. "This is the chest tube." He holds up what looks like a black coiled cord from an old-fashioned wall phone. "It goes around your chest and measures your breathing. From the outside." He motions for me to hold up my arms.

Leaning into my space, he attaches the coil around my chest. His barely-there, professional touch shouldn't send pleasant tingles dancing over every inch of my skin. But it does. For delicious, awkward seconds, I inhale his fresh-air and woodsy-cologne scent, and my cheeks grow warm again.

"There," he says, clearing his throat.

At the other end of the "chest tube" wire is a metal connector as thick as my pinky finger. He stabs it into a port on the face of the machine.

"How old is this thing?"

"Probably as old as you are."

I snort. "Either twenty-three or forty-three. Got it."

He fixes me with his gaze, pausing in adjusting the spool of graph paper. That's right. Mrs. Greenberg seemed to believe me about my predicament, but Ian had only appeared shellshocked.

"So, these memories of the future," he says, carefully. "They encompass twenty years?"

"Yes." There's no sense in beating around the bush now, especially when I'm about to be vindicated by an ancient piece of technology and a 'human lie detector.'

I glance at the machine to see what it made of my answer, but I'm not really sure what I'm looking for. I needn't have bothered. It's not running yet.

"Every moment of those years? Or just salient events?" Ian asks.

"Don't you want to turn that on?"

Ian smiles. "The test hasn't started yet. This is just me being curious."

I remember the 'natural ability' he says he shares with his aunt. Maybe this is part of the test, even if he doesn't realize it yet. If he really does have a knack for identifying truth, I want him to see the truth in my story. I want it desperately.

"Ian, I remember as much about the last twenty years of my life—or, I guess, the next twenty years of my life, as anyone would. I feel like a forty-three-year-old divorced nurse with two grown kids and a farm in Nebraska. When I went to bed last night, I was thousands of miles away, and it was twenty twenty-one. When I woke up this morning, I was in Brooklyn in the apartment I lived in with Tristan when we were first married. Every word of what I'm saying is true."

His mouth makes a grim line, and he says, "I know."

It's the first time I feel like he believes not just that I have valuable information about tomorrow, but that I'm out of place and time. It makes my throat tighten with emotion.

"Show me your hands." He's all business as he attaches finger-tip clips to both my index fingers.

I use a lot of electrodes in my line of work, but none of them look like this, with copper plates that touch the skin and thick wires coming out of them. "They're not dangerous, are they?"

"No. They measure the activity of your sweat glands. Input only, no output."

I nod my understanding.

Last comes the blood-pressure cuff, which he inflates to a point just shy of too tight. "You get used to it," he says.

"I'm familiar with blood-pressure cuffs," I say.

"Should I make it tighter, then?"

I give him a droll look.

He grins and switches the machine on with a great *thunk* of a toggle.

"Looks like I made it just in time." Mrs. Greenberg strides into the kitchen, buttoned into a dark gray skirt suit that would have been in fashion in the time of shoulder pads, only she doesn't need the pads. She's tall, broad, and formidable from her French twist to her smart Mary Janes.

She circles the table, inspecting Ian's work. Long fingers smooth over the cables coming from the video camera. One leads to a lapel mic Ian clips to his shirt. A larger mic hangs over the table on a metal framework. Ian called it a "boom" when he was setting it up.

Mrs. Greenberg stops behind the camera and swivels the viewscreen so she can see it better. "Everything looks in order." Peering at me over the screen, she says, "I'm on pins and needles to find out what hold you have over my nephew. What secrets do you possess that put our homeland at risk?" She frames the question as though she's providing the introduction for a documentary. Without waiting for an answer, she adjusts the boom mic so it points from above to a spot between where I sit and where Ian has set up the polygraph. She moves behind the camera. "Give me a sound check," she says to Ian.

"She sells seashells by the seashore," he says while she twists a knob on a small box. Satisfied, she hands him the box, and he clips it to his belt.

"Now you," she says to me.

"Uh—" I angle my face toward the mic over the table. Loudly, I say, "Peter Piper picked a peck of pickled peppers?"

Ian chuckles. "Just talk naturally."

"I can't think of any more tongue twisters."

Mrs. Greenberg smiles warmly. "*Testing, one, two, three,* always works."

I repeat the phrase, talking normally, while Mrs. Greenberg adjusts knobs on a different box. Everything seems to be working, judging by her calm face.

"This is quite the operation," I say to Ian. "I think you missed your calling."

"My calling?"

"You should be a cameraman or some kind of production person for TV." I nod at the equipment he was able to set up so quickly. "Whenever I try to set up technical stuff, it never goes smoothly. I end up saying a lot of bad words and having to troubleshoot for hours. Not you. Everything just works for you. First time, *bam*. No troubleshooting needed. It's a talent."

"Oh." His complexion darkens over his cheekbones. "Thanks. I had some broadcasting classes as part of my journalism degree." He shrugs off the compliment, as if it's the schooling that should get the credit, not him.

I'm about to tell him not to shortchange himself when Mrs. Greenberg says, "Recording now. You take the lead. I'll jump in when I see fit." She's talking to Ian.

He nods and takes a seat ninety degrees from me at the table. "Ready?"

I've been ready for this all day. "Bring it on."

Mrs. Greenberg sets a cell phone on the table with care. It's a flip phone, and the screen is lit up, but I'm not close enough to be able to make sense of any information it displays. Leaning over it, she says, "You still there?"

"I'm listenin'." A man's tenor voice is amplified through the little plastic earpiece. It sounds tinny, far away, and slightly southern.

"Who's that?" I ask.

"A friend," Mrs. Greenberg answers. Her eyes crinkle warmly, but her tone communicates finality.

I hope it's a friend who has some clout and who is primed to believe the impossible.

Ian raises his eyebrows at his aunt, but he takes her hint and doesn't ask any follow-up questions. When he clears his throat, I give him my attention.

"I'll be asking you some questions." he says as he releases a lever on the machine. The graph paper begins crawling conveyor-style across its track. One of the needles moves slightly, making a blip of dark ink. The other three draw flat lines. I wonder if those needles are working. "Answer as honestly as possible and try to sit as still as possible. Just relax and tell the truth."

Relax. Right.

I check the graph paper to see if my nerves are somehow communicated onto paper. Two of the lines have blips on them, now, but the general pattern drawn by all four pens is a continuous, flat line.

"Relax," Ian says, again.

"Easier said than done." I'm eager to get to the meat of the interview. I hope this test will verify, at least to Ian and Mrs. Greenberg, that I'm telling the truth about what I know.

I roll my head to one side, then the other, trying to relax. It's hard when I know three thousand lives will be cut short tomorrow if this doesn't work. Also knowing that if this does work, the director of the CIA might be the next person to see the recording being made.

Ian's smile is encouraging. "For the record, are you voluntarily submitting to this examination?"

"Yes." I look from Ian to the graph paper, where he makes a mark with a pen.

"Look at me or into the kitchen," he says. "Don't try to make sense of the readout. That's my job."

"Right." I force myself not to look at the slowly scrolling paper. Or at the camera three feet from my face, the mic hanging above the table, or the phone on the table with an open line to a mystery man. The kitchen sink seems a safe place to rest my gaze.

"We'll start with something easy," he says. "Is your name Lydia Clay?"

"Yes." After I answer instinctually, my brain kicks into gear. "Well, not legally. Legally, right now, my name is Lydia Watercrest." I can't help wrinkling my nose. Saying my old name makes me feel like I've undone years of therapy.

Ian makes tiny marks on the paper. I try not to look, but it's hard.

"I guess that one wasn't so easy, hm?" His smile is disarming. "How about this? What is today's date?"

"September tenth, two thousand one."

"There. That was a good one."

I can't help myself. I look at the graph paper. I see movement in the lines, but I don't know what anything means. The pens don't seem to be moving much.

"Look straight ahead," he reminds me. Only once I comply does he continue with his next question. "Did you telephone me this morning with a warning about an impencing terrorist attack?"

"Yes." Answers about the attack come much more naturally than answers about myself. There's nothing complicated about remembering an event. It's remembering where and when I am that fills me with unease.

"If you have information about a terrorist attack," he goes on. "Why did you call me and not, say, the FBI or some other agency?"

I feel myself sit taller. "I called you because you wrote about the scenario. You're 'the reporter who predicted 9/11.' If anyone could possibly believe the story I have to tell, it would be you."

"What do you mean, I'm 'the reporter who predicted 9/11?' 9/11 is tomorrow's date, is it not? To my knowledge, I haven't predicted anything. Please explain the phrase."

"You didn't predict the actual attack that will happen. But in your article, 'The New Face of Terrorism in the Twenty-First Century,' you describe a possible evolution in air terrorism that includes hijackers taking control of passenger jets. You're the first person to seriously consider the risk of airline pilots being forced from cockpits and hijackers being able to fly. Once in control, they could crash the planes or fly into populated areas. It would be easy if they had flight training, and your research showed that some al-Qaeda-affiliated Saudis were enrolled in U.S. flight schools on tourist visas."

"That it did," Ian says. "You mentioned al-Qaeda. Do you have specific names of terrorists planning this attack?"

"Yes. I know several names. Hazmi—who I called Hamzi in my notes, but you caught that spelling error—" I add with a grin. "He and Mihdhar are the ones we talked about today, but the ones who will pilot the planes are Atta, Shehhi, Hanjour, and Jarrah, with Atta being the leader of the group. There are nineteen in all. Let's see. Some of the other names are Omari, Sherri—there's two of them. Two Hazmis and two Ghamdis as well. Those are the names I remember."

My skin prickles as if Mrs. Greenberg's gaze has increased in intensity from behind the camera. I don't look at her. She'll make me nervous, and here I am, finally finding my stride.

"Thank you," Ian says. I instinctively know he's putting marks on the graph paper, but I'm over the urge to peek.

After a short pause, he says, "You told me this morning that nineteen terrorists would hijack four passenger jets departing from U.S. airports tomorrow morning. Is this true?"

"Yes. It's true that I told you, and it's true that it will happen. Unless we can stop them."

"What do the hijackers plan to do with the planes once they take control of the cockpits?"

"Crash them into buildings. Both towers of the World Trade Center will be hit. The North tower first by American Flight 11 at 8:46 a.m. Then the South tower at 9:02 by United Flight 175. Sometime around 9:30, The Pentagon will be hit by American Flight 77, and around 10 a.m., United Flight 93 will crash into a field in Southern Pennsylvania. The target for that flight might have been The White House or maybe the Capitol Building. Some people thought it could be the CIA building at Langley."

I don't miss the sober look Ian gives his aunt. I glance at her only to find her expression unreadably stoic.

"I've noticed this before," Ian says, recapturing my attention. "When you talk about tomorrow, you use phrases like, 'The tower will be hit,' and 'The target might have been

The White House.' Why say it like that and not, 'The terrorists *plan to* hit the tower,' and 'One target *might be* The White House?' To hear you talk about tomorrow, one might think you've seen these things happen already. Why is that?"

I meet his gaze and say unflinchingly, "I *have* seen it happen. Every American has seen it. The whole World has seen it. It's 9/11, the worst attack ever on American soil."

To watch, powerless, is a horror.

—Diane Sawyer

CHAPTER 16

Lydia

I DON'T BLINK as I wait for Ian's response, but inside, I'm a mess of nerves clamoring for him to believe me. He asked me to give him the full, unedited truth, and I just did. I unceremoniously dumped it on the table in front of him.

I saw it.

I lived it.

I was there.

It happened.

Please believe me.

Ian's not blinking, either. I would think he was frozen if not for the rise and fall of his chest beneath his rumpled shirt. I can't tell if he's carefully schooling his expression while he formulates his next question or if I've shocked him speechless.

It's his aunt who speaks next. "Even worse than Pearl Harbor? Where two-thousand-plus perished beneath Japanese bombers and a thousand more were wounded?"

Her words are chosen with precision. She's a different person when she interrogates, I'm learning. Gone is the warm host who sipped lemonade at my elbow and called me "dear." In her place is a drill sergeant who expects her questions to be answered honestly and thoroughly.

"Twenty-four hundred died on December seventh, 1941," I reply, looking her in the eye. "Tomorrow more than twenty-nine hundred will perish, including two hundred sixty-five passengers and crew of the four planes, four hundred first responders in New York, one hundred twenty-five Pentagon personnel, and more than two thousand people working at the Trade Center."

A pin dropping would sound like an atomic bomb in the silence that follows. Finally, the silence is broken by the tinny voice issuing from Mrs. Greenberg's flip phone.

"Dear God. Marge, tell me this person is lying through her teeth."

Mrs. Greenberg pulls out a chair and falls into it as if her knees have turned to Jell-O. She picks up the phone and holds it like an open clamshell in front of her mouth. "I wish I could, Socks. I wish I could." While she speaks to "Socks," her green gaze remains on me, sober and speculative.

She believes me.

As soon as I think it, I brace myself to learn I've misread her. I'm reluctant to rest in knowledge that's too good to be true.

"At least, she believes what she says is true," Mrs. Greenberg says. And there it is. The doubt.

Of course, there's doubt. If someone came to me with a warning about something terrible about to happen, I would be highly doubtful as well. I certainly wouldn't elevate such a warning by taking action without significant evidence.

"I'm afraid I'm as lost as an Amish electrician," Socks says. "How does this woman know what will happen tomorrow?"

"How did I know every time a subject uttered a lie?" is Mrs. Greenberg's comeback.

"You were gifted."

"*Am* gifted, Socks. I still got it." Her lips quirk in an expression that reminds me of Ian when he's being smug.

"Is this person 'gifted,' too?" His tone suggests that it goes against his nature to believe in the kind of gift Mrs. Greenberg has, but that through his acquaintance with her, he has come to accept it. "Is that how she knows these supposed flight numbers and targets? What on God's green Earth does she mean by 'the whole World has seen it?' when it's supposed to be happening tomorrow?" The pitch of Socks's voice rises with each question. I wonder what he was doing before Mrs. Greenberg called him and asked him to listen in on a polygraph exam. At the moment, he seems none too happy about the interruption. "What am I missing, here?"

"You're not missing anything," Mrs. Greenberg replies. "I have yet to determine whether Ms. Clay is gifted. What I do know is my nephew verified information she related about two of tomorrow's hijackers. And not five minutes ago, I had a conversation with her about last week's meeting of the principles. *You're* the one who told me that was going down. That meeting hasn't been made public. This girl has no ties to the government. She would have no reason to know about it, but she's the one who brought it up."

I bristle at being called a "girl," but I suppose that's what I am to her. No matter what I feel like on the inside, I look like I'm around her nephew's age. On the upside, she's working hard to convince Socks I'm worth listening to. That I appreciate.

"There's also the Massoud assassination," Ian pipes up.

Mrs. Greenberg's sharp gaze swings to him.

"What's this?" Socks says. "Speak up, son. What assassination?"

"Guerilla leader in the anti-Taliban movement," Ian says distinctly, angling his voice toward the phone. "Massoud. He was killed yesterday on a base that should have been a safe haven for him. Our government just learned of it this morning, but Lydia already knew."

"Do you mean Ahmad Shah Massoud?" Socks says. "He's dead?"

"You know him?" Mrs. Greenberg says, echoing my thoughts. I couldn't remember Massoud's full name, but Socks had it on the tip of his tongue.

"Yeah, I know him. Gave us solid intel in exchange for aid for his group. He was in the top tier of possible fixes for al-Qaeda. Hang on." I hear him talking, but his speech is muffled, like he's covering the mouthpiece with his hand. "I'm having that verified. These are significant allegations, *M*. Multiple hijackings, assassinations? If there's even a speck of truth to any of it, we need to know how this Clay knows these things."

"I'll get to the bottom of it." Mrs. Greenberg replaces the phone on the table. "Ian. Thank you, but I'm taking over."

"Of course." Ian scrapes his chair back. He hands off the lapel mic to Mrs. Greenberg, who clips it to her tailored jacket and takes a seat in front of the polygraph.

She raises her eyebrows at Ian, who indicates with a thumbs up that he's manning the camera. The look she fixes on me is unreadable in its blandness. Facing her across the polygraph machine is a totally different experience from facing Ian.

"Ms. Clay," she says. "Are you clairvoyant?"

I blink. I hadn't been expecting that. But it's an easy enough question to answer.

"No."

She makes a mark with Ian's pen. "Psychic?"

"No."

"Mentally unstable?"

I huff with humor. "No. Unless you ask my ex-husband."

She doesn't crack a smile. For a brief moment, I marvel at the fact I'm being interrogated by an expert in lie detection who may have helped her country win the Cold War. I hope this isn't a huge mistake.

"When did you become divorced from your husband?"

I swallow. I don't really like talking about my marriage, but I can only blame myself since I'm the one who brought it up.

"Um," I lick my lips. "The papers were signed on July seventeenth, twenty-twenty." I wince. Stating the year like that might not have been the smoothest move. But it's the truth. I glance at the paper and am content to see no large movements of the pens. I think movement is bad, but I'm still not sure what Mrs. Greenberg and Ian are looking for.

"By twenty-twenty, do you mean the year two thousand twenty?"

It's time for me to tell the whole, unbelievable truth. I have nothing to be ashamed of. I'm out of place and time, but I didn't do this to myself on purpose. I'm here for a reason. I'm here to save lives.

"Yes," I confirm. "I got divorced in the year twenty-twenty."

"Yet you stated today's date as September tenth, two thousand one. Are you telling me you are married at this present time, and at some date in the future, you will become divorced from your husband?"

"Yes. That's what I'm telling you. But it's not some random date in the future. It's July seventeenth, twenty-twenty." Mrs. Greenberg's gaze flicks between me and the readout. I watch her make marks with her pen. I'm intimidated but not deterred. "I know the date because I've lived it. I've lived twenty years beyond this point in time, and somehow, I seem to have been sent back.

"I know in my heart the reason is to try and stop tomorrow's attack. Because, why today? The day before the worst attack ever on American soil? When *I* lived through tomorrow, there were no warnings. The country—the whole World—was taken off guard. Two passenger jets crashed into the World Trade Center towers before anyone even realized we were under attack. At first people thought it was a Cessna that lost control, you know? Some accident. There were rumors circulating about a hijacked plane, American Flight 11, but no one knew if that was the plane that hit the North tower. From the ground, the hole looked small. The handful of witnesses who actually saw it happen gave different stories. 'It was a small plane.' 'It was a jet.' No one knew for sure. Then, twenty minutes later, the second plane hit the South tower.

"Every news outlet in New York got the second explosion on camera. The whole World realized, in that one horrible second, that the first crash was no accident. We were under attack. That's when the chaos erupted.

"All the agencies struggled to get a grip on what was happening. The FAA, NORAD, NEADS, the local flight towers and air traffic control centers, The White House—President Bush was at an elementary school in Sarasota. A Secret Service agent whispered the news of the first plane crash in the President's ear while he sat in a classroom full of second graders. The footage was shown later, over and over again. Every American witnessed the shock on his face as he was told we were under attack.

"It took almost an hour to confirm that the first crash was American Flight 11, and that the plane had been hijacked. Both towers were hit and two planes full of people vaporized in the explosions before a single fighter jet got airborne. We were slow to respond because NEADS had an exercise scheduled for that morning. Precious seconds were wasted confirming the attack was 'real-world,' not exercise." I make quotes with my hands, forgetting about the electrodes on my fingers.

Unable to help myself, I grab up Mrs. Greenberg's hand, the one holding the pen. The pen clatters to the floor. Her fingers are limp. Her eyes are wide, her brows pinched together. No one's paying attention to the polygraph.

Mentally, I implore her to feel what I feel—a driving determination to create a new end to a day already lived.

"We had no warning," I say again. "Not the first time. But someone somewhere—or the Universe, or the space-time-continuum, or a wormhole—whatever you want to call it, we've been given a second chance. This is the only warning we will get. *I* am the warning. You have to help me get this information to the right people. Please. This has to be the reason I was sent back. Help me save the ones who weren't supposed to die tomorrow."

Mrs. Greenberg's brow smooths. Her fingers grip mine as she looks deep into my soul. I can practically feel her reaching into the corners of my mind to gather evidence for her judgment. Am I telling the truth or am I lying? Do I simply believe the things I'm saying, or have I actually lived them?

I open myself to her probing. I *will* her to see it all, to know me inside and out for the benefit of tomorrow's victims.

Read me. See me.

I'm curious how Ian's handling all this, but I don't dare break eye contact with Mrs. Greenberg. I want Ian to believe me. But I *need* his aunt to believe me. She's the one who can set up a meeting with Bennet. She's the one whose endorsement could mean the launching of an operation to stop the attack.

Mrs. Greenberg slips her hand from mine and bends to pick up her pen. When she straightens, her face is composed, although a shade or two paler. "Please explain, to the best of your ability, what you experienced as 'being sent back,' as you call it. Take me through it. When did you first feel as though you were in a different time than you expected?"

I nod. It's a good question. I'm ready to talk about it. Maybe I even need to talk about it.

"This morning." I answer. "I woke up in the apartment Tristan and I had when we were first married. I thought I was dreaming, at first. Last night, I'd been in Nebraska, sitting on the porch with my daughter—Holly." I can't help smiling when I say her name. The warmth of her spirit buoys me. *You can do this, Mom.*

"We were talking about 9/11. She was born after it happened. For her generation, the attack is a chapter in their fifth-grade history book. It's hard for them to understand what it was like, to feel what we felt, those of us who lived through it.

"I was there, in Brooklyn. My apartment was on Spinney Hill. I had a perfect view across the bay. On a clear day, I could see the skyline. That day was clear as a bell. The sky was so blue that the smoke looked obscene as it extended the line of the Towers higher and higher. It was so black. And so thick." I look down at my hands, remembering. It was like seeing a patient bleed from an artery and not being able to stop it. "I kept going back and forth between my doorstep and the TV. I was watching on TV when the first tower collapsed."

My heart beats harder, like it did that day. "At first, it was hard to tell what was happening. I couldn't understand what I was seeing on the screen. Even Peter Jennings wasn't sure.

One second, the smoke was going up into the sky, like water from an upside-down faucet. The next, it started going out in every direction. It billowed from between the buildings like this massive gray blob swallowing up Manhattan.

"On TV they said the South Tower collapsed, as in the whole building. Then they showed the closeup of it happening. The floors above the crash zone pancaked on top of each other, and then the building just folded in on itself and came down.

"My living-room floor shook, I think. Or maybe it was just me shaking. All I could think was, 'I hope everyone got out.' But they didn't. Firemen were still climbing the stairs. More than three hundred of them between the two towers. Plus Port Authority cops and other first responders. Trade Center workers were making their way down. Then there were the people trapped above the crash zone. All the stairwells but one in the South Tower were severed by the planes, so everyone above where they hit—" I shake my head. "They had nowhere to go. Some went to the roof. They thought helicopters would come like in '93, but no one came. The smoke was too thick. No one wanted to risk landing on the buildings. They didn't know that time was running out. No one imagined the fires would burn so hot they would melt the steel supports and cause the building to collapse. More than two thousand civilians died while I watched on TV."

I suck in a huge breath. "When I went outside again, all I could see was this huge smoke cloud with just one building rising above. The North Tower. Alone.

"Tristan was there. He worked just blocks away. I was so worried. I tried calling him, but the phone lines were jammed.

It was horrible—like the true meaning of horror. The shock and disbelief. The fear. Were there more planes coming? Was anyplace safe?

"Not long after, the North tower came down too, and there was this incredible sense of loss. It lasted for days, like the taste of concrete dust in the air. Every breath was a reminder. Every glance at the altered skyline caused a stabbing feeling in your stomach."

Ian starts to ask something, but Mrs. Greenberg shushes him.

I feel like I'm in a trance. I talk over their interaction, lost in the past. "Holly asked what it was like, living through it. She's asked before, but I never talked about it. Tristan didn't like us to talk about it. But Tristan isn't in my life anymore. So, last night, for the first time, I told her."

I take a deep breath and release it in a shaky stream. "Afterward, she went to bed, and I stayed on the porch, sipping wine, thinking about that day. All of a sudden, I saw a shooting star." I chuckle darkly. "I know how it sounds. I was drinking. I was lost in thought. I probably imagined it. But I didn't.

"Ever since I was a kid, I've been wishing on shooting stars. The first time was on that same porch with my grandfather." The memory chokes me up. I clear my throat. "But the star last night, it wasn't any regular shooting star. It was a fireball. It was enormous—bigger than the moon in the sky—and so bright I could see the tassels on top of the cornstalks like in the middle of the afternoon.

"It was such a special shooting star that—" I laugh. "I made a special—an *impossible* wish. I wished—" I take a bracing breath. "I wished that 9/11 could be undone. I knew it couldn't possibly come true. You can't turn back time. There's no undoing the Titanic or Chernobyl or, I don't know—" I make a sweeping gesture as I think of disasters that could have been prevented. "The Hindenburg.

"I didn't care about impossible. I made my wish with the same kind of faith I had as a kid." I shrug and look at my hands. "I finished my wine and went to bed expecting to wake up on September tenth, twenty twenty-one. In Taylor, Nebraska. I had plans. Meet my new boss at the hospital. Unpack moving boxes—the farmhouse belonged to my parents. I recently lost my mother and inherited the farm—" I gasp. *Mom!*

It's 2001. My mother is still alive! So is my father! I could call them right now and hear their voices, tell them how much I love them. I could tell Mom to see a doctor about her heart. I could encourage Dad to quit smoking and get regular screenings for lung cancer.

"Lydia? You okay?" Ian's voice makes me start.

I swallow thickly and blink myself back into the here and now. I'm staring at the ivory cameo brooch at Mrs. Greenberg's throat. It reminds me of a pair of pins my grandmother used to wear in her hair on special occasions.

I can't believe I haven't thought of my parents before now.

My fingers itch to grab up my little Nokia phone. I want to call them. I want to fly to Nebraska to visit them. I want to spend as much time with them as possible. It will be many years before they die, but to me, it feels like they've come back from the dead.

"Lydia, dear?" This time, it's Mrs. Greenberg who speaks. "Please tell me where you went just now. What were you thinking about?"

I tell her. My eyes tear up as I talk about my parents, about losing Dad in 2016 and Mom in 2021 and how I just realized I have a chance to see them again, to warn them.

Mrs. Greenberg and Ian share a look.

"Would you like to stop the test?" Ian asks.

I'm tempted. I want to call my parents. But what we're doing here is too important. I'll call my parents once I know wheels are moving on an operation to stop the terrorists.

I shake my head. "No. We have to talk about tomorrow. Please. Let's not waste any more time on me. Ask about the hijackers. That's where I can give you solid, actionable information."

Mrs. Greenberg assesses me for a moment, then she removes her mic and leaves the table. When she gets back, she thrusts a glass of ice water at me. "Drink," she says. "Take a minute." To Ian, she says. "Pause the recording."

"Done."

"Good. Get her unstrapped."

I'm on autopilot as I lift my hands for Ian to unclip the electrodes. He's removing the phone cord from around my chest when Mrs. Greenberg picks up her flip phone.

"Did she say the Trade Center Towers collapsed?" Socks is saying as Mrs. Greenberg strides from the kitchen, leaving me alone with Ian.

The polygraph paper makes a limp trail that dangles off the machine and stops a few inches off the floor. The inked lines are mostly straight.

Ian helps himself to the pitcher of lemonade in the fridge, filling one of the glasses I washed. When he comes back to the table, he takes the seat at the polygraph and examines the readout.

I hope this break won't take long. I'm eager to continue. I feel like Mrs. Greenberg believes me. I think Ian does too. But I need to know for sure.

"What's the verdict?" I ask. "Am I telling the truth?"

Graph paper slides through his fingers, inky lines passing before his gaze as he answers. "I don't need this to know you are. Honesty is pouring off you like a waterfall." He looks up and meets my gaze. There's a quiet understanding there that acknowledges the weight of what just transpired. He says he believes me, but even better is the proof in his gaze.

A thousand pounds lift off my shoulders. I bow my head and blink back tears.

"I'm sorry about your parents."

I nod, head hanging. "Thanks. It's strange to know they're alive right now. I could pick up the phone and call them."

"Will you?"

I don't have to think about it. "Yes. When this is all over and behind us." It's a mixed blessing, being able to talk to my parents again. For that privilege and for the privilege of trying to right a terrible wrong, I will have to pay a hefty price.

When this is all over, I will have a lot of work to do. I'll have to wedge myself into this time and place and pretend to be twenty years younger. I'll have to let myself grieve the loss—hopefully, only the temporary loss—of my children. I'll have to come to terms with being married again despite spending years in therapy learning that I wasn't obligated to stay in a marriage that wasn't working for me. I'll stay married to Tristan as long as it's in the kids' best interest, but definitely not as long as the first time around.

It's a lot to face, but I think I can manage *if* this fireball magic results in the reversal of 9/11.

I've made sacrifices before for the greater good. I've sacrificed time with family to work overtime when needed, especially in recent years, when the COVID-19 pandemic forced every metropolitan hospital and many smaller clinics to their breaking points and beyond. Sacrifice is nothing new to me. Still, this one's going to ache for a long time.

If we can stop 9/11, it'll be worth it.

If we can't stop 9/11—I can't think about that. This *has* to work.

I roll my head from side to side, stretching my neck. I carry stress in my shoulders. Right now, they're tight as rubber bands about to snap. I reach up with my right hand and squeeze my left trapezius. It brings some relief.

Before I know what's happening, Ian's behind me. Fingers that were so gentle on the graph paper demonstrate their strength. They squeeze and press my knotted muscles. Both sides at the same time.

Despite how amazing it feels, I stiffen, unaccustomed to the touch of a man I've only recently met.

Ian's hands instantly leave my shoulders, and I miss their warmth.

"Sorry," he says behind me. "You looked like you were in pain. Want me to keep going?"

Maybe I shouldn't. I'm married, and no matter which way you look at it, a massage is a familiar touch. But it doesn't have to mean romantic things. I don't think Ian intends it that way. I think he's offering me support along with pain relief. Like a caring nurse.

"Yes, please," I say, and I accept what he offers in the spirit he offers it.

With Tristan, I always made little appreciative noises when he would massage me. Otherwise, the generous act would be short-lived. But I don't make any noises with Ian. It feels wrong. I am married, after all, in this time and place. Wonderfully, he doesn't seem to need the encouragement. He kneads my sore muscles like it's his job to work out the stress. Ian is nothing if not a hard worker.

"What you've been through," he says. "It's more than anyone should have to handle. I'm sorry."

A lump forms in my throat. "Thanks. I'm not sorry, though. Not if my being here helps stop 9/11."

The rooster clock ticks into the silence while I soak up Ian's support. I get lost in my thoughts, and I wonder what he's thinking after hearing the whole, unedited truth. No doubt, it's more than he bargained for.

"I'm sorry if you lose your job because of me."

His hands don't pause in their mission. "I'm not sorry. Don't worry about me. I'll be fine."

"Yes," I agree. "You will be."

"So, in the future, I'm some bigwig journalist, huh?"

"And author, yes," I confirm. "You're a household name."

"Because of what's supposed to happen tomorrow."

It's not a question, but I answer anyway. "Yes. Because of tomorrow."

I expect the conversation to turn toward the Pulitzers I mentioned earlier. Instead, he says, "Twenty years from now, that makes me forty-six. Is my hair gray?"

I smile. "Salt and pepper at the temples."

"Hm. I don't know how I feel about that." He sounds displeased.

"Don't knock it. It's a good look on you." He's handsome now, in a lanky, bookish way. But he'll fill out with muscle, and his features will mature to make him downright hot as a middle-aged man.

"Do I switch to contacts?" He digs into a particularly tight spot, and I melt under his touch.

"*Mmmmm.*" I have to focus to remember the question. Ah, yes. Contacts. "No. Tortoiseshell all the way." In every image I've ever seen of Ian, he's wearing his trademark glasses. The style might change slightly, but the frames are always some variation of marbled black and umber.

"If you'd said yes to contacts, I would have scrubbed this whole thing. I can't wear them. I have astigmatism." From the amusement in his tone, I gather that at this point, wild horses couldn't drag him away from our shared goal.

For a few minutes, we listen to the refrigerator hum and to Mrs. Greenberg's heels as she paces in another room of the first floor. Her voice is an alto murmur, present but undecipherable.

I wonder who she's talking to, if it's Socks still, or someone else. I wonder if she, too, wouldn't let wild horses drag her from this endeavor. From everything I've witnessed, she was all too happy to hang up her gardening gloves and come out of retirement for a day. I hope I'm not wrong. I hope she's our ticket to stopping what's coming.

Ian breaks into my thoughts. "Earlier you told me Bush will go two terms. You also suggested there are things I wouldn't want to know about The White House. Of course, that only makes me more curious. Spill it. Who moves into the Oval Office after Gee-Dub? Consider the information payment for the massage."

"You're evil. I thought this was for free."

"I'm a capitalist." He keeps kneading, and I'm too content to refuse him. Much.

"You wouldn't believe it if I told you everything. But I will say that we get our first black president."

"After Bush?"

I nod, enjoying how he attacks the worst spots until they begin to unwind.

"Hm. Who could it be? Al Sharpton?"

"I knew you would do this," I say with a smile.

"Do what?"

"Try to figure things out. It's who you are."

"So, it's not Al Sharpton?"

"It's someone you probably haven't heard of. And maybe it won't even happen. If we stop 9/11, that will change everything."

His hands still, as if the weight of that statement hits him as hard as it hits me.

"Well, I hope we still get a black president," Ian says, getting back to work. "Any women in the Oval Office in the next twenty years?"

"Sadly, still no Madam President," I confirm. "But in 2021, we'll see our first female veep. At least, that's what happened in *my* 2021."

"I was hoping we'd evolve faster than that." He sounds genuinely annoyed. "Why does progress have to be so bloody slow?"

If I weren't already a puddle of relaxation in Mrs. Greenberg's kitchen chair, I would totally swoon for this man.

At that moment, Mrs. Greenberg strides into the kitchen and sets her flip phone in the center of the table.

"Break's over," she says, and Ian and I snap to attention.

*On the one side are those who say that the
CIA missed obvious warning signs. On
the other are those who argue that it is
notoriously difficult to identity threats in
advance, and that the CIA did everything
they reasonably could.*

—Matthew Syed, BBC News

CHAPTER 17

Ian

TWENTY-FOUR HOURS AGO, if you told me I would
abandon my duties at the *Post* in favor of conducting
counterterrorism activities at the behest of a tipster, I
would have laughed out loud. Yet here I am, packing up
the polygraph and waiting with Lydia and my aunt for a
phone call from the Director of the CIA.

A few minutes ago, Marge returned to our workstation
in the kitchen and let us know her mysterious friend,
"Socks," had pulled some strings for us. On speaker
phone, his voice had sounded oddly familiar, reminding
me of Dana Carvey's *Saturday Night Live* impression of
President Bush the First. It occurred to me that it might
not be an impersonation. Bush the First *was* Director of
the CIA for a brief year while Marge worked there. It's
possible they met. But could they have become friends

close enough to be on a nickname basis and to have shared their personal phone numbers? The possibility of a former president calling my aunt *"M"* is too wild for me to process, so I don't try.

I'm still trying to come to terms with the fact that I believe Lydia's warning about tomorrow. I don't pretend to understand the science or magic or whatever it is behind the transference of her future consciousness into her present body, but I do know that Lydia sincerely believes it to be the result of a wish she made on a massive shooting star.

If it weren't for my truth sense, and the confirmation of not only my aunt's gift, but the polygraph, as well, I wouldn't believe something like this could be possible. But the evidence has been piling up all morning. Both science and intuition have validated it: Lydia has lived twenty years into the future.

She's not lying. I know it. Marge knows it, and the printout I carefully folded and slipped inside my messenger bag offers as much documentation as is humanly possible, considering there's no such thing as one hundred percent in the world of lie detection. On top of that, I have her on tape discussing Bush Junior's whereabouts tomorrow morning. No one's supposed to know *when* the President goes out of town, let alone where he'll be. It's a whole security thing. Presuming she's right, once again, Lydia knows the impossible.

As soon as I fully accepted her story, all the inconsistencies around her resolved. She's a newlywed but can't stand the sound of her married name. The paradox makes sense if, in her mind, she's been divorced for a year. Her legal residence is in Brooklyn, but she has to read her address off her ID.

That makes sense if she hasn't lived there in twenty years. She makes casual reference to a Nicolas Cage movie I've never heard of, even though I'm a fan. That makes sense if she saw it in the theater, along with millions of others, when it became an entry in the pop-culture encyclopedia. She speaks like she's worked in a hospital for years, but she's only just enrolled in nursing school. That makes sense if her consciousness has somehow reversed through space and time to unite with her younger self.

She knows specifics about tomorrow and uses the future progressive verb tense when talking about the attack, not because she has overheard an al-Qaeda planning session, but because she was an actual witness to the events.

That sense of oddness I had while looking though her notes, while taking in her hand-drawn circles for each plane, her list of times and flight numbers, the hijacker names, the supporting documentation to show there was a warning, however vague, in an obscure article by some wannabe feature writer, it all makes sense now. Lydia's notes remind me of what my notes look like when I'm preparing to write a story.

She's got the Who, What, Where, When, and How all laid out, as if she painstakingly collected the bits of information from various sources and all that's left is to type it up and put an editor's stamp of approval on it. But she's not trying to describe an event that happened. She's trying to warn about an attack that is *about* to happen.

She knows about it because she was there. She lived it.

Her description of the World Trade Center on fire was so vivid I swear I could see the smoke churning into the sky. I felt the ground shake beneath my feet as the first tower collapsed, then the second. Her shock and fear arrowed into my chest, making it hard to breathe while I stood behind the camera.

On the flip-out monitor, her eyes were distant and unfocused. She wasn't looking off to one side, trying to make things up. She was remembering.

Earlier, I tried telling her all the reasons why an attack involving passenger jets could never happen. For the first time since meeting her, I truly believe all those reasons will be swept away like pieces off a chessboard. The stars will be aligned in al-Qaeda's favor, and, left unchecked, evil will win the day. In her mind, evil *did* win the day.

She saw it. She smelled the smoke in the air and tasted the concrete dust from the collapse of New York's iconic Trade Center Towers.

The echo of that day lives in her thousand-yard stare as she described what happened. The trauma of it lives on in the shaking of her hands as she sent her memory back to those terrifying moments, which for her, took place two decades in the past.

It's unprecedented. It's inexplicable. But the documentation is there on the polygraph printout. It's in the grim set of Marge's jaw as she listened to Lydia and *felt* the truth of every single thing that came out of her mouth. It's in my chest as I, too, sensed her sincerity and her naked desire to save lives and stop evil.

"We've been given a second chance. I am the warning."

I won't let that warning go unheard.

I'm good at sensing truth. But there's something I'm even better at: telling a story.

The only problem is this story is different from any I've told before. For one thing, it hasn't happened yet. For another, the audience isn't the general public. There will be a time for that, but not now. What we need now is to tell this story to people who can show their badges to get into airports and detain persons of interest. We need to tell it to people who are passionate about counterterrorism, people who understand the threat posed by this obscure extremist group the public is barely aware of. We need to tell it to those who have been angling for a piece of Bin Laden and who have been told by those above them that "terrorism is a non-topic," but who know on a gut level the threat is real and the topic is relevant.

With an immense sense of purpose, I put away Marge's equipment and head to the sitting room to make a call. When I pass the kitchen, I see the two women sitting at the table, gripping each other's hands. I hear Lydia say, "We can stop them from crashing planes into buildings tomorrow, but if we don't do it right, Bin Laden will find another group to do it next year." Her focus is intense, and it makes me imagine her in a busy hospital directing all that passion toward helping her patients. I bet she's an amazing nurse.

My aunt's sitting room is at the front of her house. Taking a seat on a plaid-patterned loveseat, I take out my phone and notebook. It's time to follow up with Morg. I dial his desk phone at the FBI and listen to the line ring. Instead of dwelling on how appealing Lydia is becoming to me, I let my gaze roam over the garden outside the picture window.

"Come on, bud. Pick up." This is the worst possible time for him to visit the snack machine. "Pick up. Pick up."

"What up, Holms?" Morg's cheerful voice comes through. Thank God.

"Hey. It's Ian."

"I know. Same caller ID as before." He sounds like he's munching on peanuts.

"Observant."

"That's me. I put the *Eye* in FBI."

I snort. "Listen, did you get a name for me? Who's interested in al-Qaeda in your neck of the woods?"

"Yeah, I got some info for ya." I hear him shift the phone and rustle some papers. "In my neck of the woods? Almost nobody cares about al-Qaeda. But I managed to track down Ahmad Safar. He's new to mid-level management, but he was an analyst in the nineties. He investigated the Trade Center bombing and the Cole—"

"The Trade Center bombing?" My heart pounds. Lydia's description of tomorrow is so fresh it takes me a moment to realize Morg's talking about the '93 incident.

"Yeeeaaah." He draws out the word, as if questioning my sanity. "You know, that terrorist attack in Manhattan." He states it like I'm an idiot for not remembering.

"Yeah. Of course. I was just—sorry. Go on. This—" I look at my hasty scrawl. "Safar, he investigated the, uh, Trade Center bombing and the Cole, you said?"

"I did say that. You okay, buddy?"

"Meh. Not enough sleep." It's true, but not the whole story. "So, he's here in D.C.?"

"Yep. Probably somewhere on the seventh floor right now. Want me to transfer you?"

"Nah. I'll take that number though." He reads it off to me, and I jot it in my notebook. "Great. Did you find anyone else?"

"I mean, Safar's CV shows he had a partner up until his promotion, someone named—" He pauses like he's referring to notes. "Manda Zimmerman, but she's not in D.C. anymore. Her CV shows she transferred to New York two years ago."

"Thanks, bud. I owe you one."

"Yeah, you do."

I'll have to call Safar soon, but first I need to figure out what Marge is planning—and what she can work out with Bennet. At least I have a name, someone in the FBI who, hopefully, understands the threat al-Qaeda poses. That's a start. At least we don't have all our eggs in one basket.

I check in with the kitchen crew. The fragrant scent of black tea fills the space that feels like a second home to me. Marge and Lydia each have a mug in front of them. They're poring over Lydia's notes. I'm familiar with the page they're on. It's the one describing what the hijackers have in their bags.

"Newton, Mass," Marge says, reading the page. She tilts her head to one side in consideration. "Not a big city. Wouldn't be too difficult to locate the group staying there."

Lydia shakes her head. "We'd lose the others. The teams will be checking in with each other right up until they board the planes, and maybe even after boarding. We don't want someone to fail to check in and alert the others that something's up. I don't know how these things work, but what I do know is that all nineteen of them will be accounted for at their flights. Wouldn't that be the best place to get them, to minimize tipping off the rest?"

"I understand your reasoning," Marge says. "But no operative worth her salt will let a suspected hijacker anywhere near a plane. The goal is to intercept them as early in the game as possible. If we can use the names you've listed here to locate them tonight, that's the safest bet. Then, if the operation goes south, we've still got another shot."

"Even if that means some of them get away or go underground or whatever?"

"We'll catch up with them, eventually. Hard to hide once the CIA knows about you." Marge's grin suggests she misses her former occupation.

"I've got a cross-agency contact if we need it," I chime in. "An FBI agent who investigated the Cole and '93 bombing in New York. He's here in D.C."

"Good," Lydia says.

"We won't need him," Marge says.

Lydia raises an eyebrow. "Lack of communication between the agencies is one of the reasons the attack was successful in my time." She flips to a different page in her notes and points at a line of her handwriting, as if to emphasize her point.

Marge lays her palm over the paper. "If there's an attack happening in seventeen hours, we're beyond the point where we can explain what needs to happen to a large team. We need precision and coordination among a small, dedicated group. The time for cross-agency communication has passed."

Lydia opens her mouth, but Marge's ringing phone forestalls whatever she was about to say.

Marge puts the call directly on speaker. And leans close to the phone. "Retired Special Skills Operative Margaret Greenberg speaking."

We all lean in, clustered at one end of the table, me standing behind the two women.

"Hello. This is Anne Wallingford, assistant to Director Bennet." A woman's brisk voice gets right to the point. "I have Director Bennet standing by. Are you ready?"

"We are."

"I'll transfer you now." There's silence, then hold music.

Well, I'll be darned. Socks came through for us. How long will his endorsement buy us with the top brass at Langley? Three minutes? Thirty seconds? Will the Director think we're nuts?

My mind runs back over Lydia and Marge's conversation about last week's meeting at The White House. According to Lydia, Bennet and his counterterrorism head, Peck, flat-out asked for more resources to address al-Qaeda, and the response sounds like it left a lot to be desired. Bennet's probably still feeling frustration over that. If he begins to dismiss us, we should play to the strained dynamic between his counterterrorism team and The White House.

I shift from foot to foot, waiting, wondering if Lydia is as gob smacked as I am, knowing we're about to have a conversation with the most important man in our country's intelligence sector. If so, she doesn't look it. She grips her legal pad and has a laser focus trained on the little phone.

Marge doesn't appear nervous, either. She sips her tea as the foot of her crossed leg bobs from side to side.

The hold music stops. So does my heart, momentarily.

"Bennet here." The little speaker distorts the gruff voice I've heard from time to time in the occasional news bite, making it sound smaller and world-weary. Or perhaps that's the nature of the job, of continually asking for resources and being denied because what you're fighting for is a "non-topic." "Am I talking to—" There's a pause as if he's referring to notes. "Special Skills Operative Margaret Greenberg?"

"*Retired* Special Skills Operative," Marge says. "But as of ninety minutes ago, I've come out of retirement. Thank you for calling, sir."

Bennet grunts. "You have friends in high places." He sounds like he's spread thin and making this call somewhat reluctantly.

"One particular friend, anyway," she replies. "It's a testament to one's character when bonds formed in the trenches are honored on the mountain tops."

"Don't I know it," is Bennet's response. "All right. What's this I hear about an imminent al-Qaeda threat?"

"I believe the phrase you used in last week's meeting was 'imminent and spectacular,'" Marge says. "It will be both of those things, sir, unless you take immediate action."

"Last week's meeting? How do you know about that?"

"The same way I know about the plot that nineteen al-Qaeda operatives will carry out tomorrow morning, here on our soil, if you do nothing."

"Tomorrow morning? Where the hell are you getting this information?"

"You're not going to like the answer to that, sir," is Marge's response.

"I'll be the judge of that. Out with it. How the hell did a retired agent learn about a supposed al-Qaeda threat when my team's scratching their heads because Bin Laden's network has suddenly gone silent?"

Marge looks to Lydia, who whispers, "The worst kind of silence."

Marge nods grimly. To Bennet, she says, "Calm before the storm. When the intel dries up, it's time to put on your rain slicker."

"Don't beat around the bush. What do you know? No. First tell me how you gathered this intelligence when you've returned to the civilian sector."

"Do you know about the SCANATE Project?" Marge says. "You may be more familiar with its more modern name, Stargate."

A heavy sigh precedes Bennet's answer. "You're talking about that remote viewing project terminated in the seventies. Yeah, I know it."

"It wasn't terminated. It just changed into something else. You're right that SCANATE began in the seventies with the study of psychic remote viewing by coordinate, but it grew into much more than that. When funding shifted from the CIA to the military sector, its focus expanded into every area of extrasensory phenomena. Psychometry, psychokinesis, mind reading, precognitive ability. Lie Detection. The program sought to weaponize the special talents of a rare few."

"With inconclusive results," Bennet says shortly.

"In most cases, yes. But there were a few shining suns in the Stargate galaxy. Ingo Swan, Joseph McMoneagle, Uri Gellar. Me. I take it you have my file in front of you right now."

There's a pause. "More than 150 interviews between '71 and '85," Bennet says, apparently reading from my aunt's records. "Resulting in the successful prosecution of twelve active Soviet Spies. You're telling me your methods were more than just polygraphs and truth serum injections?"

Marge scoffs. "I never used injections. Didn't need them. But, yes. That's what I'm telling you. I have the innate, extrasensory ability to read people and detect the truth, and, sir, those types of skills don't disappear just because you reach sixty-five."

I stare down at the top of Marge's head. She's rarely spoken to me of her unique talent. I didn't know it extended to "reading people." I wonder if I've got a bit of that, too. There have been many times I've dismissed a potential source or paid more attention to a particular witness based on gut instincts, often before discussing the story at hand. Sometimes a mere introduction is enough for me to get a feel for whether someone has genuine observations for me or whether their motives or judgment are suspect. It's why I wasn't able to walk away from Lydia. My ears also perk up at hints I'm getting about her history in the CIA. I want to hear more about these interviews Bennet mentioned, about SCANATE and Stargate, but this isn't the time.

Another heavy sigh crackles over the speaker. "Get to the point, please." He's not a believer. But he's indulging Marge because of his frustration over al-Qaeda. I don't know if I'm "reading him" or if the same assumption would be clear to anyone listening in on this call. I can only hope Marge senses it too and steers the conversation accordingly.

"The point is this," my aunt says with lifted chin. "I'm currently sitting in my kitchen with my nephew, Ian Greenberg, who is a reporter for *The Washington Post,* and a civilian named Lydia Clay, who sought him out this morning with a dire warning. Her claim? Tomorrow morning, nineteen al-Qaeda terrorists plan to hijack four passenger jets originating from Logan, Dulles, and Newark airports with the intent to crash them into the World Trade Center towers, The Pentagon, and The White House."

Silence reigns.

I meet Lydia's eyes. Her hands are in fists on the tabletop.

I give her a nod, which I hope conveys the message that Marge has this under control.

The tension around her eyes relaxes a fraction.

The silence stretches into several seconds. I hope it means that Bennet is considering whether Lydia's warning might mesh with the "imminent and spectacular" event he, himself, brought up in last week's meeting.

Bennet speaks at last. "I don't care how big a bomb a hijacker has strapped to his chest. No airline pilot under any amount of duress will fly a plane into a building. Frankly, Ms. Greenberg, you're wasting my—"

"You're absolutely correct, sir," Marge interrupts. She pauses for the length of two heartbeats. "You see, what makes this attack so spectacular is that nothing like it has ever been attempted before. Never before has a terrorist organization coordinated a multi-pronged hijacking involving more than one passenger jet in the air at the same time." She ticks off a finger, then another. "Never before has the goal of the hijacking been death and destruction in the complete absence of negotiation." A third finger joins the first two. "Finally, sir, never before have the hijackers sat behind the controls in the cockpits and actually flown the planes." Her final statement is dropped like a nuclear warhead.

I hold my breath.

Lydia's eyes are saucers.

Marge holds her head high. Her eyes are doing that hawk-like thing where you don't dare argue with her, not if you value your life.

Quietly, deliberately, Bennet speaks. "Let me get this straight. You're saying that a civilian approached you with a concern that an al-Qaeda group is planning—tomorrow morning—to hijack multiple planes from multiple U.S. airports, at the same time, take control of the cockpits, and fly them into buildings. This is what you're telling me?" With each phrase, his incredulity builds until it reaches almost comical proportions.

"That is what I'm telling you, sir," Marge confirms. "And you'll find it much easier to believe if you restate the scenario sans sarcasm. If you'll indulge me, I'll do it for you: Tomorrow morning, nineteen al-Qaeda terrorists plan to hijack four passenger jets from three U.S. airports and fly them into the World Trade Center towers, The Pentagon, and The White House. Their intent is to take as many lives as possible, to cause as much damage as possible, and to prove to us that they are a formidable threat. And sir, their plan is so simple, so low-tech, and so outlandish that it might just succeed."

Lydia sits taller. Her brow furrows. She's no doubt about to interject that the plan will succeed—that she saw it succeed, but Marge holds up a cautionary finger. Lips pressed in a reluctant line, Lydia holds her tongue.

"In case I'm not being clear, sir, I am recommending to the director of the CIA that all agencies be put on Readiness Alert for an Air Defense Emergency on the Eastern Seaboard."

There is silence from Bennet's end.

At last, he says, "You're a former agent. I have to assume you know what you've just done."

"Of course, I do," Marge snaps. "In case the file in front of you hasn't convinced you, this isn't my first rodeo."

"And as a former agent," Bennet continues. "You understand there are penalties for fraudulent claims about our nation's security." The statement carries a dark warning.

Marge's spine stiffens. She lifts her chin. "In my forty-two years as a special-skills operative, never once did I initiate an official investigation into a subject that didn't eventually come to trial. In fact, sir, you'll see in my record I discontinued as many investigations as I launched. I've never been one to put notches in my bedpost. I'm not, nor have I ever been, interested in climbing ladders. All that has ever interested me is the truth and the defense of our homeland. I go on record here and now. Nineteen al-Qaeda operatives require immediate, emergency, multi-agency investigation. Every other iron you have in the fire needs to go on hold for the next twenty-four hours. I will personally take the fall if the investigation proves unfruitful."

Lydia gapes at Marge. I do too. My aunt has just laid her reputation, and possibly her freedom, on the line for Lydia.

I hear nothing from Bennet's end of the call, but I entertain a visual of him pinching the bridge of his nose, glasses dangling from his other hand, as he weighs the pros and cons of launching an operation based on the assessment of a former agent.

The major con, I assume, would be wasting a lot of money and risking "crying wolf." If The White House refused to take al-Qaeda seriously before, they never will if Bennet launches an operation that turns out to be baseless. The major pro, besides saving thousands of lives? Kicking al-Qaeda's ass and forcing The White House to admit they didn't take Bennet's warnings seriously enough.

I cross my fingers that the possible thrill of vindication outweighs the potential for embarrassment.

"Nineteen," is what comes from the speaker. It's a statement laced with skepticism.

I don't blame Bennet. I had the same question when Lydia first told me about the would-be hijackers. Skepticism is a healthy place to start, especially when one's gut instinct is to believe the unbelievable.

Is that Bennet's gut instinct? Am I sensing all this as part of my gift, or am I reading my own journey with Lydia into Bennet's reactions? Do gifts like these work over the phone? I'll have so many questions for Marge when this is over.

"Nineteen," Marge confirms.

"And that number is based on?"

"Five hijackers on American Flight 11 departing from Logan," is the answer, but it's not Marge who speaks up. It's Lydia, reading from her notepad. "Five on United Flight 175, also departing from Logan. Five on American Flight 77 out of Dulles, and four on United 93 out of Newark."

Marge swings her gaze to Lydia. There's a warning there, but also cautious trust.

"This is our civilian, I presume," Bennet says.

"Lydia Clay," Lydia says. "Yes, I'm the one who contacted Ian with what I know."

"Ah. The reporter," Bennet says with disdain. I'm so used to that reaction I hardly notice it anymore. "The obvious question is how a civilian can possibly know something this specific about al-Qaeda when my team hasn't heard so much as a whisper of what you're talking about." His tone rises at the end. He's agitated.

Lydia starts to respond, but Marge holds up a hand to forestall her.

"I've known Ms. Clay for a grand total of two hours," Marge says. "And in that time, she has demonstrated more accuracy, more specificity in her details, and more humility about her talent than all the subjects of Stargate combined."

"Yourself included?" Bennet asks.

"Myself included," Marge states.

Interesting. Lydia made no claim of clairvoyance or any other extrasensory skill, but Marge is lumping her in with her cohort. Maybe that's the easiest way to explain what happened to Lydia. Acquiring twenty years' worth of memories overnight is certainly beyond the scope of the ordinary. I just hope Bennet has an open mind.

"So, this is based on some frou-frou telepathy or ESP or some crap?" I hear a sharp sound at Bennet's end, and I picture him closing Marge's file and smacking it against his desk in disgust. "You expect me to sell that to the National Security

Advisor? To The White House? Ask for authorization for an emergency investigation because of a civilian who thinks she's Harry Houdini?"

Okay, so, not open-minded. Clearly, he places all individuals with extrasensory talents on the same level as magicians. He thinks Lydia is some kind of publicity-hound entertainer capitalizing on people's appetite for the strange. Whether or not Marge can read Bennet, whether or not I can, it's clear we're losing him, and we're not likely to do any better with the FBI, considering Marge doesn't have a long-standing employee record with them.

I have to do something, and fast.

"'Terrorist Plot to Bring Down World Trade Center Towers Foiled by CIA Director Bennet.'" I recite a possible headline for tomorrow's front pages, followed by another. *"'Eve of Destruction: CIA Stops Major Terror Attack with Only Hours to Spare.'* Or how about this one? *'White House Targeted by al-Qaeda, Saved by Bennet despite Denying CIA Resources to Fight Terrorism.'* Sounds better than the alternative, doesn't it? *'Tipster Dismissed by Bennet Day before Horrific Attack.' 'CIA Director Ignored Warning, Thousands Perish.'*

"Last week, you told The White House al-Qaeda's planning something 'imminent and spectacular,'" I say. At the same time, I'm having an out-of-body experience where I can't believe I'm arguing with the Director of the CIA. "You were more right than you know. Ms. Clay has the specifics your team couldn't find, and they all point to tomorrow morning. The news headlines for the next several months depend on whether you take her seriously or not, so be very sure before you write her off as some 'frou-frou' fraud. At the very least, meet her in person before making that call."

259

You can't blame gravity for falling in love.

—Albert Einstein

CHAPTER 18

Lydia

I'm still in shock as Marge—she insisted I stop calling her Mrs. Greenberg—herds me and Ian into her Town Car. I can't believe Bennet agreed to meet with us. I thought he was going to hang up after Ian suggested ignoring us would lead to being blamed for tomorrow's attack. To my surprise, and, from his expression, Ian's as well, Bennet had calmed down and agreed to hear me out before labeling me as a "frou-frou fraud." The only catch was we had to wait until the regular workday wrapped up. We planned to meet at 7 p.m., and Bennet made sure we knew what an inconvenience it would be for him to stay late when he has to appear before Congress first thing in the morning.

I have to give it to Ian and his aunt. Without them, I never could have gotten to Bennet. I just hope he'll listen. To help my case, I insisted on finding some professional clothes to wear. Ian could use a little sprucing up too, since he looks like he slept in his corduroys and button-down shirt. So, to fill the two hours before the big meeting, we're being shuttled to the mall like a pair of teenagers by their mother.

Before long, Marge slows to a stop next to a sidewalk lined with fenced maple trees, cafés with outdoor seating, and high-end boutiques. A light drizzle has set in. Whether it's the rain or the late-afternoon hour, the street is largely deserted. We get out in front of a plate-glass window displaying a family of mannequins dressed for an autumn picnic in the Hamptons. I look down at my jeans, hoodie, and sneakers, and I instantly feel like a rat in a fancy dining room. At least there aren't many shoppers around to judge me.

"Ninety minutes," Marge hollers out the window. "Meet me right back here. I've got an errand to run."

Ian salutes, and she leaves us to fend for ourselves amidst the elite of Bethesda. "Food first, or clothes?" he asks.

"Clothes. Definitely clothes." Tristan wouldn't have been caught dead in this neighborhood in anything less than pressed trousers and polished loafers and with a smartly-dressed wife at his side. It's hard not to get pulled back into old patterns of shame when, at this point in my life, I was just learning how deeply his disapproval could cut.

"Come on." Messenger bag looped around his torso, Ian leads the way with a confidence that inspires me to hold my head high. He displays no fear of judgment as he strolls beside me. In fact, as he passes other shoppers, he nods and smiles. It must be nice to have a life partner like him, smart, caring, capable, and more interested in being a gentleman to the one by his side than appearing like one to strangers.

We stroll past a toy store, a shop filled with antique baby furniture, a seafood restaurant, a trendy bar, and a quaint Italian café. The scents of dinner preparations at the food establishments make my stomach rumble. Aside from a couple tortilla chips and a cookie at Marge's, I haven't had a decent meal since breakfast. But hunger I can ignore. I'm more interested in finding myself an outfit that will make me feel as confident as I need to be when I face Bennet.

"That Italian place looks good," Ian says. "What do you say we stop there on the way back?"

"Sure." My stomach does something unrelated to hunger as I agree to what feels oddly like a date with Ian. It swoops and dives, calling attention to the attraction I've been trying to ignore. Apparently, my stomach didn't get the memo that I'm married... And with that thought, a dull ache takes up residence in my chest.

My insides are an unholy mess.

Instead of dwelling on doomed crushes or what my life is going to look like after all this is over, I scan the marquees above the sidewalk for any kind of clothing store catering to both sexes. Most display only women's clothes in the windows.

Two blocks from where Marge let us out, I see a store with promise. The window doesn't have mannequins, but there's a poster of a man and a woman dressed in "boating-chic" standing on a windy dock. I peek at Ian to see what he thinks, but he's looking across the street at a narrow shop that seems to sell nothing but men's hats. He keeps walking, and I follow.

He must know where he's going. He lives around here, after all.

We round a corner and continue all the way around the back side of the last block before Ian says, "I must be the wrong demographic for this strip. I don't know. I think we'll have to split up. I saw that haberdashery back there. Maybe they can recommend a suit shop. You'll have no trouble, though. All these are places are for women."

"Oh. Um, I saw a place, I think. Across the street from the hat shop, on the side we were on."

"Great!" We complete the circuit around the block and find the shop with the windy-dock poster. Ian shades his eyes to look through the door.

I join him, peering through the huge window. On one side of the store, I spot an array of women's outfits ranging from casual to business ready. Beyond a series of artfully-arranged racks is a wall of shoes and accessories. The other side of the store is only partially visible, but the display of satiny ties in dignified prints beside a rack of men's dress shoes seems promising.

"This is perfect," he says. "Why didn't you say something before?"

I shrug. "I guess I was deferring to you."

"That sounds dangerous," he says with a grin. This man couldn't be more opposite from Tristan if he tried.

More swooping and diving ensue, followed by even more determination to ignore my body's erroneous signals.

Ian opens the door for me, and we go to opposite sides of the shop. If anything reinforces that it's 2001, it's the styles populating the racks and adorning the polished-mahogany, headless mannequins. The front of the shop on the ladies' side is dominated by flowy tops, sequined tanks, low-rise hundred-dollar jeans, and cropped hoodies bearing logos in rhinestones. Leopard-print cashmere tops and cropped jackets in army green with faux-fur lined hoods seem to be the go-to casual look for fall. Below-the-knee leather boots with pointy toes and even pointier heels make up the season's must-have footwear along with Uggs, strappy sandals, and metallic-toned platform heels.

Toward the middle of the space, I find more professional offerings. Sequin-studded cardigans are shown over sleek sheath dresses. A dress like that is a possibility for me, but I would prefer a less flashy cardigan. I notice one mannequin wearing tailored leather slacks lacking several critical inches of sub-navel material paired with a split-hem collared shirt and a jacket so snuggly fitted it cannot possibly be closed in the front. I cringe at the triangular expanse of wood-grained lower-abdomen revealed. No way, Jose. I keep looking.

Generous expanses of wide-plank hard wood stretch between the racks and wall displays, the spacious boutique a stark contrast from the bargain stores, crowded with goods and people, where I used to scour for deals when Tristan and I were first married. Under other circumstances, I would enjoy the experience of shopping here, if not the impending jump in my credit card balance. But at the moment, I'm focused solely on acquiring an outfit I could wear to an interview for an office job, which probably shouldn't have sequins and most definitely should *not* expose my midriff.

It takes a while, but on a clearance rack under a large transom window at the back of the shop, I find a gray pencil skirt with a subtle plaid pattern. The slit up the back to allow for movement terminates just a few tasteful inches above the knee. The best part? It's my size—at least the size I am right now. A black cashmere turtleneck priced at $120 should pair nicely with the gray. To be safe, I grab the top in two sizes before searching for dressing rooms.

A recessed area between the ladies' and men's sides of the shop calls to mind a walk-in closet in a renovated mansion. Thick timbers lacquered in white frame the dressing room stalls. There are four in total, one pair facing another pair across a sitting space with a loveseat, end tables, and a wool rug with a thick pile. Through an opening, I see the men's side. Ian isn't immediately visible. I hope he's finding some good stuff.

I jiggle a dressing room door handle, but it's locked. Looks like I'll have to find an employee. The women's side is completely deserted, so I head off in the direction of the men's department. That's when I spot Ian. It's not hard. He towers over the clothing racks and stands head and shoulders above the two shopgirls assisting him.

"Definitely not," one girl is saying. "They'll be too snug. You need something roomier."

"But they're the only pair we have long enough for him." The other girl has several pairs of slacks draped over her arm, as if she's been pulling every possible candidate for him to try.

"That's all right," Ian says. "I'll squeeze in. I'll tell everyone it's a European cut. They like their pants tight, don't they?"

The shopgirls titter, and Ian blinks in surprise. He hasn't yet discovered that he's incredibly charming. His obliviousness makes him all the more alluring. To the shopgirls, that is.

I lean on the doorjamb, watching with amusement. Ian politely tests between his long fingers the sleeve of each Oxford shirt Shopgirl One presents. When Shopgirl Two displays a pair of leather loafers over her forearm, he inspects the interiors and shakes his head.

"Too small. I'm a thirteen."

I watch the shopgirls giggle together by the shoe display, and I can guess what has them blushing and whispering behind their hands. They're speculating about what other parts of Ian's anatomy might be freakishly oversized.

While the shopgirls are occupied with locating items to fit Ian's larger-than-average frame, I wend through the displays until I'm at his side.

"You're having all the fun, aren't you?" I try for a teasing tone and hope he doesn't catch the heat of jealousy burning through my comment. It's completely inappropriate. Our association is strictly professional and will be over as soon as we thwart al-Qaeda's plan. Not to mention, I'm freaking *married.*

Ugh. I don't want to think about Tristan right now. He's probably left a hundred furious voicemails on my Nokia since our brief exchange before my flight. I'll cross that bridge when I get to it. Or maybe I'll just jump off.

Ian's eyes crinkle with warmth when he sees me. "Not," he quips. "Unless it's a big-and-tall store, I usually have to special order. Places like this are hit or miss."

I can't help laughing at him. He's clueless about the subject of my teasing—the way the shopgirls are fawning over him.

"What?" Genuine confusion pleats his brow.

"Nothing."

The shopgirls come back with an array of ties and socks. Ian considers each option, approving or dismissing them in turn. I'm so amused by how attentive the shopgirls are to him while completely ignoring me that I forget to ask about a dressing room.

Heck, I'd fuss over him too, if he was in my shop.

Eventually one of the girls lets Ian know she's hung his favorites in a room. I follow the trio to the sitting-cum-changing area and finally get noticed when I hold up the outfit I picked out.

The skirt and smaller of the two turtlenecks are a perfect fit. I turn this way and that, admiring my reflection. I could get used to having this toned body again.

"Don't miss the belly pooch and stretch marks," I murmur to myself. As soon as the words leave my mouth, I want to take them back. Those body changes are precious. They are inseparable from my children. Holly and Christian.

Return them to me, I silently beg the universe. *Please.*

I emerge from the dressing room in my new outfit, feeling sober. I don't particularly want to hunt for a pair of matching shoes, but, barefoot, I head off in that direction out of necessity.

Ian is still busy behind his locked door. With no choice but to wait on me, one of the shopgirls follows me to the shoe area while the other approaches a new customer. I find my girl quite helpful when she shows me several options that would work with my outfit and brings them in different sizes. She even points out a small rack of sheer, silky stockings. I choose a thigh-high pair in the shade *barely-there*. Out of the package, they glide through my fingers with almost no friction whatsoever. I can't wait to try them on paired with the subdued black leather heels I chose. The toes are pointy enough to take an eye out, but that's the style du jour. I might as well embrace it.

Ian is still trying on clothes when I emerge fully dressed and shod, so I take my time perusing a rack of jewelry. Tristan won't like me spending money we don't have when my jewelry box at home is overflowing with presents from him, but I can't resist a string of faux pearls that look striking against the black cashmere. Surprisingly, they're reasonably priced at $35.

In my dressing room, it takes me less than two minutes to drag on the stockings, slip into the shoes, and clasp the pearls around my neck. About the time I'm finishing up, I finally hear the door of Ian's dressing room.

I open my door and peer into the sitting area and nearly swallow my tongue. Ian's standing in front of a three-paneled mirror, fingers deftly tying a Windsor knot. Gone are his limp-collared shirt and rumpled, too-roomy corduroys. In their place, a lavender Oxford shirt hugs his pecs and shoulders, the fit snug and perfect. A navy tie makes a crisp line over his placket. Slim-fitting wool trousers make impossibly long columns of his legs. The hem rests an inch too high, kissing the top line of a pair of loafers made of leather that appears both supple and strong. The missing inch does nothing to mar the pleasing style, which correlates more closely with what I'm used to in 2021 than with the styles on display at this shop.

The new clothes strike a pleasing contrast with Ian's five-o'clock-plus-24-hours shadow. With his helmet-shaped curls slightly feathered around the base of his head and tortoiseshell glasses perched on his aquiline nose, he looks like a windswept Greek billionaire fresh off his yacht.

The only sign that the shirt isn't tailor made for him is the inch and a half of wrist I can see above each of his hands. He takes care of that by rolling the fabric to his elbows, completing the mogul-at-ease look.

Good Lord. Ian is a hottie.

I'm having warm, tingly feelings, and I need to shut them down, fast.

"How did I get changed faster than you?" I ask, lightly, as I join him in front of the mirrors. "I thought girls were supposed to take longer to get ready."

"I have more buttons." He grins and shifts his tie so I can see the referenced closures. With his head bent and his attention on me, those feelings I'm trying to ignore surge stronger.

"I have a zipper," I say stupidly, turning and pointing to the back closure of the skirt.

"Yeah, you do," he says in that way that was popular around this time. In the mirror, I catch him looking me up and down, and the light in his eyes is appreciative. "You look amazing. I'd listen to anything you have to say in that."

The cashmere is a thin weave, but suddenly, it feels stifling. I clear my throat. "As long as the outfit inspires Bennet to put on his listening ears, I'll be happy."

"He'd be crazy not to," Ian says confidently. "So? How do I look?" He does a turn, shoes plodding in a slow circle.

Once I see how the wool of his slacks hugs his glutes, I can't look away. I entertain an ill-advised fantasy of him doing *Buns of Steel* exercises in front of the TV.

"Um. You look good," I say.

"You sure?" He still has his back to the mirror, and I'm still staring at his glutes. "Feels tight."

"Can you sit without splitting the pants?" I ask.

He moves to the loveseat and demonstrates that he can, spreading his arms when the seams hold.

"Then everything's perfect," I say decisively.

"Perfect?" he says, rising from his seat and joining me before the mirror. "Did you just call me perfect?" He's flirting with me, and I like it.

"I called the clothes perfect," I say.

The salesgirl chooses that moment to check in with us. She strides into the common area, clucking her tongue.

"I knew these weren't your sizes." She makes a beeline for Ian and scrutinizes his outfit. Uninvited, her hands reach for his waistband and test the fit. I see red as she says, "You've got no room for movement whatsoever, and the length—shoot, this is the longest pair we have. You know what, though, I can call our shop in D.C. to see if they have any thirty-sixes." Without a glance my way, she charges off to solve the problem.

"Brandi disagrees with you," Ian says, a spark of humor in his gaze.

"Brandi can mind her own damn business," I bite out.

Ian chuckles. "You know what I think?" He doesn't wait for me to answer. "I think you like how I look in these clothes."

"*Pfft*. Do not."

He moves behind me so my reflection blocks his to the height of his Adam's apple. He's close enough the heat from him is making my back tingle. I want him to put his hands on my waist. I want him to touch me anyway, anyhow.

But he doesn't touch me. Instead, lips a breath away from my ear, he whispers, "Liar."

Ian

I LIKE TO THINK myself above acts of immense stupidity. Regarding this act, which I have found myself committing, I have only one defense: intellect is no match for the heart.

Regrettably, I have a crush on a married woman.

I'm so far removed from any sort of romantic involvement, having been focused solely on my career since uni, that I don't even know if *crush* is the right word, according to modern vernacular. Is it a *crush* when you admire someone for being strong, brave, honest, and so intriguing you can't shake them from your thoughts, even when you know you should? Is it a *crush* when you find every dip and curve of a person's body spellbinding? When the simple action of looking into their eyes causes a spark in your chest?

This is uncharted territory for me. In many ways. I've never had feelings for someone older than me before—and Lydia *is* older. In her mind, she is forty-three and mother to grown children. And though in her mind, she divorced her husband a year ago, the reality in this moment is that she is married. To complicate matters further, some circumstance beyond the normal laws of the universe has made it seem to her as though her life has been rewound by twenty years. *"This has to be the reason I was sent back,"* she said, but what will happen when all this is over?

After she's fulfilled her mission, she'll have a husband and a life to get back to. She'll be desperate to recreate her children, and I wish her every success in the endeavor, even if the thought of her being intimate with another man makes my stomach clench painfully. She'll go to nursing school. She'll begin her career. She'll live two decades over again, with all their ups and downs.

I wouldn't want to live the last twenty years of my life over again. Not for a million dollars. And my childhood was a relatively happy one. Experiences lived have a feeling of completion about them. "Do-overs" should not be possible.

But what if they were? What if, in this extraordinary case, they *are?*

Will Lydia choose to do anything differently on her second go around at life? Might one of those differences include leaving her husband earlier? Might one of them include dating a local-politics journalist?

It seems selfish to entertain such imaginings. These feelings I have for her, though they slay me, should be given no quarter. But there's enough remarkability, not just around her circumstances, but around Lydia, herself, to perpetuate the affection that grows for her in leaps and bounds every moment we're together. No matter how ill-advised my feelings, they originate someplace deep inside that exists independent from logic.

I am their hapless victim.

As we wait for our minestrone soup and plates of pasta, I should discuss the plan with her. We're less than an hour from meeting with Bennet. It will be our one shot at carrying out the mission she believes she's here to accomplish. Instead, I ask her to tell me about her children.

She beams sadly, sitting across a small, round table from me in the Italian café near where Marge dropped us off. "Christian is nineteen." A mother's pride shines in her eyes as she swipes a chunk of torn bread through a plate of oil and vinegar. "He's a freshman at Columbia. He plans to study law, like his father. He's athletic and driven—he's on a Lacrosse scholarship. He'll make something of himself." She nods confidently, but then her smile falls.

She eats her bread, sips her ice water. When her smile returns, it's forced. "Holly is a senior in high school. She insisted on moving to Nebraska with me when Mom died." She shakes her head. "She could have moved in with her father, finished out her high-school experience with the kids she grew up with, in the city she knows like the back of her hand. But she wouldn't hear of my returning to the farm alone."

She shakes her head ruefully. "As soon as I knew she was determined to move with me, I considered selling the farmhouse and staying put. I loved New Jersey. I loved working at Kindred. With COVID rampant, I was pulling extra shifts, working seven days a week. I was needed. It was a terrible time to leave. It made sense to sell the house. But I couldn't bring myself to do it.

"Like Mom with the farm, I couldn't bear the thought of letting it go. See, when Dad died, Mom could have sold the farmland and just kept the plot with the house. She would have made enough off the sale to live off of, but instead, she chose to rent it out to another family in the area. They work the land and manage everything, and Mom paid them their share, then kept the profit. The income wasn't huge, but it was enough to keep her afloat.

"With her gone too, now, I could sell the farm, house and all, and get a good chunk of money from it—it's good land and a beautiful house. But...it's *my* house. My family's legacy. It's where I grew up. I can't part with it."

Steaming plates of pasta dusted with Parmesan cheese arrive. We dig in, and I listen to her talk about the house, which, in her mind, she's just moved back to after a long time away. She tells me how being there is helping her grieve, how it feels right, how she had been looking forward to battling something she refers to as COVID in her new rural area.

"You've mentioned 'COVID' twice now. What's up with that?" I ask.

She blinks. "Oh. Yeah. So, starting in early 2020, there will be this new virus coming out of China. There's really been nothing like it in recent history." She motions with her fork as she describes a variant of "the Coronavirus" that responds to no existing vaccine, spreads more easily than the common flu, and which has a mortality rate a staggering thirty-times greater than the flu.

Already hardworking as a charge nurse in a busy New Jersey hospital, her hours doubled when COVID hit her area, and the hours remained brutal throughout 2020 and into 2021, when her mother passed away.

"I felt like I was abandoning my patients in New Jersey," she says, leaning back in her chair with a hand over her midsection. "But I'd just lost Mom, and, God, Ian, to be honest, I needed a break. A woman can only handle so many changes at once. The divorce, Christian graduating and going off to Columbia, Mom dying." She drains the last of the water in her glass. "I needed the change of pace. I should have insisted Holly stay in New Jersey, but I think I needed her, too."

Her eyes go distant and sad. The bill arrives, and she jerks out of her reverie. "How have I been talking this whole time? We haven't done anything to plan what we'll say to Bennet. Plus, I want to learn more about you," she adds with a shy smile.

"We'll just have to stay in touch when this is all over," I say.

"I'd like that."

So would I. Very much.

There had never been a situation where hijackers ever flew the plane, which created the biggest paradox for us on that day, trying to figure out what was going on— how could a hijacker force the pilot, either by holding a gun or a knife to his or her head, force them to fly into the building?

—Ben Sliney, national operations manager, FAA Command Center

CHAPTER 19

Lydia

EVEN FROM THE SECURITY GATE a quarter mile from the parking lot, the CIA building at Langley looks massive. I stare at the complex of six-story buildings as we're waved through the checkpoint. At least three Kindred Hospitals could fit inside with room to spare.

Marge picked me and Ian up after we finished dinner at the café in Bethesda. When we opened the doors of her car to climb in, the bakery-fresh scents of bread and pastries wafted out.

"You should always bring gifts when asking for favors," she explained, inclining her head toward the stacked trays of sandwiches and danishes, beside which Ian had taken a seat and buckled in. "At this time of day, anyone Bennet can wrangle into meeting with us will be much more inclined to listen if they're not mentally running though dinner options."

Ian's aunt is a smart lady.

She drives us through a second security gate, this one guarding a parking lot emptying itself of cars in a two-lane stream. I suppose these are worker bees heading home at day's end. We drive past the mass exodus, a lone car heading in the opposite direction, and I'm reminded of another two-lane stream. World Trade Center employees descending dark and smoky stairwells in a worried drove as firemen in heavy gear trickle upward one at a time.

If we are successful in our mission tonight, four hundred firemen, cops, and security personnel will have ordinary days tomorrow. They will live on, never knowing that in another reality, they perished on 9/11.

"There's *Kryptos,*" Ian says, pulling me out of my reflection. He's pointing out the backseat window. I follow the direction of his gaze and see a sculpture in a courtyard. It's maybe ten feet tall and looks like a sheet of metallic paper freshly pulled from a typewriter and lain on its side in the shape of the letter *S.*

"I remember when that was installed," Marge says. "Nineteen-ninety. Year before I retired."

"See the letters cut out from the copper?" Ian says. "The sculptor created a code and hid four messages in those letters. Three of them have been solved. No one's been able to decipher the fourth."

Maybe later, I'll find that interesting. At the moment, I'm too busy trying not to puke up the plate of manicotti turning to lead in my stomach. I can't stop thinking about how much is at stake and how ill-equipped I am for the task before me. From everyone else's perspective, I'm a civilian nursing student with zero government ties, zero knowledge about counterterrorism, and zero reasons for anyone to listen to me. In other words, I'm nobody.

I can't believe Bennet agreed to meet me.

When I first learned we would be granted guest passes to the CIA, I imagined striding into the building flanked by Ian and Marge, the three of us moving in slow motion with a bad-ass soundtrack playing behind us, like in the movies, but the reality is not as glamorous. Marge parks the car, and we load ourselves up with food and personal items.

Ian lugs his messenger bag, which is stuffed to the gills, and a large, square container of Starbucks coffee while Marge and I each carry flimsy trays of food covered in plastic wrap in addition to a purse for Marge and a messenger bag for me.

The tray I'm holding makes it hard to watch my footing. A few feet from the front door, I nearly twist my ankle when my heel sticks in a crack between walkway slabs. The strap of my bag skids down my arm to catch awkwardly in the crook of my elbow.

I bobble the tray and manage to keep the sandwiches from tumbling over the lip by nudging it up with a knee. The sound of fabric shredding accompanies a cool draft up my legs. The slit in my skirt has expanded by who knows how many inches—I can't turn around to check.

All I can do is try not to turn my back on anyone. If I do, they'll probably be able to tell I'm wearing thigh-highs.

Way to make a good first impression, Lyd.

"Whoa! I got it!" Ian comes to my rescue, launching out a hand to support my tray while somehow balancing his bag and box-o-coffee and managing to hold the door open for his aunt with one foot.

"Thanks. I'm not normally this clumsy." I recover my hold on the sandwiches and follow Marge into a lobby large enough to double as an aircraft hangar. Immediately upon entering, we're met with the iconic CIA emblem set into the floor and depicting an eagle, shield, and compass rose. I'm actually here. It's surreal. It's terrifying.

"Think nothing of it," Ian says with a wink that makes my chest hot. He strides across the emblem after his aunt, as though he's visited the CIA a dozen times. I know he hasn't. In the car, he confessed he's never been inside. I wish I had the kind of confidence that rolls off Ian in waves.

Feeling like an imposter, I follow, periodically checking behind me to make sure no one's staring at my ripped skirt.

"I should have had the deli double up the trays," Marge says, noticing my barely-contained sandwiches. Louder, to the guard manning the information desk, she says, "Little help, please."

It's another ten minutes before we and our offerings of food and refreshment are cleared by security. Each of us wears a lanyard with a badge bearing a grainy black-and-white headshot. Thankfully, a trolley cart is found for our trays. Ian pushes it to the elevator bay.

"I see why you chose cold sandwiches," I say to Marge. "It takes forever to get in here."

She watches the floor-numbers count down as a lone elevator car descends to the lobby. "Hopefully, the coffee will still be hot."

Eventually, our party of three reaches the conference room Bennet assigned for the meeting. After all the security checkpoints, metal detectors, grand lobbies, and long hallways, the room itself feels anticlimactic. I'd imagined a dimly-lit, high-tech space sporting multiple viewing monitors manned by smartly-dressed spies, like in the movies. But this is... just a third-floor conference room. It could be picked up and dropped right into Kindred Hospital, and no one would realize it came from a place as esteemed as the CIA headquarters.

The walls are the color of coffee with too much cream, and they're scuffed where the backs of chairs have rubbed away the semi-gloss. The lighting is provided by run-of-the-mill fluorescent tubes behind ceiling panels, and the table is an ordinary woodgrain. Stray pens and stains from waterglasses testify to the room's use that day, as do the chairs left askew, looking like they were abandoned in haste by the last people to use the space. The industrial-grade carpet shows signs of wear and could use a good vacuuming. Clearly, the room has not yet been visited by the housekeeping staff this evening.

At one end of the room, a pull-down screen is held open by a thumbtack through its metal handle. At the other end, a trolly cart, like the one with our sandwiches on it, holds a projector with a pink eraser under one foot to level it. A whiteboard on one of the long walls shows a hand-drawn flow-chart in dry-erase blue.

In front of the whiteboard, erasing the writing, is a portly man of average height dressed in a shirt and tie. I wonder if he's the owner of the suit jacket draped over the chair at the head of the table.

"Ah, you made it," the man says, noticing us. He finishes his task, then turns to greet us, unsmiling. "Former Agent Greenberg, I presume." He addresses Marge first.

"Director Bennet," she replies, holding out her hand for a shake, which he reciprocates. "We've never formally met. It's a pleasure."

I blink in surprise. I don't know what I was expecting the director of the CIA to look like, but this man, like the conference room, seems so very ordinary.

"Thank you for granting us access at this late hour," Marge continues. In her low heels, she's a good several inches taller than him, and she makes no effort to round her back or make herself appear smaller. Her posture is as impeccable and respectable as everything else about her. "I hope a light dinner makes up for the inconvenience." To Ian, she says, "See if there's a kitchen or restroom nearby. Find some paper towels and wipe down the table."

Ian locks the wheels of the trolly and hurries off to do his aunt's bidding.

I busy myself pushing in chairs to help tidy the room while Bennet and Marge become acquainted.

"Director Bennet, this is Lydia Clay, our informant." I stiffen at Marge's introduction, used to hearing the term "informant" in a negative connotation on TV.

Bennet's handshake is firm and brief. Up close, I can tell he's already worked a long day. Behind frameless glasses, his eyes are bloodshot, and his lids droop with weariness. "Ms. Clay," he says.

Ian returns with a wad of towels.

"And this is my nephew, Ian Greenberg," Marge says.

Ian freezes like a deer in the headlights.

Bennet reaches to shake his hand, and a look of panic flashes across Ian's face. I realize why when he shifts the wad of towels to his other hand. His palm is glistening with moisture from a tap somewhere on this floor when he shakes the Director's hand.

"Uh, sorry," Ian says as Bennet wipes his hand on his slacks.

"The reporter for the *Post,*" Bennet says, his tone dry. "In what capacity are you here?"

"Uh, as a character witness in support of Lydia—ah—Ms. Clay. You have my word; I'm not here in an official capacity. Anything said in this meeting is strictly off the record."

Bennet raises an eyebrow. He looks skeptical but says nothing.

A squeak in the hall makes us all look up. There's a man in a brown suit who nearly just passed the doorway. The squeak was the sound of his shoes on the tile as he applied the brakes.

"Here, you are," he says entering the room, but not before craning his neck to check the room number on the wall outside. He's balding, and what's left of his dirty-blond hair looks disheveled. A pocket protector peeks from his jacket. "Sorry I'm late."

"Colin," Bennet says. "Good, you're here. This is Retired Agent Greenberg, her nephew Ian Greenberg—*reporter* for the *Post*," he adds meaningfully, "and Ms. Clay, our informant." To us, he says, "This is Colin Peck, my CTC director. If it has to do with Bin Laden or al-Qaeda, Peck's the one with the data."

I recognize the man's name, if not his face. He was one of the CIA personnel at the meeting at The White House last week. In my research, I read that he and a scant few others in the CIA and FBI were extremely disappointed in The White House's lack of reaction when faced with the threat al-Qaeda posed. This man could be an ally. He wants to bring down Bin Laden, and I'm about to give him that chance.

"Did you get a hold of Peterson?" Bennet asks Peck. The name sounds familiar to me, but I don't remember why. Maybe Peterson is an associate of Peck's.

Peck shakes his head. "Already left for the day. But I was able to reach his aide. She's tracking him down. He should be here before long." Behind his hand, he adds for Bennet's benefit, "He's got as big a hard-on for UBL as the rest of us." He drops his hand and speaks to me. "So, is it true? You have intel on an attack that's supposed to happen tomorrow?"

"It's true," I say, pleased when Peck raises his eyebrows. He looks curious and interested, not derisive. He'll definitely be an ally. He wants to believe.

Bennet, I'm guessing, will be a tougher nut to crack. He reminds me of a worn-down pencil, spent and tired of the grind. I remind myself he's been relaying Peck's warnings to The White House, and they keep dismissing him. Clearly, he believes Bin Laden poses a significant threat, or he wouldn't be vouching for his CTC director over and over again. The question is whether he has enough spirit left to go out on a limb one more time.

Bennet is the one I have to convince. He's the one who can issue orders and launch an operation to stop the hijackers from boarding those planes. He's the one who can coordinate with the FBI to bring them to trial and begin putting practices into place to make sure no one else can pull off an attack like this in the future.

Will the Department of Homeland Security be a thing if we're successful? I hope so. I don't honestly know much about it other than it was developed after 9/11 for the purpose of centralizing information relating to the security and defense of our country. I imagine it being like a hub of information, and I wonder if tomorrow's attack would have a shot at happening if such a department existed today.

Bennet and Peck are standing by the pull-down screen, speaking quietly, but I overhear Bennet use the term "frou-frou" again.

I try not to let it bother me, remembering Marge's advice on the drive here.

"I'll do the talking," she told me while I rode shotgun and Ian sat in back. She explained what would likely happen and instructed me to remain quiet unless someone asks me a direct question. She warned that my testimony would be vigorously questioned. "Keep your chin up," she said. "It's their job to judge the validity of informants. Don't take it personally and stick to your guns."

I help Marge arrange the trays on the table and uncover them. Ian pulls a startling amount of equipment out of his bag, including a laptop and the video camera from Marge's basement. He begins hooking everything up.

While I help Marge, I run through everything she told me, trying to remember my orders, my mission. I'm nervous and insecure, way out of my element. But I can't let it show.

At last, Bennet clears his throat and indicates Marge should begin. With the exception of Ian, who remains by the projector cart, we all take seats clustered around Bennet, who sits at the end of the room nearest the door.

"Thank you, Director Bennet, Director Peck," Marge begins when we're all comfortable. "Please help yourselves." She gestures over the food. "My associates and I wouldn't dream of asking you to meet at this hour without providing refreshment."

Both men take a ham and swiss on a hoagie roll, leaving the row of roast beef subs and the tray of danishes untouched. I wonder if Marge expected a larger audience. Personally, I'm okay with just two. That's fewer people to scrutinize me and accuse me of being an attention-hound or some "frou-frou" magic act.

Okay, I might be letting Bennet's words get to me despite Marge's advice.

The men dig into their hoagies while Marge fills several foam cups with black coffee and places one before each of us. I gladly sip mine. It isn't fresh-from-the-brewer hot, but it's not unpalatably cool. Ian nears my side to grab a cup from his aunt and takes the opportunity to whisper, "You get this," in my ear.

His encouragement does more to buoy me than all Marge's instructions and assurances.

While the men eat, Marge summarizes how we met and says that the tape we have to present will explain what we're all doing here. "Roll the tape, Ian." She flicks off the lights in the room and takes a seat beside me.

"Aye, aye, Captain," Ian says, and he demonstrates his miraculous ability to get technology to work for him on the first try.

An image of me sitting at Marge's kitchen table is projected onto the screen. Through a pair of speakers the size of walkie-talkies connected with wires to Ian's laptop, Marge's voice can be heard saying, *"Recording now. You take the lead. I'll jump in when I see fit."* She's talking to Ian, and from her stance behind the camera, her voice is almost too quiet to be heard. I wait for Ian to adjust the volume on the speakers, but when he appears on camera and says, *"Ready?"* his voice is loud and clear. I remember he wore a mic and Marge didn't, not until she took over the interview.

I hear myself say, *"Bring it on,"* and I wince. I sound so incredibly, unforgivably young, and I look even younger on the screen, sitting next to Ian wearing a *T*-shirt, no makeup on my face, and my hair in a ponytail. I don't like being seen looking so casual when I'm trying to make a professional impression. At least I'm dressed appropriately now. I still don't have any makeup on, but I'm happy with my clothes, and I freshened my ponytail into a French braid with a tucked end before coming here tonight.

Mrs. Greenberg's hand comes into frame as she sets her phone in front of me. *"You still there?"* she says into the phone, her voice louder this time since she's closer to the boom mic.

"I'm listenin'."

"That's George," Marge says. She's looking at Bennet, who has scooted his chair to Peck's side of the table so he can watch the screen.

George? Does she mean Socks?

"He's the reason we're here." Bennet talks over my recorded voice as I ask who's on the phone.

"A friend," Mrs. Greenberg says through the speakers, and it dawns on me why Socks's voice had sounded vaguely familiar. He's someone she knew from the CIA, and he has the clout to contact the Director directly and convince him to stay at work late to listen to a nobody tipster. My eyes bug out of my head as I realize that just a few hours ago, I spoke with former President George H.W. Bush.

"I'll be asking you some questions," Ian's voice is saying through the speakers. On the screen, I can see the polygraph device, but the resolution isn't good enough to see the paper actually scrolling past the little wire-pens. All I can tell is that one of the pens moves a little while the others remain still.

In real life, Ian hands his aunt the folded printout, and she spreads it on the table where Bennet and Peck can refer to it.

On camera, Ian is saying, *"Answer as honestly as possible and try to sit as still as possible. Just relax and tell the truth."*

It's weird watching myself on camera, reliving the moments I laid it all on the line for Ian and his aunt, but I suppose Marge is right. This is probably the best way to communicate to Bennet and Peck what's going on.

Folding my hands on the table, I watch and listen and try not to be too hard on myself for seeming so young and naive on tape. I also try not to check in with Bennet and Peck. I don't want to see their expressions of disbelief. I don't think I could take it.

"For the record, are you voluntarily submitting to this examination?" Ian.

"Yes." Me.

"Look at me or into the kitchen. Don't try to make sense of the readout. That's my job."

"Right."

"We'll start with something easy. Is your name Lydia Clay?"

"Yes. Well, not legally. Legally, right now, my name is Lydia Watercrest."

Ian makes a mark on the paper. *"I guess that one wasn't so easy, hm? How about this? What is today's date?"*

"September tenth, two thousand one."

I can't help myself. I look to Bennet and Peck and see them studying the printout.

"There. That was a good one. Look straight ahead," he reminds me when, on camera, I peer at the same strip of paper as it's receiving its markings. *"Did you telephone me this morning with a warning about an impending terrorist attack?"*

"Yes."

"If you have information about a terrorist attack, why did you call me and not, say, the FBI or some other agency?"

"I called you because you wrote about the scenario. You're 'the reporter who predicted 9/11.' If anyone could possibly believe the story I have to tell, it would be you."

"What do you mean, I'm 'the reporter who predicted 9/11?' 9/11 is tomorrow's date, is it not? To my knowledge, I haven't predicted anything. Please explain the phrase."

"You didn't predict the actual attack that will happen. But in your article, 'The New Face of Terrorism in the Twenty-First Century,' you describe a possible evolution in air terrorism that includes hijackers taking control of passenger jets. You're the first person to seriously consider the risk of airline pilots being forced from cockpits and hijackers being able to fly. Once in control, they could crash the planes or fly into populated areas. It would be easy if they had flight training, and your research showed that some al-Qaeda-affiliated Saudis were enrolled in U.S. flight schools on tourist visas."

"Jesus," Peck interjects.

"That it did," Ian says through the speakers. "You mentioned al-Qaeda. Do you have specific names of terrorists planning this attack?"

"Yes. I know several names. Hazmi—who I called Hamzi in my notes, but you caught that spelling error. He and Mihdhar are the ones we talked about today, but the ones who will pilot the planes are Atta, Shehhi, Hanjour, and Jarrah, with Atta being the leader of the group. There are *nineteen in all. Let's see. Some of the other names are Omari, Sherri—there's two of them. Two Hazmis and two Ghamdis as well. Those are the names I remember."*

On camera, I shift in my seat. I look nervous. But I sound confident. I'm actually kind of impressed with myself. I was on the spot with Ian asking those questions, but that didn't affect my recall, like it used to when I was a student. I see the student Lydia on screen, but the person I hear is the me that organizes nursing staff and coordinates with ER doctors, the grown-up me. The real me.

Ian's voice comes through the speakers. *"You told me this morning that nineteen terrorists would hijack four passenger jets departing from U.S. airports tomorrow morning. Is this true?"*

"Yes. It's true that I told you, and it's true that it will happen. Unless we can stop them."

"What do the hijackers plan to do with the planes once they take control of the cockpits?"

"Crash them into buildings. Both towers of the World Trade Center will be hit. The North tower first by American Flight 11 at 8:46 a.m. Then the South tower at 9:02 by United Flight 175. Sometime around 9:30, The Pentagon will be hit by American Flight 77, and around 10 a.m., United Flight 93 will crash into a field in Southern Pennsylvania. The target for that flight might have been The White House or maybe the Capitol Building. Some people thought it could be the CIA building at Langley."

"Is this for real?" Peck's voice can be heard over Ian's next question on the tape. "Where are we on the polygraph readout?"

Marge points at the strip and says, "Keep listening. You'll have a chance to ask questions at the end."

"*...To hear you talk about tomorrow,*" Ian goes on, "*one might think you've seen these things happen already. Why is that?*"

"*I have seen it happen. Every American has seen it. The whole World has seen it. It's 9/11, the worst attack ever on American soil.*"

It would be a mistake to redefine counter-terrorism as a task of dealing with 'cat-astrophic,' 'grand,' or 'super' terrorism, when in fact most of these labels do not represent most of the terrorism that the United States is likely to face or most of the costs that terrorism imposes on U.S. interests.

—Paul R. Pillar, 1999

CHAPTER 20

Ian

I'VE NEVER BEFORE HAD THE PRIVILEGE of seeing myself on tape with my gob hanging open in shock. It's...not attractive. I'm tempted to fast-forward the tape a few seconds, but I resist. The embarrassing moment passes soon enough.

On camera, on record with the polygraph, Lydia just dropped the "worst-attack-ever-on-American-soil bomb," and the truth behind the statement rocks me to my core now as much it did the first time.

Marge goes on to ask from her post behind the camera, *"Even worse than Pearl Harbor? Where two-thousand-plus perished beneath Japanese bombers and a thousand more were wounded?"* Maybe she asked because she wasn't sure Lydia knew how many had died at Pearl

Harbor. I know she didn't ask because she thought Lydia was lying. Both of us felt the truth in those moments.

"Twenty-four hundred died on December 7th, 1941," is Lydia's response. *"Tomorrow more than twenty-nine hundred will perish, including two hundred sixty-five passengers and crew of the four planes, four hundred first responders in New York, one hundred twenty-five Pentagon personnel, and more than two thousand people working at the Trade Center."*

The specificity of her numbers is telling in itself. But her tone, her posture, the polygraph, it all confirms that Lydia is telling the truth.

I'm familiar with the footage, having seen the interview firsthand. Instead of watching the screen, I study Bennet and Peck. The room is dark, but the light from the projector is enough for me to read their faces for hints about what they're thinking as they watch and refer to the printout. Already, I can tell Peck is inclined to believe. He's motivated, being the top brass in charge of the CTC. Bennet's harder to pin down. I think he's as eager to bring down al-Qaeda as anyone, but he's the one who has to answer for every action the CIA takes. He's the one who gets fired if things go pear-shaped.

Socks's voice can be heard next, distant and tinny, sound waves amplified through a phone, recorded by a camera, then amplified again through my speakers. *"Dear God. Marge, tell me this person is lying through her teeth."*

"I wish I could, Socks. I wish I could."

Bennet shoots a piercing look across the table at my aunt. He's evaluating her, running everything he knows about her through his mental filters, deciding if her endorsement of Lydia is worth his time.

"*I'm afraid I'm as lost as an Amish electrician.*" Socks. "*How does this woman know what will happen tomorrow?*"

"*How did I know every time a subject uttered a lie?*" Marge answers.

"*You were gifted.*"

"*Am gifted, Socks. I still got it.*" My aunt's personality shines on camera, even if she's out of frame. It comes through in her voice, the way she banters with a former President, the way she commands the interview, the way she so readily jumped into the murky fray with me and Lydia.

"*Is this person 'gifted,' too?*" Socks. "*Is that how she knows these supposed flight numbers and targets? What on God's green Earth does she mean by 'the whole World has seen it?' when it's supposed to be happening tomorrow? What am I missing, here?*"

"*You're not missing anything. I have yet to determine whether Ms. Clay is gifted. What I do know is my nephew verified information she related about two of tomorrow's hijackers. And not five minutes ago, I had a conversation with her about last week's meeting of the principles. You're the one who told me that was going down. That meeting hasn't been made public. This girl has no ties to the government. She would have no reason to know about it, but she's the one who brought it up.*"

I watch Bennet and Peck as they ping pong their attention from the screen to where my aunt sits real time. What is

Bennet making of the information Lydia was able to provide us about The White House meeting?

"There's also the Massoud assassination." That's me on the tape.

"What's this? Speak up, son. What assassination?" Socks.

"Guerilla leader in the anti-Taliban movement. Massoud. He was killed yesterday on a base that should have been a safe haven for him. Our government just learned of it this morning, but Lydia already knew."

Bennet swings his gaze my way. He looks none too pleased that I was able to confirm Massoud's assassination. I cross my fingers and hope the news has been made public by now so I'm not in a position to out Morg for giving me that super-secret software.

"Gave us solid intel in exchange for aid for his group," Socks was saying. *"He was in the top tier of possible fixes for al-Qaeda. Hang on."* I can't make out his muffled speech for a few seconds. Then, *"I'm having that verified. These are significant allegations, M. Multiple hijackings, assassinations? If there's even a speck of truth to any of it, we need to know how this Clay knows these things."*

"I'll get to the bottom of it. Ian. Thank you, but I'm taking over."

There's about thirty seconds of footage where my aunt takes my place and my mic.

"Ms. Clay, are you clairvoyant?"

"No."

"Psychic?"

"No."

"Mentally unstable?"

Lydia chuckles. *"No. Unless you ask my ex-husband."*

"When did you become divorced from your husband?"

Lydia shifts in her chair, clearly uncomfortable. *"Um, the papers were signed on July seventeenth, twenty-twenty."*

I remember that moment, when she said the date of her divorce was made final. The polygraph readings didn't budge. Realtime, Marge indicates the corresponding spot on the readout with a tap from her finger. I watch Bennet and Peck study the paper and exchange dark looks.

"By twenty-twenty, do you mean the year two thousand twenty?"

"Yes. I got divorced in the year twenty-twenty."

Bennet grumbles incoherently. He leans forward in his seat, expression stormy. Even with the evidence in front of him, we're stretching his suspension of disbelief too far. I have a feeling he's about to tell me to shut off the tape, but Marge speaks up.

"Just watch. Listen." Her quiet, urging tone causes him to relax back into his chair, if uncomfortably so.

"Yet you stated today's date as September tenth, two thousand one. Are you telling me you are married at this present time, and at some date in the future, you will become divorced from your husband?"

"Yes. That's what I'm telling you. But it's not some random date in the future. It's July seventeenth, twenty-twenty. I know the date because I've lived it. I've lived twenty years beyond this point in time, and somehow, I seem to have been sent back.

"I know in my heart the reason is to try and stop tomorrow's attack. Because, why today? The day before the worst attack ever on American soil?"

This time, when I listen to Lydia's story, it's without the filter of shock. This time, I'm able to process not only her words, but her feelings about that day, without distraction. This time, I hear the urgency in her tone, and I see the plea written all over her face. Its echo reverberates off the walls of my heart. There's no question in my mind—none—that she lived through exactly what she describes on the screen. I can't imagine anyone, gifted or not, failing to recognize the truth in what we're all hearing.

"When I lived through tomorrow, there were no warnings. The country—the whole World—was taken off guard. Two passenger jets crashed into the World Trade Center towers before anyone even realized we were under attack. At first people thought it was a Cessna that lost control, you know? Some accident. There were rumors circulating about a hijacked plane, American Flight 11, but no one knew if that was the plane that hit the North tower. From the ground, the hole looked small. The handful of witnesses who actually saw it happen gave different stories. 'It was a small plane.' 'It was a jet.' No one knew for sure. Then, twenty minutes later, the second plane hit the South tower.

"Every news outlet in New York got the second explosion on camera. The whole World realized, in that one horrible second, that the first crash was no accident. We were under attack. That's when the chaos erupted.

"All the agencies struggled to get a grip on what was happening. The FAA, NORAD, NEADS, the local flight towers and air traffic control centers, The White House—President Bush was at an elementary school in Sarasota. A Secret Service agent whispered the news of the first plane crash in the President's ear while he sat in a classroom full of second graders. The footage was shown later, over and over again. Every American witnessed the shock on his face as he was told we were under attack.

"It took almost an hour to confirm that the first crash was American Flight 11, and that the plane had been hijacked. Both towers were hit and two planes full of people vaporized in the explosions before a single fighter jet got airborne. We were slow to respond because NEADS had an exercise scheduled for that morning. Precious seconds were wasted confirming the attack was 'real-world,' not exercise."

On the screen, Lydia reaches for Marge's hand, and Marge lets the pen she's holding fall to the floor. My aunt looks as shellshocked on the screen as Bennet and Peck do sitting at the conference table.

I glance her way to find her, like me, watching the two men.

"We had no warning," Lydia says on screen. *"Not the first time. But someone somewhere—or the Universe, or the space-time-continuum, or a wormhole—whatever you want to call it, we've been given a second chance. This is the only warning we will get. I am the warning. You have to help me get this information to the right people. Please. This has to be the reason I was sent back. Help me save the ones who weren't supposed to die tomorrow."*

On screen, my aunt composes herself and resumes the interview. *"Please explain, to the best of your ability, what you experienced as 'being sent back,' as you call it. Take me through it. When did you first feel as though you were in a different time than you expected?"*

"This morning," Lydia answers. *"I woke up in the apartment Tristan and I had when we were first married. I thought I was dreaming, at first. Last night, I'd been in Nebraska, sitting on the porch with my daughter—Holly."* Lydia's smile is serene, motherly.

"We were talking about 9/11. She was born after it happened. For her generation, the attack is a chapter in their fifth-grade history book. It's hard for them to understand what it was like, to feel what we felt, those of us who lived through it.

"I was there, in Brooklyn. My apartment was on Spinney Hill. I had a perfect view across the bay. On a clear day, I could see the skyline. That day was clear as a bell. The sky was so blue that the smoke looked obscene as it extended the line of the Towers higher and higher. It was so black. And so thick. I kept going back and forth between my doorstep and the TV. I was watching on TV when the first tower collapsed.

"At first, it was hard to tell what was happening. I couldn't understand what I was seeing on the screen. Even Peter Jennings wasn't sure. One second, the smoke was going up into the sky, like water from an upside-down faucet. The next, it started going out in every direction. It billowed from between the buildings like this massive gray blob swallowing up Manhattan.

"On TV they said the South Tower collapsed, as in the whole building. Then they showed the closeup of it happening. The floors above the crash zone pancaked on top of each other, and then the building just folded in on itself and came down.

"My living-room floor shook, I think. Or maybe it was just me shaking. All I could think was, 'I hope everyone got out.' But they didn't. Firemen were still climbing the stairs. More than three hundred of them between the two towers. Plus Port Authority cops and other first responders. Trade Center workers were making their way down. Then there were the people trapped above the crash zone. All the stairwells but one in the South Tower were severed by the planes, so everyone above where they hit—" She shakes her head. Her image on the screen mesmerizes me. Her thousand-yard stare drives home that this is no act. She witnessed exactly what she's describing, and it affected her deeply. *"They had nowhere to go. Some went to the roof. They thought helicopters would come like in '93, but no one came. The smoke was too thick. No one wanted to risk landing on the buildings. They didn't know that time was running out. No one imagined the fires would burn so hot they would melt the steel supports and cause the building to collapse. More than two thousand civilians died while I watched on TV."*

"When I went outside again, all I could see was this huge smoke cloud with just one building rising above. The North Tower. Alone.

I'm lost in the dire portrait Lydia is painting. No longer am I concerned with the reactions of the other men. Instead, I'm letting the enormity of what she's saying wash over me. She witnessed, from not very far away, the two tallest buildings in North America collapse. With people inside. Her world, the one that has been rewound to this place and time, is a world that has witnessed this event along with her. What must that have been like? How did the media handle it? I imagine exclamations of inhumanity, like when the Hindenburg caught fire. An event like she's describing would have changed everything.

And now, this amazing woman is attempting to change it back.

"Tristan was there. He worked just blocks away. I was so worried. I tried calling him, but the phone lines were jammed. It was horrible—like the true meaning of horror. The shock and disbelief. The fear. Were there more planes coming? Was anyplace safe?

"Not long after, the North tower came down too, and there was this incredible sense of loss. It lasted for days, like the taste of concrete dust in the air. Every breath was a reminder. Every glance at the altered skyline caused a stabbing feeling in your stomach."

"Holly asked what it was like, living through it. She's asked before, but I never talked about it. Tristan didn't like us to talk about it. But Tristan isn't in my life anymore. So, last night, for the first time, I told her."

"Afterward, she went to bed, and I stayed on the porch, sipping wine, thinking about that day. All of a sudden, I saw a shooting star. I know how it sounds. I was drinking. I was lost in thought. I probably imagined it. But I didn't.

"Ever since I was a kid, I've been wishing on shooting stars. The first time was on that same porch with my grandfather. But the star last night, it wasn't any regular shooting star. It was a fireball. It was enormous—bigger than the moon in the sky—and so bright I could see the tassels on top of the cornstalks like in the middle of the afternoon.

"It was such a special shooting star that I made a special— an impossible—wish. I wished—I wished that 9/11 could be undone. I knew it couldn't possibly come true. You can't turn back time. There's no undoing the Titanic or Chernobyl or, I don't know—the Hindenburg.

"I didn't care about impossible. I made my wish with the same kind of faith I had as a kid. I finished my wine and went to bed expecting to wake up on September tenth, twenty twenty-one. In Taylor, Nebraska. I had plans. Meet my new boss at the hospital. Unpack moving boxes—the farmhouse belonged to my parents. I recently lost my mother and inherited the farm—" She gasps.

On the tape, I say, *"Lydia? You okay?"*

"Lydia, dear?" My aunt's expression on the screen is concerned. *"Please tell me where you went just now. What were you thinking about?"*

"My parents," she says, eyes distant. *"They're still alive right now."* She takes several breaths that make her chest heave. *"Dad died in 2016 from lung cancer, and Mom—"* She tucks her chin as she seems to swallow a lump in her throat. *"Died this year. I mean, in May 2021."* She looks at Marge, then toward the camera, where I'm standing. *"I could see them again. I could call them right now and talk to them. They're*

alive!" On the screen, her hands brace on the table, like she's about to stand.

"Would you like to stop the test?" It's me asking her that.

She blinks, then shakes her head. *"No."* A look of determination settles on her face. *"We have to talk about tomorrow. Please. Let's not waste any more time on me. Ask about the hijackers. That's where I can give you solid, actionable information."*

On screen, my aunt studies her, then leaves the table. She comes back with a glass of water for Lydia and tells me to pause the recording.

In the meeting room, I pause the playback and look to my aunt for further instruction.

She gets up and turns on the lights.

Lydia stands as well. Hiding her face, she says, "Excuse me, please," and she hurries from the room.

I don't think. I just give chase.

Lydia

SORROW, THICK LIKE syrup, coats my heart as I relive the moment on the tape when I realized I have a second chance to see my parents. And as I think about Christian and Holly. As I face a future where several thousand lives might be saved but where my own life may move forward looking unfamiliar and uncertain, possibly barren of my children's love.

I can't hold in the flood of sadness. It's all catching up with me, everything that's happened.

I run from the room, only allowing myself to release the building sob in my chest once the door shuts behind me. My insides twist with agony as tears blur my vision, my perfect vision that doesn't require glasses because I'm so damned young right now. I'm in the wrong body. This is all wrong, and I don't even know if what I'm trying to do here is going to work.

What if this is all for nothing?

My teary eyes spot a ladies' room just a few steps from the conference room. I plow through the door. A moment before it closes, I hear Ian's voice. My name is an echo in the hall. He sounds worried.

"I just need a minute," I call out as I throw myself into a stall. Sitting on a toilet, I give in to the urge to double over and weep.

After having Christian, I went through a period of postpartum depression. I'd felt so alone, so changed, so lost, for no reason other than my neurotransmitters were messed up. Tristan didn't understand. He offered no hope, only criticism. "You have to pull it together, Lyd. You're a mother now. You have to be the one to be up with him at nights. I can't afford not to sleep. I have to be sharp for court tomorrow."

I remember being on my hands and knees on the chipped tile of our tiny bathroom, pouring gut-deep wails into a bunched-up bath towel. Even in those dark moments, I tried to put Tristan first. I tried not to wake him with my depression.

I feel like that now, lost and alone, wracked with grief in a bathroom.

I don't have a towel to sob into, but my hand over my mouth holds back the worst of it.

I hear the main door to the restroom open. Marge must be coming to check on me.

"I'm okay," I lie. "I just need a minute."

"I call bullshit on that." It's not Marge who followed me in here. It's Ian.

The shock of being in a ladies' restroom with a man puts the brakes on my outburst. "What are you doing! Get out of here!"

"I'm pretty sure you're not actually going to the bathroom, and I'm also pretty sure we're the only ones in this part of the building. It's after seven, and the halls are dead quiet. Come on. Get out of that stall and tell me what's going on." His new loafers can be seen through the rectangle of space beneath the stall door. "Come on," he coaxes. His long fingers drape casually over the top of the door, not like he's trying to open it. More like he's trying to forge some kind of connection with me. "Tell Uncle Ian all about it."

I can't help it. I laugh. "Uncle Ian? I'm twenty years older than you!"

"Yeah, but I'm still taller."

I bunch up a wad of toilet paper and use it to dab at my face. At my sniffle, he speaks again.

"Seriously, Lydia. Is it your parents? That couldn't have been easy to hear. I'm sorry."

"It's okay." I unlatch the door and start to open it.

He takes over, swinging it wide and taking in my appearance. When he focuses in on my face, his eyes are full of compassion. "I'm sorry," he says again. "This has to be hell for you, being back here in the past when your life has moved beyond this point, knowing people you lost are back too, being without your children. I can't imagine what you're going through."

I sniff again. I probably look like a swollen, red-faced mess. "Thanks."

"Come here." He pulls me in and wraps his arms around me.

I stiffen at first. Then his warmth seeps into my skin, and I melt against his chest. Our height difference means that when I bury my face against his shirt, my ear is at the level of his heart. I hear it beating solidly, reassuringly.

The tears start again, but this time, they're silent.

He rubs gentle circles on my back while he tells me his aunt is answering Bennet and Peck's questions.

"Bennet doesn't believe, does he?" I tried not to look his way, but couldn't help myself a time or two. What I saw was not reassuring. He didn't quite roll his eyes at the part where my on-camera self talked about the towers falling, but his flattened lips and snarkily-cocked head reminded me of Tristan when I would offer explanations for why I was late or why I didn't answer his call or whatever the problem du jour happened to be. I always had good reasons, but he didn't see it that way. If he was inconvenienced, he assumed I'd done it with ill intent. That's what Bennet looked like, like he thought I was putting on an act in order to get out of trouble or gain attention. But why would anyone possibly lie or act or exaggerate something like this?

"I can't face questions right now," I admit. "I need a few minutes."

"Of course," he says. "I don't blame you. You're being put on the spot here when you're trying to process what any rational person would call a traumatic experience. We should probably be sending you to therapy to talk through your feelings, not demanding you relive your memories about tomorrow." He blinks. "Wow, that sounds really strange to say, but I've totally accepted it. You know that, right? That I believe you?"

I nod against him, enjoying his scent, which is woodsy while also reminding me of sipping coffee in a library. It's nice being held by Ian. More than nice.

At some point, my arms snake around his waist. I'm holding on to him as he comforts me, and it feels *right*.

"Do you want to go outside with me and give your parents a call?" he asks quietly.

I do. It blows my mind that I could actually *speak* with Mom and Dad right now. I could fly out to Nebraska and hug them both. But I can't afford that kind of distraction. Not yet. I have to pull myself together. I have to find a way to convince Bennet that the things I'm saying truly *did* happen. They will happen again if we do nothing.

"No." I squeeze Ian, then force myself to release him.

His arms fall to his sides, and he steps back from me. There's a question in his gaze. He wonders why I don't want to talk to my parents.

"I need to stay focused on the task at hand." I go to the sink and splash water on my face, then pat myself dry with paper towels. "I can do this," I tell Ian. Or maybe I'm telling my reflection. My eyes are red-rimmed and swollen. I run cold water on a wad of paper towels and press them to my eyes to ease the puffiness. "I have to do this, or it's all for nothing."

"Of course, you can do this," Ian says, and his tone is mildly annoyed, like he can't even fathom questioning my ability. He appears behind me in the mirror. He rests his hands on my shoulders. "I'm sure you've been through some tough situations as a nurse. Right? I mean, you did it for, what, almost twenty years? You said you were a trauma nurse, right? I bet you had to come up with all kinds of creative solutions to help save lives, or even just to improve the lives of the people in your care, and in a hurry, too. This is like that. We don't have much time to convince Bennet to work with us, but you'll rise to the occasion here just like you've done a thousand times in your line of work."

He's right. Generally, I'm a rule follower, but there have been times I've bent rules and pulled strings and cobbled together solutions to problems that, at first, seemed insurmountable.

"But why would Bennet even listen to me? I'm nobody. I don't belong in this building, in these clothes. In this body. At this point in time, I'm just a student. A naive newlywed who doesn't even know how to stand up for herself. How am I supposed to stand up for all those people who will suffer and die tomorrow?"

"Excuse me?" Ian sounds more than mildly annoyed now. His brow is furrowed, and his mouth is turned down. "Did you just call yourself *nobody*?" He doesn't wait for my answer. Turning me by my shoulders, he says, "Would *nobody* have called a journalist out of nowhere and demanded he meet with her that very day? Would *nobody* have fearlessly convinced him that the impossible is possible? Would *nobody* have been chosen by the universe for this mission?"

I blink. "Chosen?" I know I entertained the possibility before, but it just seems so far-fetched. Why would anyone choose *me* for something so important?

"Oh, I'm sorry," he says, voice thick with sarcasm. "I forgot, people get sent twenty years into the past all the time. I'm sure it's as common as seeing a rainbow...or a shooting star." He gives me a gentle shake. "What happened to the woman who phoned me this morning, the one who marched off immediately after meeting me, expecting me to follow? Where's the woman who reminded me that I believe in miracles?"

Where indeed? That Lydia seems to have faded into the background. The longer I'm here, the more I forget the woman I've become.

Could Ian be right? Was I chosen for this? Was my seeing that fireball intentional? Did some consciousness somewhere single me out to carry out this mission?

"Look how far we've come," Ian says, as if he can sense that my confidence is on the verge of rebuilding itself. "We're at the CIA. *You* have the attention of Director Bennet. Who else could have gotten this far under the circumstances?"

Ian is right. But we're not here just because of me. "You," I answer. "You could have gotten here. You did the research. You wrote that article. You have your aunt and all of her connections."

"No." He shakes his head decisively. "I was focused on my job. I had no reason to think anything out of the ordinary would happen today. Not without you making me believe it. This is all because of *you,* Lydia. Don't lose your confidence now, not when we're so close."

I'm not used to having someone believe in me. It feels amazing. Ian's encouragement flows over my skin and through my pores and lights a fire inside me.

When I realized what was happening this morning, I came up with the idea of contacting Ian, "the reporter who predicted 9/11." I practically bent over backwards to convince him to work with me. I wheeled and dealed, just like in the hospital when I need more resources for my department or when I advocate for a patient. I held Marge's hand at her kitchen table and poured out my heart to her until she agreed to help.

If I could bend a busy journalist and a former CIA agent to my will, I can do the same with Bennet. I'm a nurse, dammit. I can move mountains.

"Ian?"

"Yeah?"

"I really do need to go to the bathroom, now," I say with a grin. "Then, I'm going to go back in that room and make the suits listen to me."

"Atta girl." He chucks me under my chin before leaving the restroom.

I'm going to stop 9/11, and I'm not taking no for an answer.

*To do what nobody else will do, in a way
that nobody else can do, in spite of all
we go through ... that is what it is to be a
nurse.*

—Rawsi Williams

CHAPTER 21

Lydia

THERE ARE THREE NEW PEOPLE in the conference room when I return. Marge is pouring coffee and handing each of them a cup. Someone has found creamer and sugar. There must be a kitchen nearby.

Stepping into the room this time, I feel different. I feel like I belong here. If Ian is right, and I was chosen for this, then maybe I'm the only person who could possibly pull this off. Maybe the facts I researched about 9/11 by reading all those books has given me the exact tools needed to stop tomorrow's plan in its tracks.

A slender man not much taller than me talks with Peck across the table while he munches a danish. He's wearing a royal blue dress shirt and yellow tie that complements the caramel color of his skin. With his dark hair and aquiline nose, he looks like he could have some Middle-Eastern ancestry.

The other new arrivals are a woman in a rose-pink skirt-suit with her hair in a loose bun and a man with untidy, thinning hair who appears closer to my age than to Bennet's and Peck's. Trendy, rectangular glasses give him a look of refinement that clashes with his wind-blown look. The woman has large, pretty eyes that track Ian as he tinkers with the tech at the back of the room. A hot poker of jealousy jabs me in the stomach, but I do my best to ignore it.

The man with trendy glasses sits next to the girl in pink. He has a sandwich in his hand and a danish on his napkin. Like Bennet, he looks worn out from the day or from his job, maybe both.

"Are you all right, dear?" Marge tugs on my elbow, guiding me into a corner where we can't be overheard.

I nod. "I am, thank you." When I smile at her, it's not forced. I really do feel better. Ian's belief in me has made a world of difference. "I'd like to say a few words, if that's okay with you."

Her eyes widen. "Of course. But there are new arrivals. Allow me to introduce you."

"That's all right. I'll take care of it."

Marge looks at me like I've lost my mind. I realize she's never met the real Lydia.

"It'll be okay," I tell her. "I'm back."

She studies me for a moment, then inclines her head in acquiescence.

"Everyone," I say loud enough to call attention to myself. I'm standing at the head of the table, blocking the screen. "Everyone, take your seats, please. We have a lot to do and not a lot of time to do it in." I'm in charge-nurse mode, and I have lots of jobs to hand out. I need my staff to listen up and get to work, and I'm not afraid to assert myself.

Bennet, who had been talking on his cellphone in the far corner, does as told, and everyone already seated turns their heads my way.

Ian beams at me. He's the reason I'm finally feeling in my element.

And I really *am* in my element. I've led meetings of doctors, nurses, and support staff hundreds of times. I can totally do this.

"Thank you." I have the attention of everyone in the room. Even Marge and Ian have taken seats and watch me expectantly. "I'd like to thank Director Bennet for organizing this meeting tonight. Thank you," I say to him. "You didn't have to do this, but I guarantee by this time tomorrow, you'll be glad you did.

"I'd also like to thank Retired Special Skills Operative Margaret Greenberg for providing refreshments. Thank you, Marge."

"You are very welcome," she says, smiling warmly.

"Thank you, Ian, for running the tech, and thank you all for being here at this late hour. I appreciate it very much.

"For those of you who don't know already, my name is Lydia Clay. I have intelligence about an attack scheduled to take place on our soil tomorrow morning. I am the only one with this intelligence, and the only one who can tell you where to go and what to do to stop it."

I let that sink in while I check in with everyone in the room. The new arrivals look more concerned and skeptical than shocked, which tells me they must have been apprised of the situation while I was in the restroom. Bennet appears resigned.

I want him to be involved, so I ask him if he would carry out introductions for the new arrivals.

After raising an eyebrow at me, he motions to the new arrivals in turn and introduces them as Bill Peterson, Deputy Director of the CTC (the man with trendy glasses), his aide, whom Bennet doesn't bother to name (the girl in pink), and Ahmad Safar (blue shirt). The clipped tone of his voice suggests he doesn't care for Safar. I wonder if it's a prejudice thing, but then Bennet continues the introduction.

"Safar headed a counterterrorism joint task force between our agency and the FBI last year. The task force was disbanded, but somebody—" He glares at Ian, who smiles disarmingly in response. "Thought it would be a good idea to involve the FBI in this matter."

"Safar investigated the '93 World Trade Center bombing and the USS Cole," Ian says. "I phoned him earlier, before we left my aunt's. Thanks for coming, Ahmad."

Way to go, Ian! I hope he can tell I'm pleased he overrode his aunt and brought in someone from the FBI.

"It is my pleasure," Safar says. "Thank you, Director Bennet, for allowing me access to this meeting. I assure you, I am here in a strictly supportive role." I notice he wears a badge with a grainy picture like the one I'm wearing. Everyone who already works here has color photos.

Bennet's response to Safar's gratitude is a frowning grunt.

Before I lose momentum, I lay out the details of what I know. Moving to the dry erase board, and consulting my notes, I recreate the page with the circles representing tomorrow's flight numbers, talking through what the circles represent. To my astonishment, I see Peterson's aide and Peck taking notes. Peterson gives me his avid attention while he finishes off a sandwich and reaches for his pastry.

"There are nineteen hijackers in total," I say, pointing to the circles in turn. "Five on each flight, except for United 93, which will have only four. These two will turn around shortly after takeoff and head for Manhattan." I draw lines from the top two circles and write WTC in big letters. "Their targets are both towers of the World Trade Center. This one's coming here, to D.C." I tap the circle for American Flight 77. "The target is The Pentagon." I hear a gasp and some murmuring, but I plow forward. "Ninety-three is also coming back in this direction, but I'm not sure what the intended target is. I saw it crash in a field in Southern Pennsylvania. Some people speculated the target was The White House, the Capitol Building, or even this building we're in right now."

"Um, how did you *see* it?" Safar speaks up.

"How I saw it is kind of hard to believe, but a polygraph exam strongly suggests I'm telling the truth." I start off addressing Safar, but I direct the rest to the whole room. "I believe I've been given an—" I look to Marge, remembering her summary of the Stargate Project, "Extrasensory vision of the event. To me, the vision is indistinguishable from memories of my everyday life. It feels, to me, like I lived through tomorrow already." I leave it at that. Bennet hasn't shut me down yet, so he must believe my story at least a little bit.

Safar's expression is skeptical.

"Believe me or don't," I say as I begin writing the hijacker names I remember inside the circles. "Argue over the validity of polygraph exams, if that floats your boat. But do it later. Right now, we have four groups of al-Qaeda terrorists to stop. Regardless of how I came by the information, much of it has already been verified." I nod in Ian's direction.

Everyone at the table swivels their head to look at him.

He returns my smile, and I can practically hear him in my head, telling me I can do this.

"These men have been living in the U.S. on tourist visas," I say, returning my attention to the board. "Please forgive my misspellings, of which I'm sure there are many. My memory, sadly, is not photographic. That's why I have blanks here in place of some of the names.

"What I do know is that each of them has been quietly abiding by our laws, attending non-extremist mosques, and training to either fly or be muscle."

Bennet whips off his glasses. Leaning on his elbows, glowering at me, he says, "Now, wait just a minute, Missy. How do you know any of this? You say in the recording you *supposedly* witnessed the plane crashes because of some magical nonsense." He motions with his glasses as they dangle from his hand by a temple piece. "You expect me to believe it because Agent Greenberg can somehow tell you're not lying—

also magical nonsense." He motions to Marge with an agitated hand, oblivious to the daggers she's hurling his way with her stare. "On top of all that, you want me to believe you saw these *supposed* hijackers planning and training? You drag me and Peck to this room and feed me some bullshit story and expect me to—what? Call The White House for another meeting where I get told to keep my eyes and ears open like I'm not already doing that? Where I get told that unless I have proof Bin Laden's got WMDs, I'm not authorized to delegate resources to his group?"

I flinch at Bennet's tone, tempted to return to the meek insecurity that shrouded me when we first arrived. I also don't appreciate being called, "Missy." Out of the corner of my eye, I see Ian tense up. We can't afford for him to stand up for me and alienate Bennet. This is the time to bring people together for a common cause, not to divide them.

I pull myself up taller and address Bennet. "You're absolutely right, sir." His face is flushed as his frame leans back in the chair and makes its joints groan. Ignoring his narrowed eyes, I go on. "Premonitions, polygraphs, Stargate—" Marge used that term earlier to refer to a CIA program to weaponize extrasensory abilities. "These are all fallible."

I remember when we were at Marge's and spoke by phone with Bennet, he said something about "mixed results."

"I don't understand what went on in Stargate," I say to Marge. "But am I correct in assuming extrasensory abilities were never proven one-hundred percent accurate?"

"You are correct," she says. "However, polygraph exams, when administered by a trained professional—even one without extrasensory abilities—are highly reliable on the order of ninety-plus percent." Her eyes flash, and I'm reminded of the mighty bird of prey depicted on the CIA's seal.

"I don't make authorizations of this magnitude based on data that is fallible," Bennet says, slapping the table.

"Then you should," Marge counters. She splays her hands flat on the table, like she's ready to rise and give Bennet a piece of her mind.

I step forward and place a hand on her shoulder, letting her know I've got this.

"I believe we can all agree that anything less than one-hundred percent means potential fallibility," I say. "And I completely understand that the director of the CIA can't take action without solid, reliable proof of my claims. Unfortunately, I can't offer you that. The means don't exist to flawlessly examine what I've experienced."

Marge begins to stand, but I pat the air to tell her she's not needed just now. She looks like she could punch a hole in the wall by spitting sunflower seeds, but she sits back down.

"So here is what I propose." I smile her way, then give Bennet my attention since he is the decision maker. "I propose you don't put *me* to the test. Instead, you'll put my information to the test."

I gesture toward Ian. "Mr. Greenberg has already done some of the work, but it will need to be verified by your team, Mr. Peterson."

Peterson has a napkin covered in crumbs in front of him. He jerks to attention, looking eager to help. He's Peck's Deputy Director for the CTC and appears receptive to taking orders.

"You and your aid—I'm sorry, I didn't get your name," I say to the woman.

She sits up taller. "Sharon." She casts an anxious look Ian's way. It's almost like she has some kind of history with him. More jabbing hits my midsection, which I, once again, ignore. "Sharon Hansen."

"Great. Nice to meet you, Ms. Hansen. So, you and Mr. Peterson will investigate the flight training angle. All four of the pilots have FAA-issued pilot's licenses. That should be straight-forward enough to check. The licenses would have been issued recently, like in the past few years. I also have the names of several U.S. flight schools." I tap my notes. "Will you please verify that Hazmi and Mihdhar attended and flunked out of Flight Training International, or FTI, in San Diego? Neither of them will pilot a plane tomorrow, but they have the training to do so. Also, find out if a flight school owned and operated by a man named Dekker had students by any of these names." I gesture to the board.

Sharon scribbles furiously in a spiral-bound notebook.

Peterson nods. I think the coffee's finally kicking in for him.

"There's also an Airman or Airmail flight school in Oklahoma, I believe. Run this list of names by them as well. If you find connections, as I suspect you will, and if it's not too late, see if you can contact their instructors. Find out what they thought of the students, if they harbor any suspicions about them. Let's verify, first and foremost, that this group has the ability to pull off what I say they're going to pull off. If none of these men have been to U.S. flight schools or have pilot's licenses, we have our answer. I'm full of nonsense. But if they *are* registered with the FAA, you might consider taking me seriously."

I check in with Bennet. He's still glowering at me, but his glasses are back on his face, and his coloring is returning to normal. Since he hasn't kicked me out yet, I take it as a good sign and continue.

"Oh, and while you're doing that," I say to Peterson and Sharon, "please find out everything you can about me. Do I have any secret government connections that would give me access to the news about Massoud's assassination or the Vigilant Guardian operation scheduled for NORAD tomorrow? Does the data on me suggest any logical way for me to know the names of al-Qaeda operatives?"

I jot Massoud's name on the board along with *Vigilant Guardian* and *NORAD*.

When I'm done, I turn to CTC Director Peck. "Sir, would you please call the airlines and find out if passengers by these names are on the flight numbers I say they are? I also remember some of the names of the flight attendants and pilots that made the news. Write down your email address before you go, and I'll have Ian send you those names as well so you can check them."

Peck folds his arms across his chest and studies my writing up on the board. He appears pensive. "I can do that, of course, but I have a question for you, Ms. Clay." I'm instantly nervous, but I don't let it show. Peck's one of the people driving the intelligence community's interest in Bin Laden. He's on my side.

"Of course. Fire away." Internally, I cringe, feeling like I've just said 'bomb's away' in an airport.

"Where's the money trail for all this? My team's all over al-Qaeda's financials, and we haven't seen anything beyond a couple thousand changing hands here and there."

I nod. "That's a good question. It turns out, an attack like this is very cost effective. You wouldn't see the movement of the type of large sums that raise red flags. Flight lessons were paid for in cash. The men worked, earned their own way, lived quiet lives. They sent money to family overseas, behaving like a lot of immigrants do. Not to mention, from what I remember, you didn't have many of these men on your radar. Am I right about that?"

Peck concedes with a tilt of his head. "We knew about Mihdhar and Hazmi, but the other names don't stand out."

I open my hand in a there-you-go gesture. "So, you were looking at the al-Qaeda end and looking for cells in the U.S. receiving large deposits, but what you actually have here are a few spread-out individuals receiving small deposits and living quiet lives."

"Wait a minute," Safar says. "You knew Mihdhar and Hazmi were in the country, and you didn't share that intel with us?" He's glaring at Peck.

Peck pulls a face of disgust. "Oh, like your 'joint task force' is all about the sharing. I get a memo about Massaoui *after* you already arrest him, and it mentions nothing about al-Qaeda. So, don't lecture me about sharing intel."

"Are you two serious, right now?" I ask. "If your agencies had half the organization and half the single-minded sense of purpose al-Qaeda does, you might have been able to spot this attack without help from me. Stop nitpicking each other and start communicating. Now, Mr. Peck, did I answer your question about the money trail? Are you good to look into the flight manifests?"

He throws a sulking look at Safar, but nods.

Safar sucks in one cheek, looking chastised.

"Mr. Safar, you investigated the '93 Trade Center bombing and the USS Cole, yes?"

He pulls himself up in his chair. "Yes. We are on Bin Laden. All over him, actually. We've got teams in Yemen and Scandinavia right now disrupting the cells responsible for those attacks."

"Excellent. So, you have the experience to know how best to approach and detain these guys. You know what needs to be done to make sure they're tried for their attempted attack. I can tell you that all the proof you'll need can be found in their luggage. Between their carry-ons and checked bags, you'll find weapons like knives with blades shorter than four inches—"

Safar flips open a notebook and starts making notes.

"And devices that look like bombs," I continue. "They'll use these items to take control of the cockpits of all four planes, killing the pilots and injuring some of the crew and passengers in the process. You'll also find in their bags handwritten instructions, in Arabic, for carrying out this plot, including their plans for martyrdom, a summary of end-of-life preparations they're to carry out, flight training VHS tapes, and flying equipment like altimeters and course trackers and stuff like that. You'll want to pay special attention to Atta's checked bag."

I tap his name within the circle of American Flight 11. "I know where a couple of these men are right now—at least the general area, but what I know for *sure* is where all nineteen of them will be tomorrow morning: at the airports listed here." I tap the dry erase pen on the board. "They'll all make it through security without major issue and board their flights. If they get on and those planes get airborne, we'll be too late. People will die.

"If my information pans out, we'll have precious little time to plan an actual operation to stop these guys. We'll need teams in place at these three airports, ready to act if Bennet gives the go-ahead. Can you organize that?"

"Yes," Safar says, "If Director Bennet authorizes it."

I look to Bennet.

He looks like he's sucking on a lemon as he stares me down.

I don't blink. I don't back down. He's no more intimidating than some of the surgeons I've crossed.

"You're the Central Intelligence Agency, aren't you?" I ask quietly, sincerely, speaking just to him. "Don't rely on my intelligence. Go collect your own. The most you have to lose is a few hours of these people's time." I motion to the room. "Please. Don't be the man who ignored the warnings and let 9/11 happen." I put all my compassion for tomorrow's victims into the plea and mentally cross my fingers and toes.

It feels like the whole room is holding its breath.

Bennet spits out the lemon on a curse. "Two hours," he says. "We reconvene here in two hours to evaluate the information you all are able to gather." He stands and includes Marge in the glower he fixes on me. "We'll put the information to the test, Ms. Clay, Ms. Greenberg. And if there's nothing in it, you *both* will be held legally responsible for the expenditure of resources."

He sweeps his gaze around the meeting room. "You have your assignments. Get on those phones."

The room clears out until I'm left with Marge and Ian.

"Holy shit," Ian says when he reaches my side. "You just gave orders to a room full of CIA top brass."

Damn right, I did.

*I would rather work with five people who
really believe in what they are doing than
five hundred who can't see the point.*

—Patrick Dixon

CHAPTER 22

Lydia

THE CAFETERIA IS TECHNICALLY OPEN, but there are no smells of cooking food, and the refrigerated offerings, like salad and yogurt, are locked behind lowered gates. Ian and I find a bay of vending machines at the back and start feeding bills into them. After taking on a room full of CIA agents, I'm starving. I also need a quiet place to do something I've been putting off.

I need to call Tristan.

It's nearly eight p.m. He would have gotten home from work a while ago. Not finding me there, he would, of course, try to call me to find out where I went, but I've had my phone off all day. I probably have a full voicemail box to look forward to, but that can wait. What can't wait is the guilt I'm feeling over my radio silence. For all Tristan's faults, he doesn't deserve to be left in the dark. Well, not *completely* in the dark. It's not like I can tell him his young wife has been taken over by her consciousness from twenty years in the future. Or that I'm at the CIA headquarters helping our country thwart a major terror attack. But I can at least let him know I'm safe and planning to return home sometime tomorrow.

Ugh. Tomorrow.

Today I am focused on my mission, stopping 9/11. But by this time tomorrow, whether I succeed or fail, the reason for my being sent back in time will have expired. By this time tomorrow, I will be faced with reliving the next twenty years of my life. I'll worry every day whether my children will be the same Holly and Christian I love with all my heart. I'll have to make things work with Tristan, at least until my children are born.

But it's not all bad. I'll also get to call my parents. I'll go see them. I'll hug them and tell them how much I love them and encourage them to take good care of their health.

Going to nursing school will be a snap. I'll ace all my tests and nail my internship. Another bright side is getting to be a nurse for another twenty years. I'll probably even get to see some of the same patients again. I'll get to fix mistakes I've made. When conflicts arise, I'll have a unique perspective, to say the least.

I'll live life better this time. I'll be kinder, more intentional about things. I'll appreciate this second go-round and not take it for granted.

My chips hit the bottom of the vending machine. When I pull them from beneath the flap, I notice my reflection in the glass. Straightening to my full height, I force a smile and try to absorb the resolution into my soul.

You're going to make the best of this, I tell myself, but my new conviction comes with a good dose of reluctance.

I don't *want* to live the next twenty years again. I can't stand being in a time where my children don't yet exist, where they might never exist. My soul revolts at the thought of going home to the Spinney Hill apartment and climbing into bed beside a young Tristan.

I feel numb as I follow Ian through the cafeteria seating area, chips and soda in hand. But instead of pulling out a chair to sit, Ian leads me to an outdoor courtyard lined with wooden benches, manicured bushes and tufts of ornamental grass. The centerpiece of the courtyard is lit with spotlights situated on the ground. It's the sculpture he pointed out from the parking lot, the one with the codes written on it.

I take a seat on a bench and study the letters, which are punched out from the sheet of metal, leaving void spaces that look like gilt glyphs in a book of magic.

"What does it say?" I wonder out loud, as I tear into my bag of chips.

I don't really expect an answer, but, of course, Ian has one for me.

"The first passage says something about light and shadow and the nuance of illusion, only, illusion is misspelled with a *Q* in place of the first *L*." He tears into a bag of pretzels and pops one in his mouth, taking his time over his monologue.

I'm in no rush, either. We've got some time to kill. I enjoy my snack as well and wait patiently for more.

"The second passage gives coordinates for some secret buried nearby and that only WW knows the details. It's assumed WW is William Webster, who was director when the sculpture was installed. Some people think the sculptor gave Webster the solutions for all four passages.

"The third passage is from the 1922 account of when the tomb of Tutankhamun was opened. It leaves off when one of the tomb's explorers asks another what he sees when he peers inside. The next line in the account is 'wonderful things,' but that part isn't included in the code. The fourth passage hasn't been solved yet." He shrugs and cracks the top off a Coke bottle.

"Weird." My response reflects how braindead I am right now. I feel like when Tristan would tell me the details about some case he was working on, getting into the nitty gritty of obscure laws. I would fail to see in Tristan's story whatever made his eyes light up with intellectual fascination. In contrast, my eyes would glaze over.

Ian laughs. "I suppose it is weird. But I'm guessing it's the kind of thing code breakers get a kick out of."

"I guess I was expecting secret-to-life type stuff or quotes from presidents, not random excavation passages and secret coordinates."

"And misspellings."

"What, are you the spelling police?" I ask.

"Someone has to enforce proper spelling."

We share a smile as we consume our junk food.

"What do you think Marge is doing right now?" I ask.

Ian crumples his empty bag and disposes of it in a trash receptacle. "I think she was going to update Socks."

I shake my head, still amazed I've spoken with a former president. "Friends in high places, indeed."

"I had no idea my aunt was friends with Bush the First."

I picture Marge hanging out with George and Barbara, having a barbeque and watching fireworks together on the Fourth of July. "*M* and Socks. Buddies from the CIA."

When Ian laughs, his Adam's apple moves. I love the crinkles beside his eyes, which will deepen with time, making him even more handsome than he is now.

"You did amazing in there," he says, green gaze locked on mine. There's a familiarity in the way he looks at me that wasn't there before. I shouldn't like it, but I do. Oh, I do!

I also like his praise. I'm not used to receiving such open approval from a guy I like. With Tristan, I always felt just shy of acceptable. If I were just a little different, a little more this or a little less that, I would be worthy of him. So, I had better be thankful that someone of his caliber paid me any attention at all. They weren't explicit words he ever told me, but the message was implied in daily nitpicks. My inferiority and his magnanimity were the themes of our marriage.

"I imagine that's how you are at work," Ian goes on. "Taking charge, handing out jobs. When you know what needs to be done, you make sure it happens. And people listen to you. Your confidence is contagious."

"I guess I was confident in there," I say, amazed at the truth of the statement. But it wasn't *my* confidence that was contagious. "It's because of you, you know."

"No. It's because of you."

"I respectfully disagree." I pick up his hand and hold it in both of mine. Earlier today, I would have fought the urge. Not now. Even if I don't plan to act on this attraction I feel for Ian, he has become my friend. "Being back here? It's like I'm falling back into old patterns. I might be confident now, as a grown woman, a mom, a nurse with years of experience. But in 2001, I wasn't any of those things. I doubted myself at every turn, you know? I started to feel that way again, but you snapped me out of it. What I did in there, that was the me I've become. I sort of forgot about her until you reminded me in that bathroom. So, when I say that was all you, I mean it."

Ian gazes at me wordlessly, tenderly. His hand rotates, and soon, he's holding both of my hands in both of his. His thumb strokes my wrist.

I wonder what's going on in his head. I want to ask, but I don't. The answer could be dangerous.

Will there be a time when I might be able to press my lips against his? What will become of our friendship after tomorrow? He mentioned staying in touch, but I'm not sure that's a good idea. He'll inevitably begin dating someone, and I'll feel jealous and hurt because *I* want to be with Ian. Not to mention, I'll be married to Tristan. Us remaining friends is an emotional train wreck waiting to happen.

"Peterson's aide, Sharon—you two seem to know each other." The words sort of tumble out of my mouth.

One of his eyebrows lifts in an amused expression.

We're still holding hands. It's nice. Almost platonic, but not quite. A little forbidden. The prolonged touch speaks volumes in a code only our hearts can decipher.

"I interviewed her a few months ago," he says. The quirk of his lips tells me he's picking up on my jealousy but diplomatically not calling it out.

"Something tells me you shared more than just an interview. She was tracking you with her eyes like a rabbit tracks a cat from the safety of a thornbush."

Ian chuckles. "So, it's not just me she reminds of a rabbit."

We laugh together. I'm unforgivably relieved that his tone holds no sign of romantic affection when he talks about Sharon.

"I bought her drinks," Ian admits. "And may have flattered her a bit to help her open up. She shared some insights about Peterson's work in counterterrorism. Off the record. But she pointed me in the right direction. She's how I heard about Mihdhar. I think she's watching me so closely because she's worried I might out her."

"So, it was drinks and information sharing, not a date?" I'm being obvious. I don't care. Ian knows I'm into him. I know he's into me. There's no sense in denying what we feel, even if we're deciding not to act on those feelings.

"Not a date," he confirms, grinning down at me. "I would spring for more than two rounds of drinks if I were treating someone special to a first date. I'd at least buy them a nice dinner." He winks, and I remember our hour at the Italian restaurant.

My cheeks grow warm.

We sit like that for a while, hand in hand, my head on his shoulder, watching the moon rise above Kryptos. When I can't justify putting it off any longer, I take out my Nokia and turn it on.

"Thank you, Ian. Your support—it means the world to me. I wouldn't have made it this far without you."

"Without Marge, you mean."

I smile. "Without both of you." I sigh, resigned to my task. "Would you mind giving me a few moments? I, uh, need to call Tristan. He'll be worried about me."

Ian nods. "Of course." He squeezes my hand before letting it go. "You sure you don't want me to stay?" His frown broadcasts his concern.

Over dinner, we talked about Tristan—in general terms, but enough that I think Ian could tell I'm not exactly looking forward to being married to him again. I also think he understands why I have to try to smooth things over with Tristan. Without him, Holly and Christian will never come to be.

"I'm sure." I watch Ian until the cafeteria door shuts behind him, trying not to think about how fine a backside he has. Another sigh escapes me, this one wistful.

Regretfully, I turn my attention to my phone and note the symbol on the green-yellow screen that tells me I have a voicemail. Something tells me that if I check, I'll find more than one. I would bet my favorite pair of hospital-grade Dansko clogs that upon finding me absent from the apartment and not being able to reach me at home, Tristan checked with my parents to see if they knew where I was. I probably have multiple messages from him and them.

Since I don't want to hear any more of Tristan's voice than absolutely necessary and I can't handle hearing my mom or dad's voice, I don't bother calling up the voicemails. Instead, I bring up Tristan's contact, one of the few I have stored in the phone's memory, and hit Send.

Tristan picks up before the first ring is through. "Lydia. Where are you? Is everything all right?" He sounds panicked, which seems sweet on the surface, but I know him. As soon as he realizes that I'm not in any danger, he's going to be furious with me for taking off without consulting him first.

"I'm fine. I'm just calling because I didn't want you to worry. I, uh, decided to travel to D.C. for the day. I'll be back tomorrow night. Please don't worry. Nothing's wrong. I just... needed to get out of town for a bit." I wince, anticipating an eruption.

Tristan is silent, but I know it's because he's processing an explanation that's at complete odds with everything he knows about his meek, attentive wife.

Three...two...one.

"D.C.? Needed to get out of town? You sound like you robbed a bank, or something. And what the hell happened to our bathroom? It looked like there was some kind of struggle."

Ah, yes. The vase-mirror incident. "Um. I..." *Needed to know if I was dreaming.* "Saw a spider." The lie is lame, but the best I can do on short notice.

"You saw a spider," he deadpans. "And you went to the bookcase, got the vase my mother gave us, and threw it at the mirror. To kill a spider."

"Yep. That's what happened." The pens on Marge's polygraph would be dancing a jig.

"Are you kidding me, right now?" On the Richter scale, his anger is around a three. He's warming up. "Do you have any idea how worried I was when I saw that mess? I almost called the police. Do you know what stopped me?" He doesn't wait for me to answer. "Your rings. You took your rings off and left them beside the bed." He's a quiet, simmering, and frightened four.

"Oh, I, uh, had some kind of allergic reaction and my fingers swelled up." My pants are *so* on fire. "Look, I'll be back tomorrow, and we'll figure everything out, okay? Please, don't worry about me."

"Don't worry about you. You expect me not to worry when you take off your goddamn wedding rings, destroy our bathroom, and take off without a word? We're going to have to pay for that mirror, by the way, or we'll lose our deposit. And where do you think we're going to get the money for a trip out of town? Are you staying at a hotel? Did you take the train? I don't even know where to start with you."

His breathing picks up, telling me he's pacing and gesturing wildly. Pacing means he's at a five. "We're still paying off our honeymoon, Lydia. The tropical honeymoon *you* wanted. Dammit, you know how tight money is with you going back to school. Not to mention, you're a married woman, now. You don't just up and go out of town. Husbands and wives discuss these things."

Okay, he has a point with that one. Not that he gives me a chance to tell him as much.

"Why D.C., anyway?" he goes on. "You don't even know anyone there."

I bristle at his know-it-all tone. "I actually do have a couple of friends here. You don't know them. I figured I'd pay a visit before school starts next week."

Technically, I am visiting friends. Ian and Marge. But I didn't plan my trip here as a pre-semester fling. I've always been more the type to get a jump on the next semester's material during Spring break when everyone else was going to the Jersey Shore. So, yeah. I'm lying to my husband. It doesn't feel good, but it does feel justified.

"So, you don't have to worry about me," I say brightly, demonstrating how not-a-big-deal this trip is. "I'm staying with my friend, Marge, and I'll be home sometime tomorrow."

"Marge, huh? How come I've never heard of her before? And what am I supposed to do for dinner tonight? I've been waiting for you for hours. You just take off without warning and leave me to fend for myself? That's not what I signed up for last month." He's referring to our wedding. His tone is so cutting it would have drawn blood if I were the Lydia he married.

I'm so far from that Lydia, thanks to Ian's encouragement, that I actually laugh at his annoyance. "What you signed up for? Are you serious? I seem to recall you being able to turn on a stove burner or order takeout without my assistance before we tied the knot. What you signed up for." I say the last part to myself, shaking my head.

"Are you—are you laughing at me?" There's the six. Funny. We're climbing the Tristan-rage scale, and I'm not affected one bit. My therapist would be proud.

"I suppose I am. You make it sound like I've left you on the moon and run off with your oxygen tank." I can see through the overly-dramatic poor-Tristan act. It's manipulation, pure and simple. He knows I'm a compassionate person, so he plays on that to get me to do what he wants. It's a vile way to treat someone you're supposed to love, someone who loves you. And I did love him back then. Enough to overlook the wretched way he made me feel whenever we fought.

At the same time, I am married to him. On some level, he feels responsible for my safety and wellbeing, and having me go out of state without telling him is out of character for the Lydia he married. He probably doesn't deserve it, but I take pity on him.

"Look, I should have let you know I was going. I sort of... got a wild hair and just felt like doing something spontaneous. I'm sorry I didn't take your call earlier, but—"

"Take my call? Jesus, Lydia. We're not colleagues. We're *married*. You don't *decide* whether to 'take my calls.' When I call you, you pick up the damn phone. How would you like it if I took off out of nowhere to hang out with friends you don't know? Overnight? Without my wedding ring? And didn't answer when you called fifteen friggin' times? What the hell is this? Are you having second thoughts? Is *that* what this is?

After everything I've done for you? Everything my *family* has done for you?"

Just like Tristan to bring his family name into the fight. God forbid a Watercrest be put out by a mere farmer's daughter.

"Don't forget, Lydia. You're the one who married up, here."

Oh, wow. There it is. This is possibly the first time he's played the marrying-up card in our marriage this time around.

"Remember," he goes on. "I'm the one who stuck up for you when my parents wanted me to dump you for Gretchen Rhodes."

Ah, yes, Gretchen. Heiress to the Rhodes family fortune, built on the Rhodes & Rhodes telecommunications firm. How many times had Tristan wondered out loud if Gretchen would have done what I had done to upset him?

I remember clearly how old Lydia responded to Tristan's musings about Gretchen. She blanched and cried and felt terrible about her shortcomings and gave in to whatever Tristan wanted. Apologies, promises of change, and a good, firm stroking of his ego would be the currency he deigned to accept for his forgiveness, which old Lydia would have been relieved to obtain.

I blow out a furious breath. I'm angry with myself for saying "I do" to this jerk in the first place. I'm angry with myself for staying with him as long as I did and allowing him to grind my burgeoning adult confidence into dust. I'm angry with myself for being angry with myself, because it's taken years of therapy to forgive the Lydia that made these decisions in the past.

It's not her fault. All she wanted was to be loved, and Tristan could be very affectionate when he wanted to be. He drew me in with charm that only ran skin deep. Beneath, he was an emotionally-manipulative egoist who knew how to play a farm girl with big-city dreams.

You didn't do anything wrong, I remind myself. *If you're going to be angry, be angry with* him.

But not too angry, says a small voice in my head. *Remember Holly and Christian.*

"You there, Lyd? Or are you not talking to me now? That's very mature." His disdain puts Director Bennet's to shame.

"You want to talk to me about maturity," I say. "How's this for maturity? Up yours, you narcissistic, mean-spirited jerk. Oh, and by the way, Gretchen Rhodes is going to become a nudist and get a reality show where she winds up being disinherited for dating Marilyn Manson."

I punch the end-call button with aplomb and power down my phone. I think I just saw ten on the Lydia-rage scale for the first time in my life.

Rising from the bench, I smooth my skirt. "That went well," I mutter before heading into the cafeteria to look for Ian.

Ian

It's PEACEFUL IN the cafeteria at night. I'm leaned back in a comfortable chair in a small meeting room off the main dining room. A TV in the corner had a remote Velcroed to its side, which I used to turn on the evening news.

ABC's *Eyewitness News* weatherman, Sam Champion, is giving tomorrow's forecast over a video feed from earlier in the evening, showing New York's skyline at sunset. "This shot, showing you lower Manhattan, and everything is actually in pretty good shape," he says in his easy-going, amicable voice. "...as we work into clear, but for us, bright sunny skies. Sixty-five degrees at seven o'clock in the morning. And sunny and pleasant for the rest of the day. Eighty degrees—it's kind of a guilty pleasure as beautiful as this weather is going to be."

Sorry, Sam. But Lydia beat you to the forecast, and there's nothing pleasurable about her version. *"The sky was so blue that the smoke looked obscene as it extended the line of the Towers higher and higher."*

There was a time in my life when I prayed to God when I wanted or needed something. I haven't done it in a long time, but I make a faltering attempt. I look up to the ceiling tiles and reach out with my heart. *Let this work,* I say, keeping it simple.

My watch tells me we're getting close to the two-hour mark. Since I've been up for a ridiculous number of hours without sleep, I abandon Eyewitness News in favor of the coffee vending machine I noticed on our way into the cafeteria. The front of the machine promises café-style espresso drinks, but as I scrutinize the mud-colored sludge in my cup, I have serious doubts.

"That any good?" Lydia finds me at the lid dispenser, trying to convince myself that if I can't see the coffee, it won't offend my palate.

"No," I conclude, tilting the cup to show her that the mud color on top darkens to tar-pit black beneath a thin layer of foam. "This is supposed to be a cappuccino."

"Good luck with that." She smiles a little too brightly. When she swipes a wisp of hair from her cheek, there's a slight tremor in her hand.

"You okay?"

"Fine. Is it time to go back upstairs?"

I have a feeling the talk with her husband didn't go so well. I want to ask about it and offer support, but everything about her manner suggests she's ready to put the phone call behind her.

She looks pointedly at my watch.

Sighing, I check the time. "We've got fifteen minutes."

"Might as well head up. Maybe some of the others will be there by now." She marches off, and I can't help my smile. It seems my Lydia is most likely to take charge when her world is askew. The talk with Tristan went poorly, so she's even more determined to take on al-Qaeda.

I don't envy the terrorists right now.

I use my long legs to catch up to her before we reach the elevators. Her smile as she meets my gaze is a little too aggressive. She shows a little too much of her teeth, a warning for me not to push for answers.

Shifting her weight from foot to foot as we ascend to the third floor, she says, "I can't wait to see what they found."

"Me, too." I'm positive Lydia's information is correct. But the question is whether the CTC director and deputy director and an FBI agent were able to find supporting documentation. If they were, Bennet can authorize an emergency investigation and an operation to detain the hijackers. If not, then further investigation will require approval from higher-ups, which

Bennet isn't likely to get based on the CIA's history of asking The White House to support their fight against terrorism. I gather from Bennet's earlier comments that unless the intel has to do with weapons of mass destruction, The White House isn't interested. Unfortunately, no one has ever considered that a passenger jet might fit that description. Tomorrow will change that paradigm.

Side by side, we reach the meeting room. Looking through the open doorway, I have to do a double take. The space is empty and organized, showing no signs of recent occupation. Even the whiteboard is clean.

Is this the right room? The plaque beside the door says it is.

Someone has erased Lydia's reproduction of her page about the planes. Her list of hijacker names is gone. It's like it never was.

My chest grows tight. This is all wrong.

Beside me, Lydia gasps. She clutches the sleeve of my shirt. "Where is everyone?" She plows into the room and goes straight to the whiteboard. "My notes!"

Immediately, she grabs up the blue marker and begins drawing the four circles, recreating what was there when we left the room.

"Don't bother," says a weary voice behind me.

I spin around to find Director Bennet frowning as he lumbers through the door and takes a seat.

Lydia wheels on him. Uncapped marker in one hand, she leans over the table and grips the back of a chair. "You promised two hours. There's still fifteen minutes. You can't call this off. I know what I know, dammit. This is *happening*. If your people haven't found anything, they're not looking hard enough."

"Take a seat, Ms. Clay." Bennet's tone brooks no argument.

Lydia pushes back from the chair with a sound of disgust. The marker makes squeaking sounds as she practically destroys the tip recreating her work.

"I will not sit down," she says. "You *have* to listen to me." Her voice shakes with panic, but determination makes it strong. Tears fill her eyes as she writes out the flight numbers again. "Everything you'll need to prove what they're planning to do will be in their bags." The tears begin to fall. A sob bursts from her as she keeps writing and talking. "They're going to kill so many people! Please!" She wipes her eyes with her sleeve, then presses an arm across her midsection. Doubling over, she says, "Oh, God! I can't!"

My arms go around her. "Hey, hey. Take it easy." I help her stand up straight and bring her to a chair. Glaring at Bennet, who glares back over the rims of his glasses, I guide her to sitting, and I take the chair beside her.

If he's going to throw us out, he needs to hurry up and do it, while we still have time to go to the FBI. I can contact Morg for after-hours numbers and figure out who might be able to help us. Maybe Safar is still in the building.

Bennet watches while I rub soothing circles on Lydia's back.

I feel her shudder beneath my hand.

"This isn't easy for her," I say.

"That's apparent," Bennet says.

"So many people are going to die tomorrow," Lydia whispers, staring at the woodgrain.

She's been through so much. Waking up twenty years in the past, carrying this burden of incredible knowledge, arguing, I assume, with her husband, from whom she's supposed to be divorced, and, most importantly, worrying about her children.

"No one's going to die," Bennet says.

Lydia hiccups. "They are," she insists, splotches of anger and grief reddening her delicate skin. "And you're going to just let it happen! You're supposed to protect us! You're the one who's supposed to know about terrorists, not me. You're the CIA, dammit!" Her shoulders shake as she unleashes her fury.

"No one's going to die." Bennet speaks over her, his tone sharp. "Because we're going to grab these sons of bitches before they get on those planes."

CHAPTER 23

Ian

LYDIA HICCUPS AGAIN.

My hand freezes on her back at Bennet's declaration. "Are you saying…" I trail off, hoping I'm drawing the right conclusion, that he believes us.

"If you'll get ahold of yourself, Ms. Clay," Bennet says. "And give me a chance to speak, you'll know that I've relocated this operation to the situation room. My team has confirmed much of what you've claimed."

"What?" Lydia asks. She's spent her whole day trying to get someone to listen and take her information seriously. Now, she's wary of trusting that she's accomplished her goal. I feel it, too. Having such a powerful ally in stopping this attack seems almost too good to be true.

"I'm not ready to concede this has anything to do with shooting stars or magic," Bennet says. "But I can't argue with the facts." He opens a plain manilla folder and refers to the papers inside. "Atta, Jarrah, and Shehhi all hold commercial pilot's licenses with the FAA, issued between 1999 and 2001. Hanjour's license is registered with the FAA but was issued by an independent contractor after a failure to obtain the license through the FAA directly."

He shuffles papers, bringing a new one to the top. "A training exercise by the name Vigilant Guardian is, in fact, scheduled to take place tomorrow morning at ten a.m. I've notified NORAD of this new threat and requested to speak with central command to cancel the exercise."

He shuffles papers again and pins me with his gaze. "Massoud's assassination hasn't yet been picked up by the Associated Press, Mr. Greenberg, which leaves me scratching my head as to how you were able to confirm it. But." He slaps the folder closed. "Assassinated he was, yesterday morning at his Northern Alliance base in Afghanistan. Not even The White House knew about it yet, not until I called the Vice President half an hour ago. Are you suggesting, Ms. Clay—" He gives her his undivided attention. "That Massoud was taken out by al-Qaeda?"

Lydia sits taller. Cheeks wet, she clears her throat and says, "I don't think that was ever confirmed one hundred percent, even in my time. But it's the hypothesis everyone accepts because of the timing. How it happened right before 9/11, like they were trying to make a big statement, you know, show the whole world who's boss, so to speak. Just like the attack here, they went in stealthy. The assassins got into the military base with camera equipment and press passes under the guise of interviewing Massoud. Then, when they were close to him, they detonated their suicide bombs."

Bennet stares at Lydia, no doubt struggling to absorb everything she's saying. I had difficulty at first, too, but I learned to trust my gut where Lydia is concerned. Bennet's expression fails to give away whether he believes what she's saying about Massoud or not. But considering how much of her information has been verified, I'm guessing he's leaning toward believing her.

"And you know this how?"

"It was in the news. And written about in books." She inclines her head toward me, and I have this weird feeling she might be referring to a book written by a future yours-truly. "You have to understand, from my perspective, 9/11 was—it was *the where-were-you-when* moment for, like, *everyone.* It was all anyone talked about for months. It dominated the news. Countless books were written about it, and in most of the retellings, sir, the CIA comes out with egg on its face.

"It's why I came here and not the FBI. From everything I've read, you had some of the information, but nobody here at Langley connected the dots. No one comes right out and says 9/11 was the CIA's fault, but the implication is that you missed important signs."

"What signs, goddammit?" The table shudders as Bennet strikes it with his meaty fist. "We've been burning the midnight oil trying to connect dots. Do people think we're gods? That we're omniscient in matters of national security?"

"That's what people expect," Lydia says. "Unfair as it is. But like I said, you have more information about the terrorists at your fingertips than anyone else, and you and Peck have tried, multiple times, to get more resources for this fight, and multiple times, you've been denied. I know how that feels. I've pushed for more resources, more staffing, more everything at Kindred, but no matter how squeaky a wheel I am, the funding always goes to the fancy new MRI machine. No one cares that our stock of Neosporin is out of date or that we're reusing masks. We're expected to combat COVID with breathing machines we've had to clean by hand because we've run out of the sanitizing solution the protocol calls for."

Bennet and I both stare at her. I've heard her mention COVID before, but Bennet's raised eyebrow shows he's a little lost.

"The point is," Lydia says with a wave of her hand. "I know what it feels like to get blamed when things go wrong. No one cares that you went to the National Security Advisor for help and she said no. No one cares that you think Bin Laden is planning something to do with planes when they're only interested in hearing about WMDs. They don't care because they have no idea how destructive a plane can be. They have no idea the hijackers can fly or that they'll turn those planes into missiles. Right now, al-Qaeda doesn't have any WMDs, but in twelve hours, they will. They'll steal them and use them to turn Manhattan and The Pentagon into war zones, and the whole world will try to blame you."

"But that's not going to happen now," I say quickly. Bennet's face is turning purple, and I'm worried he's going to have a stroke and we'll lose our best chance at stopping this plot. "Because fate is handing you perfect, 20-20 hindsight." I gesture toward Lydia.

Bennet leans back, arms crossed over his chest. "I've interviewed a lot of people in my day, but I've never heard a story quite like this one."

Is it my imagination, or is that an admission of belief?

Narrowed eyes fixed on Lydia, he says, "Peterson dug into your background. He found no hint of government connection or any other possible way you could have known about any of this. Yet, here you sit describing an attack you witnessed with such clarity and detail that I can practically see it in my mind's eye." Eyes closed, he gives his head a shake, like he can't believe he's about to say what he's about to say. When he opens his eyes, he rises from the table and says, "You're going to have a lot of explaining to do—you too, Mr. Greenberg—but that will have to wait. Right now, I need you both downstairs, in an advisory capacity, because, apparently, you know more than an entire foreign intelligence service devoted to protecting our homeland."

He strides from the room, and Lydia and I scramble out of our chairs to follow.

"If it makes you feel better," Lydia says, stopping Bennet in his tracks. "The FBI didn't connect the dots, either."

Standing in the doorway, Bennet grunts, as if he doesn't care, but the twinkle of satisfaction in his eye tells a different story.

"These guys came here legally," Lydia says. "They lived under the radar and put together a plan so simple and cost-effective that no amount of watching their financials would have made them stand out."

Bennet turns to go, but Lydia stops him with a hand on his elbow.

"Your challenge, sir, if you don't mind me saying so, isn't just stopping these nineteen men. It's so much more than that. You have to do it in such a way that the world knows how bad this could have been. Because things need to change. The CIA and FBI need to be talking to each other, not competing with one another. Airport security needs to be completely revamped. The FAA's method of issuing pilot's licenses needs to be assessed. Arresting and trying the hijackers will be just the beginning."

For the first time since arriving at Langley, I witness Bennet smile.

"One thing at a time, Ms. Clay. One thing at a time."

He has no idea to whom he's talking.

Lydia

IAN AND I FOLLOW Bennet, exchanging looks of triumph behind his back. I show two thumbs up, and Ian does a fist pump.

"Save the celebration for when this is all over," the director says, and I have to assume that like every parent on the planet, he has eyes in the back of his head.

We take the elevator to the first floor, then we follow Bennet to another building, where we take another elevator to a level beneath the ground that requires Bennet to scan his badge for access. The elevator opens into a sleek lobby looking into a glassed-in room with a guard posted at the door.

Beyond the bullet-proof glass I can make out several bays of computer monitors and a bank of flat-screen televisions running what look to be news programs with their scrolling ticker ribbons at the bottoms of the screens. A CNN logo swoops into the center of one TV, confirming my suspicion. Personnel in suits and a few in military uniform man the computers. There's a huge whiteboard with writing all over it. At the center are my four circles representing the endangered flights. An officer in an Air-Force-Blue coat uses a roll of tape to secure pieces of paper to the board. From outside the room, the papers look like headshots. I can't wait to get a closer look.

The guard holds a machine-gun-looking weapon and nods solemnly at Bennet as the director scans his badge and enters the glass room with us in tow.

Once inside, I can see just how high-tech the space is. The computer monitors are all white on black, designed to be easy on the eyes in low lighting. An electronic table in the center of the room shows a map of the world with glowing dots demarking, I assume, places of interest. Some of the dots are in the Middle East. Others are on the Eastern Seaboard of the United States.

Besides the Air Force officer, I see Peck and Peterson sitting at a pair of side-by-side computers. Peterson has a land-line phone pressed to his ear. Safar has a laptop open on his knees and hunches over it near the TVs. Marge sits under a goose-neck desk lamp, taking notes with a phone receiver pressed to her ear. There are a few other people I don't recognize, including a man in Army camouflage from his dust-colored combat boots to the hat atop his shaved head and a woman in a skirt-suit the same color as the Air Force officer's.

The energy inside the room is infused with purpose, and suddenly, I feel right at home.

"This is more like it," I say to no one in particular. The conference room upstairs had left me uninspired, but this space reminds me of a nurse's station on a ward. I can see everything that's going on and feel in control of it all, not that I'm the boss here, but I can't shake a strong sense of ownership over this operation.

"More like what, Ms. Clay?" Bennet asks.

I grin and rub my hands together. "This is the kind of space where a girl can make things happen."

"Glad it meets your approval." Though he is unsmiling, there's a twinkle in his eye. He strides off to consult with the Air Force guy in front of the whiteboard.

"I think he's warming up to me," I say to Ian.

"Impossible not to," he replies with a crooked smile. "Now, go get to work, lady." He honest-to-God slaps my butt before heading off toward his aunt. A pleasant tingle warms the real estate where his palm landed, and I relish it as I make my way to the whiteboard.

When Bennet sees me, he says, "Lieutenant General Campbell, this is our civilian informant, Lydia Clay. Ms. Clay, this is Lieutenant General John Campbell of the United States Air Force. He serves as the point person for military support to the CIA, and, given the hour and the urgency of this operation, I thought it best to bring in the big guns."

Campbell reaches out to shake my hand. He's a broad man in his late fifties, and he and Bennet must have read the same memo about saving polite smiles for off-duty hours. "Nice to meet you, Ms. Clay. I've only just arrived. Still getting my bearings. What do we have, here, sir?"

Bennet walks the Lieutenant General through the circles and terrorist names. The papers he was taping up are, in fact, headshots. He's got Atta's face connected by a blue line to Atta's name within the circle for American Flight 11. There are also headshots for Shehhi, Hanjour, Mihdhar, and one of the Hazmis.

The woman in the Air Force skirt suit shows up at that moment and tapes up a headshot of Jarrah. "There," she says. "Now, we've got all the pilots."

I observe the proceedings, impressed they've gathered so much information so quickly. I can't quite believe this is actually happening, an operation to stop 9/11. If this works, then everything I'm bound to go through over the next twenty years will be worth it. Well, almost everything. I hug my arms to my chest as I think about Holly and Christian.

I'm sure I'll be able to smooth things over with Tristan. The fight we just had was nothing compared to some of the gems I recall from our first go-round at supposed marital bliss. But even if we make amends, how will I be able to pretend I love him long enough to conceive our children? What if I conceive, but the babies we have aren't *my* Holly and Christian?

"Director Bennet." The man in Army fatigues approaches. I'm all too happy to shelf the thoughts in my head in favor of listening in. "My team is working on a plan of attack. If you'll come this way, you can see the departure times for the four flights are closely clustered between 7:45 and 8:10, making a multi-airport interception the most streamlined and clandestine approach." The Army guy and Bennet move to a computer monitor, and I follow, Bennet's little shadow.

The two men discuss the best location to intercept the hijackers. It sounds like they're leaning toward doing it outside the airports to minimize possible casualties. Thanks to my information, they know some of the hijackers will claim to have bombs on them, so the caution-level is high. I can appreciate that. At the same time, the plan won't work.

"Atta and Omari will arrive at Logan from their early-morning Portland flight," I say.

Both men turn and stare at me.

"Hi, I'm Lydia Clay, the civilian informant who brought this matter to Director Bennet's attention." If Bennet's not going to introduce me, I'll do it myself. I hold out my hand to shake, and the Army guy accepts. His grip is a little too intense, but I refrain from shaking out my abused fingers when he releases me.

Bennet clears his throat. "General, pardon my *faux pas.* I should have made the introduction. Ms. Clay has been an extremely valuable asset to this operation. Ms. Clay, meet General David Abrams. He'll be our point person for support from Special Forces. His team will work in tandem with our agents to intercept the hijackers."

I notice four black stars stacked along the general's sternum against the camouflage and swallow a sudden lump of nerves in my throat. "Nice to meet you, sir," I say, battling the urge to curtsey. "Um, as I was saying, Atta and Omari will arrive by plane, so you won't be able to, uh, intercept them outside the airport. Also, the four teams of hijackers will be in communication with each other before their flights. I don't have specific details, but I know they were calling each other on their cell phones, possibly to let the other teams know they made it through security, or that things were going according to plan. So, if you intercept a team and they fail to check in, it could alert the other teams before they can be captured.

"If you want my advice—" Bennet's eyebrows climb his forehead, but I plow onward. "You'll have undercover people at the gates or even on the planes, for the earliest flights. I mean, you know where they'll be since all nineteen of them will make it through security. Don't do the intercept-thing until they've made their phone calls and assured the others that things are going according to plan."

"You think I don't understand how to intercept terrorists, Ms. Clay?" Bennet faces the board and fusses at me over his shoulder, as if I'm not important enough to face directly. The back of his neck is turning red. "Is that really what you think?"

"I don't think that. Of course, you do. But *I* understand what it's like to watch a plane fly into a skyscraper and emerge out the other side as a fireball spanning ten floors."

His shade darkens. "If you think I'm going to let hijackers get anywhere near those planes, Ms. Clay, you need to get your head examined. The *only* reason I'm willing to do this outside three metropolitan airports is that it's a Tuesday morning, and it's the choke point all these assholes are going to funnel through. If there was any possible way to get at them all sooner, I would." He points at the board and begins talking with the general.

"I've already agreed to get my head examined," I point out, undeterred. "And I hear you. I do. But why would you take the chance you might miss some of them when you know they're not going to try anything until the planes are airborne?"

"I don't know that," General Abrams says. With heavy arms crossed over his barrel chest, he half-turns my way. "No one can possibly know that. Your intel, according to Director Bennet, says these men will be armed with knives and possibly bombs. We're not going to *hand* them civilians to use as hostages."

I shake my head. "You're still thinking about hijackings as being about hostages and negotiations." I address my next comment to Bennet. "'A Failure of imagination.' That's what people said about you after the attack. They said this was able to happen because no one imagined terrorists might take control of passenger planes with suicidal intent.

"As far as these nineteen men are concerned, they're *not* armed. Not yet. They're not looking to take a few dozen passengers hostage. They want to bring down the World Trade Center. They want to destroy The Pentagon, and to do that, they need those planes airborne."

I face the general. "Imagine you're an interloper in an airport in a foreign country, which you hate. You've just made it through security. You're relieved. Your comrades are phoning in, saying they've also made it through. The plan is working!"

Peterson and Safar have joined us. Ian breaks from his powwow with Marge and comes to my side. Everyone's listening to me, and I feel like I'm giving a pep talk at the hospital.

"At this point, these guys are gearing up for the technical part of their mission. They're nervous, praying, preparing to die. They know they have at least ten minutes of taxiing and takeoff before they need to act. Maybe they're enjoying a last moment of peace before fulfilling their purpose and meeting their end."

The Air Force duo is back, joining the group around the board. No one's stopping me, so I keep going.

"None of the passengers or crew on the planes know it, but the planes *aren't* going to take off, not until your operation is complete. The tower knows you have a team on each plane, and they won't issue permission to take off until you give the word. There's no danger to anyone on board because you'll be there. You'll have the upper hand. You'll know exactly where these guys are sitting and what they're armed with. Your teams will be the shield between the hijackers and the passengers. The hijackers will be taken off guard, and you'll 'intercept' them, most likely without a fight. They won't know you're on all four of the planes, so they'll want to cooperate, go along with you, and not raise alarm. They won't want to compromise the other groups.

"Then, think of the power you'll have over these guys in the interrogation room." I don't let on that all my knowledge of CIA operations comes from watching Netflix. "None of the hijackers will know you have the groups from the other planes in custody as well. I mean, it's win-win."

Bennet's face is doing that purple thing again. General Abrams has sucked his lips between his teeth. He looks like he's trying not to laugh.

"I appreciate your enthusiasm, Ms. Clay," Bennet says. He looks like he's holding onto his composure by a frayed thread. "And I'm in your debt for bringing this matter to our attention. But I'll thank you to leave the logistics to the experts."

"This isn't the movies," Abrams says, smirking. The expression doesn't become a man of his age and rank. It makes him look juvenile. "In the real world, we don't wait until the last possible moment to grab the bad guys. It's my job to consider every possible outcome and minimize loss of life and damage to property, and I don't need help from a civilian to do that."

Ian's hand flattens across my lower back, and I appreciate the support. It helps me stay focused on the goal and not on the sting of the general's reprimand.

"Fine. I get it," I say. "'Thanks for the tip, but we'll take it from here.'" I sigh and reorder my thoughts. "Just promise me one thing. Promise you won't let those planes take off until you have all the hijackers in custody." I meet Bennet's gaze. "If you owe me a debt, pay it by keeping those planes on the ground."

That's the big *E* on the eye chart. If they're going to risk letting some of the hijackers being alerted to their operation and slipping through their fingers, they can at least make sure none of them can somehow make it into the air.

For Bennet's ears alone, I say, "If the planes never take off, 9/11 can't happen."

He holds my gaze, like he's considering it. "I'll see what I can do, Ms. Clay. Now, if you and Mr. Greenberg will return to the lobby—"

The lobby? As in on the wrong side of the reinforced glass? He's kicking me out? Unacceptable!

"I'll be good," I promise. "I won't interfere. Please, let me stay."

Bennet angles his head toward the guard manning the door from the inside. The guard comes over.

"Show Ms. Clay and Mr. Greenberg to the lobby, please, and don't let them back in."

"No!" He can't shut me out. "I know things! I can help!"

The guard takes my elbow and drags me away from the board. I look pleadingly to the corner where Marge sits, and she simply watches with her hawklike gaze. Why isn't she sticking up for me?

Ian follows me and the guard, shoulders rounded.

"At least let Ian stay," I shout at Bennet, who's turned his back on me again.

Abruptly, he shoots a glare at me and strides to stand toe to toe. "Do you have any idea how difficult it is to be me right now? Any idea how busy I am, and how much energy you are sucking from me with your misguided attempts at aid? Do you think I want planes flying into buildings? Do you?"

His anger stops me in my tracks. He's so purple, he's practically glowing. "No, sir. I don't." I didn't know I was being an energy vampire. I'm trying to make his job easier, not harder.

"Then you will do as you're told and *sit* in that lobby until you are invited to contribute. Do you understand?" He punctuates the command with a finger jabbing into the air in the general direction of the door. "Or I could have you escorted from the premises entirely."

"Lobby," I say. "I'll sit out there and be quiet," I promise. *Like a good little doggie,* I add in my head.

He wheels around to leave me at the mercy of the guard, apparently satisfied.

When the guard indicates with a hand that Ian should follow us, I say to Bennet's back, "Please let Ian stay. He'll be quiet." Bennet's gaze is murderous. I toss Ian a pointed look. Bennet takes two steps to bring himself toe to toe with me again. "Someone needs to be able to tell the story of what happened here," I hurry to say. "The World needs to know how close this was, how bad it could have been. They need to know what you laid on the line to make us safe, and they need to know that change is needed or this could happen again. Please. Let Ian tell your story."

"Nothing leaves this room without your approval," Ian says, lifting two fingers in a Scout's honor gesture.

To Bennet's credit, he takes a brief moment to consider. His response is a curt nod before he returns to the board.

Ian's sympathetic face is the last thing I see before I'm expelled from the situation room.

*Nothing could have ever really prepared
us for what happened—or how fast the
events would unfold.*

—Thomas Von Essen, commissioner,
FDNY

CHAPTER 24

Lydia

IT'S SURREAL WATCHING the close-captioned CNN broadcast through the reinforced glass. I can't read the text from here, but I can tell what the stories are about from the images. There's a video package of President Bush at an elementary school in Florida with a large headline that reads, *President Bush Touring FL Pushing for Education Reform*. Tomorrow morning, he'll be at a different school, one that will be made famous as the location where he heard about the attacks.

Hopefully, it *won't* be made famous this time. I'm crossing my fingers that Booker Elementary will be mentioned in tomorrow's news with no greater fanfare than the school shown on screen right now.

Another package runs, this one showing a closeup of a woman in a suit followed by an image of the Capitol

Building. The headline announces, *Elizabeth Dole to Run for Senate.* Another shows images of prescription drug bottles followed by a man in a suit and finishes with pictures of former President Clinton. After a few minutes, the Secretary of State's face graces the screen followed by images of a largely African American crowd holding protest signs.

I don't remember, like, any of this, but Ian's probably intimately familiar with every single story.

Occasionally, he holds up a note to let me know what's going on inside the situation room. Using my notepad, which I have the misfortune of being separated from, he writes me black-Sharpie messages, like, *They're contacting FAA now* and *NORAD canceled exercise.*

I find a dry-erase marker and a ream of printer paper behind the reception desk. Since the guard doesn't seem to care what I'm doing as long as I don't go near the door, I send messages back.

Do they know evidence will be in checked bags?

Have they grounded the flights?

What's Marge doing?

I feel like I'm in fifth grade, again, passing notes when the teacher's not looking.

Ian doesn't always answer. He spends a lot of time at a station near the back of the room, where his aunt periodically makes phone calls. He's on his laptop. I hope he's writing about all this, because what good will it do to stop 9/11 if there will be another 9/11 next year or the year after? So many things need to change.

I get that Bennet's focused on the immediate action and not the big picture, but it's tough to be ignored.

At least no one's going to die tomorrow.

That's the important thing. That's what I was sent back for.

The hour hand on the clock over the reception desk creeps along, moving painfully slow and too fast, all at once. People come and go from the room, more coming than going.

The call has been put out, and despite the late hour, staff are hurrying in to be of service. Even from the wrong side of the door, I can tell the situation room is filled with high energy. For the CIA, this is game day, only, they don't have a tidy schedule with predictable events, like an NFL team. They have to be ready when needed, and boy, are they needed tomorrow.

Make that today.

It's been 9/11 for a few hours, and I'm on pins and needles. They have to pull this off. They have everything they need, unlike the first time around. This time, the dots have been connected for them. This has to work.

After much pacing, note-passing, and worrying, the clock insists it's five a.m. Atta and Omari will be in Portland, now. Soon, they'll arrive at the small, regional airport, where they will board a plane that will ferry them the short hop to Boston.

Ian's been giving me radio silence for more than an hour, but at last, he appears on the other side of the reinforced glass. The note in his hand says, *Atta & Omari spotted in Portland. B letting them board plane. A not happy. Scrambling to get 2 spec. ops. on board, undercover, keep eye on them.*

B must be Bennet, *A* must be General Abrams, and spec. ops. must be Abrams's special operations team. Earlier, I heard Abrams sending teams to all the involved airports, so he must have men in place right now, waiting for instructions. It looks like Bennet is trusting me on this one and letting Atta and Omari, in their business shirts and pants, board the plane with their hidden knives and equipment that will help them pilot American Flight 11.

I'm relieved. I stand by my assertion that it would be unwise to capture any of the hijackers before they can check in with the others. I just hope those special ops guys are subtle. If I were Atta and Omari, I'd be seeing potential threats to my plan everywhere. If Atta sees muscled-up men with concealed-firearm bulges sitting right by them, he might order the rest of the hijackers to abandon ship.

I can't stand the thought of these evil men not being caught.

Because I have nothing to do but think, I push myself to remember everything I possibly can about today's timeline. I know when each of the planes takes off and when they hit their targets, but it's harder for me to recall specific times before the flights, like when the hijackers arrived at the airports or when they made it through security. I wish I'd paid attention to reports about them placing calls to each other. I know I read a log at one point that detailed their cell phone records for today, but I can't recall specifics.

I do remember one thing that might be helpful, though it's probably too little too late. I write a note directly to Bennet: *If you have any idea where UBL is right now, get him. Because he's going to disappear & we won't get him for 10 yrs.*

I press it against the glass and try to catch Bennet's eye. The man seems determined to ignore me, but Ian steps up. He taps the director on the shoulder and points to my sign.

Bennet reads it, then picks up a handheld radio. On this side of the glass, I hear his voice through a device on the guard's belt. "Enough with the signs, Ms. Clay. Do I need to have you removed from the building?"

I crush the paper in my fist. This waiting on the sidelines is unbearable. So is the smell of coffee infusing the air as more people march through the lobby with Starbucks cups and paper cups like the one Ian tossed in the cafeteria. I'm hungry and thirsty, but I'm not about to leave. I need to be here in case anyone needs me, in case Bennet realizes what an asset I can be.

At last, six a.m. rolls around. Atta and Omari will soon be airborne.

The situation room is packed, now. Bennet's suit coat is long gone, and his shirtsleeves are rolled up. The long dry erase board is covered with printouts and writing. People come and go from its shadow. Clearly, it's the hub of the operation.

Nearly every phone in the room is pressed to someone's ear. There are no cell phones visible. They're all landlines.

A new armed guard relieves the one Bennet instructed not to let me in. Trying not to be conspicuous, I watch the old guard leave and notice he didn't say anything to the new guy. That means he didn't relay Bennet's order about me. Maybe I could try getting in.

Or maybe I should be good and stop irritating Bennet. I don't want to end up removed from the building.

It's a tough call, but I end up doing the mature thing and not upsetting the apple cart. Instead, I stand at the glass, chewing a fingernail, reading the face of every person in the room, in turn, trying to draw conclusions about what's happening. An hour passes like that, and finally, just before seven a.m., Ian holds up a note.

All 4 flights arranged to have delays. Take-off times all 8:20 now, boarding at 8.

Oh, cool. That's a good idea. I hadn't thought of that. By delaying the flights, Bennet can ensure all the hijackers are at the gate areas around the same time. That should give them time to place their check-in calls.

Okay, *maybe* Bennet's doing a good job in there. Maybe I should give him credit for how much faith he's put in me, and maybe I should try to relax a little. More than once, I've gotten employee reviews suggesting I need to work at relinquishing control. I'm trying to do that here, but it's a challenge. I'm not wired for sitting on the sidelines.

At 6:45, Ian holds up another sign. *Atta & Omari on ground in Boston.*

The relief I feel makes my knees weak. I knew they wouldn't do anything on the short flight, but just knowing those two men were in the air with innocent people had a thread of tension pulling my shoulders tight.

Periodically, Ian lets me know when certain hijackers have been spotted. I'm keeping track with tick marks on a sheet of paper and am up to four, including Atta and Omari, at Logan, and two at Dulles when someone taps my shoulder.

I turn to find Sharon, Peterson's assistant, bearing a tray of coffee and bags of goodies from Starbucks.

"Here you go," she says with a smile, handing me a cup. "They're all the same, lattes with no sweetener. That's what Peterson likes. I figured you and Ian, and Ian's aunt would still be here, and you might be getting hungry."

I take the grande-sized drink and a bag with a blueberry muffin in it, and I want to fall at her feet in thanks. "You are seriously the best," I tell her.

She beams, then asks, "What are you doing out here?"

"Bennet doesn't like me," I pout. I soothe my hurt feelings with a sip of hot heaven.

"Hm. Well, I can't do anything about Bennet, but Peterson's another story."

She shows her badge and goes inside, and I track her progress as she hands out coffee and treats to Ian and Marge and then Peterson, who hasn't moved from a computer monitor opposite the whiteboard in hours.

The look on Peterson's face is pure rapture when he sees Sharon, or rather the coffee she holds out to him. I see her bend to talk in his ear, and he finds me with his gaze. Like Bennet, he's shed his coat and loosened his tie. Lack of sleep shows in dark circles under his eyes, behind his glasses.

A moment later, Sharon comes back to the lobby. "Peterson says you can come in, but you have to stay with him and out of Bennet's way."

"You are officially my new favorite person," I tell her, and I feel bad for my earlier jealousy.

Keeping my head down and putting Sharon between me and Bennet's line of sight, I re-enter the situation room and slip into a swivel chair at Peterson's side.

"Thank you," I tell the CTC deputy director.

"You looked miserable out there," he says with a half-smile. "Don't be too hard on Bennet. He's got a lot on his plate right now."

"I can understand that."

"I believe you, you know," Peterson says. "I've read all about the Stargate Project, and I can't believe I actually got to meet *The* Margaret Greenberg. If she says you're telling the truth, that's gospel. Bennet knows it, too, but he has to work with people like Campbell and Abrams, skeptics, you know? He has to be able to back up every decision with data or it won't fly."

"And Peterson's the data guy," Sharon says, proudly.

"Remind me to give you a raise," Peterson says.

"Looks like the note passing is done." Ian gets my attention with a hand on my shoulder, and it's insanely good to be near him again. Squatting to be on a level with me, he says, "So, this was too much to write down, but a little before seven, Atta placed a call that lasted three minutes. Shehhi answered a call at the same time, so Peck's team assumes the two were checking in."

He rests one hand on the arm of my chair, and a frisson of awareness rushes over every inch of my skin at his nearness. I find myself placing my hand on his. I crave connection with him after hours apart, and now that I have it, I can think more clearly.

"They assume?" I say. "Can't they tap into the cell phones to listen in?"

Ian shakes his head and takes a sip of coffee. "No. They can pull logs of call times after the fact, but from what I've overheard they can't just jump on the signal and listen in."

"That's both disappointing and comforting," I say.

Sharon grins. "Don't feel too comforted. They can't pull off a tap in this kind of emergency situation, but if they need to listen in, and they have a little time, they can work miracles."

There are too many people in front of the board for me to read what's been added, so I ask Ian for an update. "How many of the hijackers have been spotted?"

He stands and faces the board, tall enough to see over everyone's heads. Inclining his head to me, he reads, "We knew about Atta and Omari at Logan. They've also spotted Suqami and two Shehris." Suqami. That was one of the names I couldn't remember, one of the blanks in my notes. "The five of them have checked in for American Flight 11. Also checked in at Logan for United 175 are..." He shuffles to get a better view. "Shehhi, the pilot, another Shehri, two Ghamdis, and Banihammad." He takes his time over the unfamiliar name of Banihammad, another of my blanks. "From what I heard just before you came in, it looks like there were some hiccups in security, but the board shows they're all through, now, and under surveillance. Bennet's livid, by the way."

"Why?"

"He can't believe airport security has let all these guys through."

"What about Flight 77 in Dulles? You told me about Mihdhar and Moqed." Moqed was another blank of mine.

"Looks like for Dulles, we've got three new check-ins," Ian says. "Hanjour, the pilot, and two Hazmis. Guess this is a family affair."

I tick off fingers. "That's all of them for the first three flights. Awesome." So, none of the hijackers for American Flight 11 and 77 and United 175 were alerted that they were being watched. It's almost too good to be true. "Who's checked in for United 93?"

Ian cranes his neck. His brow furrows as he shakes his head. "Hold on." He leaves me to get closer to the board. I see him sidle up to Bennet, who's having a heated discussion with an equally red-faced Abrams.

When Ian returns, he says, "Something's screwed up with the United computer system. No one can get their hands on a list of passengers who have checked in. But Abrams and Bennet both have guys all over Newark. Parking lot, departures drop-off, check-in counters. No one's spotted our 93 guys. Abrams thinks you must have it wrong. He wants to focus on Logan and Dulles, but Bennet's arguing that we need a team to monitor the gate, just in case we missed something."

I agree with Bennet. I also find it odd that the hijackers for Flight 93 haven't been spotted yet. The clock on the wall says it's a quarter to eight. My memory plugs in 8:42 as the moment of take-off for United 93, but the scheduled time had been much earlier. The first time around, the flight took off later than scheduled because Newark is a high-traffic airport, apparently, even on a Tuesday. The hijackers would have arrived at the airport in plenty of time for the *scheduled* take-off time. That means they should have checked in by now.

"What if they noticed the 'undercovers,' and ran for the hills?" I ask.

"Impossible," Peterson says. "We've literally got every quarter covered. If those four came in by car or bus or metro or friggin' helicopter, we would have seen them before they saw us. They never showed. It's as simple as that. Cold feet, I guess. I mean, this was supposed to be a suicide mission, right? I wouldn't blame them for backing out."

I shake my head. Something feels off.

"Or one of the other hijacker teams saw something and tipped them off," Ian suggests.

"No," Peterson says. "All the other hijackers are acting normal. Trust us. We're the best in the world at this. Here. Take a look." He clacks on his keys, and says, "This is the video feed at the United check-in counter."

I swivel my chair and practically glue my nose to his monitor. I'm searching the passengers arriving at the desk and those in line, looking for faces to match Jarrah's headshot. Peterson has a color printout of the headshots of most of the terrorists beside his keyboard. The grid of photos reminds me of the one shown on the news. One difference is that the quadrant of the grid allocated to Flight 93 has only one image. Jarrah's.

"We're looking for..." Peterson uses an orange highlighter to circle Jarrah's face. "Him, and anyone arriving with him."

I don't need Peterson's cheat-sheet. I know what Jarrah looks like. Out of the nineteen hijackers, there were three faces, three sets of eyes, that haunted me, even appearing in my nightmares from time to time. They were Atta, Hanjour, and Jarrah, pilots for American Flights 11 and 77 and United 93. For some reason, the face of Shehhi, the pilot for United 175, didn't stay with me. Maybe he just didn't look evil enough to haunt me. But looks aren't everything. He still flew a plane full of innocent people into a populated skyscraper.

I study the monitor. The timestamp shows we're watching in real time. Flanking the United counter with its five check-in stations are two men in street clothes who I can guess might be CIA or maybe Abrams's special ops guys. They stand casually, one with a cell phone pressed to his ear, but their gazes are a little too intent as they sweep the arriving passengers.

God. The passengers. Some of the people on this screen right now might be checking in last minute for Flight 93. I focus in on individual faces. I would recognize certain heroes, like Jarrod Streeter, Jason Trick, Matt Braden, and Tim Forsythe, men who were honored for their bravery in standing up to the hijackers. But the resolution on the security monitor is far from perfect. The feed is black and white, and the actual faces of the people are small.

"How do you see anything on this?" I ask Peterson.

"You get used to it," he says with the ease of someone who's watched a lot of surveillance tape.

"So, besides Jarrah, who else are you looking for?" Flight 93 was the one where I had the most blanks in my notes. I only knew Jarrah's name, plus Qahtani, the possible fifth for Flight 93. But Qahtani never made it into the U.S., so he's irrelevant. "What other names have you uncovered?"

"None yet. But Safar ran a background check, and he's working with local law enforcement to find out who has connections to him. Don't worry. We'll catch these guys." He wears a reassuring smile.

The time stamp rolls past 8:00, and I'm drumming my fingers on my knee, desperate to see Jarrah check in, but there's no sign of him. Even if he were to walk up to the counter right now, he would be running late according to his scheduled takeoff time. From what I remember, all the hijackers were on time for their flights, and, even if some of them hit snags with security, they all made it through and ended up boarding in time for takeoff.

This feels wrong.

"How long have you been monitoring the check-in desk? Could you have missed Jarrah?"

Peterson motions to the people sitting along the same bank of monitors as him. "It's not just me. We're all on it. We've been on it all morning. Plus Abrams's guys at their headquarters in North Carolina. Plus the spec-ops team and our team on site. See them there?" He taps the monitor with the capped end of the highlighter.

"I see them. They're a bit obvious."

Peterson ignores my comment. "There are teams outside, too. We've got people all over."

I don't like this. So many opportunities for Jarrah and his team to get a whiff of the operation. I mean, I'm glad they're not going to end up taking over the flight and crashing it into a field in Pennsylvania, but the thought of those men getting away to possibly plan another attack sometime in the future leaves me feeling unsettled.

Suddenly, the room erupts in cheers.

Whoops and *Atta-boys!* flood my ears, tearing my attention away from the monitor. Abrams is slapping Bennet on the back. Peck is grinning from ear to ear.

He comes our way and claps Peterson's shoulder. "We got 'em," he says. "Fifteen spiteful bastards in custody without issue. We're going through their luggage right now." He reaches to shake my hand, and I reciprocate, numbly. "Ms. Clay, you're a hero."

Papers fly through the air, and I remember the bits of singed paper floating over the streets of Manhattan, numerous as the stars in the sky.

Fifteen hijackers in custody.

That means the Logan and Dulles flights won't hit the World Trade Center or The Pentagon. Two thousand-plus lives have been saved because Ian listened, because Marge believed, because Bennet acted.

Two thousand-plus mothers and fathers, sisters and brothers, aunts and uncles, and grandparents and grandchildren will see another Thanksgiving, another Christmas, another wedding, another funeral.

I try to feel relief, but I can't. I don't know why, I just can't. It's like, I've been working toward this goal for twenty-four hours, and now that I've accomplished it, I can't rest in the knowledge.

My ears fill with ringing. It's so strong it drowns out the ongoing celebration.

"Lydia?" Ian's voice seems to come from far away.

"Ms. Clay?" Bennet's sweat-beaded face appears before me. He's squatting like Ian had been before, holding onto the arms of my chair. He looks concerned.

"She's in shock," someone says, and a cup of water appears in front of me.

I drink.

It's over. 9/11 isn't going to happen. Just like that, it's over. I drink again.

But past the ringing, past the celebrating, past the concern of the people crowding around me, I remember that I still haven't seen Jarrah.

I shake my head and thrust the water away. Someone takes it from me and says something, but I don't bother to make sense of the words.

I grip Bennet's arms and say, "What about Jarrah? What about ninety-three?"

"It's over," Bennet says, smiling. The man is actually smiling, and it takes years off his face. "We got them. Because of you."

"I heard fifteen," I say. "What about the other four?"

"Must have been spooked by our teams. Don't worry. We'll find 'em. The point is: no one's hijacking any planes today. We did it. *You* did it."

"It's over." The quiet voice belongs to Ian, who stands to my right. His hand is on my shoulder, and I don't know how long it's been there. "It's over," he says again, and it's that quiet assurance that pulls me through my shock and out the other side.

It's really over.
We stopped 9/11.

At 8:46 on the morning of September 11, 2001, the United States became a nation transformed.

—9/11 Commission Report, Executive Summary

CHAPTER 25

Lydia

I'M JUST BEGINNING to relax into the knowledge that 9/11 isn't happening this time around when a woman in Air Force garb leads Bennet away by the elbow.

"Congratulations, sir. Do you still want us to track the flights?"

"Yes. Stay on them 'til they reach their destinations."

I blink, sure I must have heard wrong. Surely, he didn't let the planes just take off like normal, as if the passengers and crew hadn't just dodged the mother of all bullets. Wouldn't there be questions and interviews as part of the operation? I mean, the terrorists have been stopped, but what about the investigation?

"They didn't let the planes take off, did they?" I ask Ian.

It's Peterson who answers. "No need to ground them, now. But just as a precaution, we've got two undercovers on the flights from Logan and Dulles, either our guys or Abrams's. Safar's teams are handling the arrests and luggage search. We're covering this from every angle. Nothing to worry about."

Except Jarrah.

"What about Flight 93? Are there two undercover people on that plane? Are people looking for the other four hijackers, the ones who never showed up?"

"Everyone we have at Newark is looking for those four. We even pulled the undercovers designated to get on the plane to help scour the airport."

"You pulled the undercovers?"

"To help in the search. We'll find these guys." Peterson nudges my elbow with his. "Relax. We're on it. The plane is completely safe."

It's hard for me to reconcile how quickly the CIA was able to locate names and photographs for the other fifteen terrorists, several of which I represented with blanks in my notes, and the dearth of information on the group of hijackers bound for United Flight 93.

"Lydia." A calm, authoritative voice makes me look up to find Marge smiling warmly. "It feels wonderful being vindicated, doesn't it?"

I force a smile. "Yes. It definitely does." The sparkle in her eye tells me she's known the feeling herself a time or two.

"How are you feeling?" Ian asks, taking Bennet's place close in front of me. I smell faint traces of coffee on his breath and feel soothed.

"Good." I try to keep the smile in place, but it feels forced.

Marge cocks her head. "What is it?"

"I heard it, too," Ian says.

"Heard what?"

"The lie," he answers. "You don't feel good. Not even remotely. Why? What's wrong? Is it your ex-*er*-your husband? The phone call earlier?"

"No." I try to put what I'm feeling into words. "I—I know it must sound strange, but I can't shake this feeling that this was all too easy. Where's Jarrah and his group? How could they just let the planes take off, not knowing what happened to those four? Why did they pull the undercover agents from Flight 93?" I shake my head. "Something just doesn't feel right."

"We'll find them," Peterson says, obviously listening in. "They won't get far."

"At least, we know they didn't get on the plane," Ian says. "That's the important thing."

I frown. "Yeah. I guess." Everyone is so sure the operation worked. Why don't I feel relief?

I lean into Peterson's space. "So, this is the feed from the United counter at Newark. Do you also have access to the gate for Flight 93?"

"Of course. But you wouldn't see anything out of the ordinary there. If Jarrah and his team never checked in, they obviously wouldn't make it through to the gate. Trust us. We haven't seen Jarrah or anyone else suspicious."

I study Peterson. He appears so confident. But how can he be?

"*Nothing* suspicious? Isn't that suspicious all on its own? I mean, when I flew yesterday, knowing what was going to happen today, I saw suspicious stuff everywhere. You're telling me that of all the people you have at Newark, no one's seen *anything* suspicious?"

"I mean, there was plenty of chatter on the radios," he admits. "But Jarrah was definitely not there. Face it. He's a no-show."

I read between the lines of what he's saying. "Let me get this straight. Your people at Newark are looking specifically for Jarrah, but other than that one face, they have nothing else to go on. You can't get access to United's passenger list, so you're working off of this headshot, and this headshot alone?" I tap on the paper beside Peterson's keyboard.

"I suppose, you *could* say that." Peterson's tone is defensive.

My mind begins racing. What if Jarrah had his face partially hidden and slipped past? What if the other three hijackers all made it onto the flight because the teams in place to stop them didn't know what they were looking for?

"Why don't we take a walk," Marge suggests. "You could use some fresh air and maybe a second cup of coffee."

Peterson looks relieved.

I get up from my chair reluctantly. I'm trying to focus on the fact that the World Trade Center will continue on as a Manhattan landmark for generations to come. Vaguely, I hear Sharon asking Peterson if he needs anything, and him responding that a second cup of coffee sounds good.

Marge, Ian, Sharon, and I start to leave the situation room, but Marge is called back by someone I don't recognize.

"I'll join you in the cafeteria as soon as I can," she says.

"Spill it," Ian says when we reach the elevator. "Something's wrong. Tell me."

"I don't know," I admit. "Something just feels off, but I can't put my finger on it."

When our trio reaches the cafeteria, it's a little after nine. Unlike my first time here, this morning, it's filled with the scents of eggs and bacon. Bright lights help a few dozen CIA employees wake up while they fill their stomachs.

I follow Ian and Sharon blindly, my mind busy working out why I feel so uneasy about Flight 93. I finally realize what the problem is as Ian frowns into another cup of mud-colored imposter-coffee.

"In my time," I say, thinking out loud. "The passengers of Flight 93 fought back."

"You mentioned that," Ian says.

"They did?" Sharon appears with a tray, on which sits a heaping plate of eggs and sausages. She sets down the tray and takes Ian's cup, pouring out the sludge into the overflow return of the machine. "Move over. I know how to make it good."

Ian stands back, and Sharon pulls four clean cups from the dispenser and begins filling the first with a combination of button presses that miraculously creates an aromatic, non-sludge-like flow.

"The hijackers took longer to take over that flight, compared to the others," I say while the first cup fills. "So, the plane actually made it into Ohio airspace. By the time they took control of the cockpit and turned it around, they had a good forty minutes to fly back to D.C., where we think they were headed. During that time, once the passengers knew they were hijacked, they made calls. Lots of calls."

Sharon watches me, wide-eyed, and the first cup overflows. "Shit!" She moves the cup, swearing again when hot coffee splashes onto her fingers. The flow continues another second before stopping. "That's the risk of making it the good way," she says, shaking off her hand.

"That'll leave a mark. Here," Ian says, handing her a wad of napkins.

Undeterred, Sharon sets the machine for "the good way" part two. "Go on," she encourages. "Lots of calls."

"Lots of calls, right. So, the passengers are hearing accounts from friends and family. They hear about two planes crashing into the World Trade Center. They hear about The Pentagon. They're realizing we're under attack."

This time, Sharon's ready when cup two is close to full. She expertly slides it to the side while sliding cup three into place beneath the stream.

"They powwow and decide they're not going to let the hijackers take out another building."

"Wow," Sharon says. "That's crazy awesome."

Ian says, "Crazy brave."

"Yes. It is," I agree. "They staged a revolt. They attacked the hijackers in first class and subdued them and tried to break into the cockpit. The pilot, Jarrah, panicked, and ditched the plane. It went down at 10:02 in Pennsylvania, miles from D.C." I do a long blink as I relive the pain of hearing their fate. "They couldn't save themselves, but there's no doubt in my mind they saved the lives of others. They made sure 93 didn't reach its target, whatever it was."

"They were heroes," Ian says.

"*Are* heroes," Sharon says. "They're the same inside, even though they're not going to face a life and death situation this time."

We both look at her. I don't know what Ian's thinking, but I'm amazed she's accepted the miracle of my situation enough to utter the phrase, "this time" so casually.

She caps the last cup of coffee and sets it on her tray. "Breakfast is on me," she says, and she takes off toward the cashier, carrying her heavy load.

Ian and I follow. At the register, Ian grabs a handful of individually packaged, oversized cookies. "These are on *me,*" he says.

We take a seat at a cafeteria table. Sharon lifts the plate of eggs and sausage, revealing more plates stacked underneath.

"Thanks for breakfast," Ian says.

Sharon blushes as she uses a fork to scrape a portion of food onto each plate. I feel a faint reminder of that jealousy from earlier, but it's lost its bite. Probably because I'm starting to really like her. Despite Ian's assurance that her focus on him is strictly related to their interview, I can tell she's into him. Maybe that's for the best. Maybe she and Ian will get together once I've returned to my life. The thought brings me no pleasure, but it's not like I have the right to protest.

We all dig into our eggs, and I pick up where we left off near the coffee machine. "So, in my time, the passengers on Flight 93 had warning about what the hijackers were planning.

Recordings after the fact prove that Jarrah made a cockpit announcement—it never actually made it to the passengers, since he didn't know how to use the intercom—but he told everyone to stay seated, that there was a bomb onboard, and they were headed back to the airport. So, it's clear the plan was to keep the passengers calm and compliant while they flew it into some government building or other."

Sharon watches me with rapt attention.

Ian forks up a sausage. Pausing with it halfway to his mouth, he says, "Maybe it feels wrong this time because things have shifted. The operation worked, and fate adjusted itself. Surely, that has to leave some kind of mark or scar on—I don't know—the space-time-continuum. Maybe that's what you're sensing." He bites into his link of meat with gusto.

"That's not it." This feeling has to do with Flight 93, specifically. I'm sure of it. "I think it's that this time, the passengers won't have any warning."

"Of course, they won't," Sharon says. "There won't be any hijackings this time. They won't be warned because they're not going to be hijacked at all. You heard what Peterson said. We're all good."

"Right." Ian beams at me.

"Right," I say, uncertainly. "No hijackings this time." But there's a tug on my gut I don't like.

Ian's Blackberry rings. "Probably my editor firing me," he says cheerfully before answering.

But when he connects the call, his face goes serious. "It's Marge," he mouths as he continues to listen. "You're kidding."

His face darkens. His gaze grabs mine. "We're on our way," he says, and he hangs up.

"What is it?"

"Flight 93 is off course and not responding to air traffic control."

Ian

I SHOULD HAVE KNOWN better than to dismiss Lydia's gut feeling that something was wrong. I guess I was too busy being elated that her persistence and honesty paid off I didn't bother considering that something might go wrong.

Lydia, Sharon, and I sprint back to the situation room. When we arrive, the mood is deadly serious. Gone are the congratulatory backslaps and handshakes, and in their place are hushed, hurried voices talking into phones.

One voice rises above the rest. "I don't care. Get them airborne now!" It's Air-Force Lieutenant General Campbell.

Marge meets us at the door. In a rushed whisper, she says, "They've just scrambled four F-16s."

"God," Lydia says. "They'll be armed this time. NORAD cancelled the exercise."

My breakfast feels like a rock of jackhammered cement, pressing unbearably on my internal organs. Lydia was right to still be worried.

"How did this happen?" I ask.

"No one knows," Marge answers. "Every team swears up and down they never saw Jarrah or any likely associates."

"I knew that didn't make sense," Lydia says. She elbows through the room to the monitor where Peterson had been sitting.

He's not there, anymore. Instead, he's at the whiteboard with Bennet and Peck, looking far less confident than he was half an hour ago. His thinning hair looks like it's been pulled at by frustrated fists, and, like his two bosses, his shirt is pitted out. Speaking of which, mine is too, after that dash from the caf.

"Sharon," Lydia barks. "Can you pull up the feed from the gate, time stamp, let's see—" Lydia looks at the clock and rolls her eyes upward to do a mental calculation while Sharon scoots close and takes control of the keyboard. "If 93 took off when it did last time, that would have been 8:42. But in my time, they boarded way before then. The take-off time was supposed to be closer to eight, if I remember right. But who knows what time they would have boarded with Bennet's adjustments. I want to see the passengers as they're milling around, waiting to get on."

"I can scan through the feed to see when they boarded, then work backward from there." Sharon uses a ball-in-socket mouse to bring up footage from the security camera in the gate area and then back it up.

"I'll go get one of the bigwigs," I say, but Lydia stops me by snagging my beltloop with a finger. It's an intimate gesture that makes my heart leap.

"There's no time," she says, bringing my focus back to where we are and what we're doing.

"What do you mean, there's no time?" I say. "They're the only ones who can help. Whatever time we have is irrelevant."

"What are you thinking?" Sharon asks, eyes intent on the computer screen.

"I have an idea," Lydia says. "But first, I need to know how they got on board."

By "they," she means the hijackers. I need to know, too. We were so sure we were in the clear. I stood by and watched as Bennet pulled strings and called in favors and refused to back down against a four-star general in order to work a miracle. For all his bluster, he'd taken Lydia's warning to heart. He'd *listened.* And he'd done what had been necessary to protect us.

I'd been so impressed, not just with the action he'd taken, but with the sense of fatherly authority pulsing off him while he did it. *He really cares,* I remember thinking. *He will grieve bitterly if people die today. He's a patriot and the perfect man for this job.*

But he was overly confident. We all were.

Lydia tried to tell us something was wrong. It was too easy. But we didn't listen. *I* didn't listen. Even when I sensed the truth in her words.

"There," Lydia says. "Wait. Go back. What's that?" She points at the screen.

"I don't see anything," Sharon says.

"Go back and play it again."

I lean over Lydia's shoulder, hand braced on the arm of her office chair, and train my eyes where her finger had been. The black and white footage shows people handing their tickets to the gate attendant for inspection, then having it handed back, then disappearing into the jetway. I see a man in a business suit move through. Then a woman with a young child in tow. There's a pause in the line. Then a man in slacks and a dress shirt walks through, followed by another, then a woman in jeans and a male passenger together, and a rotund, bald man in a suit coat.

Not to put too fine a point on it, but so far, none of the passengers appear to be of Middle-Eastern descent. Unless al-Qaeda recruited some hometown help, which, sadly, isn't beyond the scope of reason, none of these passengers can be the hijackers.

"What did you see?" I ask.

Sharon starts the segment over. I watch closely. Suit guy, lady with kid, pause, business casual, business casual, jeans, ballcap, and so on.

"There," Lydia says, pointing at the empty place behind the lady with the kid.

"I don't see anything," Sharon says.

"Exactly," Lydia says.

"I don't get it," I say.

"Play it again."

Sharon obeys.

While the tape plays again, Lydia says, "Look at the line. It's heel to toe. Everyone's eager to get on. Why's there a blank space there?"

I squint at the space.

"Maybe they're giving the mom some room," I suggest. "To be polite."

"No," Lydia says, decisively.

"Oh, my God!" Sharon says. "I see it!"

"See what?" I ask.

Sharon backs it up and pauses the video at the exact moment a blank space in the line is level with the gate attendant.

It's Lydia who answers. "Look. There." She points. "Is that a ticket? Can you play it in slow motion?"

Sharon does as asked.

"Yes. Right there," Sharon says. "It's like a ticket is changing hands, but there's no passenger. The ticket just appears, the gate lady looks at it, then hands it back, and it disappears again."

Sure enough, as the people in the line move, the space, about the size of an average passenger, produces a ticket out of nothing, and then absorbs is back again. And if I squint, I can see faint waves in the air, like heat coming off a car engine.

"What the hell?" I say.

"What if the fireball that sent me back was good," Lydia says, "and whatever is causing that passenger to be invisible... what if that's...evil?"

We're at war.

—George W. Bush, 9:45 am on 9/11 aboard
Airforce One

CHAPTER 26

Lydia

SHARON PLAYS THE ENTIRE boarding procedure at 2x speed, and it reveals a total of four invisible passengers. Two of them happen when the first-class passengers board, and the other two when the coach passengers get their turn. Each instance features a paper ticket appearing out of nowhere to be checked by an airline attendant and then disappearing again.

When I first saw the blank space in the line, I didn't think anything of it, but then I realized that the size of the space remained consistent as the passengers stepped forward, one at a time. It was like a train speeding past, and one of the cars is missing. Not just the cargo on top, but the whole car, connecters and all. The rest of the train moves as if the car is attached as it should be, but, somehow, it's invisible. Then, on playback, I saw that ticket appear out of nowhere, and I knew something was working against us. Something was helping the terrorists get on that plane.

"Invisible passengers," I say, voicing my thought.

"This is unbelievable," Ian says.

"Do you think we'd see the same thing at the check-in counter?" Sharon says. "Or the security checkpoint? I can pull up the feed." She gasps. "What if whatever's causing this…this glitch is the reason we can't pull the check-in records from United's network?"

I've moved past the how, and my focus has shifted to what action we need to take.

I look at the clock. It's 9:37. If the flight is going according to the schedule I'm familiar with, the hijackers would have taken over around 9:30, and the passengers would be well aware of the fact. "Did the plane take off at 8:42?" I ask.

Ian says, "I'll check."

Sharon says, "We need to tell Peterson. He believed you about your memories going twenty years into the future. He'll believe this."

"What if he doesn't?" I exchange a worried look with her. "If 93 took off at the same time, 8:42, then it's going to be heading back this way already. And this time, the passengers won't have any idea what's coming. They won't know to fight back."

"We have to warn them," Sharon concludes.

"We don't have time for bureaucracy," I say, but it lacks conviction. What if I'm wrong? Bennet surprised me before. Maybe he'd do it again. But we'd lose precious moments explaining the invisible passengers to him.

"Take off was 8:42," Ian confirms. Marge is with him when he returns. "I told her what we suspect. Sharon, can you play the feed for her?"

Sharon does, and Marge watches. She sees the first ticket materialize out of nowhere and gasps. Sharon fast-forwards to the next, and the next, and the next.

"My God," Marge says. "Lydia, how much time do we have to work with?"

"Shouldn't we tell Peterson?" Sharon says.

"Less than twenty minutes, if the passengers fight back," I say. "If they don't fight, which—they have no reason to right now—then I don't know. We're off script, here."

"We should tell Peterson." Sharon.

"We will," Marge says. "But right now, they're all like chickens with their heads cut off, yelling at the FAA and demanding to know why the jet's not showing up on radar."

"They turned off the transponder when they got in the cockpit," I say. "They're not transmitting anything we can use to track them. But I know their flight path from last time. They will have turned around over Ohio, and they're heading back here, going through southern Pennsylvania. The trip to Penn will take—" I look at the clock. "Another seventeen minutes, give or take."

"Give or take?" There's a hint of panic in Sharon's voice. She's at her best when she has something to do, and it just so happens I have a task that *only* she can do.

As a trauma nurse, I'm good at thinking on my feet. Since hearing Ian say those awful words, "Flight 93 is off course," I've been working out a plan of attack. It's almost like I was ready for the news, and like my brain had been working on the problem already.

I thought about Jamie Lynn Streeter, the pregnant wife of Jarrod Streeter, who was said to have been the ringleader of the passenger resistance. I think about Matt Braden, the gentle giant who never shied away from a fight when someone weaker needed someone to stand up for them, and who also happened to be gay. I think about college quarterback Tim Forsythe and his wife, Diane, who fed him valuable information from the ground. I think about Judo champion Jason Trick, who told his wife by airphone that some guys were planning to storm the cockpit.

These heroes cannot die. Not this time.

"You told me earlier the CIA can work miracles when they want to," I say to Sharon. "You're CIA. Can you get me four cell phone numbers?"

She glances in Peterson's direction. He's with the others at the whiteboard. "I'm not supposed to without authorization."

"You're authorized," Marge says. "What are you thinking, Lydia?"

I write down the names of the four passengers who led the rebellion on Flight 93 on four sticky notes. "There are four men on the flight who will be ready and willing to fight. They just need a reason. Let's give them one."

Ian

SHARON'S DESK SITS outside Peterson's office on the fourth floor of the same building where we met him, Peck, and Bennet. She only has access to the software for searching cell phone carrier records if she accesses it from her computer.

Marge, Lydia, and I surround her as her fingers fly over the keyboard.

She scrawls phone numbers on the Post-it notes Lydia gave her, each bearing the name of a passenger on United Flight 93. Finished, she hands the little squares to Lydia, who passes them out, one to each of us.

"Here's the plan," she says. "We get on our phones and call these men and tell them what's happening. We get to the point as quickly as possible and tell them they have to get into the cockpit as quickly as possible. Whatever they have to do, do it. First time around, they started to have some success by ramming the door with the drink cart. So maybe this time, they should start there. Once they breach, Jarrah will try to ditch. We need to make sure Dan Garrison is standing by. He's a licensed pilot."

I'm amazed. She knows so much about the flight. The information is readily available to her, and she wields it with confidence. But there's just one problem.

"How will we reach them?" I ask. "Phones are supposed to be turned off in flight."

"And what about reception?" Sharon adds. "Can you even use a cell phone on a plane?"

"Reception shouldn't be a problem," I answer Sharon. "Cell phones work on planes the same way airphones do, but they have to be turned off to limit interference with the flight and communication equipment."

Lydia says, "Everyone with a cell phone will turn it on the second they're hijacked. The hijackers will say they have bombs. The passengers will be scared. They'll call their loved ones." She swallows, and the compassion on her face is raw. "To say goodbye. But the bombs are probably fake. No evidence of explosives was found at the crash site. Even if they're real, though, their only hope is to take back that cockpit."

This is so surreal. I look at my note. I have Tim Forsythe.

"These buildings are fortresses," Sharon says. "For the best reception, we should go to the roof."

"Lead the way," Marge says. While we jog to the elevator, she offers some last-minute advice. "Tell them you're calling from the CIA—they don't need to know you're not employees— and that hijackers have been arrested trying to get on three other flights with the intent to crash them into the World Trade Center and The Pentagon."

We exit the elevator and take a final flight of stairs to a steel emergency exit.

Sharon waves her badge in front of a panel. When she pushes through the door, there's no alarm. "I made sure to get access. I take a smoke break, once in a while," she adds with a shrug.

"Tell them there's likely an axe somewhere onboard," Marge says, breathless from running up the stairs. "The flight attendants should know where."

"Who do you have?" Lydia asks me as we pour out of the stairwell onto sunbaked concrete. A breeze lifts the fringes of hair that have escaped her braid.

"Forsythe."

"I have Braden," she says, thumb flying over her keypad. "Our guys are sitting next to each other," she turns her back on me, presumably as the phone begins to ring.

I dial Forsythe on my Blackberry, and my stomach does a nervous flip as I listen to the line ring. I cold-call a lot of people in my line of work, but it's never been life or death. 'Til now.

After three rings, a man answers. "Hello? Who's this?" His tone is urgent.

"My name is Ian Greenberg," I say crisply and quickly. "I'm calling from the CIA. Mr. Forsythe, we know your plane has been hijacked."

"God! You do? Thank God! They've killed the pilot and copilot. What do we do?"

My breath is sucked from my lungs. The pilot and copilot are dead. This is all too real. I'm also amazed that Lydia called it, once again. This guy is ready to act. I hope the others are, too.

"Listen carefully. The men flying your plane intend to crash it into a public building. Three other groups of hijackers were arrested attempting to get on other flights this morning. Their intended targets were the two World Trade Center towers in Manhattan and The Pentagon. We think your group is targeting The White House or the Capitol Building."

"Oh, my God. Oh, my God."

"Don't panic. I need you to help. Can you do that?"

"They say they have a bomb. What do we do?"

"There's no bomb. It's a fake."

"What? Wait—hang on a second." I hear Forsythe say, "It's the CIA. You?" There's a pause. "The bomb's not real. They're gonna tell us what to do. Okay, I'm back. Tell us what to do. We're in."

Lydia's a couple yards from me, speaking to the man beside Forsythe. That must be whom he's talking to. If they're both "in," that means Lydia's having success, too. I hope this works.

Yahweh, if I haven't used up the day's miracles yet, could I have one more?

"We need you to break into the cockpit," I tell Forsythe. "You have to do it fast, because as soon as you breach the door, the hijacker pilot will try to ditch the plane. Start with the drinks cart. Use it as a battering ram. There may be an axe on board. Ask a flight attendant. There are four of you we're calling. Get with the others. Make sure you find Dan Garrison. He's a passenger but also a pilot. Get him to the cockpit as fast as you can. Understand?"

"Ram cockpit, Dan Garrison. Got it. We do this now?"

"Yes, now. Get with the others. Go. Hurry. You can do this." *You almost did it once before,* I add, mentally. I want them to succeed this time. I want it so bad I can taste it.

Lydia

"You've got this, Matt."

"All right. Do I stay on with you?" Matt Braden has a deep, earnest voice. I've read so much about him and the others on Flight 93. I can't believe I'm actually talking to him right now.

"Just put the phone in your pocket and do what you have to do. I'll be here."

"'Kay." Everything becomes muffled as he tucks me away to focus on the task at hand.

This has to work. This has to work.

I have a moment's doubt. Should we have brought Bennet in on this?

My grip threatens to crush my Nokia as I strain my ears for any and every scrap of information I can lay claim to. When I get a call-waiting beep, I curse and glance at the screen. *Not now, Tristan. Dammit.*

I ignore the call and keep listening. I hear several male voices and some female voices. I was expecting more panic, but everyone's talking in turn, and no one's shouting. The whole operation seems remarkably civilized.

I peek at Ian. He sees me and gives a thumbs up. When I look at Marge, she's got a finger poked into one ear to keep out background noise, but she nods to show it's going well with Jarrod Streeter. Sharon's talking into her phone and doesn't see me. I have to trust she's getting through to Jason Trick.

Some minutes pass while the voices talk, and then I hear something that makes me hold my breath.

"Ready? Okay. Let's roll."

Jarrod Streeter has just uttered the rallying cry he made famous, loud and clear enough that I heard it from Matt

Braden's pocket. If I were the hijackers, I'd be shaking in my boots.

A roar goes up as the charge begins. There's a battle taking place, and the prize is the sky.

Silently, I hurl my prayers into the universe. I hope whatever, or whoever, sent me back here is listening, because it's not just ordinary people fighting this battle. There's something else going on, something beyond what we understand. Whatever made those hijackers invisible might be on that plane. I hope whatever sent me here is on it, too.

Too much time is passing. The battle rages, men shouting. A woman screams. A man yells, "We're going down!"

I have to strain to hear. The wind is getting loud.

I want to ask Matt what's happening, but he needs to concentrate. He's literally fighting for his life, along with the others.

"Oh, my God! Look!" Sharon points into the air.

The noise is getting louder and louder still. It sounds like we're in a wind tunnel, but the air is relatively still.

I follow Sharon's pointing finger and see something in the sky. It's dark for a moment. Then it lists to one side, and the sun reflects off it in a blinding ray. It's growing larger.

A sickening sensation makes it feel like the building has dropped out from beneath me.

It's a plane, and it's wildly banking from side to side as it falls from the sky.

Ian

IT CAN'T BE. I shake my head, willing it not to be true, but the stone weighing down my insides tells the truth. I don't have to ask Forsythe what's going on up there. I can see for myself. Flight 93 is coming down.

I'm no expert in estimating altitude, but I don't live far from the airport, and planes that low are usually coming in or taking off. And they're usually tail down. This plane has its nose down, and its trajectory will bring it darn close to where we are.

I would guess the altitude to be 5,000 feet and dropping fast.

"No!" Lydia shouts.

Instead of running away from the massive jet screaming toward us, she runs to the western edge of the roof, as if to meet it. She's running fast, right toward the four-foot wall separating her from a six-story drop.

"Lydia!" I sprint in her direction. I can barely hear myself over the jet.

The phone call with Forsythe is forgotten. My only concern right now is getting to Lydia. I need to keep her safe.

I reach her at last, sides heaving, and hook her with an arm. I'm only satisfied when I have her tucked against me.

She's rigid, her neck bent toward the sky. Her lips move. I can't hear her, but I can read what she's saying. I'm saying it too.

"Pull up. Pull up. Pull up."

A hand lands on my shoulder. Marge. She stands stoic beside me, hair whipping in a wind that kicks up, as if the air around us knows something big is about to happen.

"Come on," I chant. "Come on."

I hate this helpless feeling. The plane is maybe at 2,000 feet now, and if someone doesn't pull it up, like, now, it's going to crash into the sprawling parking lot where Marge's car is. Or maybe into the building.

Was the CIA building a target, or is it coincidence that it's coming here? Are we simply in the path for a more prominent target? The White House or the Capitol?

My ears pop as the air pressure changes.

The plane is nearly on top of us.

I crush Lydia to my chest and hold on.

The screaming engines reach a piercing crescendo, and I look up to see the underside of tail elevators block out the daylight in a dark, speeding *V*.

Wheeling around, I watch, dumbfounded as the jet gains altitude. It's listing to one side, but it's climbing. Slowly, but surely, it's climbing.

A sudden gust of wind rips Lydia from my arms.

She tumbles to her knees and rolls as we're buffeted by hurricane-force winds. I only remain upright by clinging to the wall.

Marge holds on, too, her gray hair torn from its updo.

When the wind settles and I can walk without being bowled over, I rush to Lydia's side.

She's lying prone, face down, with one arm bent over the top of her head and the other making a wrong-way *L* at her side.

"Lydia! No!"

Like Marge's hair, hers is in disarray. I sweep it away from her face to see blood coming from broken skin at her hairline.

"Lydia!" I bend close and shout at her to wake up.

Marge is there. Then Sharon.

"Let's roll her over," Marge says. "Miss Hansen, call 9-1-1."

Marge and I work together to gently put Lydia on her back. We're extra careful to keep her neck straight, in case she has any damage to her vertebrae.

Lydia's a mess. She took a hard dive when that wind hit us, and her body's paid the price. She clearly has a broken arm and a bad cut on her head that probably has a concussion in tow, but I thank my lucky stars that she's breathing.

"Lydia, wake up." I tap her cheek. "Come back to me. Come on."

Her lashes move. She blinks, then gasps as she opens her eyes.

"Where am I?" She studies my face. "Who are you?"

CHAPTER 27

Lydia

"Mom? Mom. Wake up, Mom."

I bolt upright, flailing in darkness. My arm connects with another person.

I instantly think of Ian. I was just blown out of his arms as Flight 93 careened toward the CIA headquarters, of all places. The last thing I remember was eating concrete as a blast of wind from the jet engines sent me flying "ass over teakettle," as Mom would have said.

"Ouch! Mom! Are you okay?"

That's not Ian's voice.

A light clicks on, and my parents' old bedroom comes into focus, as does Holly, who's scowling at me and rubbing her cheek, where I must have smacked her in my panic.

"Holly!" The second my gaze lands on my precious daughter, healthy and whole and *her,* I haul her into my arms. "Oh, my gosh, Baby! It's you!"

Tears of relief splash onto my cheeks as I smother her with kisses and run my hands all over her. I touch her curly brown hair, and I smooth my hands over her gently-winged eyebrows, and I cup her fresh, confused face in my hands, and I just look at her. It's *her.*

I'm back!

I'm in bed at the farmhouse in Nebraska, wearing the leggings and *T*-shirt I went to bed in after seeing that fireball. And my darling Holly is here with me. She's blessedly unchanged.

"Uh, of course, it's me," she says. Her expression says she's questioning my sanity.

I laugh, filled with joy. It's indescribably good to see her.

But I quickly sober. What about Christian?

"Have you heard from your brother?"

"My brother?" she says again, looking at me as though I've lost my mind.

My heart drops through the floor.

"Why would I *hear* from him when his room is right beside mine?"

I blink. "His room is beside yours?" To say I'm confused would be an understatement.

"Yes." Holly drags out the word, concern evident. "Are you okay? I mean, you've been sleeping, like, all morning. I figured you were just tired from unpacking. But maybe you're coming down with something." She presses a palm to my forehead, like I used to do with her to check for a fever.

I glance at the clock. It's just past one in the afternoon.

"Is it...September 11th?"

"No. It's the tenth. Wait! Weren't you supposed to go into the hospital this morning to meet your new boss?" Panic flashes across her face.

Shoot! I was. I'm disoriented from my...experience. "You're right. I'll call her." I throw my legs over the side of the bed.

Holly stops me with hands on my shoulders. "Maybe you should take your time. You're acting...weird. Just sit there a minute, okay? I'll go get your phone and a cup of coffee." Keeping a sharp eye on me, she backs out of the room. I hear her pad down the stairs, and then voices float through the house, hers and Christian's.

Christian is okay! But what is he doing here?

Phantom pains linger in my arm and head. And my knees burn as though they've been freshly skinned. I went down hard on them when the jet flew over us, not more than a few hundred feet over our heads, if my guess is right. I wrestle my leggings up and see smooth, unharmed skin that's due for a shave. The pain fades as I make the mental adjustment. I'm not hurt. I didn't fall and tumble across the roof of the CIA building in the wake of a crashing jet airplane.

I gasp.

The passengers! Did they pull it up? Did they make it?

I launch myself out of bed and dive for my tablet, finding it on the bedside table, where I always keep it. Fingers flying, I search Google for United Flight 93. The top result out of three million has the headline: *"Miracle over Langley: United 93 Passengers retake control of jet in nick of…"*

My knees feel weak. I slump into the wicker-backed rocker where my robe is draped and skim more headlines.

"Flight 93 Passengers Share Incredible Story of Survival amidst Hijacking Horror."

"Inside the Close Call of United Flight 93: Mystery Caller from CIA Never Identified, Passenger Matt Braden Says He Spoke with an Angel."

"Major Terror Disaster Averted by Quick Thinking CIA on 9/11/2001."

"Four Phone Calls to Flight 93: How Passengers were able to Get Licensed Pilot and Ticket Holder Dan Garrison to Cockpit in Nick of Time."

"F-16s Scrambled, Find Missing Jet Minutes after Passengers Save the Day."

"Death Toll of 3 on 9/11/2001 Could Have been Much Worse, Says CIA Director Bennet."

"Mom? What's going on?" A young, male voice brings my gaze up from the screen.

"Christian!" I rise and throw myself into his arms, landing kisses on his face, like I did for Holly. Then I lean back and inspect him all over for differences. I see none, other than the incongruity of him being here, when before my experience, he'd been living with his dad, opting to make Tristan's condo his home base for college. "What are you doing in Nebraska? You love New York."

"I love *you* more," he says, good humor mixing with concern.

"What about school?"

Holly strides in with a steaming cup of coffee, which I gladly take from her. "He's flying out tomorrow, remember?"

No. I don't remember. This is all different. But my kids are the same, and that's what matters.

We did it! Ian and I actually stopped 9/11! We saved nearly three thousand lives!

Death Toll of 3.

My heart aches as I realize those three must be the two pilots and one crew member from Flight 93. I wish we could have saved them, too. At least I know I did my best. I held nothing back, and neither did Ian.

Ian.

I miss him with a twisting, dull pain in my chest. I couldn't have done anything to help those people without him, without his aunt. He was my rock as I floundered in a unique, supernatural strangeness. I wish he was my rock, still. I wish he was here with me, celebrating with me, meeting my children and sharing my joy that they're alive and well.

Holly hands me my phone. "I'm sure your boss will understand. Just tell her you're sick."

"I'm not, though."

"I hate to argue, Mom," Christian says. "But you're clearly not completely well. What's going on with you?"

I paste on a smile. "Nothing, honey. Just an intense dream."

"I'll say." Holly mock-rubs her cheek. "Mom clocked me one when I tried to wake her up. I think you missed your calling as a boxer."

Holly and Christian leave me to ready myself for the day. I take their advice and call in sick for my meet-the-team day at my new hospital. My boss is understanding, and we agree to postpone the meeting for two more days. My first shift will begin as scheduled, next Monday, giving me plenty of time to move in, get settled, and wrap my brain around my new life.

I take a long, hot shower with my mug of coffee close by. As the caffeine rushes through my senses, memories begin to worm their way through my consciousness. *Different* memories.

It's like there are two sets, now. One set is growing stale. It's the set representing my first run through of the past twenty years. The second set is fresh, like bread out of the oven. The fragrance is strong and overwhelms the stale set.

The fresh memories begin with recent events and work their way backward.

Christian and Holly accompanying me on the drive out here takes the place of Holly and I making the trek alone.

Tristan and I divorcing after only six years of marriage, when the kids were still small, takes the place of persevering in a hurtful, unhappy marriage until my kids were grown.

September 11th being annually hailed as a day of triumph takes the place of 9/11 remembered as the greatest terror attack in American history.

Waking up in a hospital in D.C. with Tristan fawning all over me takes the place of...the moment of blackness between the jet flying over me and Holly shaking me awake. I remember being told I had amnesia, that I lost about twenty-four hours, and that a reporter by the name of Ian Greenberg found me on a sidewalk in Washington, D.C., looking like I'd been hit by a car.

Since that's not what happened, I wonder if Marge and Bennet put their heads together to erase my involvement in the operation to stop the hijackers.

What must that have been like for poor Ian? Having me not remember him? Watching me treat him as a Good-Samaritan stranger?

I dress for the day in stretchy jeans that give a nice shape to my forty-three-year-old, stretch-mark-riddled midsection and a casual top with a wide neck that hangs off one shoulder to reveal the strap of a jersey-knit tank top. It's good to be back in the body I've grown comfortable with. It's good to be home.

It's like I've lived the past twenty years twice, but while inside those years, it felt like the first time. Nowhere in my dual set of memories do I spot any sense of frustration or repetition. When I woke up this morning, it was like I'd just left Ian's side on that rooftop.

I'm relieved. I didn't want to relive those years. I didn't want to worry that my children wouldn't be my children. If I have any regret, it's that I never got to warn my parents about the health issues that would claim their lives.

But I realize I wasn't sent back to tinker. I had a singular purpose, and I fulfilled it. I know in my heart my parents are somewhere, looking down on me, and that they are insanely proud.

Ian

DUST RISES BEHIND my new Subaru as I traverse the long, gravel drive to the address I have been waiting twenty years to visit. Ripe corn plants make walls on either side of me, and when I round a bend, a two-story farmhouse painted a weathered white comes into view. Not far behind the house are two barns, one large and red, the other small and constructed of raw timbers. From the second barn, the nose of a farm tractor peeks out.

Surrounding the house is an acre or so of knee-high grass, and wrestling a mower through the overgrowth is a leanly muscled man, shirtless.

The corners of my mouth pull down.

Did I miss something in my research? I've been keeping tabs on Lydia since the day she changed the world and then changed into a different person, right before my eyes. I knew when her husband rushed to her side after her "accident," which Marge and Bennet arranged to cover her involvement at Langley. I celebrated privately as I read the birth announcements of her two children, Christian and Holly. I knew when she and Tristan became divorced. It had happened more than a decade earlier than in the recollection Lydia previously had. I knew when she got promoted to charge nurse over the ER at Kindred Hospital in New Jersey. I learned what she meant by "COVID" as the whole world battled a deadly pandemic caused by the Coronavirus. I knew when her parents died and she inherited this very farm.

From her Facebook page, I know she is single.

So, what is this strapping man doing mowing her front lawn?

As I shut the car door, he lifts his head and silences the mower. Approaching me, he says, "Can I help you?"

The man is young and stands half-a-head shorter than me, making him around six foot. His face matches pictures on Lydia's Facebook. This is her son Christian, who is about to begin his freshman year at Columbia. I replace my frown with a cordial smile.

"I'm looking for Lydia Clay. Name's Ian. Ian Greenberg." I stick out my hand, and he shakes it.

"Ian Greenberg. Like, the author?"

I didn't go back to work at *The Washington Post* after 9/11. In fact, around the time Bennet's sting was taking place to capture fifteen of the hijackers, Carmen had left a voicemail on my Blackberry letting me know I was fired. By the time I got the message—well after Lydia had been delivered safely to the hospital with her husband *en route* to be by her side, I had five-thousand words written and approved by Bennet, describing the atmosphere inside Langley as the Director led an operation like no other in the agency's history. I would love to have seen the look on Carmen's face as it went to print on the *New York Times* front page first thing Wednesday morning.

Since then, I've written features galore and won not just two Pulitzers, but four between my journalism and my books. I wonder how many of them Lydia has on her shelf or if she has a 9/11 shelf at all anymore.

"That's me. And you must be Christian. I'm an old friend of your mom's."

"Really?" His face is warm and open and tanned from outdoor sports.

"She probably hasn't mentioned me. It's been a long time." So *very* long. "She home?"

"Yeah. Yeah, man. Lemme go get her for you." He jogs up the porch steps and disappears inside. Before slapping shut, the screen door emits a large hound with a mottled gray and brown coat.

The dog wags its tail tentatively as he comes closer to check me out.

"Hey, buddy." I squat down and let him sniff my hand. When he gives me the go-ahead, I scratch his ears and make myself a new best friend. "Jester, huh?" I read the name on his bone-shaped tag. "Nice to meet you. We'll be seeing a lot of each other. I hope."

His tongue lolls out, and his liquid eyes smile in the way dogs have, letting me know he'd be okay with that. If his approval were the only one needed, I'd move in tomorrow.

While I pet Jester, I look around and get my bearings. The house has a wrap-around porch that could use a good painting, and between the front door and a big picture window is a two-seater swing. Is that where Lydia saw the fireball?

The hinges on the screen door shriek again, and I look up.

The dog's tail wags even harder at the sight of the woman coming down the porch stairs. If I had one, it would be wagging too.

Lydia.

She's in her forties, now, and more beautiful than ever. Her hair is up in a loose ponytail, and she's dressed in comfortable work clothes, form-hugging jeans and a *T*-shirt that exposes one creamy shoulder.

My heart runs a marathon as I stand and take in the smile blooming on her pretty face.

"Hi," I say.

"Ian." She breathes my name as she breaks into a run.

I catch her on a leap and crush her to me. She remembers!

I hadn't been sure she would. Within a few seconds of her coming to on that rooftop, I knew she was no longer *my* Lydia. During that fall, she transformed back into the Lydia that belonged in 2001.

My heart had broken in two.

It took a while, but I began thinking about the Lydia that had existed in her version of 2021, the one that saw a fireball and made an impossible wish for something so good and pure, what angel could refuse granting it? I couldn't imagine that Lydia completely disappearing along with all her memories of the twenty years she lived before coming back to the past. That Lydia had to go on. She was too special to simply cease existing.

If she had to go on, then where could I find her? I racked my brain and came up with an answer that would require patience. I might be able to find her in 2021, on September 10th.

I was right.

I set her gently on her feet and frame her face with my hands. She's so small compared to me, perfectly petite and perfectly beautiful.

"I've waited a long time to do this," I say, and I lower my mouth to hers.

Her lips receive my kiss, and her arms wind around my neck. It's not a long kiss, but it contains the power of a stick of dynamite.

Lydia breaks it with a laugh and studies me with eyes that dance with happiness. "It feels like I just left you," she says, and she does this joyful sob thing and kisses me again.

I'm happy to let her do whatever she wants with me.

"I wish it felt that way for me too," I say when we finally break apart. "But this—you—are definitely worth the wait. Are Holly and Christian...?" I leave the question hanging. I remember that was her greatest concern, whether changing 9/11 would result in her children being changed.

"They're fine. They're *them*." Her eyes shine with a mother's love. "It's been twenty years for you." She lays a cool hand along my bearded cheek. "I'm sorry."

"I'm not. I'm glad you didn't have to live your life all over again." I lean into her petting. "How did it work, though? I mean, do you know that things have been different? Like your divorce was much earlier."

"You know about that?"

I nod, unashamed that I've been stalking her online.

She laughs. "It's weird. I'm still getting used to it. It's like I woke up this morning with two sets of memories."

"That sounds confusing." I'm probably grinning like a fool, but I don't care. I'm just so *relieved*. Now *this* is *my* Lydia.

"It is. The kids have to keep reminding me of things. You know, Christian was living with Tristan in the old version of my memories. I was so surprised—and delighted—to see him this morning."

"You're good, then? Everything's good?"

"Everything's good," she assures me. "Everything's amazing, actually. Ian, we did it!"

"You did it," I say.

She shakes her head, ponytail bouncing. "No. No one could have done what you did, Ian. You, your aunt, it all worked perfectly because you knew how to take the information I had and get it where it needed to go."

I soak in her praise, like a hound soaking in ear scratches. "We did it together."

"Together," she says. "I'll buy that." Her smile falters. "Not that I'm complaining, but what are you doing here?"

"Checking out my new hometown."

She blinks. "What? You're seriously thinking of moving here? You do know this is Nowhere, USA? The major news stories are agricultural. That's a big change for a Pulitzer-winning author and writer for the *New York Times*." Her lopsided smile tells me that her new set of memories contains information about my career.

"I've got nothing against agriculture, but I was actually thinking of a career change."

"Oh?"

"Did you know the University of Nebraska has a campus in Kearney and they have a communications program?"

Lydia's eyebrows climb her forehead.

"And did you know they've recently hired a new associate professor to teach their journalism courses?"

"They have?" Her coy smile tells me everything I need to know. She's happy to hear about my relocation.

"They have," I confirm. "In fact, I was thinking about taking my new girlfriend over to campus today to show her around. I've got this sweet office with a slanting floor and a window that doesn't open."

She beams at me. So. Damn. Beautiful.

"Girlfriend, huh?" she says with a hand on her hip. "I don't remember agreeing to that."

I twine my fingers through hers and drag her close. My body lights up just being close to her. I can't wait to see what it does tonight, when I get her alone.

Bending to her ear, I echo one of the first things she ever said to me. "If you give me an hour of your time, I think I can convince you."

She smells amazing, like coconut shower soap and coffee. Her gaze is heated as she reaches up to hold on around my neck. "You have thirty minutes," she says, and her lips claim mine.

Time is passing. Yet, for the United States of America, there will be no forgetting September the 11th. We will remember every rescuer who died in honor. We will remember every family that lives in grief. We will remember the fire and ash, the last phone calls, the funerals of the children.

—President George W. Bush

Thanks so much for reading *Terror Undone.* I hope you enjoyed it. For more information about the book, including images of Lydia's notes and a summary of what's fact and what's fiction, see the appendices at the back of this ebook.

This is the first novel in my new Turn Back Time series. I plan to write more adventures through time for Lydia and Ian, and I hope you'll subscribe to my newsletter so you won't miss out when future books are released.

Did you know I also write highlander romance? If you loved the magic and emotion of Lydia's story, you'll find just as much charm and even more magic in my Highland Wishes series. The best part? These four romances are **FREE on Kindle Unlimited!**

Not a KU member? No problem. Simply click the cover to purchase the first book, *Wishing for a Highlander.*

What are you waiting for? Jump into
your next Jessi Gage series now!

*"I give this story five stars out of five and look forward to
more fantasy tales from this enchanting author."*

--The Romance Reviews

*"Darcy and Melanie's story is funny, touching, and unfor-
gettable. I loved this book, and you will, too."*

--Romance Author Julie Brannagh

**Be careful what you wish for. It might just come
true.**

Single-and-pregnant museum worker Melanie voices
an idle wish while examining a Scottish artifact, that a
Highland warrior would sweep her off her feet and help her

forget her cheating ex. The last thing she expects is for her wish to be granted. Magically transported to the middle of a clan skirmish in the sixteenth-century Highlands, she comes face to face with her kilted fantasy man.

Tall, handsome, and heir to his uncle's lairdship, Darcy Keith should be the most eligible bachelor in Ackergill. Instead, thanks to a prank played on him in his teenage years, he is known for being too large under his kilt to ever make a proper husband. "Big Darcy" runs his deceased father's windmills and lives alone at his family manor, believing he will never marry.

But a strangely dressed woman he rescues from a clan skirmish makes him long for more. When the woman's claims of coming to Ackergill by magic reach the laird's ears, she is accused of witchcraft. Darcy determines to protect her any way he can, even if it means binding her to him forever.

Grab WISHING FOR A HIGHLANDER now!

Sign up for my newsletter to find out about new books as soon as they're available.

Indie authors like me rely on you, the reader, spreading the word. I appreciate every little thing you do, whether you tell a friend about my books or leave a review at Goodreads and Amazon.

Appendix A

Lydia's Notes

<u>9/11/2001</u>

American Flt 11 - North tower 8:46 a.m.
United Flt 175 - South tower 9:02
American Flt 77 - Pentagon 9:30 – 9:40
United Flt 93 - Southern Pennsylvania, 10-ish

Look up flight times.
Stop from taking off.

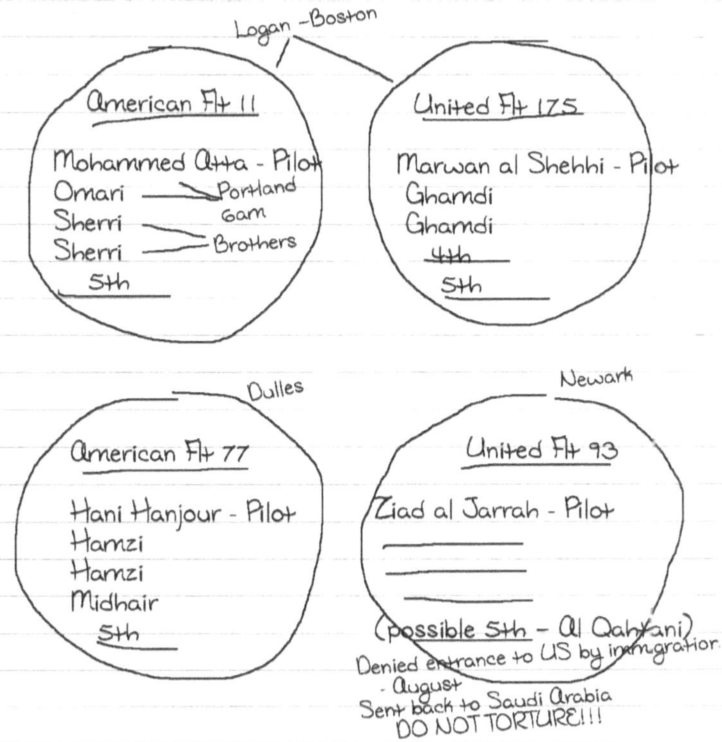

FBI - able to help, won't believe.
CIA – able to help, may be more likely to believe than FBI.
FAA – ?
Local Police –

Problem is ME – No one in right mind
will listen to me. I am nobody.

Need an Abigail Chase!

- PI motivated by cash

* Reporter!

not yet located at
One Franklin Sqaure
Old address:
1150 15th Street NW

Where is Ian Greenberg in 2001?
- Washington Post
- "New Face of Terrorism in the
Twenty-First Century" – Aug 26, 2001
- suggest planes as means
- builds on Cole & embassy bombings: If we
apply same motivations (to cause as much
damage as possible) to planes scenario,
"we could see major air-travel catastrophes
the likes of which we've never before imagined."
"It would be a mistake of deadly proportions
not to consider the terrorist mind capable
of evolutionary thinking."

First person to suggest
planes as terror implements...
Still no idea planes can
be used as missiles

Don't think he knew
abt his article being
online!!

Verifiable Info

- Massoud assassination in Afghanistan
  (probably al Qaeda)
- Midhair & Hamzi flunked out of flight school
  - instructors alarmed because only interested in
    controlling a plane mid-air, not in takeoffs or lancings.
    - Montgomery Field.

- Some were in US on tourist visas
  - reported lost passports, got replacements to remove
    record of suspicious travel
- Used their real names
- Abided by law, kept heads down, trained to fly or
  to be muscle, attended non-extremist mosques,
  had gym memberships
- Midhair & at least one other on watchlist for other
  countries for al Qaeda association
- CIA knows some are in US
  - Did not share with FBI or place on watch lists or no-fly
    (No-fly list useless, has only 16 names on it
    at this point in time, no one knows who maintains it or
    how it's used to screen passengers)
- FBI knows Bin Laden was interested in planes as weapons
  as early as 1996. US had a terrorist in custody who
confessed to plans of crashing a plane into the CIA building.
    Not sure if CIA, FBI or other govt org

More about Terrorists' time in US...

- Atta already had pilot's license (from Egypt, I think)
- Several hijackers spent time in Hamburg, Germany
    - Atta & Shehi met there and came to US from there
- Dekker, Owner of flight school in Florida
- Airman something or other, Flight school in Oklahoma
- Several carried out cross-country travel, multiple trips
    to learn airport security & procedures
- ATMs used to get out cash, empty bank accounts
- Letters or packages, cash sent to family, girlfriends
    in FL, Germany
- Blue Nissan Altima, Atta & Omari drive from Boston
    to Portland on evening of 9/10 for early morning flight
- Some stay at hotel in Newton, MA (I think) - hookers hired
- Preparations underway for end of life, religious martyrdom
    - prayer, reflection, shaved body hair.
- Rolling luggage that looks like pilots' bags
- Atta's checked bag will get lost & never make the connecting
    flight from Portland.

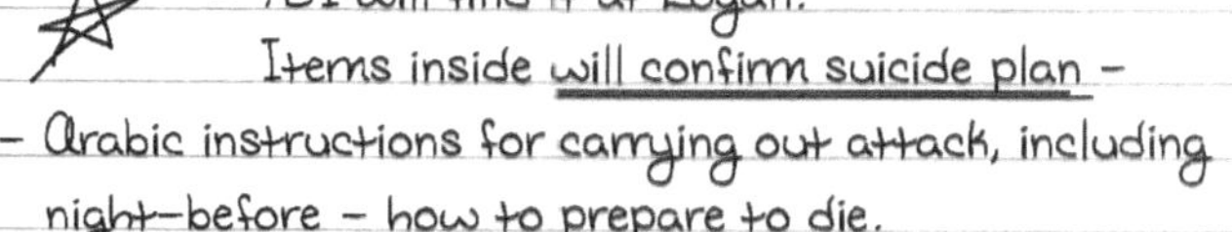

        - FBI will find it at Logan.
            Items inside will confirm suicide plan -
    - Arabic instructions for carrying out attack, including
        night-before - how to prepare to die.
    - Items in carry-on bags; folding knives under 4", mace,
        VHS for flying Boeing jets, flight computers, red
        bandanas, Koran

Ian Greenberg

Pre-9/11

- New Face article
- ? No others that I could find

Post-9/11

9/11 The Whys and Wherefores

The Terrorist Mind

The Making of 9/11

A Generation Raised on Terror

+ countless articles

What do I know about Ian?

- Genuinely seems to care about counter-terrorism
- Future works will show how passionate he is abt TRUTH and helping people understand
- Atheist / devout Jewish upbringing (Muslim mother, family issues
- believes in miracles - Oprah
- Massively talented ... 2 Pulitzers

How can I get Ian to help me stop 9/11?

- Be honest
- DONT tell him about fireball / wish / morning from Twilight Zone!!!
- Give info he can verify
- Appeal to his morality
  (Ian is a good perseon, at least, he seems to be)
  - Lives at stake 3,000 +
  - we have an opportunity to undo al Qaeda's win!

Appendix B

Fact vs Fiction

Terror Undone is a work of fiction that explores an alternate outcome to real events. It is not meant to inform or educate, but to encourage and entertain those who enjoy imagining a happy outcome to one of the worst days in American history.

Fact

The numbers, originating airports, and hijacker targets of the four flights featured in this book are fact.

The names of the terrorists (though different spellings appear in different sources, I tried to keep the spelling of the hijacker names consistent throughout this book)

The assassination of anti-terrorist militia leader Ahmad Shah Massoud is fact, as is the prevailing theory that it was done by al-Qaeda.

The names of presidents are fact, but any dialog from a past president is completely fictional.

Everything Lydia remembers about the terrorists is fact, including their flight training, their movements, and the contents of their luggage.

Fiction

Lydia and Ian are fictional characters. Everything Lydia remembers about Ian's career is fiction and is not based on any real journalist. Ian's passion for counter-terrorism and his Washington Post article that Lydia finds when she begins searching for him are totally fictional and a product of my imagination.

All CIA, FBI, and other "agency" personnel are fictional, but some are based on real men who tried their best to protect us.

All descriptions of the CIA building, inside and out, are fictional with one exception. The Kryptos sculpture is real.

While the names of United Flight 93 passengers were changed, many of the characteristics of those heroes are fact. It was important to me to honor those brave men and women by being true to as much as I could.

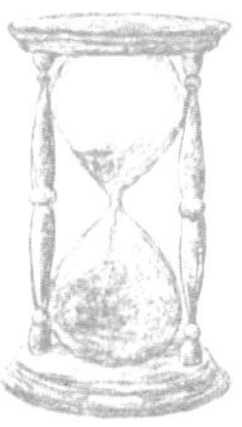

About Jessi Gage

USA Today Bestselling Author Jessi Gage is addicted to happy-ever-after endings. She counts herself blessed because she gets to live her own HEA with her husband and children in the Pacific Northwest.

Jessi has the attention span of a gnat...unless there is a romance novel in her hands. In that case, you might need a bullhorn to get her to notice you. She writes what she loves to read: stories about love.

Use the contact page on www.jessigage.com and drop her a line. There is no better motivation to finish her latest writing project than a note from a happy reader! While you're visiting her website, sign up for Jessi's newsletter so you never miss a new release.